Mandy Magro lives in Cairns, Far North Queensland, with her daughter, Chloe Rose. With pristine aqua-blue coastline in one direction and sweeping rural landscapes in the other, she describes her home as heaven on earth. A passionate woman and a romantic at heart, she loves writing about soul-deep love, the Australian rural way of life and all the wonderful characters who live there.

www.facebook.com/mandymagroauthor

www.mandymagro.com

Also by Mandy Magro

MANDY
MAGRO

Return To Rosalee Station

mira

First Published 2018
Second Australian Paperback Edition 2021
ISBN 9781867237778

RETURN TO ROSALEE STATION
© 2018 by Mandy Magro
Australian Copyright 2018
New Zealand Copyright 2018

This is a work of fiction. Names, characters, places, and incidents are either the product of the author's imagination or are used fictitiously, and any resemblance to actual persons, living or dead, business establishments, events, or locales is entirely coincidental.

Published by
Mira
An imprint of Harlequin Enterprises (Australia) Pty Ltd.
Level 13, 201 Elizabeth St
SYDNEY NSW 2000
AUSTRALIA

A catalogue record for this book is available from the National Library of Australia
www.librariesaustralia.nla.gov.au

Printed and bound in Australia by McPherson's Printing Group

MIX
Paper from
responsible sources
FSC® C001695

To the love of my life, my darling daughter, Chloe Rose xx

Wounds may heal, but they always leave a scar …

My Dearest Matt,

I'm so sorry to do this in a letter, but I've tried every other possible way to tell you how I'm feeling and we always end up in an argument. I honestly can't handle fighting with you anymore, so this is my last resort to try and get through to you. Please, babe, I need you to understand that I'm broken too, just as I understand you've been through hell and back. I'm doing my very best to help you through this, while at the same time trying to keep my own head above water. But truthfully, with the way things are between us, I feel like I'm drowning. I don't know how much longer I can stand by and watch you slowly killing yourself. I can't live like this any longer. I won't live like this any longer. Something needs to change. I wish you would go and talk to my psychologist about it all, and the fact you refuse to makes this even harder for me to comprehend and to be there for you when you won't even try and help yourself. It's like you don't want to get better. We're both in a world of pain, but we have to find a way to keep on living, and hopefully together. Please, I'm begging you to listen this time. You need to figure out what it is that will help you heal your heartache, once and for all, before it spells the end for us.

Sometimes
You are so withdrawn from me
I can't help but wonder
If I am still someone special to you.

Sometimes
You act as though
I am intruding in your world
When all I really want
Is to have you by my side.
Sometimes
I feel as though
I have asked you too many questions
As though I have somehow loved you too much
Maybe desired too much from you
When all I want
All I long for
All I pray for
Every single day
Is to understand you better
So I can love you better
So we can be back to what we used to be

I love you so much, Matt, and I can't imagine my life without you by my side. Please, baby, please think about what you are doing to yourself, and our marriage, and get some help, before it's too late.

All my love,
Sarah xoxo

PROLOGUE

Malanda, Far North Queensland
Present day

Something needs to change … the ultimatum circled torturously in Matthew Walsh's mind.

As much as he hated to admit it to himself, he had to agree. Self-medicating with booze was doing neither him, nor Sarah, any good. Her words played over and over again in his head, every one of them so very true.

Shifting uneasily, he hung his dusty, wide-brimmed hat on his knee and tried to stop from shaking. Sitting still was no easy feat these days. Not when it felt as if the weight of the world was pressing down upon his chest, and every one of his nerve endings hummed. Like a moth to a flame, he couldn't help himself when the drink gave him some reprieve – but it was high time he found a way to control it. The heartbreaking letter Sarah had left him on the dining table felt as if it were burning a hole in his pocket. He choked back tears – he didn't deserve to cry. His darling wife had reached her limit, and after the godawful year they'd had, he couldn't blame her one little bit.

Staring in a daze at the pile of magazines on the coffee table, and noticing that one of them was almost two years old – so much for fresh tabloid gossip – he tried to steady his breathing. The last patient of the day, he was thankful for the empty waiting room. Late afternoon sunshine poured through the glass front door and bathed the Malanda Medical Centre in golden light. What Matt would give to be lying in the sun in one of his paddocks instead of sitting in a doctor's surgery facing his fears. His leg bouncing anxiously, he watched the sixty-something secretary gather her things at the desk and then hurriedly shove them in her handbag before reapplying her already bright pink lipstick.

Rubbing her lips together, she bustled over to him. 'The doctor knows you're here, love. He's on a phone call and won't be much longer. I'd usually wait around with you but I need to run, have to pick the grandkids up from daycare for Marne.' She dashed past him, frazzled but smiling. 'Say hi to Sarah for me, won't you?' she called over her shoulder.

'Will do, Shirl. And say g'day to Bob for me too.' Matt tried to smile as he watched her wrestle the door open and then disappear outside.

The surgery door opened and Doctor Lawson stepped out. 'Sorry to keep you waiting … come on in, Matt.'

His Akubra in hand, Matt stood up, wandered in and sat down awkwardly. He hung his hat back on his knee and drew in a slow, steadying breath. 'Thanks for seeing me at such short notice, Doc. I know you're staying back later than usual and I really appreciate it.'

The doctor followed Matt in and settled himself in his high-back leather chair, and crossed his legs. 'Not a problem at all. I realise you've been having a hard time of late, which is to be expected after what you and Sarah have been through.'

A hard time? More like the worst time of his thirty-four years on this earth. Matt nodded, knowing full well the entire town would know of his situation at home, including the doctor, so it was no surprise to hear him say so. 'Yeah, it's been a damn tough year, that's for sure.'

'I have no doubt.' His lips set in a grim line, the doctor clicked and unclicked a pen – the sound grating on Matt's already frazzled nerves. 'So tell me, what can I do for you today?' His kind eyes moved over Matt as if already assessing him.

His heart in his throat and his stomach churning with nerves, Matt dug deep and found the nerve to open his heart just enough to get what advice he needed from the doctor. Each and every word was a struggle, an admission he needed help – and that made him feel even less of a man, and even more like the drunken fool he was. He was ashamed it had come to this, abashed he'd denied it for so long – but there was no more hiding from it, or from himself for that matter. Sarah was right. Enough was enough. If he wanted their marriage to have any kind of hope for a happily ever after, he needed to stand up and be the man he once was. The stench of stale alcohol was his shadow, as too was the past that haunted him every waking hour, even reaching into his nightmarish dreams that held him hostage every single night. He needed to find a way to climb out of the dark hole he'd fallen into.

The words tumbling from him, he finished his last sentence with a self-conscious smile, and then waited for a response he was almost too scared to hear.

'Well, you've come to the right place, Matt. I can most certainly help you through this.' The doctor's compassionate smile almost brought Matt undone.

'Great. Excellent.' Matt could hear the strain in his voice, and he coughed to try to cover it up. He wished he could get rid of the horrific images and the bloodcurdling screams from his head without the aid of alcohol, but he'd learnt all too well over this past year it was impossible. His only option had been to drink himself into a stupor to silence it all, if only for a little while. 'Sarah's right, I'm slowly killing myself, and ruining the hope of there ever being any chance of our marriage working.' He choked back a sob. If he allowed himself to cry, he was afraid he'd never be able to stop. And men weren't supposed to break down – it was his job to try to keep it together, to hold the fort, to make sure all the special women in his life were looked after. And he'd failed with that, miserably.

'Matt, you've taken the first step in asking for help.' His brows furrowed, Doctor Lawson adjusted his thick glasses and then folded his hands on his desk. 'So how many drinks, per day, would you say you're having?'

Ashamed, Matt's initial reaction was to lie, but he knew that wasn't going to get him anywhere. 'Probably eight or nine, maybe more on the really bad days.' He decided to leave out the fact he could devour an entire bottle if the moment called for it.

'I see, and what's your drink of choice.'

'Whiskey, sometimes rum.'

The doctor drew in a slow breath. 'Although the initial stages of alcohol withdrawal are over in a few weeks, your dependence may take anywhere from six months to a year to totally overcome, and even then you'll have to be mindful of falling back into the trap of thinking alcohol will solve all your problems for a few years after that.'

'I know it's going to be a tough journey, Doc, but I'm willing to give it my best shot.' Turning his gaze to the family photo of the doctor, his wife, and their two children in their twenties, Matt had to fight from feeling resentful. So, looking anywhere but, he tried to remain calm, steady, focused – a hard thing to do when he was craving his next drink like a parched person craved water.

'Righto, well, let's get this show on the road. Are you open to taking some medication, to help with the side effects of withdrawal that you're most certainly going to experience?'

Drugs to get him off the drink? It didn't make an ounce of bloody sense. 'Nope, I'm not open to that. I just want you to let me know what I'm in for, and how to handle it, without making me addicted to another kind of drug in the process.' It was said a little too harshly, and Matt regretted his tone instantly. This is what he always did to people who tried to help – took his frustration out on them. Poor Sarah. He bit his lip shut to stop from saying any more.

'I see.' The doctor's gaze narrowed.

Silence hung heavy. Matt hankered to escape the confines of the little room, but he planted himself firmly in the seat and gritted his teeth. It had taken him a long time to gather the courage to come here, too long in the grand scheme of things, and he wasn't about to chicken out now.

The doctor readjusted a few already straightened papers on his desk. 'I *really* do think you need to reconsider my suggestion for medication, Matt.' His tone was serious and authoritative. 'It's no easy feat, getting off the drink. And I would suggest you also think about going to counselling.'

'Go to a counsellor? No, thanks.' Matt shifted uncomfortably beneath the doctor's unyielding stare. 'And I *really* don't want to do this with pills, either.' Acknowledging the doctor's disapproving expression, Matt shrugged. 'Sorry, but taking something to get off something is just jumping from the frying pan and into the fire, in my opinion.'

'As you said, that's your opinion, Matt, and with all due respect, I totally disagree with you. The medication is offered for a very good reason … especially if you're thinking about doing this in the middle of the outback where help isn't at your beck and call, as you mentioned when we spoke on the phone.'

'I'll have plenty of help there, if I need it – my mum and dad, my sister, my best mate.'

'That's all well and good, but they can't do what medication will do.' Doctor Lawson breathed a weary sigh. 'Look, I totally understand your concerns, but the Valium will help in the short term, and then the Naltrexone will guide you through until you feel strong enough to do it on your own.'

'Thanks, but no thanks … it'll be another thing I need to wean myself off.' Determined to stand fast with his decision to go cold turkey, Matt cleared his throat and feigned a confidence he was far from feeling. 'If it makes you happier, though, I'll take a script for both, just in case of an emergency.'

Doctor Lawson held up his hands in defeat. 'Okay, but for the record, I really don't like the idea of you going it alone out there, Matt.' He reached for his prescription pad. 'Can you do me a favour and fill the scripts, so you have the tablets on hand if you get to the stage where you feel you need them? There's not many chemists out near your parents' station, I'm gathering.'

'Correct.' Happy to meet on middle ground, Matt nodded. 'Yup, it's a done deal, Doc. I'll make sure I have the tablets with me before I head out to Rosalee … but that doesn't mean I'm going to take them.' Matt's word was genuine – he would get the script filled at the very least.

'That's a good start …' Doctor Lawson stopped writing and looked up. 'So thank you.' He tipped his head a little to the side. 'May I ask, on more of a personal level seeing you and Sarah are like family to Marg and me, how is she feeling about you heading out there and doing this without her around?'

Matt swallowed. Hard. 'I haven't told her yet.'

'Oh, right, okay. That's probably something she should know sooner rather than later, don't you think?'

'I know, I'll tell her.' Unable to look him in the eye any longer, Matt stared down at his weather-beaten boots. 'I just want to stop. Now. Before it's too late.'

The pen still poised, Doctor Lawson raised his eyebrows. 'Too late for you and Sarah? Or too late for you?'

Matt suddenly realised what the doctor was asking him. His throat so tight with emotion he couldn't speak, he quickly shook his head, and then stole a few moments to recover. 'I'm not suicidal, if that's what you're asking.'

'Are you one hundred and ten percent sure of that?' The look in the doctor's eyes suggested he was unconvinced.

Even though he'd contemplated it many times, and come very close to following through with it, Matt rolled his eyes and forcefully made himself appear completely shocked by the accusation. 'Of course I'm sure.'

The doctor regarded him over the rim of his glasses, to the point that Matt squirmed in his seat, and then looked back down at his prescription pad. 'Be sure to talk to someone if you do feel suicidal at any time, okay?'

'Yup, of course.'

Ripping the sheet of paper off, he passed it to Matt. 'Like I explained, after drinking so heavily for the past year, you're going to experience the height of the withdrawal symptoms in the first few days. Irritability, poor concentration, feeling shaky, irregular heartbeat, difficulty sleeping and nightmares, just to name a few.' He smiled sadly. 'And then there's the physical symptoms … trembling hands, sweating, headaches, nausea, vomiting, lack of appetite, and possibly even hallucinations. So please, don't try to be a hero – use the tablets if it gets too bad.'

'You have my word, Doc, thanks.' Matt took the script, folded it, and then shoved it in his pocket along with Sarah's letter. He was terrified of what lay ahead, both for him and his marriage. How in the hell were they ever going to get through this, and out the other side, if he didn't rediscover the man he once was, the man that Sarah had fallen head over heels in love with?

CHAPTER

1

Rosalee Station, Central Australia
Where it all began, eight years earlier

A month off turning twenty-six and Matthew Walsh felt as if his life was finally falling into place. The thunderous sound of the mustering chopper's blades sliced through the silence – his dad was flying off to Mount Isa to do the banking and pick up some supplies. Why drive for ten hours when you could fly? It was one of the perks of a lucrative cattle station. Usually Matt would have gone with him, but nothing was going to drag him from his bed before she woke. He wanted to be the first thing she laid her dazzling, emerald-green eyes on. It was only quarter past seven, but the corrugated-iron roofing of the cottage creaked and groaned beneath the blazing outback sunshine. With the air-conditioner on the blink, the fan spinning madly above wasn't doing much to ward off the heat – but without it, it was suffocating. The curtains flapped in the breeze and dappled sunlight flittered over the room like golden licks of flames – it was going to be another beautiful day in Central Australia. The temperatures would be scorching, and the relentless flies would drive most people batty, but he still loved every square inch of the treacherous, sun-baked, red-dirt country like only a true-blue cattleman could.

He smiled at the gorgeous woman cuddled into him, her arm draped over his chest. If he could, he'd stay in bed and make sweet, hungry love to her all day long, but there was work to be done. He'd been watching her sleep for the past half an hour; the peacefulness of her face and the soft, in–out of her breath was mesmerising. Never had he felt such intense, soul-deep love before. And as each day passed, as they spent more and more time in each other's company, and planned their lives together, the love he felt for her only grew stronger and more encompassing. Matt just hoped nothing ever changed, that she would never fall out of love with him, hoped he never did anything to hurt her, even unintentionally, because this, right here, was what true love was all about. He wanted to make her happy, every single day from here on in, for the rest of her life.

Looking to where he'd hidden the dark blue sapphire engagement ring, in the third drawer under his clothes, he wondered if she was going to say yes. His heart raced like a bull at a gate just thinking about it, and nerves sent his stomach somersaulting. It would crush his entire world if she knocked him back – but he wasn't about to dwell on that thought for too long. He'd already asked her parents for their permission, and they'd gladly agreed, so now it was all up to Sarah. Would she think this was too soon, too fast? Most would say five months wasn't long enough to get to really know someone, but for Matt, everything between Sarah and him felt so right, so natural, as though they'd already been together before, in some previous lifetime, and he couldn't imagine this life without her in it every day.

The bellow of cattle travelled through the open window and he turned to gaze out at the land he called home. Leaving here, and his family, was going to be bittersweet. But Sarah Clarke was worth it, and he could finally make his dream to live closer to the coast a reality. The offer they'd put in on the Tranquil Valley property had been accepted, now they had to wait for the usual twenty-eight days cooling-off period before they picked up the keys to their new home. He couldn't wait to start their life together, and make plans for the family they'd spoken endlessly about. Two kids, maybe three, and he and Sarah would be living their dream. Remembering their many deep and meaningful conversations, he shook aside his concerns about asking her to marry him. It was the natural next step in a very committed relationship.

Glancing at the two upended wide-brimmed hats on his dresser, he felt a rush of contentment. He'd finally found his one in a million cowgirl – a sweet, sassy, tender-hearted woman who'd own his heart for an eternity. His family and his mates all loved her, and who wouldn't with her fun, generous spirit? Inhaling her intoxicating scent, he thought about how the universe worked in such mysterious ways. After his run of bad luck in the love department, he had started to think the universe was conspiring against him, and he truly believed he was never going to meet the lady of his dreams. But here she was, right beside him. He found it hard to believe this goddess of a woman loved him as much as he loved her. Found it hard to believe they were about to buy their very own property together. Found it hard to believe he was finally leaving Rosalee Station. Things were moving fast and usually that would terrify him, but in this case he wouldn't want it any other way now that he'd won her over. He would do anything for Sarah Clarke – he was willing to lay down his life for her, move mountains for her. He felt like the luckiest man alive to be able to wake up to her every single morning.

In awe of her beauty, both inside and out, he gently pulled her closer, loving the way he could feel her heartbeat against his own. Her dishevelled blonde curls lay scattered across the pillow. Peering down at her pink-painted toenails poking out of the bottom of the doona, he smiled. A true country girl at heart with determined grit that would outdo most men, she also had a feminine side that he wholeheartedly adored. She was the epitome of balance and perfection.

A four-wheel motorbike roared past the window, Slim and Liam's laughter carrying with the noise of it. A pair of larrikin stockmen, always up for a laugh, Matt couldn't help but chuckle with them. He wondered what adventures they were up to today – there was never a dull moment when in their company. Duke barked excitedly from the back porch, a doggy greeting as the bike roared past and quickly faded off into the distance. Thank goodness for the makeshift chook wire fencing closing off the latticework of the verandah, otherwise Duke would be running like billyo after them. With all the commotion, Sarah stirred, her arms tightening around him. His heart skipped a beat.

'Good morning, handsome.' Her bright green eyes looked sleepy as she smiled up at him.

'Hey there, my beautiful.' Her lips appeared even sweeter first thing in the morning and he craved to taste more of her. Leaning in, he placed a tender kiss against their softness, the simple touch firing his body to voracious life. 'How'd you sleep?'

'Like a log.' Yawning, she stretched with the grace of a cat.

'Me too … I reckon it might have been because of all that lovemaking tiring us out.' He smiled wickedly, and she returned a sassy grin of her own.

'Well, there's much more where that came from, my handsome cowboy.'

'Is that so?' He trailed his fingers featherlike down her side, loving the way her skin covered in goosebumps and her nipples hardened against his chest.

'Yup, you've just seen the start of it.' Smiling ruefully, she threw back the thin cotton sheet and slipped from his reach. 'But I'm afraid any more hanky panky will have to wait until tonight, seeing as your dad wants us to fix the pump at the top dam.'

'Come back here, you sexy minx.' He grabbed a good handful of her behind, playfully trying to force her back to him.

With a mischievous glint in her eyes she skilfully rolled away from him, onto her side, dragging the sheet with her. It left him completely naked, his longing for her evident. Her gaze travelled downwards and a coy smile curled her lips. Holy hell, she could make him hot for her within seconds. He ached to be at one with her, but he used every bit of his willpower to not pull her back to bed.

'Make sure you save that thought, Miss Clarke.' He wished he could have his wicked way with her, but at this time in the morning (which was considered a damn good sleep-in) there was work to be done, as usual. He climbed from the bed and sorted through the basket of clean clothes he was yet to fold, aware her eyes were on him the entire time. And he loved it.

Sarah came in beside him, pulling out some fresh clothes from the same basket. 'You want some Vegemite on toast and a cuppa before we head off?'

'Yeah, thanks, that sounds ripper.' His jocks now on, Matt tugged his jeans up while watching Sarah slip on her red G-string and then a black lacy bra. How in the hell was he meant to keep his hands off her all day while knowing about her sexy underwear beneath her jeans and button-up paisley shirt?

Catching his eyes, she grinned and stopped buttoning, leaving her bra visible and her ample cleavage tempting. 'You like what you see?'

Momentarily speechless, he smirked and nodded, the luscious curves of her womanly body doing things to him he couldn't put into words right now.

'Good, because for the record ...' She closed the distance between them. Reaching up on her tippy toes, she wrapped her arms around his shoulders and pressed her body into him. 'I really like what I see too.'

With his hands around her waist, Matt lifted her from the floor. She wrapped her legs around him and their lips met, passionately, hungrily.

Reluctantly pulling back before he tore off what little clothes she'd put on, he captured her eyes with his and smiled. 'Where have you been hiding all my life, you beautiful, sexy woman?'

∽

Sarah devoured the view of Rosalee Station from the highest vantage point, Rocky Ridge. It was her and Matt's favourite spot. With a showman's pizzazz, the full moon hung high and bright among the squillions of stars. Over a million acres and twenty thousand head of cattle separating them from their closest neighbour, this was outback living at its finest.

It had been a long day of hard yakka, the top pump proving to be an absolute bastard to fix. Regardless, she loved working beside her hunk of manly man, watching how his muscles flexed beneath his shirt, and loving the way they would constantly catch sideways glances, their longing for each other knee-buckling. Freshly showered after her day of tough physical work, and pressed up against him, she floated way above cloud nine. Never in her wildest dreams would she have believed she'd find herself a man so worthy of loving, a man who reciprocated the profound love she had for him. It went beyond anything she'd ever imagined feeling when and if she was lucky enough to meet 'the one'.

Their lips brushing against each other's, Matt then graced her with a toe-curling smile, sending her insides tumbling even more before he tucked a tendril of hair behind her ear. She gave him a coy smile of her own as his fingers left a trail of heat wherever they touched. Contentment settled deep within her heart and soul. Everything had finally fallen into place. What had she done so right in her life to deserve all this? Although over the moon with happiness, there was a small part of her that was terrified it was all going to blow up in her face, that this deep love was too good to be true. She wished the tiny voice of pessimism in her head would shut the hell up. She was twenty-three, with her whole life ahead of her, and she couldn't be happier with the possibility of spending it with this amazing man. She had to focus on that and ignore her fears. There'd been no red flags. No hints of any bad times to come. He was wowing her with everything he did – and especially with this. She'd never been on a stargazing date before. It was the most romantic setting in the world, and she couldn't help smiling with delight at the dazzling beauty of it all.

Matt had spread a blanket on the bonnet of his LandCruiser and she cuddled into him, enjoying his warmth that protected her from the chilly night air. All around them, the flat, copper-red landscape of Rosalee Station stretched on into the never-never, with nothing manmade ruining the spellbinding view. It was Mother Nature at her finest. She heard the *thump, thump* of grey kangaroos approaching, the mob making a wide berth around the LandCruiser before hopping away. Beyond where she could see, dingoes roamed amongst the rocky cliffs and scribbly gums, their howls distant but distinct. It was an unnerving sound she'd grown accustomed to during her life as camp cook, but certainly not one she liked. The sky above them sparkled like a swathe of velvet encrusted with glimmering diamonds, and the blackness of the night surrounded them, making her feel as though she and Matt were the only ones to inhabit this magical outback world. He pointed out all the different stars and constellations, explaining the myths behind each one, and she was amazed by his knowledge. Could he get any better? Not only was he handsome as hell on the outside – his towering frame and muscular physique was drool worthy – but his mind was extremely attractive too. Matt Walsh was undeniably the entire package. And he was all hers. And she wasn't letting him get away. Ever.

Snuggling closer still, she breathed in his fresh scent from his shower mingled with his spicy aftershave and a hint of leather. He smelt so good, earthy and manly, and she loved the way her body melted into his as they cuddled. It was as though they were made for each other – two peas from the same pod. With only moonlight to guide him, Matt pushed a ringlet of blonde hair off her forehead and kissed her gently on the lips, sending the already flickering flames dancing wildly in her soul. Then running his hand softly down her face, he looked deeply into her eyes. The intensity snagged her breath and made her feel giddy all at once.

'I love you, Sarah Clarke, with all my heart and soul. And I can't wait to begin the rest of our lives together in Malanda.'

She smiled dreamily back at him, her heart reaching for his. 'I love you too, Matt. This is the life I've always dreamt of, and I'm sharing it with the most mind-blowing man in the world. I still can't believe we're together.' She sucked in a shuddering breath, her emotions almost getting the better of her. 'We were on different journeys in our lives not long ago, and now here we are, together, wrapped in each other's arms, talking about our future. It's absolute heaven!'

He smiled tenderly. 'It surely is, my beautiful, sassy, sexy cowgirl.'

Sarah felt heat rise on her cheeks. 'Wow, now that's a compliment and a half, lucky me.'

A peaceful silence descended, and they gazed at the stars for a few more moments, lost in their thoughts. 'Hey, how about a song?' His voice was husky. 'Any requests?'

But before she could answer he pulled gently out of her arms and slid off the bonnet, his boots stirring the dust as he landed. 'Hmm . . . I reckon I'm in the mood for some Garth Brooks.' She smiled like a lovesick teenager as she watched him nod and then flick through his CD case.

'You know how much I love old Garthy boy, and I've got the perfect tune in mind.' Holding a CD up and shaking it, he then leant into the cab to put it in the CD player, skipping forward a few songs.

'To Make You Feel My Love' finally played.

'Oh my god, I freaking love this song!' Sarah called out into the night as the first bars rang out softly.

The driver's door squeaked as Matt closed it. 'Good, because it reminds me of you every time I listen to it.'

A bubble of bliss erupted in her heart. 'Aw, that's so sweet.' She sang along to herself as she waited for him to join her back on the bonnet.

But when he came back to her, he didn't climb up but instead held out his hand. 'Can I have this dance, my beautiful princess?'

Sarah didn't think the night could get any more romantic, but it just had. 'Yes, you may, my spunky cowboy,' she replied with a gentle smile.

Sliding down off the bonnet and into his irresistibly strong arms, she rested her head on his chest, lost in happiness as she listened to his heartbeat. Matt took the lead and waltzed her gently around, one hand cupping the curve of her back while the other tenderly held her hand. And without another word needed, they danced, their boots sliding across the red earth beneath them and the moon spilling its silvery light across their faces.

I have found the love of my life, Sarah thought.

Above them, millions of stars shone down from the beautiful country sky, creating a picture-perfect romantic atmosphere. The country love song was nearing its end when Matt stopped dancing. Their eyes met, and then held. Something unfathomable and so deeply intimate passed between them. Sarah's heart fluttered and then flew. Leaning in, he feathered a kiss, so soft and gentle, she felt as if she were floating on a cloud. The fire between them flamed even brighter, intensified, and then burst into a plethora of sparks throughout her. Taking her by the hand, he cleared his throat as he dropped to one knee. No. He wasn't. Couldn't be. No man would commit like this so quickly. Was she imagining it? He blinked as if warding off tears. This was oh so beautifully real. Time screeched to a halt. Her heart melted and then welled as she blinked back hot tears of her own. He pulled a little black box from his top pocket and opened it, revealing the most beautiful engagement ring she'd ever seen, nestled amongst red velvet. She stared at it, her eyes wide and her mouth open, trying to make sense of what was happening. This *had* to be a dream, and if it was, she never wanted to wake up. She almost pinched herself to confirm it wasn't.

'You okay, baby?' Matt's voice was a whisper.

She nodded, unable to speak.

He gave her hand a tender, loving squeeze.

Beneath the silvery moonlight, the sapphire sparkled like one of the glimmering stars in the velvet black sky. It was her favourite gemstone, and he knew that. Her hands fluttered to her chest. Her breath whooshed out in a sweet sigh. She stood, speechless, her whole body tingling with unadulterated happiness.

Matt graced her with a trembling smile. 'Sarah Clarke, I've loved you from the very first moment our eyes met. And I reckon, with how deep my feelings run for you, maybe even before that. You're everything I've ever wanted in a woman, and more. I want to kiss you goodnight every single night, and the first thing I want to see every morning is your beautiful, smiling face. I want my heart to be your shelter, and my arms to be your home. I want you to be the mother of my children. I want to grow old with you, and sit on rocking chairs on our back verandah and reminisce about our lives. So, Sarah, will you make me the happiest man on this earth and marry me?'

Sarah found it hard to process the perfection of the magical moment, every single word hitting her heart. Tears of pure joy rolled down her cheeks. 'Yes,' she said. 'Yes, of course I'll marry you, you beautiful man.'

'Oh thank god for that.' He breathed a sigh of relief like he'd been holding his breath for an eternity. 'With how pale you went, I was worried you were going to say no.'

She smiled, his nervousness endearing. 'Now why would I go and do something stupid like that?'

He grinned waywardly. 'Stranger things have happened.' Taking her hand, he slid the ring on her finger. Looking up at her, he smiled like a man who had just won the lottery.

She launched herself at him, dropping to her knees and wrapping her arms around his neck. 'You have made me the happiest and luckiest girl alive. I love you so much, Matt.'

'Love you too, baby. There'll be no getting rid of me now.'

'Oh trust me, I'm not ever going to be getting rid of you. You're mine forever and ever.'

'Me and you, forever and always.' His strong hands settled on her back as their lips met.

Their kiss held so many promises and so much love she thought her heart was going to burst. Then he pulled her even closer still. His big, strong arms wrapped tightly around her, possessively, tenderly. She wanted to stay like this forever, in his arms, and now, she never had to live a day without him by her side. She clung to him and rested her head against his chest, listening to his pounding heart. The heart that belonged to her.

CHAPTER
2

Rosalee Station, Central Australia
Seven years later

It was a brand new year, a fresh start to achieve the resolutions she hadn't last year. Like starting yoga, and doing a few cooking classes, maybe Thai and Japanese, or even German – Sarah loved anything to do with food. It was the way she relaxed and wound down after splitting her time between motherhood, being a good wife, and the farm – not an easy juggling act, but she did it, and enjoyed every tiring, backbreaking second of it. She and Matt had a goal in mind – to do the hard yards for another couple of years, and then sell up to hopefully make a profit. As much as she loved living in Malanda, where the climate was cool enough to have a fireplace, and the feed for their cattle was endless, she missed being close to her friends and family in Mareeba, especially now Eve was old enough to form bonds and needed company. She thanked the powers that be for having a man like

Matthew Walsh in her life – he lived by his motto that as long as they all stuck together, and he had his bucking bulls to breed and train, he didn't care where they lived.

Humming to herself, she packed the last of the glasses from the top rack of the dishwasher away in the cupboard. Sunlight poured through the kitchen's bay window, igniting the sun catcher into an array of colours, and the smell of freshly brewed coffee and sizzling bacon filled the room. As usual, the homestead was a hive of activity, and Sarah loved the feeling of wholesomeness she always had when they found the time to visit her in-laws. She glanced outside. The sky was an eggshell blue without a cloud in sight, and ripples of heat blurred the silhouettes of the horses off in the distance. The land seemed to stretch on forever, with little speckles of green sprouting amongst the endless brown thanks to the arrival of the wet season. Even so, today was faultless. It was the right weather to spend a few hours out on horseback, for some time to herself, away from mummy duties while Matt took Eve fishing. Not that she would ever complain about the time she spent with her daughter. Being a mum was the ultimate gift. It was just that, sometimes, it was nice to relax in silence. She felt a twinge of guilt even thinking so, but as her mum had assured her, the longing for alone time came with the territory of being a mother.

The ABC radio played softly in the background, the announcer proclaiming that it was a perfect first day of the year, albeit sweltering hot. Sarah had to agree. Despite the eyelash-adhesive flies, the red dust that got into places it shouldn't, and the unrelenting heat that made you sweat before you'd even had time to dry off from a shower, this was her favourite time of the year to visit Rosalee Station. Although it was New Year's Day, the festive vibe of Christmas still lingered in the Walsh homestead. With the mustering season done and dusted early, and the guys she'd grown over the years to regard as brothers still here for another week before chuffing off to their out-of-season jobs, they all had time to relax and cherish the little things. And it was the little things that meant so much to her. Sarah smiled, feeling as though life couldn't get much better.

Judy bustled in and dunked her hands into the soapy water in the sink. 'It's a beautiful day in paradise, isn't it?' Her smile was wide and warm as she dried them on a tea towel.

'It sure is.' Sarah matched her smile.

'I hope the boys get here soon. I don't want breakfast to get cold.'

'I don't reckon they'll be too far away, Judy. Their bellies would be growling by now.'

Judy nodded in agreement as she went over to the stove.

While thinking about where she would venture to in the saddle, Sarah busied herself lining up nine dinner plates. Bacon, sausages, eggs, baked beans, mushrooms, grilled tomatoes, hash browns – her stomach ached with the thought of the feast Judy was preparing. She'd learnt that copious amounts of food was a given here. A sudden gush of hot air filled the room and she turned to see her hunky, spunky husband walking through the back door of the homestead. She graced him with a tender smile and Matt grinned at her from beneath his wide-brimmed hat, his brown eyes mischievous, as always, before he took his hat off and hung it on a hook, revealing his freshly clipped brown hair. Her heart swelled at the sight of him, covered in red dust from head to toe. There was something so raw and primal about a man of the land. And besides that, what wasn't there to love about her good-hearted, hard-working cowboy? Even now, after seven years together, he still made her heart flutter and her knees weak.

'Daddy!' Dropping her crayon next to her drawing, six-year-old Eve Walsh leapt from her seat and into Matt's arms, her chaotic blonde curls framing her petite features. In looks, she was most certainly her mother's daughter, but in spirit, she was Daddy's little girl.

Cuddling her tightly, Matt dusted her cheeks with kisses. 'Morning, sweetheart, did the tooth fairy come last night?'

'She sure did.' Her smile widened, revealing the new gap at the front. 'And she gave me a whole ten dollars.'

'Wow. You're a mighty rich six-year-old. I might have to ask you for a loan.'

Eve tipped her head to the side. 'What's a loan?'

Matt chuckled. 'Not something you need to know about just yet.'

'Okay then.' Eve crumpled her nose up. 'You really stink, Daddy.'

Matt rolled his eyes, which matched the colour and intensity of his daughter's. 'Don't beat around the bush, will you, Eve?' He smiled cheekily at Sarah over Eve's shoulder. 'You're becoming more and more like your mother every day.'

'Oi.' Sarah tossed the tea towel from her shoulder in his direction. 'I beg to differ.'

Matt successfully avoided it by ducking to the side. Eve giggled as she wriggled free of his arms and hopped back up to the table to continue drawing.

'What are you making, sweetheart?' Matt peered over Eve's shoulder.

Eve pointed to three stick figures holding hands. *My Family* was written above it. 'This is me, you and Mummy.' She smiled up at him. 'And I'm about to draw Duke. Do you like it?'

'Nope ... I *love* it.'

Eve grinned a smile that would outshine the sun.

Padding towards Matt, Sarah gave him a quick peck on the lips. Catching a whiff of something disgusting, she swiped at the air. 'Good god, you really do stink.' She smiled. 'Reminds me of the day we wrestled each other in that putrid mud ... it took me days to get the smell out of my hair.'

'Ah, sweet memories ... we were young lovers back then.' He smiled charmingly. 'And FYI, before you both hound me, I'm going to run through the dip before brekkie, which by contrast smells divine, Mum.' He licked his lips. 'I'm bloody starving.'

'You've got five minutes before it's on the table, love,' Judy Walsh called from where she was dealing with two frypans and a pot on the AGA stove. She turned and wiped her hands on her bright yellow apron. 'Is your father far away?'

'Nope, he was right behind me. He just stopped to give Duke and Stella a drink on the porch. The poor buggers needed one after jumping around like frogs in socks.' He chuckled and shook his head. 'You can't half tell Duke's glad to be here.'

Judy picked up the bowl of eggs she, Sarah and Eve had collected from the chook pen less than an hour ago. 'Good, because the rest of the crew will be here any minute, and I don't want breakfast going cold.'

Setting the table, Sarah's heart sank as she thought about the fact one of the chairs would be empty this year. It had been a blow, getting the news that Stumpy, Rosalee Station's seasonal chopper musterer for the past ten years, had died in a helicopter accident five months ago. Mustering by air was a dangerous job, and sadly, it had taken a few of their friends over the years. It came with the territory but that didn't make it any easier to accept. Tears stinging her eyes, she quickly blinked them away, sucked in a breath and put a smile on her face. Stumpy wouldn't want her mourning; he'd want her, and everyone else, to celebrate his fifty-eight years of life. Which is exactly what they'd done at his wake. Getting through his funeral had been tough, but the wake had been one hell of a send-off, leaving everyone with hangovers that had taken them all a few days to get over.

The back door creaked open again and Steve walked in, looking as dusty and dirty as his son. Duke and Stella skidded in at his side, their tails wagging like the clappers. Duke's nose was as red as the mud on both the men – he'd obviously been digging. Sarah smiled at her long-time furry mate, the grey on his muzzle showing his thirteen years. Stella, Judy's dog, was half his age, but Duke kept up with her in the rascally sense. After Judy told them to get on their beds, both dogs curled up in the corner on their rugs.

With a weary sigh, Steve hung his hat on the hook beside Matt's. 'Well that took way longer than expected.'

Matt came back in, smelling one hundred percent better than before. 'Tell me about it, old fella. That bloody waterline was clogged up to the eyeballs. No wonder there was hardly any water getting through to the troughs.'

'Yeah, it sure was.' Steve gave Matt a pat on the shoulder. 'Thanks for helping out. You come here for a holiday and I've had you working almost every day.'

'No worries, Dad, I like helping out when I'm here. And with the drunken larrikin state the boys were in last night when Sarah and I made our stealth exit from the workers' cottage, I'd safely say they would've needed their beauty sleep this morning.'

Steve chuckled and shook his head. 'Yeah, I'd say so, knowing that lot. They'll never learn.'

Matt was fresh and clean but the stench on Steve's clothes filled the kitchen, and Sarah stepped away from him to find some fresh air. Retrieving the tea towel from the floor and then tucking her unruly curls behind her ears, she went back to drying up the few containers left in the dishwasher – why in the heck they never dried in a machine hot enough to boil an egg was beyond her. 'Would you like me to make the toast after this, Judy?'

'Yes please, Sarah. The bread is in the freezer.' She turned to her husband and wrinkled her nose. 'You having a shower before brekkie, too, then, love?' Judy's tone was more telling than questioning.

Steve chuckled. 'I'm gathering that's an order, my darling wife?'

'You're gathering right.' With a cheeky smile, Judy then focused on cracking eggs into a frypan almost big enough for paella. 'Everyone still like their bum nuts over-easy?'

'Yeah, thanks,' was the collective reply.

Thirty minutes later, nine of them were sat at the table, bellies full and plates basically licked clean. Conversation flowed freely, as did the pot of coffee, the laughter loud and contagious. Her cuppa cradled in her hands and sitting beside Matt's sister, Georgia, Sarah gazed across the dining table at the two people who meant more to her than life itself. She was so grateful for the little family God had blessed her with. Giggling, Eve pulled a face at her dad, and Matt returned the gesture with one that made Sarah's heart melt. Eve was certainly Daddy's little girl. Look out anybody that ever hurt her, and Lord help her very first boyfriend.

'So where did you two sneak off to last night?' Slim said as he leant back in his chair, his belt undone and his hands folded behind his head. 'One minute you were on the dance floor, boogying like there was no tomorrow like the good old days, and next minute you were both gone.'

Sarah stifled a laugh as she spotted his belly button poking out from beneath his shirt – some things never changed. 'I was buggered … can't keep up with you mob anymore.'

'Oh, don't tell me you've gone soft in your old age, Sarah?' Liam grinned, his Irish accent pronounced, and then graced her with a wink.

'Nope, not soft at all … it's called growing up,' Sarah shot back playfully, enjoying the banter.

'I'm too young at heart to ever grow up. I'm a party animal from way back.' Liam smothered a yawn.

Patrick jumped into the conversation, his bloodshot eyes in stiff competition with the red shirt he was wearing. 'Yeah, look at you go, bro.'

'Hey don't you start, Patrick …' Liam looked at his brother. 'I outlasted you by a long shot.'

'Oh no, you didn't.' Patrick said it like he was from the Bronx.

Liam pointed accusingly at him. 'If my memory serves me right, you were facedown in the lounge chair by eleven-thirty, didn't even make the countdown.'

'Ah, well … I was looking for spare change down the side of it.'

'Oh, pull the other leg, Pat,' Slim said, and chuckled.

Georgia yawned noisily beside Patrick, her red-rimmed eyes not much better than his. 'I'm with Sarah, it's about time we grew up, huzzbuzz.'

'Never.' Patrick shot her a playful look. 'I will disown you as my wife if I ever hear you say that again.'

Georgia gave him a firm slap and Patrick winced.

Liam leant forward, his forearms resting on the table. 'So what's on the cards today, Walshee?'

'I'm taking Eve fishing, you wanna join?'

'Yay, I love fishing!' Eve squealed, wiggling in her seat.

Liam shook his head. 'Oh, thanks, but no thanks … this Irishman needs his beauty sleep.'

'You boring old fart,' Matt said with a devilish grin, scarcely ducking away from a poke in the ribs with Liam's fork.

'How 'bout you, Patrick?'

'Count me out. The missus has got me under the thumb today. Apparently two months in our new place is long enough to have fitted the toilet-roll holders – but I beg to differ.' He shot Georgia a sideways glance, succumbing to another firm slap from his wife.

'How 'bout you, Slim? Got any plans for the day?'

'Thought you'd never ask.' Slim grinned. 'I'd love to join you … once this food goes down.' He sat up, fumbling with the top button of his jeans as he turned his attention to his left. 'That's if you don't mind, Eve?'

'I'd love you to come along, Uncle Slim. You're the bestest fun.'

Slim smiled from the heart. 'Aw, thanks, darling.'

'Well, I've got to get back to it. No rest for the wicked, as they say.' Steve stood, his chair scraping as he pushed it out.

'What have you got to do, Dad? I thought we were all supposed to be taking it easy,' Georgia said as they all began gathering plates and cutlery from the table.

'Oh, this and that,' Steve muttered, carrying a couple of mugs to the sink.

'You know your father, Georgia, got bloody ants in his pants. He almost sent me round the bend when we were caravanning.

I couldn't get the bugger to sit still for longer than a couple of hours.'

Georgia balanced a pile of plates in her hands. 'I don't know how you did it, Mum.'

'Hey, this old bloke has feelings you know.' Steve smiled as Judy tucked her chair back into the table.

Sarah helped Eve down from her chair. Grabbing a wet wipe from the packet she always had nearby, she cleaned her daughter's greasy hands. 'I think you should go and brush your teeth and have a trip to the loo before you and Dad head off.'

'Okay, Mummy.'

'Good girl.' Sarah smiled proudly, always amazed by Eve's willingness to do as she was told. She watched Eve dash off down the hallway, with Duke hot on her heels. Eve's laughter carried with them into the bathroom. The two had been inseparable since the day Sarah had come home from the hospital with Eve bundled in her arms, Duke looking extremely protective of his tiny friend.

'Thanks for breakfast, Judy,' Liam said, rubbing his stomach. 'I think I need to go and sleep it off now. I feel like a beached whale.'

'Me too,' Patrick added before placing a kiss on his mum-in-law's cheek. 'You're the best cook ever.'

Georgia poked him in the ribs. 'Hey, I thought I was the best cook ever.'

Patrick jumped back, rubbing his side. 'Will you stop bashing me up, Mrs McDonald.'

'Never,' Georgia said with a wicked grin. She started rinsing dishes in the sink, splashing water up the window, before stacking them into the dishwasher.

Judy wiped the droplets of water away with a cloth. 'You go, love, too many hands make for more work.'

'You sure, Mum?'

'Of course.' Judy plucked the plate from her daughter's hands, and being a creature of habit re-rinsed it. 'I like to be the Queen of my kitchen, as you all know very well.' She waved her hands in the air, smiling. 'So out you all go, be gone with you.'

Slim plonked a serving plate down on the sink then plucked the last piece of bacon from it and shoved it in his mouth. 'You sure, Mrs W?' he mumbled through the mouthful.

'Sure I'm sure. Go and get ready for your fishing trip.'

Amidst the usual chaos, Sarah started to wipe down the tomato sauce bottle and the table around it. Eve had tried pouring it but when she gave it a hit, the sauce had exploded over her plate, onto the table and into a pool on her fried egg.

Matt's arms circled around Sarah's waist as he tugged her into the hallway, away from prying eyes and ears. She enjoyed the feeling of his body pressing up against her. 'Hey there, sexy.' His voice was hushed and husky, making her toes curl.

'Hey there, handsome,' she purred back.

'You going my way?' He nibbled on her earlobe, sending goosebumps skating over her skin.

'Maybe.' She grinned naughtily over her shoulder. 'Depends what you're offering.'

'That's for me to know and you to find out,' he whispered in her ear.

She spun to face him and they enjoyed a fleeting kiss, their lips barely touching before Georgia walked out and told them to get a room, and everyone else mumbled in agreement.

'Love you, my beautiful,' Matt said, loud and proud.

'Love you too.' Sarah smiled.

Eve skidded in beside them, as did Duke, both of them breathless. 'Ready, Daddy.' She pulled on her favourite pink cap and jiggled excitedly on the spot.

Unwrapping her arms from around Matt's shoulders, Sarah knelt and took Eve's hands in hers, marvelling, as always, at how tiny and fragile they were – such a contrast to her daughter's fierce, effervescent nature. 'Now, you make sure you're a good girl for Daddy today, and don't go in the dam without someone going in there with you, okay?'

'I promise I won't, Mummy.'

'Cross your heart?'

Eve nodded as she did the movements. 'Cross my heart.' And then she clutched the half-moon pendant on the gold chain around her neck, reaching out to touch the other half of it hanging from Sarah's necklace. 'Heart to heart, Mummy, I promise I'll be a good girl.'

Sarah's heart filled with so much love she thought she might burst. She clutched the pendant Eve had given her for Christmas. 'You know what?'

Eve shook her head. 'No.'

'You're the most beautiful soul I have ever met.'

'What's a soul, Mummy?'

'Never mind, I should have said you're the most beautiful girl.'

'Ahhh, then why didn't you just say that, Mummy? You silly billy.'

'Don't worry, Sarah. I got this.' Matt placed his hand on Sarah's back and patted it reassuringly. 'I've been her dad for a while, so I kinda know how to take care of her.' He flashed her a playful grin. 'She'll come home safe and sound, although probably smelling like fish and mighty grubby.'

Sarah nodded, grinning. 'I know she will.' She pushed to standing and grimaced. 'Sorry for sounding like I don't trust you with her; mother's instinct, can't help myself.'

'Relax and enjoy your day. You deserve it.' Matt brushed a kiss over her cheek.

'I will, and I'll probably be back from my ride before you two, so I'll be waiting for you,' Sarah said.

'Come on, sweetheart.' Matt took Eve by the hand. 'Let's go catch us some fish for dinner.'

Eve punched the air. 'Yeah!'

Sarah felt a little piece of herself walking away with Matt, and even though she knew she was worrying about nothing, she couldn't help but feel like she should be going with them, just to keep an eye on things. She shook the feeling off, chastising herself for being so overprotective, but at the same time she couldn't help herself. 'Please make sure she puts her seatbelt on, Matt.'

Matt turned and graced her with one of his trademark knee-buckling smiles. 'Stop worrying, will you? I got this.'

She smiled. 'Okay, sorry.'

Just before they stepped outside, Eve turned and blew Sarah a kiss. Like they always did, Sarah caught it and held it to her heart, smiling from the inside out as she did the same and Eve caught it from the air, holding it to her chest and smiling.

Sarah's heart melted – a mother's love was infinite.

CHAPTER

3

Tranquil Valley, Malanda, Far North Queensland
Twelve months later

In a split second, her life had been turned upside down and inside out, and just like the previous one, it was a New Year's Day like no other. Tumbling through a deep dark abyss, with a hazy nightmare gripping her tightly, Sarah woke with a start. Her hand instantly went to the half-moon pendant lying against her chest. The room was dark, but the tiny sliver of light peeking between the blackout curtains alerted her to the fact the day she'd feared had arrived. Dread rose like floodwaters in her chest. A whimper escaped her. Sobs fought to surface, but she dug deep and fought off the wave of emotion – she'd become good at doing so these past twelve months. There would be plenty of time for crying when she got there, when she faced the harsh reality head on. For now, she wanted to save her strength, knowing that exhaustion was a part of her daily life. She was holding on to what was left of her world, but only barely, gripping whatever she could to keep it together for yet another day – not thinking past the next twenty-four hours. That's how she'd gone on this long, barely keeping their lives together, by living in every pain-filled moment because that's just what she had to do.

Rolling on her side and with the lingering images of the nightmare still upsetting her, she struggled to catch her breath. She couldn't put her finger on the details of her nightmare, but she would have preferred going through the horror of her bad dream all over again rather than having to face her reality today. She shivered, the sheet in a bundle at her feet and the doona nowhere in sight. With the fitful sleep she'd had, she gathered it would be on the floor at the foot of the bed. It was summer in the tropics, but typical of Malanda, the temperatures were well below what they were in her hometown of Mareeba.

Rolling over, she reached across the king-size bed, longing to find some comfort in the man she loved with every inch of her being. But she was not shocked to discover that Matt wasn't there. What had she expected? She punched his pillow, feeling cheated, unloved, uncared for. It was rare to find him here anymore, the couch was more his thing these days. Anything to not be near her, to not look in her eyes, to not see the hurt in them, which he blamed himself for. Sarah had to admit that in her times of utter despair, she sometimes silently blamed him for it too. And although she denied she did in every one of their arguments, she knew he sensed it – their connection was too strong for him not to. She wished she could control the unwanted feelings that clung to her deepest, darkest self … but she was only human. Both of them were holding on to what was left of their marriage, but was it because they were too scared to say goodbye? Had the letter she'd left for him on the table two days ago achieved anything? She wasn't sure, because he hadn't even mentioned it to her. For all she knew he could have screwed it up and thrown it in the bin.

Closing her eyes, she tried not to let her thoughts get away from her, but as usual, it was a fruitless battle. She felt as if she were living with a ghost. The conversations and cuddles she and Matt had once shared, their laughter and love, the hopes and dreams they'd been striving to make their reality, were now all things of the past. And yet she'd foolishly thought, given the gravity of the day, he may have somehow pushed his demons aside and tried to find comfort in her, and they could have found solace in one another. It was exactly twelve months since they'd lost their darling Eve. Her daughter's six years of life were all she had to remember her by. But Matt had another love now, one that wasn't doing him, or them, any favours. If only she could do something to snap him out of it, to help him through it, to rid him of his dependence on the booze to numb his anguish. As much as she wished she could be his rock, the pillar to hold him up, she had to fend off her own battles and deep-seated grief. It would be so much easier if he were right there beside her, if they could be there for one another, then the pain wouldn't be so raw, so suffocating. But it was as if they were strangers sharing the same house, with nothing to say to each other. They existed, that was all. Even though he'd survived the accident, she'd lost him, too, on that fateful day. The very thought tore her already broken heart to shreds.

Her mobile phone vibrating from the bedside table startled her. She picked it up and peered at the caller ID while also noticing a text message from her best mate, Lily. She'd read it in a minute. She sucked in a breath and tried to steady what she knew would be a trembling voice. 'Hey, Mum.'

'Hi, my love, how are you?' Maggie Clarke's tone was soft, compassionate.

Still shivering, Sarah tugged the sheet up and over her. 'Yeah, you know, just trying to keep myself together.' Her voice sounded way stronger than what she felt.

'Oh, love, I really do wish there was something I could do to take your heartache away.' Maggie sniffled and Sarah could picture her mother trying to do exactly the same thing on the other end of the line – keep herself together. 'I hate feeling so damn helpless.'

'I know, Mum, but nothing anyone says or does is going to bring her back.' Eve's petite face filled her mind. She bit back raw emotion, not wanting to upset her mother any more. Eve had been a diamond in their lives. It had been a tough year for all of them losing her.

'Mmm.' There was a short pause before Maggie cleared her throat. 'How's Matt going?'

'Yeah, you know.' Sarah tried to brush shaky fingers through her wild bed hair.

'Actually, no I don't.' Maggie sighed softly. 'Please, Sarah, tell me how things are going. I feel so cut off lately, especially with you refusing to talk about what's going on under your own roof. I'm your mother, love. I'll help you through anything.'

Sarah sighed. There was no use sugar-coating the situation any longer. Her mum, along with everyone else at the dinner table, had seen the worst of her frayed relationship with Matt only a week ago at Christmas lunch. Her father had had to drag Matt out to the shed for a man-to-man talk. So her mum and dad deserved to know the truth. 'To my knowledge he still hasn't shed a tear to this day, Mum, and he drinks all the time to numb his grief. I've tried to help him through it, but I honestly don't know what to do anymore. He's like an empty shell and I don't know how much longer I can live like this.'

'Oh, love, I don't think there's anything you or anybody else can do. The way he lashed out at you over Christmas dinner, accusing you of blaming him for everything, was harsh and uncalled for.'

Sarah's breath was ragged as the need to defend Matt overcame her. 'I know, Mum. He'd drunk way too much. But surely you and everyone else who was there understands that he's dealing with some massive guilt.'

'I do understand, love, we all do. But there comes a time when enough is enough, and from what you told me on Christmas Day, you've suffered a year of this and it's only getting worse. Like your father said to you, Matt has to want to try and work through it himself, and until he does, he's his own worst enemy.'

'Yes, I know, and I think he does too. He's in a really dark hole, Mum. It scares me to think how much deeper he could fall.' She sucked in a juddering breath. 'In a way I feel abandoned by him because of it, as much as I try not to. And I'm resenting him for it, so much so I'm actually thinking about asking for some time apart.' Sadness clawed at her throat. Her reserve broke and she cried quietly, doing her best not to let her mother hear. She'd wept rivers in front of her loved ones, and had reached a point where she felt they'd shouldered way more than their fair share of her heartache.

'Oh, my sweet daughter, I wish I could hug you right now.' Maggie's pained voice tugged at Sarah's heartstrings even more. 'I spoke to Matt's mum about it a few days ago and Judy is beside herself with not knowing what to do. We all are.'

'Yeah, I know, poor Judy, she called me yesterday for an update.' Sarah's throat pinched tight. 'I just wish he'd let me in, because I know if he could do that, we could work through it together.'

'Sorry to say, but I don't think that's going to happen, love. He really needs to go and see someone, get some help.'

'Don't you think I've tried to tell him that?' The words were snapped and Sarah instantly regretted her harsh tone.

'I'm sorry, love, I know you've tried. I'm so worried about him, and you. Please don't think I'm being heartless here, because you know how much we love Matt, but he should be there for you as you are for him, not shutting you out. And certainly not turning to the drink to numb the pain.'

Sarah cleared her throat and calmed her breathing. 'Don't apologise, Mum. I shouldn't have snapped at you.' Sighing, she shook her head, her cheeks wet with tears. 'I'm trying not to get mad at him, trying to understand why he is how he is. Yes, he was the one behind the wheel, and yes, he should have put Eve's seatbelt on, like I asked him to, but it's not like he deliberately rolled the ute. He's hurting, like I am. It's just that he doesn't talk about his feelings, whereas I do … which is why I'm further into the bereavement process than he is.' The tears continued to well and spill. 'I don't know how much longer we are going to last like this, and the thought of us breaking up kills me.' She sobbed now, the pain too much to conceal.

'Oh, love, I understand it's hard, but please try not to think like that. Matt loves you; that hasn't changed.' The phone was muffled, giving Sarah a few brief moments to try to pull herself together. She could just make out her dad's deep voice in the background.

'Your father says you should come and stay here for a few days, love.'

'I can't, Mum, I'm not leaving Matt here by himself.'

'Jimmy and Liam are there, so it's not like he'll be by himself.'

'Yes, but they're here to help out around the place, not to watch over Matt.'

'They're two of Matt's closest friends, Sarah, I'm sure they wouldn't mind.'

'Maybe not, Mum, but Matt would certainly mind me asking Jimmy and Liam to basically babysit him. He's feeling less of a man now, I don't want to make him feel any worse.'

'Matt doesn't need to know you've asked.'

'Mum, please …' Sarah's patience was wearing thin.

There was a moment's silence before Jack's deep voice came down the line. 'Hey, sweetheart, how are you?'

'Pretty shit actually, but I'll be right, Dad.' Conversations with her father were always more direct and to the point than with her mum.

'I know you said you don't need me and your mum there today, but we really feel like it would be good for you, and Matt, if we were.'

'It's the peak of the fruit picking season, Dad, and with Peter at the mines now and Daniel recovering from his knee surgery, you have to be there to hold the fort.'

'Yes and no, Sarah … there's ways around it. I could always pull Johnny Marsh from the paddock to watch over the shed crew.'

'Then who's going to watch the paddock crew, Dad? You know how slack that lot can be if there isn't a boss around. And it's a three-hour round trip to Malanda.'

'And?'

'And, you and Mum need to be there. Simple.'

'Sarah, you're more important than the farm.' Jack's voice was becoming sterner, even though Sarah could tell he was doing his best to bite his tongue.

'Look, I know you both love me to bits and want to help, but I'll be right.'

'Aha.' Jack sounded far from convinced. And to be honest, Sarah wasn't convinced she'd be all right today either, but having her parents there wouldn't ease the painful significance of the day. If anything, she would be even more of a mess and just crumble into their arms. And she didn't want to make Matt feel like her parents were judging him. Yes, they loved him, but they loved her more. Blood was always thicker than water. Also, Matt had shocked them, and her; the way he'd exploded at her halfway through Christmas lunch was inexcusable. His profanity was not like anything she'd ever heard from him before.

'I'll come and visit in the next couple of days, okay?'

'But, Sarah …'

'Dad, please stop.'

Jack sighed weightily. 'Okay, sweetheart.'

Barely holding herself together, Sarah knew she had to get off the phone before she cracked. Her parents wouldn't take no for an answer then, and for some inexplicable reason, she really wanted to prove to herself that she could make it through on her own today. There were going to be plenty more anniversaries of her daughter's death to contend with, so step by step, she had to go through the motions. 'I better go and get ready, Dad. Please tell Mum I love her.'

'I will. Love you, Sarah.'

'Love you too, Dad.' And she hung up before she broke down and wept uncontrollably, only to feel another surge of emotion engulf her as she read her best mate's text message.

Daniel and I are thinking of you today, my beautiful friend. I know you'll want time to yourself this morning, to filter through everything, so I'll ring you later this arvy to see how you're doing. Please know that if I could take away your heartache, I would. And please remember, I'm here to catch your tears and hold you tight, anytime of the day or night. Daniel sends you his love from his hospital bed. The bugger is climbing the walls already, and driving the nurses nuts, and he's still got six weeks of healing before he can walk properly – Lord bloody well help me! I'll be sure to light a candle today, for Eve. I love you a million, babes. Xo

Sarah texted back a quick thank-you message, a faint smile tugging at her lips as she imagined her ants-in-his-pants brother confined to bed rest for so long because of an old bull riding injury. She promised Lily they'd definitely catch up for a phone chat later. But her wispy smile vanished as quickly as it had appeared when she placed the phone down and returned to the crushing reality of what lay ahead today. The darkness of the room suddenly felt oppressive. She switched the bedside lamp on, squinting a little from the brightness. Choking back the damn relentless tears, she threw her legs over the side of the bed and the coolness of the timber floorboards beneath her feet somehow felt reassuring. Duke was instantly by her side and raising a paw. He rested it on her knee, his big brown eyes full of concern for her. Placing her hands on either side of his grey-speckled face, she leant down and kissed his muzzle, and then hugged him to her, thankful for her best mate's tireless support in his very own doggy way. She wasn't sure how she would have got through her darkest of days without Duke by her side.

Sitting back up, she ruffled his ears. 'I love you so freaking much, buddy.'

Duke barked a reply, his tail rhythmically tapping the floor. He nudged her hands with his cold nose.

Sarah gave him another loving pat. 'Come on then, I better let you out for toilet duties.'

As if understanding every word, Duke tap-danced over to the closed bedroom door.

Her body feeling a hundred years old, Sarah stuffed her feet into her slippers and then dragged herself up. Padding towards the door while trying to straighten out her aching back, she groaned. Grabbing her thin cotton robe from the floor, she pulled it on and tied it up. It was time to find out what state Matt would be in for the day, and her instincts told her it wasn't going to be pretty. She knew where she'd find him, the man who had once given her so much love, so much contentment, and the thought made her already heavy heart sink further. If only he'd let her in, if only he could let go of the guilt and stop blaming himself, if only they hadn't gone fishing that day, if only she'd followed her gut and gone with them … So many goddamn *if onlys*. Hindsight was an absolute bitch.

Making her way down the hallway, with Duke close by her side, she slowed as she passed the framed family photos that reminded her of wonderful days gone by but also deepened the cavernous aching hole in her soul. She had one particular favourite, and she forced herself to stop and look at it. Eve was in her pixie costume, flashing a wide grin that matched Matt's, who was standing beside her, holding her hand. Her cheeks were dusted with fine freckles and her eyes were full of the world's wonder. Anguish pounded Sarah like fists. She wrapped her arms around herself, as if trying to hold herself together. Next to it was another of her favourite photos – a snapshot from Christmas two years ago. Eve was cuddled in Matt's arms, both of them still in their pyjamas. Duke was at their feet amongst piles of scrunched-up wrapping paper and opened presents, Eve's reindeer headband perched on his head. Her vision blurred, Sarah sucked in a sharp breath. She felt a wild impulse to scream, to punch something, to run until she had no strength left. The emotional rollercoaster was relentless; it never stopped for her to get off.

Unable to stand there any longer for fear of losing what little self-control she had, she continued towards the staircase that led downstairs. She tried to keep her eyes looking forwards but the pull as she passed Eve's bedroom door was so strong that she couldn't take another step. She squeezed her eyes shut to stop the tears when her emotions engulfed her. She felt as if she were caught under a wave, struggling to resurface. The world spun in crazy circles beneath her feet. She bit her lip as the images came flooding back like a tidal wave that forced her to remember every tiny agonising detail ... the screech of brakes on gravel, heavy footfalls running across the verandah, Slim's cries for help, Judy's screams as she met him in the doorway, Sarah's own heart-wrenching cries as she overheard the words a mother never wanted to hear and collapsed to the floor.

The world had blurred, spun, sped up, slowed down, as she'd begged God for his mercy. The Flying Doctor was called, but by who, she couldn't recall. The time between the earth-shattering news and getting to where the ute had rolled had felt like a lifetime. The bull Matt had hit lay dead on the rutted dirt track, the ute upended on its roof beside it. Diving from the LandCruiser before it had even stopped she'd found her darling Eve, ashen, lifeless. And the blood, there'd been so much blood. Eve's platinum curls were soaked in it. Down on his knees, Matt had her tiny body in his arms, cradling her to him, sobbing, begging her not to die. Sarah had found herself doing the same, pleading with God to take her life for her daughter's. But no amount of begging had relieved them of the heartache no parents should ever have to endure. They'd been powerless as they watched when their beautiful, vivacious, kind-hearted Eve had taken her final, gasping breath. Hours later, Sarah was still clutching her lifeless daughter, screaming at anyone that dared try to take her from her arms.

Bracing her hand on the wall to stop from falling, she rested her forehead against Eve's closed bedroom door – leaving it open would be like pouring salt on the wound. Duke whined at her feet, and she gently told him to shush. He did, and rested up against her leg. A pretty, handmade, pink and purple plaque hung from a hook, only inches from her cheek. She reached up and traced the words with her fingertips, *Eve's Room*, treating it as if it were made of the frailest glass. Eve had been so proud of her efforts that day she'd made it, with speckles of paint splattered all over her face, hands and clothes. It had been one of the billion moments Eve had warmed Sarah's heart beyond belief. She wished with everything she had that she could hold her daughter tight, and tell her how much she loved her over and over again; that she could watch her grow older, year by year; be there to see her get married and have children, and grace the world with her beautiful soul. But that was never going to happen. God had taken Eve well before her time, and cheated Sarah of a parent's dream to see their child grow up and make a life of their own. She was never going to see Eve's beautiful smile, or her sparkling eyes, or feel her little hand entwined in her own, or hear her sweet voice, ever again. And the pain of that was asphyxiating. If she could die, without passing this same pain on to her loved ones, she would. The emotion she'd pushed down bubbled to the surface, and this time, she gave in to it, hot tears falling onto her cheeks. Sliding down the door, she sat with her back against it and cradled her knees in her arms, her grief spilling in loud sobs as Duke buried in close beside her.

Once she felt as if she had no tears left, Sarah stood on shaky legs. She wiped her face, straightened her shoulders, and took deep calming breaths. Tugging her unruly hair back, she pulled the hairband from around her wrist and shoved her hair into a messy bun. She took a step, and then another, physically and mentally having to force herself onwards – something she'd learnt to do over the past twelve months. Running her hand down the banister to steady herself, a sensation of anger mingled with her sadness as she descended each step. Duke was only one step behind her. This wasn't right. She and Matt should be comforting each other. He should be there for her, as she wanted to be for him. With the way he was acting, it was as if she were the one to blame for it all. And, feeling such a way, she was really reaching the end of her tether. Something had to give, had to change, before the dwindling spark of love she had left for him extinguished and left them wondering about what could have been if things had been dealt with differently. And she was desperate for that *not* to happen. As angry and hurt as she was, Matt meant everything to her.

She walked into the laundry and opened the back door for Duke, who bolted across the verandah and down the steps, relieving himself as soon as his paws had hit the grass. Job done, he took off in a trot towards the horse paddocks. Sarah was never really sure what he got up to for the hour or so that he'd be gone, but he always returned puffed out and ready for his morning snooze on his rug. Catching sight of her beloved stockhorse, Victory, his head down as he grazed and the morning sunlight sending his coat aglow, her heart brimmed with love. Victory was twelve years old now, and she'd been telling him her deepest confidences for eight wonderful years. Eve and Victory had also shared a beautiful bond. Eve had been horse mad – nothing could drag her away from hugging Victory or watching the television if there was a horse movie or documentary on. Like mother, like daughter. Close by, Matt's newest addition to their equine family, Marshmallow – named by Eve – rubbed her face up against the timber of a fence post. In contrast to Victory's bay colour, the Appaloosa's coat was pure white and speckled with tiny reddish spots. Quick to lay her ears flat with any horse that got in her way at feed time, she was a gentle giant with humans, and their pet chicken, Chilli. It wasn't unusual for Chilli to be seen riding bareback on Marshmallow or Victory – a sight that had always sent Eve into hysterical laughter. The memory stabbed Sarah's bleeding heart.

She stole a few moments to appreciate the land she and Matt had called home for the past seven and a half years. The homestead, sitting on the highest point on the land, had a commanding, uninterrupted view of their property, Tranquil Valley. Like a sea of green, paddocks rolled out in front of her, dotted with horses, cattle and prized bulls, and occasionally spotted with jacaranda trees in bloom. In season, the ground beneath the trees would be covered in a purple blanket. Eve had always loved lying under the trees, on the flowers, where she believed the fairies lived, thanks to Sarah's magical tales, which her own mum had told Sarah when she was a little girl.

Feeling the pull of the earth and the desire to ground herself, Sarah kicked off her slippers and padded down the back steps. Her bare feet touching the grass, she felt a little fire of hope that she would get through today. Wandering over to where the rope swing was tied to a sturdy limb on a big old gum tree, she plonked down on the wooden seat. The ground was worn into a trench at her feet. So many times she'd pushed Eve on the swing, her excited giggles infectious as she'd reached for the clouds with her tippy toes. The sudden need to feel what her daughter felt all those times overcame her.

Pulling her hair from the messy bun on top of her head, Sarah shook it free, her hands coming to grip the rope on either side of her. And then she kicked her legs out and leant back, driving the swing forwards. Back and forth, higher and higher, she pushed the seat up until she felt as if she were weightless. It was so … freeing. She tipped her head back, her long hair trailing out behind her, and looked to where two eagles floated effortlessly, feeling as if she could reach out and touch them. She stared up, in awe of the sky and its limitlessness, her spirit lifting a little, and then she allowed the momentum to slow, until her feet were skating across the ground, eventually coming to a stop. Her eyes settled on the horizon, and she followed where the green dipped into a valley then rose up into shadowed hills. Malanda was a good hour and a half's drive from Mareeba – her hometown – but it was as if it were another world away. Verging on the edge of the outback, Mareeba could become terribly thirsty in the dry season, whereas Malanda had green, rolling hills all year round that were often shrouded in mist, giving the impression this land was somehow closer to heaven than anywhere else. If only that were so, she would be closer to her beautiful Eve.

CHAPTER

4

Walking away from the house, Sarah acknowledged she was putting off going back inside, avoiding the moment when she and Matt would sidestep the elephant in the room. It happened every waking hour, and eventually something would have to give. Opening the door to the chook pen, Sarah jumped aside as Makka, the rooster, strutted out; cocky and assured, he was the king of the castle. His six feathered girlfriends followed. Chilli, the smallest and oldest of the chickens, did her usual mad dash across the gravel drive towards the horse paddock, where she would hang out with Victory and Marshmallow for most of the day. Sarah would find her egg there later, tucked away in the corner of a lavender bush – as it always was. Deciding to check for eggs in the pen a little later, when she had her basket to put them in, she turned and wandered back to the house, her steps getting heavier the closer she came to the back door. Out here, she felt free, as though she could somehow, some way, get through the day, but back inside, as much as she loved every character-filled inch of her home, it was a different story. The land was where she did her healing, and her soul searching. She'd never been one to stay indoors of her own choosing unless she was cooking, and she'd all but lost the love for that the day Eve had died.

Now back inside, and with her eyes taking a few moments to adjust to the dimness, she took determined steps down the hallway and towards the lounge room. Reaching the doorway, she tugged her robe in tighter, more for comfort than the bone-nipping cold. A gap under the curtains let in enough light for Sarah to see the dust particles flickering like jewels, but otherwise the room was dark. The stench of stale alcohol hit her and she knew Matt was in there. Walking around the dark shape of the coffee table, she flicked the lamp on beside the couch. The shadows disappeared and were replaced with Matt's bearded face half buried in one of the cushions. An upended packet of salt-and-vinegar chips covered her favourite cowskin rug. One crunched beneath her foot as she took a measured step forwards, and she cursed beneath her breath.

'Matt, are you awake?'

He mumbled something about leaving him alone – his voice low, gruff, tired – and then rolled onto his side, away from the light, and from her. Today of all days, why did he have to be a bastard? Hurt fired through her veins, and punctured her to the very core. He was still in his dirty work clothes from yesterday, and the dinner she'd made him of steak, mash and veggies sat uneaten on the coffee table beside an almost empty bottle of bourbon. As much as her heart bled for him, her anger intensified. There was only so much pity she could have, and only so many times she could peel him off the floor or the couch; only so many times she could beg him to go and get help before their relationship was irreparable. Like a rubber band pulled to its limits, she felt something inside of her snap. Her fists clenched at her sides, a tsunami of rage rose from deep within. She wanted to scream at him, punch his chest, make him hurt like he was hurting her. But she clamped her lips shut. She was determined not to start anything today. What good would it do? If she spoke what was on her mind right now, in the heat of the moment, their marriage would be well and truly over. And she didn't want that, especially on the anniversary of Eve's death.

'Matt, come on, it's time to wake up.' She prodded him. He didn't move. She prodded him again, this time raising her voice. 'Matt, bloody hell, wake up would you?'

Matt swiped at the air, trying to push her fingers away from his ribs. 'Yeah, righto.' His voice was groggy with a hangover. He groaned like an old man as he sat up. His eyes, which used to be as sharp as a hawk's on the hunt, were now lifeless and red-rimmed, and under them dark shadows loomed. 'I'm awake.' He couldn't even look at her.

'Do you want me to make you a coffee?' *To sober you up …* she wanted to add, but bit her tongue. It would only lead to an argument. Today was Eve's day. There was no room for anything else.

He finally dragged his bloodshot eyes from his socked feet to her face. There was so much sadness in them she had to fight from buckling at the knees. She longed to reach out and hold him, to kiss him and remind him how much she loved him, to tell him they'd get through this. But she knew from experience that he didn't like it when she did – he said it made him feel like a pity case.

He rubbed his face as if trying to will himself to return to the land of the living. 'Yes, please, but only if you're making yourself one. Don't want to put you out.'

She fought the urge to huff. 'Making you a cuppa is not putting me out, Matt, and I'm going to have some Vegemite on toast while I'm at it. Want a piece?' She didn't have an appetite whatsoever, but she would do anything to get him to eat something, anything, other than junk.

He shook his head. 'Don't think I could stomach it just yet, but thanks.'

'You have to eat.' She looked to where his jeans gaped at the waist. 'You're withering away to nothing.'

'Does it matter?' He shrugged, but even that was half-hearted.

'Yes, of course it matters.' Sighing, Sarah sat down beside him. Moments passed. Silence hung heavily, uncomfortably. Souls that used to reach for one another, resisted. She placed her hand over his, and he flinched, as though stopping himself from pulling away. She sucked back a sob. 'Are you going to come with me today, to see her?'

Matt stopped bouncing his leg. 'Do you want me to?'

'Of course I do. Why wouldn't I?' There was a hint of anger in her tone, but she couldn't help it. She was over trying to make him realise she loved him.

He scratched at his unruly beard. 'To be honest, it doesn't sound like you do.' He pulled his hand out from under hers and clasped his fingers together, his elbows on his knees and his knuckles turning white. 'I can't blame you if you don't want me there, seeing as it's my fault.'

A jolt of pain shuddered through her heart – an open, silent wound. 'Please, Matt, not today.'

He turned to her, his eyes stormy, challenging even. 'Why not today, Sarah?'

Words evading her, she shook her head, blinking back hot, heavy tears. She hated this distance, this isolation from each other. Looking to the coffee table, she spotted Eve's kindergarten photo that was usually on the fridge. She panicked with the thought of it being ruined. Reaching out, she picked it up, and then looked from Eve's smiling face to Matt's distraught one. Her bottom lip quivered with emotion.

He gently took it from her. 'I'll pop it back up. Sorry I snapped at you.' He stood, unsteady on his feet. Shoving his free hand in his pocket, he cleared his throat. 'I'll go and make us that cuppa, and get you some Vegemite on toast.'

Anything to get away from me … she wanted to say. 'Thank you, but no toast for me either, just a cuppa,' she whispered. 'I'm going to go to the loo and wash my face, and then I'll catch you in the kitchen.'

'Yup, take your time.' He turned on his heel.

Watching him walk away, Sarah would have given almost anything for Matt to turn back and comfort her. To feel his arms around her would mean the absolute world.

Ten minutes later she was sitting opposite him at the kitchen table, her hands wrapped around her cup of tea. She silently watched Matt's fingers fidgeting with anything he could reach and his shoulders bunched tight. He looked at least ten years older than his thirty-four years. 'So did you get my letter?'

'Yup.' His reply was short and certainly not sweet.

'And?'

'I'm going to try and do something about it.'

She huffed, exhausted with his refusal to talk about their problems. The phone conversation with her parents at the forefront of her mind, she couldn't hold back anymore. 'I really think you should go and talk to someone, sooner rather than later.'

'I know you do, but as I keep telling you, and everyone else that wants to give me their two bobs worth, talking to some shrink, some person I don't even know, isn't going to help me like it helped you.' He spoke without looking at her, choking on his words, clearly trying desperately not to cry. He inspected the holes in the peppershaker. 'Why won't any of you goddam listen and respect that?' His gaze was angry when he raised it to hers.

'Matt, we're only looking out for you. Tell me, then, how else are you going to heal the heartache if you bottle it all up?'

'By facing it head on, dusting myself off, and getting back in the saddle of life. But it's not proving easy, especially when everyone around me is telling me what I should and shouldn't be doing.'

'Drinking isn't doing you any favours, Matt.'

'Maybe not, but it numbs the pain for a little while, so I can sleep. I'll lose it completely if I don't get some kind of rest.' The expression in his eyes was hard, direct and deeply honest. There was raw pain in his voice. He cleared his throat and clasped his hands tightly on the table. He went to say something but then stopped himself. She could see his pulse beating fast in his throat.

'I understand you need rest but medication can do that too, you know. Help you relax enough to sleep.'

'I'm not going to take drugs, Sarah.'

'But you'll go and drink yourself into a stupor. Where's the bloody sense in that?'

'Please, Sarah, lay off, would you?'

She bit back, hurt. 'Lay off? Really?' So much for not arguing today – old dogs no new tricks.

'Yes, Sarah, please lay the hell off.'

Sarah's heart ached beyond belief. 'I can't live like this anymore. *We* can't live like this anymore.'

'Don't you think I know this?' He sighed and ran his fingers through hair that used to be shaved short, but had been left to grow wild, the same as his scruffy beard.

Her anger bubbled, intensified, erupted – until it was out of her control. 'You either go and get help, or we're ...' She screeched to a stop, cursing herself for speaking out in anger.

His fingers stopped strumming the table; his expression showed he was as shocked as she was with having said such a thing. 'We're what?'

Speechless, she stared at him. Her mouth opened and closed. She bit her bottom lip.

'We're what, Sarah?' His eyes narrowed. His jaw clenched as he waited for a response. When he didn't get one, he said it for her. 'Over?'

Her breathing slammed to a stop. She wanted to take the words back. Quickly, before she gave him an easy way out of their mess. 'Matt, I'm sorry ... I didn't mean it like that.'

Staring at her for a few more excruciating seconds, he sat back and held his hands up. 'Yes you did, and I can't blame you. I'm the one that's sorry.' His hands dropped to his side. 'I've ruined what we had, and everything in your letter is true, I need to take responsibility for it.'

'No, Matt, you haven't *ruined* us. You're just grieving in your own way, that's all.' She reached across the table to try to touch him, but he sat back even further in his chair. She withdrew and wrapped her hand around her coffee cup. 'If you could go and talk to someone, and find help to give up the booze ...'

'Sarah, stop, please just stop.' He shot to standing, his chair tumbling behind him and crashing to the floor. 'I can't have this conversation with you again. I honestly can't do this anymore.'

'Do what anymore?'

'Have you breathing down my neck all the time, reminding me how much of a failure I am.'

'I'm only trying to help you.'

'Well, take it from me, you're not helping, everything you say is only making me feel worse.'

She looked down at her cup and nodded. There were a million more things she wanted to say, but she didn't for fear of digging herself deeper into the shit with him. Walking on eggshells was something she'd never have believed she would have to do with Matt, but here she was, doing just that. And a big part of her was sick of it.

'I went and saw Doctor Lawson three days ago.'

'You did?' Hope rose in her chest.

'Yup, and I'm going to try and go cold turkey.'

'You are?' She knew she didn't sound convinced.

'I am. He's given me a script for Valium and some other stuff to help, but I'm going to try and do it myself if I can. Not really keen on taking drugs to get over the drink.' He carried his cup to the sink and after rinsing it out, upended it in the draining rack. Turning to face her, he folded his arms across his chest. 'You happy now?'

'Yes, of course. That's great that you went to see him, but why haven't you told me until now?'

'Because there's more to it than that, to talk about, and we haven't really said two words to each other since I went to see him.'

Sarah thought it was a lame excuse, but she'd learnt to pick her battles. 'Okay, fair enough.'

'I'll come to the cemetery with you, and then I think I should make plans to go sort myself out.'

'Go where?' She looked at him, hoping he was about to say a rehab clinic.

'The only place I can go, back to Rosalee Station. We need some time apart, to think, and to find ourselves again. This, us …' He waved his hands from her to himself. 'We're not working.'

Emotion made it impossible for her to speak. She took a sip from her cup and then sat staring at the clock above the stove. Time just kept on goddamn turning.

'Sarah, please, say something.'

Sucks when the shoe is on the other foot, hey, Matt? she wanted to say. But didn't. She didn't want to do this, didn't want to acknowledge they were so very close to the end. 'What about the farm?'

'Don't worry, I've already spoken to Jimmy and Liam about looking after everything while I'm gone, so the load's not put on you.'

She finally turned to look at him, the skinny, unkempt man standing before her looking nothing like the Matt she'd fallen in love with. 'You have? When?'

'Yesterday.'

'So you've been planning this and you haven't thought to talk to me about it?'

He shrugged like it was no big deal. 'I am now, aren't I?'

'No, Matt, you're not *talking* to me about it, you're *telling* me what you're going to do – there's a big difference. Don't forget, I'm part of this relationship, and it's not all up to you how we work this out.'

'I reckon it is up to me, when I'm the problem, Sarah.'

She sighed, shaking her head. 'I'm not happy about the guys getting told before me. It's like a kick in the face.'

'I'm sorry, I really didn't mean to make you feel like that. I was just worried about how you'd react, and I didn't want you to try and talk me out of it. We need some space, before we end up hating each other, and I desperately need some time, alone, to try and pull myself back together.'

Sarah felt completely and utterly exhausted, as though the fight had been knocked out of her. 'How long are you going for?'

'I'm not sure yet. All depends on how long it takes.'

'You're not sure?' She did her best to hide her rising anger. 'I wish I could up and leave, and run away from it all, like you are.'

Hurt creased his face. 'You think I'm running away?'

She refused to answer, knowing she could only say 'yes'.

Matt began to pace, back and forth, back and forth, his steps grating on Sarah's already frayed nerves. 'I'm not running away, I'm running to it, to where we lost Eve. I can't explain it but my instincts are telling me that's where I need to be. And with Georgia and Patrick needing to go to the city for the birth of their baby, it'll help Dad out, having me around while they're away.'

'Your mum and dad knew about this before me too?'

'Yes, I spoke to them yesterday as well, but asked them not to say anything because I thought it was my place to tell you.'

After only speaking to Judy yesterday, Sarah felt cheated by her mother-in-law. 'Damn straight it is, Matt. And you should have told me first.'

'Bloody hell, Sarah, I'm sorry.' He stopped and waved an arm in her direction. 'And for the record, you *can* just up and leave, if you want some time with your family. Jimmy and Liam have it well and truly covered here.'

'This is my home, Matt. Our home. Eve's home. I don't want to abandon it, or our animals for that matter.'

'You're not abandoning it or the animals, Sarah. And neither am I.'

'Yes, you bloody well are, and at the same time you're abandoning me when I need you the most, just like you have the past twelve months.'

He remained quiet, the deep sadness in his eyes letting her know her arrow had hit its mark. Hard. She felt bad, but at the same time truth sometimes hurt, and she was only speaking the truth of how she felt. 'Why do we need to be apart to get through this, Matt? Aren't two people who are supposed to be in love meant to push through things together?'

He drew in a long, deep breath. 'In most situations, yes, you're spot on, but when it comes to mourning and grief, everyone is different, Sarah. You like to talk about things, and get everything out in the open so you can dissect it and put it back together, and I admire that about you. Whereas, I have to do it internally, on my own, and in my own time, and you can't seem to accept that.'

'Yes, I can.'

'No, you can't.'

They were at a standstill. Sarah imagined what it would be like here, in their home, without Matt. As much as they were living like strangers, he was still *there*. She couldn't bear the thought of not seeing him every day. Panic lodged in her throat. 'But, I love you, Matt.' She didn't look back up, too scared that when she did he'd be gone.

'I love you too, Sarah.'

His reply felt all too automatic, mechanical. A wave of grief almost overwhelmed her and her stomach tightened. Her head spun. An army of *what ifs* marched through her mind. What if he fell further, darker, deeper? What if he never came back? What if he fell out of love with her? What if he already had? What if she fell out of love with him? 'Can't you stay, please, and work through things here, with me?' She hated sounding so desperate, but she was.

Matt paused, his Adam's apple bobbing. For a second, she thought he was going to say, 'Yes, let's do this', but he shook his head. His eyes brimmed with tears he dared not shed. He looked away from her and folded his arms. 'I really wish I could, but I think I've proved I can't. I'm so sorry, but I can't put you through this any longer. I know I need to get my shit together and it isn't going to happen here.'

'Okay then.' What else was she meant to say? She gave up trying. There was nothing left in her heart to give.

He sucked in a breath. Their eyes locked. Intense. Earth-shattering regret and heart-faltering unhappiness somehow bound them together. It was excruciating. Her thoughts were a jumble of emotions – fear, anger, sadness and despair. She swiped at the tears on her cheeks, angry with herself for not having more resolve, for not being more like Matt. She was so sick and tired of crying. 'You do what you have to do to get through this, and I'll do the same,' she choked out.

'Thank you.' It was said with a relieved sigh, as though he'd been holding his breath for an eternity. His expression softened and for the first time in so many months she caught a fleeting glimpse of the deep love he had for her within his tortured gaze. His long, jean-legged strides closed the cavernous distance between them. Like a caged bird longing to be free, her heart fluttered and swooped about her chest, frantically trying to get to his. Then, to her surprise, he knelt down beside her and took her hand, his thumb running over her fingers. She drew in a long, steadying breath. His strong, warm, hardworking hand was holding hers, and he wasn't showing any signs of letting it go.

'I hope you know that I'm doing this because I love you so much, Sarah.'

Her head dropped in a barely discernible nod, as her heart drained every bit of energy from the rest of her body in a bid to keep beating. She was completely broken.

His arms went around her shoulders and he pulled her close to him, possessively, desperately. 'I love you, baby.'

'I love you, too.' Grabbing a handful of his shirt, she buried her head in his chest and cried so damn hard she thought she'd never, ever, be able to stop.

CHAPTER
5

When there's a problem, don't rush to fix it; otherwise you may make matters worse ...

Matt's late grandfather's voice echoed in his head, his wise words striking a chord. His and Sarah's relationship was beyond a quick fix; only time would tell if they were meant to stay together.

His heart aching beyond belief, he stroked Sarah's back as her anguished cries echoed in the otherwise silent kitchen. He'd gone and broken her heart. Again. And that crushed him. Before he left for Rosalee, he knew he needed to make an effort to show her how much she meant to him, otherwise he'd leave and she might see that she'd be better off without him around. By admitting to himself he had a problem, going to the doctor for help, and now letting Sarah know his plans – as hard as it all had been – a weight had lifted from his shoulders. That should help him to make their last hours together memorable without the need for drowning his sorrows with booze. He hoped. He wasn't sure if she'd accept his peace offering, or if he'd be able to do it sober, but at the very least he had to try.

Everywhere his eyes settled, he had memories of Eve – spilling her milk all over the breakfast bar, stirring cake mixes with chocolate covering her lips while Sarah watched over her, she and him balancing fruit loops on the tips of their tongues to see who could hold it there the longest – he'd always let her win. And this was the same in every room of the house. There used to be so much life, so much happiness, and so much promise for the future, with Eve around. The house had felt like a home, his and Sarah's lives had felt complete. They'd even been talking about having another child, a brother or sister for Eve to boss around, and love with her big, kind, beautiful heart. And in a blink of an eye, all of that had vanished. Eve was gone. Forever. He was never going to cuddle her in his arms again, or kiss her goodnight, or see her smiling face in the morning, or take her to her first day of school, or walk her down the aisle, or hold her children. The agony of that thought was beyond anything he'd ever imagined was possible. And now, within the home that was meant to be filled with the love of a family, it felt as if death lurked in every corner, and hung from every ceiling, as if it were a palpable force that couldn't be reckoned with, reminding him every second of every excruciating day that Eve was gone all because of him.

Drawing in a shuddering breath, he used all his resolve not to shatter into a million tiny pieces as Sarah's trembling body shook against his. He was meant to be her rock, and just like he'd failed Eve, he'd failed Sarah too. He'd caused this pain, this utter heartache, for her. And yet here she was, being her usual magnificent self, loving him and supporting him regardless of his massive flaws and faults. This woman was perfection in its most exquisite form. He didn't deserve her or her love. In fact, he didn't deserve to live, to breathe the air when Eve couldn't. Through no fault of her own, Sarah's unconditional love made him feel guiltier, and even more like he should rot in hell. If he could have given his life that day, in place of Eve's, he would have in a heartbeat. But God didn't work like that, and neither did the devil, so he had to live with the crushing weight of it for the rest of his life. In his eyes, although oppressive, it was too small a penance. He should have died that day, and last night, when he'd stared down the barrel of his shotgun in the tractor shed. Drunk out of his mind, he'd contemplated pulling the trigger. It was only the thought of Sarah being the one to discover his body that had stopped him. And now, somewhat sobered-up and in the light of day, the realisation of what he'd come so close to doing was a colossal reality check.

If only he'd done things differently that day … their life was the butterfly effect at its darkest.

As a father, it was his job to protect his little girl with his life, and he'd failed, miserably. Eve had trusted him to always take care of her, to keep her from harm, and he'd done the complete opposite. He'd run the events of those fateful few minutes over and over in his mind, to the point where he'd started to feel insane. He shouldn't have ignored Sarah's request to fasten Eve's seatbelt, shouldn't have based his decision on the fact he'd hooned around the station as a young kid without ever having the need for one; shouldn't have looked down at the stereo to tune it in; but there was nothing he could do to change all that now. Remorse engulfed him. Choked him. He hugged Sarah even closer, wishing there was some way he could erase all her heartache, all her tears – everything that had been caused by his one stupid, thoughtless mistake – the mistake that had taken his darling Eve's life and devastated Sarah's. He closed his eyes, willing the building tears away. He would not break down. He didn't deserve to cry. Ever.

Burying his head into the soft curve of Sarah's neck, he breathed in the woman he loved with every fibre of his being. It had been a long time since he'd held her like this, since he'd shown her how much he cared for her. Way too long. But in all the times he'd ached to do so, he hadn't been able to bring himself to, and the only reason he could now was because he was doing the right thing by leaving. He could see it in Sarah's eyes, the blame she held for him, even though she refused to admit it. But how could he hold that against her when he blamed himself? Standing on the razor-sharp edge of grief, he hadn't wanted to take Sarah with him if he fell, so he'd kept his distance, for the sake of her, to protect her from the darkness that seemed to be smothering him. While deep down he knew, *he knew*, all he was doing was breaking her exquisite heart even more by creating a chasm so wide and deep between them that he wasn't sure if he'd ever find the strength to cross it and be at one with her ever again.

But she didn't need to know that right now …

Her tears soaked through his shirt. Time seemed to drift into nothingness as he watched a ray of sunlight slowly creep across the wall, over the door of the fridge, and then disappear. His knees ached from where they pressed into the tiled floor, but he wasn't moving, he was going to hold Sarah until she didn't need him to hold her any longer. It was the very least he could do, especially on a day like today, the anniversary of Eve's death. The sound of a four-wheel motorbike revving to life burst the bubble they were in. It was Jimmy and Liam heading off for their day's work. Thank goodness for the pair of them, happy to work for minimal wages as long as they got the workers' cottage rent free.

Sarah's tears eventually stopped, but he still held her, somehow wanting to make up for all the times he hadn't. Too little, too late, he thought. How he wished he had her strength. With slow movements, she untangled from him. She inhaled a deep, shaky breath, one that spoke of her emotional exhaustion. Bloodshot eyes gripped his, silently pleading for him not to leave. But he had to. There was no other way. 'This is the right thing to do, Sarah,' he said ever so gently. He was saying it more to himself than to her.

'I hope you're right.' Her voice was a whisper. She wrung her hands together. 'Are you sure you still love me, Matt?'

He blinked hard, his breathing ragged with sorrow. It was the easiest question he'd ever had to answer, but the words weren't finding a way past the lump in his throat. There was so much he wanted to say to her, but he didn't have the strength right now – it would have to wait. Maybe he would never get to say it. 'I love you more than ever, and tomorrow, I will love you more than today, and then the next day, I will love you even more than that. There is no limit to how much I love you, Sarah, please believe that.' Her face pale and drawn, he waited for her to respond, at the same time feeling responsible for the devastating sadness in her spirit, in her soul.

Her lips trembled. She nodded. Her mouth fell downwards before she attempted to smile. 'You have no idea how nice it is to hear that.'

His chest felt as if it were about to explode from the pressure of the sadness building in his heart. Cupping her cheek, he wiped her tears. 'It breaks me, seeing you in so much pain. I wish I could do something to take it away for you.'

She placed a trembling hand over his. 'Please come back to me, Matt, once you've done what you have to do. I don't want to lose you too.'

'I will.'

'You promise?'

He nodded, but inside, he was unsure of the answer. How could he return to her when he wasn't even sure if he could find himself? Unless he was whole, complete and able to give her the life she deserved, the love she deserved, he wouldn't be coming back into her life. As much as it would kill him, he would rather see another man who was deserving of her love come into her realm and take care of her big, beautiful heart.

'Are you driving?' Her voice was soft.

'To the cemetery?'

'No, I think you'd still be over the limit … I meant to Rosalee?'

The drink was his vice, and by Christ he knew how weak it was of him to give in to it. Shame burned hot throughout him. He shook his head. 'I was thinking I might fly to Mount Isa and then I can catch the mail plane with old Stan.'

'Do you need help booking your flights?'

'Already done it yesterday.'

Shock was written all over her face and it stabbed at his stone-cold heart. 'There wasn't going to be any way of me talking you out of this, was there?'

'Nope, as hard as it is, and is going to be, this has to be done.' Leaning in, he brushed a kiss over her lips before standing. 'I'll go and have a shower and freshen up. Won't be long. Okay?'

'Okay.'

He dragged his gaze from hers, feeling like the biggest bastard that had ever walked the earth, leaving her like this. But it was the lesser of two evils. If he didn't find himself, and stop drinking, he was afraid he was going to do something reckless and stupid. It was time he grabbed hold of the reins of his life again. He just hoped he had the strength.

Pulling her visor down to ward off the midday sunshine, Sarah sat up straighter, trying her best to hold it together. Her head spun, her soul ached, and everything around her felt surreal, as though she were looking through an hourglass. When she'd rolled out of bed this morning, she didn't think life could get any harder, any more heartbreaking, any more challenging – but it was about to. Murphy's bloody law. How in the hell was she going to get through this when it felt as if all that was left of her were the broken pieces? How was she going to cope without Matt around? Was he telling the truth about coming back to her? Part of her didn't believe him when he promised. Searing pain shot through her heart – she couldn't bear the thought of losing him forever, or the thought of going this alone, more alone than she already was. Maybe she should go and stay with her family, just for a little while? Staying at Tranquil Valley without Matt and with only memories of Eve to keep her company would be absolute torture. She could take Victory and Duke with her, maybe even Chilli the chook, and Liam and Jimmy could look after the other farm critters along with their prized bulls. As much as a part of her didn't want to leave the sanctuary of her home, she knew that spending time in Mareeba would help her through. And maybe, now she didn't have Matt to focus on and look after, it was time she thought about herself. A sudden urge to punch the steering wheel came over her, but instead, she gripped it tighter, noticing her quickened breath.

Why did life have to constantly be so goddamn hard?

She glanced over to where Matt sat in the passenger seat, his forearm resting on the windowsill and his eyes towards the unfurling sea of paddocks. A shadow of his former self, he was a man lost within his heartbroken guilt-filled world. After almost eight years by his side, she knew him like the back of her hand, and had to admit he was right. Matt being Matt, he needed to get through this on his own terms and in his own time. Usually a person of immense pride, and stubborn independence, it would be the only way he'd come out the other side with his manhood in tact. She tried not to think of the moment she'd have to say goodbye, with something telling her it was going to be a while before she saw him again. But, no matter the outcome, she had to let him go, had to let him do what he felt he needed to.

If you love something, set it free; if it comes back, it's yours forever . . .

Dragging her eyes back to the highway she drove on auto-pilot, not taking much notice of the passing houses or the lush green landscape that used to bring her so much joy, a big part of her feeling numb. The bright yellow sunflowers she'd picked for Eve, from the garden where Eve had planted the seeds with her very own tiny hands, lay in the centre console, alongside a water bottle she would use to fill the vase. Glancing in the rear-vision mirror, she caught sight of Duke in the tray of the LandCruiser, his lead pulled taut as he tried to gulp the air over the side of the tray. Her lips tugged at the corners, although a smile didn't eventuate – her forever companion, as always, brought her some comfort.

Slowing, she flicked her blinker on and turned into the Malanda cemetery car park, as she had countless times before. Anxiety gripping her, her heart took off in a frenzied gallop as she pulled to a stop. She stole a moment to take a breath, willing her hands to stop trembling as she pulled the handbrake on and the keys from the ignition. Coming here never got any easier. Time didn't heal wounds, it just taught you to live with them.

She grabbed the flowers and the water bottle.

Tugging on his wide-brimmed hat, Matt finally looked to her, his face pale. 'You okay?'

Unable to get a word past the lump in her throat, she nodded, but knew her eyes spoke otherwise. She pushed open her door and stepped out. Matt did the same and joined her. Neither of them spoke. A pair of magpies flew overhead, squawking. Reaching out, he took her hand and their fingers entwined. Looking to where Eve rested, Sarah was swiftly reminded of the weight of her empty arms and the hollowness in her heart. With Matt gently urging her forward, she used every bit of strength she had to walk on. They passed a woman bent low over a grave, fixing flowers. She looked to them and forced a smile, wiping tears from her cheeks. Sarah acknowledged the woman's heartache with a gentle, knowing smile. It felt as if the cloudless blue sky was mocking her. It wasn't meant to be a picture-perfect summer's day. It should have been dark and stormy with the heavens crying tears of raindrops on the freshly mowed grass beneath her feet. This was a reminder of the darkest day of her life, and she wanted God to somehow acknowledge that he'd taken her beautiful Eve way before her time. That was, if he even existed – she'd lost count of the amount of times she'd asked herself this question.

Reaching the gravestone, she looked down at the flowers that had wilted over the past five days, and felt an engulfing wave of guilt for not visiting sooner, to get rid of them and replace them with fresh ones. Her vision blurring, she let go of Matt's hand and dropped to her knees. The pain in her heart was all too much to bear. This was her baby, the child she'd carried, the child she'd desired with every fibre of her being, and conceived in unconditional love. The very thought of Eve, lying in this deep, dark, cold grave, tore her heart to shreds. Her throat constricted. Sobs racked her body. Her breaths came in torturous gasps. Reaching out, she traced Eve's name with her fingers, mouthing the inscription on the tombstone, her other hand gripping the half-moon pendant hanging from her necklace.

> *She who leaves a trail of glitter is never forgotten.*
> *I will sleep in peace until you come to me.*
> *Our darling Eve, forever in our hearts.*

Matt knelt down beside her, his face ashen, his jaw clenched. He placed a hand on her back, and left it there. No words could express how much that meant to her. Her husband was finally by her side, if only for today. Pulling the dead flowers from the vase, she emptied the putrid smelling water off to the side, and then filled it with fresh water and the sunflowers. Placing it back, she tidied up the shells she'd placed there a few months back, ones Eve and she had collected from their trips to the beach, and straightened the rainbow-coloured wind catcher.

'Love you, sweetheart, so, so much,' she whispered.

Then, as if she were back there, the day of the funeral flooded her mind. The viewing had been the funeral director's idea; apparently it was a way to help accept a loved one had passed over. But all it had done was intensify Sarah's already crushing grief. It was a moment of heartbreaking finality, a devastating reminder that death was forever. The tiny hands folded across Eve's chest and the eyes behind the closed lids had been so painfully lifeless. Lifting Eve's unresponsive fingers in hers, she'd held on to them for dear life, shocked by the coldness of her little girl's hands and her cheek as she had kissed it, her heart cramping in pain. It had taken both Matt and her father to drag her away from the open casket, her throat raw from her anguished cries. Then before she knew it, she was standing at the graveside, the priest saying things she didn't want to hear, condemning Eve to the ground. *Earth to earth, ashes to ashes, dust to dust.* She could recall the feel of the dirt digging into her knees when she'd fallen while watching Eve's tiny coffin being lowered to her final resting place, could still smell the dank earthiness of the freshly dug grave, could still hear her own mother's deep soulful cries from beside her.

Then she crashed back into reality and the world around her began to spin. Needing to lie down, she did so and curled onto her side, her face resting against the grass. Matt lay down beside her, his hand resting on her thigh. They lay like that for what felt like forever, watching as the clouds gathered, met and darkened, until the scent of rain hung heavily.

Finally, God was acknowledging his part in all of this.

'Sarah, we should go before it buckets down.' Matt's voice sounded a million miles away.

'Mmm.' But she didn't move. She didn't want to go.

He sat up and took her hands in his. 'Come on.'

Reluctantly, she allowed him to pull her up to stand in front of him. Turning towards the car park, she felt as if she was turning her back on her child, and every single step she took away from the grave felt as if her boots were made of lead.

'Mummy will be back, sweetheart,' she whispered under her breath as she felt Matt's hand on her back and he slowly, tenderly, pressed her forwards.

CHAPTER

6

Twilight was quickly approaching. While giving Liam and Jimmy a wave as they drove past, Sarah couldn't help but notice the pity and compassion behind their smiles. It was an expression she'd become accustomed to over the past year, seeing it in almost everyone she came in contact with. Would it ever stop? With their work done and dusted for the day, and having paid their condolences over a cuppa, the two eligible bachelors were on their way to the pub. Friday night at the Malanda pub was the big one. Lacking a little in the looks department, Jimmy made up for it with his addictive personality, and he didn't have much trouble wooing the women. Neither did Liam, whose roguish good looks and Irish lilt made the women flock to him like bees to honey, as did the guys' cheeky cowboy personalities. Round these parts, every woman loved to lasso herself a cowboy, but not many of them had that special something to tether these two men for long.

Sarah settled herself down in her favourite spot on the wide, wrap-around verandah, sighing softly. A small part of her felt envious of Jimmy and Liam's normalcy – her life was far from it and she doubted it would ever go back to being normal again. If only a person could rewind time. Looking past the sun catchers and wind chimes she had collected over the years, some of them she had made with Eve, she smiled at the state of Jimmy's LandCruiser, almost every inch of it covered in mud. The unmistakable twang of country music faded as it disappeared down the driveway. She still had to go and talk to them about heading over to her family's fruit farm for a few weeks, but it could wait until tomorrow – she'd done enough for one day.

Climbing the front steps, Duke joined her, and after walking around in a circle three times he plonked himself at her feet, his eyes staring up at her.

Sarah's heart swelled as she looked down at her furry forever friend. 'I'm okay, buddy, you rest.'

With a doggy sigh, as if he didn't really believe her, Duke's eyes dropped closed and he was snoring within seconds. Gently, Sarah ran her foot over his coat, noting how grey it was becoming. Her heart clenched. 'You've still got a few good years in you yet, buddy, so don't be going anywhere soon, you hear,' she whispered.

Knowing she'd got through the first anniversary of Eve's death, Sarah breathed a small sigh of relief while trying not to think about the many more to come. Lightly pushing her foot against the wrought-iron railings of the verandah, she enjoyed the feeling of the chair-swing moving back and forth; the creak of the chain it was hanging from was strangely comforting, as were the sounds of the dusk chorus. Soft birdsong mixed with the rhythm of frogs and nocturnal insects, and frogmouths blended with the chirruping of crickets, the distant bellows of cattle and relaxed whinnies of horses all lulled her tortured heart and soul into peace, if only for a few blissful moments. Then the early evening Aussie rooster joined Mother Nature's melody, the currawong's singsong distinctive as the last rays of sunshine breathed fire into the sky. Only a country sunset would dare wear such bold slashes of orange, hot pink, red and deep purple. Before long, she wouldn't be able to see the tree line that bordered their property, the shadows stretching to invite the darkness.

It was almost an hour later when Sarah stepped inside the house. Wandering through the lounge room, she looked to the couches that were positioned at just the right angle around the coffee table for conversation rather than watching the television in the corner – not that there had been much tête-à-tête this past year. Padding into the bathroom and closing the door, she listened to the rumble of the four-wheeler approaching the homestead and then coming to a stop. Matt was home from checking on his bucking bulls. She stripped off her clothes, avoiding catching her reflection in the mirror. The curvaceous woman she once was now looked tired and way too thin, and she really didn't feel like facing up to that tonight, didn't feel like acknowledging how tear-stained and haggard her face looked, or seeing the emptiness in her eyes.

Drawing back the shower curtain, she turned the taps on, making sure the water was hot enough to leave red marks on her skin. The old pipes rumbled in protest before easing off. The gentle hiss and the patter of the water beckoned her. There was nothing like a scorching hot shower to ease aching muscles. Steam quickly rose, enveloping her, and she stepped beneath the warm spray, closing her eyes and tilting her face so the water would wash away the traces of her tears. With a shuddering breath she reached for the shampoo, her heart squeezing at the sight of the pink Peppa Pig body wash beside it. Eve had loved Peppa Pig. They would sing the song together, and Eve would snort at exactly the right moment, sending them both, and anyone else around, into fits of laughter.

Scents that made her think of a fresh pine forest mingled with the mist as she lathered her hair up, rinsed it out and then applied the conditioner. Waiting for it to work its magic on her curls, she glanced down at her womanly bits and wondered if she should shave. It really could use it down there. For a split second she considered it, but then she shrugged. Why bother when Matt wasn't interested in touching her that way? Then she thought, *Why the hell shouldn't I if it makes me feel that little bit better about myself?* Plucking the razor from the holder on the wall, she got to it, even deciding to do her legs while she was at it – she'd done her underarms this morning. Grabbing the bar of oatmeal soap, she washed herself down, loving the way the grainy bits scrubbed her skin.

Resting her head against the coolness of the tiles, she allowed the water to massage her aching back as she gave the conditioner a little longer. She imagined it washing all her worries and heartache away, and sending them spiralling down the plughole with the soapsuds. She chuckled sarcastically at the thought – if that happened she'd damn well clog the pipes up with her sorrow. The idea both amused and troubled her. By the time she stepped from the shower and reached for her fluffy towel, she felt a tiny bit better and actually felt a pang of hunger. Her stomach growled in agreement. She hadn't eaten since yesterday, so knew she'd better have a bite. Opening the bathroom door so the steam could escape, the scent of something yummy caught her attention. She stopped drying her hair to pop her head around the corner of the door, peering down the darkened hallway as if she would be able to see what it was. She sniffed harder, her mouth watering with the unmistakable aroma of pea and ham soup. But how in the hell could that be possible when it took hours to cook?

Tipping her head upside down, she wrapped the towel around her hair. Grabbing her robe, she tugged it on, remaining naked beneath. Making her way down the steps she headed towards the kitchen, stopping in her tracks as she passed through the lounge room. Her eyes widened. She blinked, wondering if she was imagining it. Soft light flickered from a lone candle – one that had sat unlit since her birthday almost a year ago. The rose and vanilla scent was beautiful. One of her favourite country artists, Chris Stapleton, played from the stereo, and the heartfelt lyrics of 'Tennessee Whiskey' somewhat calmed her tormented heart and soul. Wandering over, she turned it up. Her eyelids flittered closed. She pulled the towel from her head and tossed it to the couch, her blonde spiral curls now cascading down over her shoulders. Like a feather on a gentle breeze, she drifted into the melody, losing herself completely. Her hips gently swayed to the seductive tempo as she let the lyrics of sweet love carry her away to another time and place, where nothing mattered, nothing hurt her, to when she and Matt were happy and so very much in love. Time faded, stood still, and rewound. She was twenty-three again, and holding on for dear life as Matt chased a rogue bull on the four-wheeler with her cuddled in tightly behind him. Those were the days, when they were young and carefree and so full of hope with seemingly reachable dreams.

If only she'd known then what she would be going through now ...

While listening to the beautiful melody that reminded her of the smoky, southern honky tonk bars she and Matt had visited on their trip to America to watch the PBR finals, just before she'd found out she was pregnant with Eve, a sound caught her attention and pulled her back to the present. She flickered her eyes open and turned to see Matt resting against the doorframe, a tea towel slung over his bare shoulder and his beard gone so she could see the hard chisel of his jaw. Although a little too much on the skinny side, he was still one hunk of a man with tattoos adorning all the right places, especially the one that read *Eve*, inked over his heart. He had always been a sentimental kind of guy. A little embarrassed he'd caught her dancing, she graced him with a coy smile before she reached for her towel. She needed to get her hands busy before she ran them down the contours of his chest.

He folded his arms. 'Hey there, baby.' His voice was husky, somehow suggestive, and his eyes were glazed with longing, the smouldering heat within them making the ground spin beneath her.

The impact hit her like a physical force. Caught off guard, and a little breathless, she fought to remain on her feet. 'Hey there, you.' She stammered every word out. 'What are you doing?'

'Taking in the sights.' He chuckled softly. 'I love watching you dance, Sarah. I still remember the night I met you, when I stood back and watched you dancing with the boys at the workers' cottage.' He smiled distractedly, as if he were back there. 'You had me hook, line and sinker from that moment on.'

'I did?'

'Yeah.' His smile was filled with wicked suggestions.

Heat licked through her like a fire. Where had this man come from? And where had he put the Matt she'd grown so used to over this past year? She felt a little lightheaded, the combination of lust and shock overwhelming her. She leant against the back of the couch. 'You feeling okay?' She had to ask as she looked for signs that he might be drunk, or on his way there.

'Yup, all good.'

'You sure?'

'As sure as I can be.' He shrugged gently. 'I feel a huge weight has been lifted off my shoulders after telling you I need time to myself to heal, that's all.'

She cleared a sudden lump of raw emotion from her throat. 'Okay, well, that's good.'

She admired his perfect lips, an urgency to kiss them claiming her. A quivering sensation rolled through her limbs. As if a magnet, her eyes were drawn downwards, to the zipper of his jeans, snagging only momentarily on the way the waistband was slung low around his hips. Her heart raced off in a wild gallop. It took every bit of her resolve to drag her eyes back upwards. 'How long have you been standing there, watching me?'

'Not long enough.' Fierce passion blazed in his eyes.

Her cheeks flamed as though this was the very first time he'd shown an interest in her, and as much as she enjoyed the sensation, it also felt strange. Even though she was miserable about it, she'd grown accustomed to the chasm between them and didn't know how to act without it separating them. She gestured past him with a glance over his shoulder. 'You cooking up a storm in the kitchen, are you?'

'Yeah, sort of … I thought I'd whip us up some dinner.'

'Really? That's not like you.' She regretted her words instantly.

Hurt crossed his face but he quickly recomposed himself. 'I found some pea and ham soup in the freezer. It's all heated up and I'll turn it on again so it's ready to go when we are.'

She smiled. 'You could have done that the modern way, you know, and used the microwave.'

'Nah, not good for you, all that radiation heating the food up.'

Neither is all the alcohol you drink, she thought, before chastising herself for it.

Another song began, and this time it was Faith Hill and Tim McGraw's 'I Need You'. Sarah looked to the stereo. 'Wow, I love this song, maybe even more than the last one.'

'I know you do.'

She dropped her gaze, emotions overcoming her. 'Is this our playlist? The one I made for you?' She cleared her throat and looked up at his handsome face.

'It sure is.' He tossed the tea towel from his shoulder to the coffee table and stepped towards her. Quickly closing the distance, he held his hand out to her. 'Can I have this dance, my beautiful princess?'

Recalling the last time he'd said those exact words, Sarah tumbled back eight years, to the night he'd asked her to marry him. His gesture and gentle voice, combined with the poignant memory of them dancing beneath the stars at Rosalee Station on their stargazing date, stole her breath. Her heart swooped and then soared. The giddy happiness made her head spin. Reaching out, she gripped his hand to stay upright; the love flowing through her was so strong she thought her heart might burst.

Pulling her to him, Matt placed a hard kiss against her lips. It was hot and heavy, and left her flabbergasted. With his face only inches from her own, she wanted to say something, anything, but couldn't get the words past the lump of emotion building in her throat. She flung her arms over his shoulders, trailing her fingertips over the back of his neck as their eyes met and locked.

The atmosphere ignited. Invisible sparks flew between them. The room was fiery hot. His hand came to rest on her waist and his other on the small of her back, his thumb gently caressing her arch. She couldn't smell a hint of alcohol on his breath, and that gave her hope that he was going to come back to her from Rosalee Station whole again. Swaying to the music, she allowed him to lead her. They had shared so many special moments just like this, arm in arm, swaying to country love songs. Many a night they'd spent in here, or out on the lawn, once they'd put Eve to bed, sharing much needed adult time. Music was their thing, their way to connect beyond words.

'Do you have any idea what you do to me?' he whispered into her ear.

'I think I do …' His breath was so warm, so evocative – goosebumps covered her every inch. 'But please, tell me again.' Her voice was muffled. Her head now resting against his chest, she could feel his heart pounding beneath her cheek.

'You own my heart and soul, baby. I'm so deeply in love with you, it sometimes feels like I'm drowning in emotions and I can't breathe past it.' His hands clasped at the nape of her neck, his firm but tender hold alerting her to the fact he was desperate for the comfort he'd knocked back from her for so long now.

'I feel the same, Matt. I really truly do.' She gazed up at him from beneath lashes wet with tears. 'I'm so sorry I haven't …' She was about to say, *supported you more, loved you more.*

He pressed a finger to her lips. There was a moment's silence. 'Don't you dare apologise, baby. You've done nothing wrong. Actually, you've done everything right. It's me that should be begging for your forgiveness. I haven't been there for you like I should've been. I know that, and I hate myself for it. I've let you down, in every possible way. Like I did with Eve.'

She shook her head. 'Please, don't say that.' She watched him try to blink away the tears as he drew in a deep breath, her heart breaking with the sight. Part of her prayed for those tears to fall, for him to drop to his knees and sob like there was no tomorrow. He needed it, needed the release that would give him. But within seconds, he had himself under control. She placed a hand on his chest. 'Please, Matt, don't beat yourself up any more than you already have. I understand you're in a world of pain.' Her words were soft, spoken as though in a daze as she continued to drink in the sight of him.

'Yes, but so are you, and I should be there for you. I want to be there for you … but …' He choked on his words, stalled, and shook his head. He cleared his throat, once, twice, three times. 'I'm so sorry I have to go, but I can't see any other way past this, past my demons.' He pulled her to him, close and tight. 'I'm so sorry, baby,' he murmured into her hair, his voice finally breaking.

She scrambled to find the right words, but they were jumbled in her mouth. Standing on her tippy toes, she brushed a kiss across his cheek. 'You got this, baby,' she whispered into his ear.

'You're so damn strong, Sarah, I wish I could be more like you.' His hands came to cup her face. 'It's going to tear me apart, leaving you, but staying here is tearing *us* apart. Even though it's unintentional, I can't hurt you anymore. I need to do something about my drinking before there is no *us* any longer, before it's too late to right my wrongs … before you fall out of love with me.'

She wasn't stronger than him, it was just she didn't have the cross to bear that he did … having to live with knowing that he was the one who'd rolled the ute, who had left Eve's seatbelt off. Sarah couldn't even begin to fathom the weight of his guilt. Her poor, darling man. Hot tears blurred her vision. Before she had a chance to respond, his mouth swooped down to touch hers, so softly at first she almost buckled at the knees. But she clung to him, their kiss becoming hungrier, more desire-fuelled and desperate. It was long and deep, an exchange of promises too powerful to need words. The magic of his touch, his taste, the strength in his arms as he pulled her close, brought it all back – the desire that had been put on pause re-ignited, sizzled, blazed. Fiery passion snatched her between one raspy breath to the next. Her body roared to life. She wanted to climb beneath his skin, to feel him inside of her, to be at one with him. She wrenched her mouth away from his, gasping. 'Make love to me, Matt.' But after so long, did she even remember how?

'You sure?'

'Mmmm.'

Picking her up, he carried her in his arms, across the cowskin rug, down the hall and towards the staircase. Her arms draped around his bare shoulders, she rested her head against his chest, feeling as if she'd just arrived back to her one true home after way too long away from it, from him.

Stepping into their room, he crossed the floor, and gently placed her on the bed. Silvery moonlight had the room softly aglow, enhancing his chiselled features even more. His lips twitched and hinted at a wayward smile.

'You're overdressed,' he said, as more of a demand than a statement.

She slid her robe off, quietly relieved she'd shaved. And then he just stood there, looking down at her like only a man deeply in love could. 'You're so beautiful, Sarah. I've missed this, missed you.'

'I've missed *us*, Matt,' she whispered. 'Now, come and make love to me like you damn well mean it.' She smiled enticingly.

'Oh, trust me, baby, I'm planning to.' Sliding his jeans and jocks off, he eased down on top of her, a sexy jumble of limbs, his weight partly on his elbows.

An alpha male at his finest – shivers danced over her flesh. Hunger poured out of her, hot and urgent and unstoppable. She wrapped her arms around his neck, pulling him closer, raising her hips until she could feel his throbbing erection pressing into her. Softly, she trailed her nails down his back, stopping to clutch the perfect curves of his butt. He drew in a breath when her hands travelled over his waist and came to skim ever so teasingly over the tip of his longing. Her fingertip wet from him, she brought it to her lips and licked it away.

'Oh god, Sarah, you do things to me that I can't put into words.'

'Well, show me then.'

His hands framed her face and he took biting kisses, luring her into a dizzying, lust-filled trance. She kissed him fervently, as though starving for him, and in truth, she was, and had been for a very long time. Trailing his lips down her neck, he paused to kiss and bite her in exactly the way he knew she loved him to. He kissed her breasts softly, teasingly, coaxing until they burned under his touch, until she begged him to bite down on her nipple, just hard enough to teeter her on an erogenous edge that she always loved to dangle from with him. He travelled down further, kissing her stomach, her hips, inside her thighs, and then he paused, his tongue tracing over her most sensitive part so lightly, so teasingly, so erotically that every single one of her nerve endings stood up and took notice. She arched into him with satisfaction, silently, urgently, pleading for more ... so much more. And he met her demand with vigour, taking her to a place where nothing else mattered, until she was gasping for air. But just before she tumbled, he stopped. She almost cried out, but like him, she wanted this to keep going and never end.

Coming to his knees, he knelt before her. Sliding his hands from her ankles, up her thighs, trailing over her pleasure spots, and back down again, he guided her to wrap her legs around him. Not letting go of her gaze for a second, he slid inside her with one slow, tantalising thrust, uniting himself with her, and then stopped. She tightened around him, clenching so hard she almost fell over the edge instantly. Inch by inch, he slowly pulled out, and then thrust into her again. She gasped. His hands gripping her hips, he shuddered with pleasure, as did she. Their eyes caught, and snagged. His already chocolate brown eyes seemed to darken. She reached up and pressed her hands against his chest. Muscles bunched beneath her hands. His skin was smooth, hot. He leant into her and kissed her throat, biting down just hard enough to balance her on the brink of pain and pleasure. She found herself lost in the exquisite sensations. Then he moved, in and out, slowly, the drag delicious. Her thighs clamped against his hips. She moved against him, pulling him deeper and deeper inside of her every time. They matched each other's rhythm. Greedy for the end goal, she rolled him over and straddled him within seconds. Pinning his wrists to the bed, she moved exactly how she needed to, to reach the pinnacle. Close now, so damn close, she cried out. Tension sizzled down her body, making every muscle taut. Her entirety begged for release. Possessively, he flipped her onto her back and set a rhythm that felt oh so perfect. Her body tightened as she clenched harder and harder around him. The hammer of his heartbeat, the musky scent of man, the connection enveloped her, and rendered her senseless. She fought for breath as he took her right to the edge, refusing to let go until she did.

'Come with me, baby,' he breathed, raw and hot and husky. His body tensed above her, and his face glazed with pure ecstasy.

And she did, so hard and so intense, she didn't think she'd ever be able to catch her breath. He stayed with her, giving her strokes that catapulted her even further. Then he shifted over onto his side, his arms around her. Limbs entwined and utterly spent, they collapsed into oblivion. She drew air into her lungs as if she'd just run a marathon, as did he. They held each other for as long as it took for both their breaths to ease and slow. And then, she drifted and floated before falling into the deepest sleep she'd had for the past year, wrapped tightly in her husband's arms.

CHAPTER

7

A rooster crowed. Horses whinnied. A kookaburra called out, laughing to its mate. It was a little after six. Bright sunlight flooded the bedroom. Sarah stirred and woke to find herself on her own. Again. Her heart went to tumble, but she mentally caught it and firmly put it back in place. She had to look at the positives. At least this time there was a difference – last night she hadn't crawled into bed alone. For the first time in as long as she could remember, Matt had come to bed with her, and made love to her like he meant it. It was a strange yet beautiful experience, considering they were parting ways today. In the heat of the moment, and as she'd drifted off to sleep wrapped in his arms, it had given her hope that there might be a chance he would change his mind about leaving. But now, in the harsh light of day, she felt like a fool and, in a way, selfish for even allowing herself to have such a thought. He was right. He had to go. Had to find peace. It would be the only way they'd survive. If he stayed here, continuing to drink his woes away, their marriage would be well and truly over.

She pressed her ring finger to her lips, her wedding band still shining. Eloping to Vegas to tie the knot in a little chapel had seemed like a great idea at the time, saving a heck of a lot of money and killing two birds with one stone as they'd also attended the PBR World Finals. It had been Matt's idea, and keen to be his wife she'd run with it. But in hindsight, she would've loved to have had the wedding she'd always dreamed of – a country themed marriage on the beach, with all their loved ones around to witness her and Matt's love. Maybe, if they could get through this, she would still be able to have her wish. Maybe they could do it all over again with a vow renewal ceremony, and do it right this time.

A weighty sadness pressed down on her, nearly bringing her to tears. She had to fight off the temptation to pull the sheet up over her head and stay there forever. It was time to grab the reins of her life and try to find a way to deal with what was about to happen. She came from a long line of strong women, and had been through her fair share of shit to prove she was akin to her ancestors – she could get through Matt leaving too. She didn't have any choice. A part of her, a very small part, was worried she might get used to his absence, or even worse, he'd get used to hers – but there was only one way to find out.

Climbing from the bed, she walked to the ensuite, wondering why Duke was nowhere to be seen – Matt must have let him out. Even though he was her dog, Duke was going to feel Matt's absence too. After washing her face, she brushed her teeth and then pulled her hair up into a bun. There was no way in hell a brush went anywhere near her hair when it was dry, or she'd look like she'd stuck her finger into an electrical socket. Then she pulled on her favourite denim shorts and a long-sleeved shirt, tugged on her Ugg boots, quickly made the bed and picked up the few clothes Matt had dropped on the floor (a habit she'd never got used to and one that irked her no end), and tossed them into the laundry basket as she wandered past. Then, taking a deep breath and with determined steps, she soldiered out the bedroom, down the hallway, descended the steps two at a time and walked into the kitchen, ready for a good morning kiss and cuddle. She was sure things had improved between them – how could they not after a night of making love?

'Morning, Sarah.' Already sitting at the table, Matt didn't break a smile and didn't stand to kiss her. Instead, he remained engrossed in his mobile phone. His dishevelled hair was damp from a shower. He must have had one in the guest bathroom and as much as it shouldn't, it really pissed her off. It was always the little things that grew into something way bigger, way more provoking.

'Morning.' She forced a smile.

Silence hung in the room. Last night now felt like a dream; the energy between them had gone right back to how it had been the past twelve months – detached, cold, heartbreaking.

He placed his phone down on the table. 'Sorry I didn't stay in bed until you woke up, but I'd been lying awake for hours and ...'

Spooning a heaped teaspoon of coffee into the mug she'd just banged down on the counter, she cut him off. 'No worries, I'm used to it.' Anger and resentment bubbled inside her. Clenching her jaw, she made sure to keep her back to him. It was easier to be hard-hitting and stay angry with him when she wasn't looking into his soulful eyes.

Matt sighed as if to say, *Here we go*. 'Used to what?' There was an edge to his voice.

'Waking up on my own.' Her tone was cutting. She stole a glance over her shoulder as she pulled the sugar bowl down from the shelf above the kettle. 'What did you think I meant?'

His brows knitted into a frown. 'Exactly that, but I wanted to make sure. I never know what I'm in the shit for anymore. It's always something different with you.'

His words stung, burnt her, and scratched at her soul. She was far from a cantankerous woman, which is exactly what he was making her out to be. 'Yeah, well, maybe if you weren't so goddamn selfish, and didn't get so goddamn drunk all the time, I wouldn't have so much to bloody well complain about.' She stormed past him to get the milk from the fridge. Swinging the door open, it slammed against the kitchen bench. She plucked the carton out and slammed the door shut, taken aback by the rage coursing through her.

'We don't need to do this.' His tone was cautionary.

'No, we don't.'

He laced his hands behind his neck. 'I'm sorry I didn't stay in bed with you, Sarah.'

'Righto, whatever.' Shrugging, she focused on putting one foot in front of the other. Pouring in a splash of milk, she stirred her coffee into a storm, the teaspoon clanking noisily. 'Like I said, I'm used to it.' She wanted to scream at him, wanted to tell him he shouldn't have made love to her if he intended to be so distant in the morning, wanted to tell him he was pushing her to her limits, wanted to tell him to never come back just because she was so damn hurt and mad, but she bit it all back, pushing it to where she'd pushed everything else this past year. What good would it do, going over the same old things again?

Matt smiled sadly. 'Fair enough.'

She glanced at her watch. Less than an hour and they would have to head to the airport. 'You almost ready to go?' She tried to keep her voice even and the tears from her eyes.

'Yup, got to pack a couple more things and then I'm good to hit the road.' He brushed his hands over his face, his five o'clock shadow only deepening the dimple in his chin she'd always found so endearing. 'I don't need you to drive me to Cairns.'

Sarah flinched. 'Why? Who's taking you?'

'Liam needs to go there anyway, to get some parts for his LandCruiser, so he's offered to take me.'

'Oh, righto ... you reckon you could have let me know before now?'

'Sorry, slipped my mind.'

'I wouldn't have minded getting away for the day, you know.' The small piece of her heart that was somehow still intact suddenly cracked. 'It's like you can't get away from me quick enough.'

'I didn't mean anything by it, Sarah, I was just trying to save you the trip.'

'Okay, well, thanks.' She felt as if she were balancing on the tightrope of love, the drop so deep, so dark, that if she fell she would surely die because Matt couldn't be arsed to catch her. A part of her felt like he'd just used her for sex before heading out to the station, or maybe it was some last ditch effort to remind her what he could be if he tried. But she wasn't going to mention it, wanting to hold on to the rare intimate night they'd shared, just in case it was their last. 'You had breakfast?'

Matt held his cup up. 'Having it.'

She nodded. Matt cleared his throat then began thrumming the table top. The clock above the oven ticked loudly, but otherwise silence pounded the walls. She turned away from him and kept herself busy making toast she really didn't feel like eating, cursing beneath her breath when she popped it down for a second time and then burnt it. Storming to the bin, she tossed it in. Then, on the brink of tears, she stared out the window while taking sips of her coffee.

'Sarah, are you okay?' Matt's voice was soft, tender.

Her heart yielded and reached for his. She hated how one minute she could be so mad at him and the next minute loving him, and vice versa. *What do you fucking think?* she wanted to yell, but said, 'Yup, all good, thanks.' She pushed the window open wider, desperate for fresh air. A breeze whipped through, lifting the curtains, and as it did she caught a whiff of rum. Spinning on her heel, she glared at him. 'Is there alcohol in your coffee?'

His lips clamped shut. Shame filled his gaze. He shook his head in one jerky movement of denial, which told her everything.

'What the fuck, Matt? Great bloody start this is.'

'I'm nervous about leaving and I wanted to take the edge off.'

Disappointment pummelled her insides like a boxer's fists. She eyed him incredulously, shaking her head.

He offered her a disillusioned smile. 'And there it is.'

'There what is, Matt?'

'That look, the one you give me every single day. The one that lets me know how much of a disappointment I am to you.'

'Well, what do you expect? I can't help the way I feel, when you're the one making me feel that way.'

'Yes, you're right, I am the one making you feel like that, unintentionally by the way. And that's why I need to get the fuck out of here, so I can get my shit together.' He stood abruptly. Breathing heavily, he gripped the edges of the table. 'I'm not a complete and utter failure, Sarah. I am a good man beneath all of this, not that you want to acknowledge that. A piece of me died the day Eve did, and I don't know if I'll ever be the man you fell in love with, the man you want me to be again. What then, huh?'

She went to say something, anything, but he'd verbally slapped her into bewilderment. Had she really made things that hard for him? Was she so deep in her own grief that she hadn't noticed she was doing to him what he was doing to her, just in different ways? Her chest and throat tightened, the reality of their situation landing on her like a tonne of bricks. She forced herself to breathe deeply. Unable to look at him any longer, she turned back to the window, wrapping her arms around herself as if to stop from breaking.

Matt's footsteps came up behind her. His hand came down upon her shoulder. She stiffened beneath his touch. He guided her to turn around, and when she did, she was met with his wretchedness, and a deep-set heartache she knew so well. This mess they were in – they'd done this to each other.

Matt's lips trembled. 'I'm so sorry.'

'Please, Matt, stop saying sorry.' Her chin quivered but she raised it stubbornly. She. Was. Not. Going. To. Cry.

'But I am, and you don't seem to believe me, so I feel like I have to keep saying it until you do.'

'I'm sorry too, for a lot of things.' Her voice was choked. She churned inside with newfound guilt.

Cradling her head in his hands, he kissed her forehead, and then her nose, cheeks, and slowly trailed his lips to her mouth. His kiss was full of love and sincerity. They said things so much better without uttering a word. As mad as she was, as hurt as she was, she tumbled into him, wrapping her arms around his shoulders. Their tongues danced to their own rhythm. Their breaths mingled. Her tears welled, and much to her annoyance, she couldn't hold them back. They rolled down her cheeks, heavy and persistent. Without a word, Matt began to kiss them away. Why couldn't they be like this all the time? A whirlwind of emotions pounded her. She released the grip she had on his shirt, and flattened her hands against the hard planes of his chest. 'Stop, Matt, just stop.'

Releasing her, he stumbled back a step, confusion clouding his eyes. 'I'm only trying to make things right, before I go.'

'This isn't going to make us right ... it's going to take a lot more than this to fix what we've broken.'

He nodded, sad and slow.

'I can't do this like you can,' she said.

'Do what?'

'Pretend everything is okay when it's not.'

'I'm not pretending, Sarah. This is me, trying to show you I love you.'

'A little too late for that now, isn't it?' She stopped.

The look on Matt's face showed he was as shocked at the words that had left her lips as she was.

Taking another step back from her, he shoved his hands through his hair – a sure sign of frustration. 'You know what?'

'What?' She folded her arms.

'As much as I love you, and as much as I hope we can sort things out and be happy again, I'm tired of trying to make up for my shortcomings.'

She eyed him as if he were speaking another language. 'What are you on about?'

'What more can I fucking do, Sarah, to show you how much I love you?' It was half question, half accusation. 'I have loved you with every inch of my being. I even gave up my life at Rosalee Station to be here with you, and yes I have dug my own hole with my drinking, but do you think you could lay off me a little bit? I'm trying to make things better.'

'You might be trying to make things better, but only under your own terms, the way you want to do them. That's exactly how it's always been when it comes to any big decision in our lives.'

He threw his hands up in the air. 'I give up.'

Her head pounded and she felt as though she'd run for miles carrying a heavy burden. 'You know what, come to think of it, so do I.' She pointed at him, fierce and determined. 'You don't get to do this. You don't get to turn your back on me when I need you the most, and then make love to me and kiss me like there's nothing to worry about. I'm tired of being dragged around in your unrealistic world, Matt.' Anger stabbed her from within, as if a beast was fighting its way out. On auto-drive, she tugged the wedding ring from her finger and shoved it towards him. 'Here, take it back.'

'What are you doing, Sarah?'

'What I need to do to get through this.'

'You're breaking it off?'

Was she? She had no idea. Her heart pounded so hard it hurt, each beat a stab to her chest. Her hands went to her hips. 'You don't get to say that to me. Don't you dare put that on me ... you're the one breaking it off by leaving, Matt, remember that.'

He shook his head. 'I'm not taking your wedding ring.' He held his hand up and pointed to the gold band they'd picked together, snug around his finger. 'And for the record I'm not taking mine off. I'm not giving up on us like you obviously are.'

'Fine, take it how you want. You do what you have to, and I'll do what I have to.' Storming to the table, she slammed the ring down. 'If the man I fell in love with is still inside there somewhere, come back to me. But if you don't find him, please, don't put me through all of this for nothing. I can't live like this anymore, Matthew Walsh. It's killing me.'

Sarah could feel the ache of tears behind her eyes. Unable to look into his tormented gaze any longer, she spun away before she crumpled to the floor. She thundered to the back door, stumbling blindly into the daylight outside. She needed to get away from Matt. Right now. Before she said anything else she was going to regret. She'd already gone too far but there was no turning back. She'd made her bed, now she had to sleep in it.

Stomping out, she kicked off her Uggies, and not caring that she was sockless, tugged on her work boots. She should really go and get a pair of jeans on too, but there was no way in hell she was going back into the house right now. She'd have to just Daisy Duke it.

Racing up the steps, his nose covered in red mud and with bits of garden mulch clinging to his fuzzy coat, Duke skidded into her side, almost barrelling her over. He was panting like no tomorrow, with his tail wagging like the clappers. Sarah shook her head at the state of him. Clearly, he'd been having a much better morning than she had.

Tapping her foot, she tried her very best not to break a smile. 'Have you been digging up my garden again, you cheeky bugger?'

His tail came to a sudden stop. He looked up at her from beneath wrinkled eyebrows, guilt written all over his muddy face.

She waggled a finger at him. 'You know better than that, but you can't help yourself, can you?' Then giving in and smiling softly, she knelt down and gave him a kiss on the muzzle. 'Love you, boy.'

His tail took off like a chopper blade whirring to life, and he licked her fair up the cheek.

Grimacing, she wiped off his slobber, and then standing she gestured to the horse paddock with a tip of her head. 'Come on then, let's go let the chooks out and see how Victory and Marshmallow are going today.'

Clearing the steps two at a time, she took determined strides down the pebbled garden path and out the front gate. Crossing the drive, she jumped on the four-wheeler, motioned for Duke to jump up and join her, which he did, and then revved it to life. Daring a glance back at the house, she spotted Matt standing at the lounge room window, watching her. She quickly looked away, pretending she hadn't noticed; her heart honestly couldn't take any more anguish.

*

Almost an hour had passed when Sarah saw Liam pull up under the shade of a flame tree – she was well aware it would soon be time for Matt to head off. She'd been giving Victory a brush down, but now she stopped and peered over his neck. From the driver's seat, Liam gave her a tip of his hat in greeting, and she smiled back. The passenger door opened and Matt stepped out. Her heart tumbled towards him, and her throat choked with raw emotion. Jumping up from where he'd been snoozing in the shade, Duke ran over to welcome him. Matt gave him a ruffle on the head. Needing to do something, anything, Sarah went back to brushing Victory, keeping one eye on Matt as he approached her with long-legged strides.

Tossing the brush in the bucket, she straightened. 'You off?'

'Yup.' His mouth set in a firm line, he gave her a stiff smile. 'You calmed down a bit now?'

She breathed in deeply as though suddenly winded. 'Yeah, you?'

He nodded. 'Yeah, sorry about all that before.'

'Stop saying sorry.' She folded her arms, sighing heavily. 'We're both in the wrong here, and both doing and saying things out of frustration and hurt.'

'So you didn't mean to take your wedding ring off?'

Unable to give him the answer he wanted, she chewed the inside of her lip, desperately trying to find the right words to say. As much as it pained her, she was going to stick to her guns now she'd pulled the trigger, hoping it would make him take the break seriously. Giving up the booze was vital if their relationship was going to have any chance of recovering. She had to jolt him back into the man he once was, had to force him into a corner so he came out fighting.

With too many silent seconds passing, he shook his head. 'Actually, don't answer that.' He leant in as if to kiss her on the lips, but she turned her cheek. She couldn't have that kind of intimacy with him right now. It would tear what resolve she had left into absolute pieces.

Brushing a quick kiss on her cheek, he stepped back and then shrugged as if defeated. 'Can I at least get a hug before I go?'

His look of despair cut her to the very core; just knowing that she'd helped cause it was ripping her to shreds. She cleared her throat and took a step towards him, her arms outstretched. 'Yeah, of course you can.'

They wrapped their arms around one another, but this time, it felt as if it were a cold goodbye. Sarah's hope that they would make it through this tumbled that little bit more.

'Okay, well, I'll let you know when I'm there.' With a sad smile, Matt shoved his hands in his pockets.

'Yeah, that'd be good.' Her heart ached. He looked tired, oh so tired.

'Just remember my mobile doesn't work out there, huh?'

'Yup, will do.' Her voice was strained as she choked back emotion. 'I've got the cottage number if I need you.'

He paused, his gaze holding hers that little bit longer, and then he turned, walking away from her, from their home, from *them*.

She called Duke to her side as she watched Matt go and check his backpack was secure in the back and then climb into the LandCruiser again, shut his door and then pull his seatbelt on. Revving the battered old beast to life, Liam gave her a gentle smile as they drove past, but she couldn't return it. She felt numb, empty, dead on the inside. Praying her ultimatum hadn't cost them their future, she watched the four-wheel drive disappear down the drive in a cloud of dust, at the same time feeling as if her entire world was fading away with it.

CHAPTER

8

Sarah was getting smaller and smaller. Matt looked down to make sure his racing heart hadn't completely torn from his chest. He sucked in a quiet yet desperate breath in a bid to stop his galloping pulse. Even though he could still see her, he felt further away from her than he'd ever been. His heart felt as if it were gripped within a vice, the hold becoming tighter as Liam drove away. She stood confident yet haunted, willowy yet strong, her blonde curls blowing about her pretty face and her hand shielding her eyes from the sun. She was perfect in every way. Even now, she was doing what she had to, to take care of him – by letting him go with the faith he was going to get better. But was he? He was going to give it his best shot, but he honestly didn't know if he could ever put all his broken pieces back together. It was going to take a damn miracle to do so. He wished he had her strength, then they never would have ended up with this crater between them. It was all his fault.

His hand going to her wedding ring in his pocket, he watched her for as long as he could, until a trail of billowing dust stirred up by Liam's four-wheel drive swallowed her reflection in the side mirror. Hopefully, he would return whole, to ask for her hand in marriage once again. Closing his eyes as if to block out the pain, in a terrible moment he imagined never seeing her again, imagined everything blowing up in his face and Sarah telling him she was over him, that she'd met someone else stronger and more deserving of her love, and never to come back. Panic rushed through him. He almost yelled for Liam to stop and turn around, but he dug his boots into the floor and gritted his teeth. He had to do this – for both their sakes. He was no good to her a broken man. The walls they had built were too high, too strong, for either of them to break through or climb over right now. They needed time and space to heal, away from the complexities of their battered relationship, and within their own worlds.

Rattling over a cattle grid, they hit the dirt road that would lead them to the highway, and to Cairns. 'You right, mate?' Liam's voice sounded a thousand miles away.

Turning from where he was staring out the passenger window, Matt offered his long-time mate, one he classed as a brother, a grim smile. 'Yeah, as right as I can be, thanks, buddy.'

Liam kept his eyes on the road. His thumbs tapped the steering wheel restlessly. 'Wanna talk about it?'

'You know me, I'm not really one for D&Ms.'

Liam sighed as if frustrated. 'I know you're not, but it might help to talk about it …'

On the defensive immediately, Matt cut him off. 'Yeah, yeah, I've heard that a thousand times, from you and everyone else. I don't need no counselling. I know what's wrong, I need some fucking time and space to deal with it, away from everyone's endless bloody demands.'

His brows raised, Liam blew air through his teeth. 'Geez, mate, righto, no need to get your knickers in a knot … I'm looking out for you, and so is everyone else, that's all. Take it as a compliment that we all care about you so bloody much, rather than it being a burden.'

'Yeah, you're right, sorry.' Matt tried his best to soften his tone. He knew Liam was doing what any good mate should do. It was just, well, he didn't want to talk about it. End of story. 'People have to understand I need some time to get my head around everything. We don't all deal with shit the same way, and just because my way might not be what everyone else thinks is best for me, it doesn't mean it's wrong.'

Groaning, Liam shook his head. His jaw clenched, as if he were biting back what was on the tip of his tongue, and that irked Matt to no end. 'Well, come on then, spit it out.'

Liam shot him a sideways glare. 'Spit what out?'

'You're biting your tongue so hard right now it might as well be bleeding.'

'Righto, but before you crack the shits, remember you asked me to do this.' Liam sucked in a breath, and then blew it noisily away. 'Sorry to be so blunt, I just hope you're going to do what you promised Sarah you'd do, and go out to the station to get yourself on the straight and narrow, not to hide yourself away so you can drink your fill and not be seen. Otherwise, you're going to lose the best thing that's ever happened to you.'

Even though Liam had tried to coax him into giving up the drink, tried time and time again to persuade him into talking about his deepest, darkest feelings, never before had he been so damn frank. It was like a punch to the face and it took Matt a few seconds to recover from the verbal blow. Even then, he had nothing to say in his defence. Liam had hit the nail right on the head, and the truth damn well hurt. A hell of a lot.

Silence sizzled and hung between them.

'So you got nothing to say to that, Matt?'

Determined to stay poker faced, so Liam didn't know he'd hit his mark so damn hard, Matt remained silent.

'Blimy, if it isn't uncomfortable enough in here with the aircon on the blink.' Taking his hat off and tossing it upside down on the seat between them, Liam wiped the sweat from his brow and then heaved a sigh. 'You're a stubborn bastard, you know that, Walshee?'

Matt nodded, with the hint of a smile. 'Yup, sure do.'

'Shite, mate, we all want to see you happy again, and not blaming yourself for the accident. You deserve peace after everything you've gone through this past year, and so does Sarah for that matter.'

'I know, buddy, and don't you think I want peace, especially for Sarah? I love that woman, with everything I've got, and then some. So much so that I'd rather her live a happy life without me than have to put up with my bullshit any longer.'

'Yeah, I know you do, and don't talk like that – you two are made for each other.' Liam smacked the steering wheel. 'Life can be so cruel, can't it? If only we were back in the day when everything was easy, and we could have a craic. We used to have so much fun as young lads.'

'Yeah, true.'

Liam quietly chuckled to himself.

Matt tugged at his seatbelt, easing it off a little. 'What's so funny?'

'Remember that time Patrick, Slim and me painted our faces with boot polish so we would remain incognito in the dark, and stalked your crazy ex? What was her name again?'

'Brooke.' Matt smiled. 'And yes and no – I wasn't there to witness it but the photographic evidence is up on the workers' cottage wall to prove it.'

'Oh, that's right. I forgot Sarah got the photo blown up and framed as a present for Slim.' Chuckling, Liam slapped his hand on his jeans. 'I know it wasn't under the nicest of circumstances, seeing as we caught Brooke and Chris in the act, but it was a bloody hoot and a half sneaking around in the dark like that, I tell ya.'

Matt rolled his eyes, grinning. 'With you three larrikins, I could only imagine.' He exhaled a slow breath. 'And if it wasn't for you lot doing that, Sarah and I might have never got together.' He pulled a horrified face. 'And I might still be shacked up with Brooke living a very miserable existence.'

Liam looked aghast. 'Oh no, don't even speak of it.'

'Good riddance to bad rubbish with that chick. She was a bloody nightmare and a half.'

'Touché, buddy.' Grabbing a chico baby from the half-empty packet, Liam shoved the bag towards Matt. 'I wonder where she and Chris ended up, or if they're even still together?'

Matt took a handful of the iconic Aussie lollies – they were his favourite. 'I doubt it – they're both too shallow to commit to anyone for too long.'

Liam tossed three of the chocolate lollies in his mouth. 'Jimmy mentioned a while back he thought he'd seen Brooke walking down the street in Mareeba, but I told him he was being an idiot.' He shrugged. 'What in hell would she be doing up north?'

Matt threw his hands up in the air. 'Who bloody well knows?'

Now winding down the Gillies Range, they sat in silence for a few kilometres, the wind whipping through the windows, hurling the minty wrappers that had been tossed onto the dash into a frenzy.

Catching one before it flew out the window, Liam grinned triumphantly and then rested his forearm on the sill. 'Feel like a few tunes then, to pass the time?'

Matt plucked a minty from where it had rolled into the centre console, unwrapped it and popped it in his mouth. 'Yeah, sounds good.' He garbled every word, the lolly almost sticking his teeth together.

'Your pick, buddy.'

'Ha, you're game … I might pop on a bit of your Sinead O'Connor …' He playfully started to sing the lyrics to one of her hit songs.

Liam looked fierce, stupidly so. 'Hey now, there'll be no ditching Miss O'Connor. She's Irish for one, and secondly she's got one hellava voice.'

Matt grinned. 'Each to their own, buddy.' Grabbing Liam's CD binder from the floor, he rifled through it, choosing one that was upbeat … a compilation of B&S hits. He couldn't risk hearing any country love songs today – they would break him. He thought about the days when he used to go to the country shindigs, far and wide, with all the boys in their beefed-up utes with stickers covering almost every square inch and enough aerials to pick up a radio signal from the moon. Those were happier times and they seemed a lifetime ago. Oh to be young again, without a worry in the world, instead of feeling as though his entire biosphere was crumbling around him. But then whose fault was that – the mess he was in? Eve's smiling face and the sound of her addictive laughter filled his mind, and the vice around his heart tightened. He reminded himself why he was at this point in his life, and he didn't deserve for any of this to be easy.

Pushing the disc into the CD player, he turned the music up, liking how it helped to drown out the sound of his relentless inner voice. Liam tapped the steering wheel in rhythm with the Garth Brooks song 'Ain't Going Down 'Til the Sun Comes Up', a broad smile on his face. Matt couldn't help but smile along with him as a flashback of him and Liam, and Patrick and Slim, dancing like billyo under a star-studded sky amidst fellow B&S'ers, with paint covering their entirety and beers held high, claimed him. If only he could get back that happy-go-lucky bloke he once was. Easier said than done when every action had a reaction.

The party song ended and 'Learning to Live Again' started. A fitting song for his situation, Matt thought, and shook his head. Could he ever learn to live again? Only time spent out at Rosalee Station was going to tell. Pulling his Akubra over his face, he stretched his long legs out as far as possible, amidst empty Coke cans and salt-and-vinegar chip packets, dropped his head back, and tried to get some shuteye. The knot in his stomach was growing bigger and tighter with each kilometre he travelled away from Sarah, and sleep would be his only possible relief.

He was almost there. Matt sighed and looked out the window of the mail plane, in awe of the brightness of the country sky.

Black soil plains had turned red, running creek beds were now stone dry, and the rocky ridges reached higher to the heavens the further inland they got. He spotted the old Toyota bonnet – the cursive letters he and his sister, Georgia, had painted boldly stated the name of the property above a huge red arrow pointing the way for the welcomed weary traveller. There were no road signs out here, no rest stops with free tea and biscuits. But his mum, being the wonderful country woman she was and a proud member of the CWA, was always keen to welcome visitors into the homestead for a good chat over a cuppa and a homemade pumpkin scone or two. On the one-million-acre station, smack bang in the dead heart of Australia, there was barely a tree to be seen. With unsealed roads and an inescapable freedom, it was a world of both beauty and fear, where droughts were inevitable and the storms, when they finally came, would crack and boom with thunder and lightning worthy of a standing ovation. The magnificence of it drew people from far and wide – travellers, workers, people running away from their pasts, and then people like himself, needing the isolation to help them heal a scar so deep only the remoteness of the outback would suffice.

Looking down at the mirages created by the intense desert warmth, he could almost smell the torturous heat from the cockpit of the mail plane. He was not so keen to step into the murderous forty-five degree day after becoming accustomed to the moderate temperatures of Malanda. Rosalee Station was a place unto its own, but one he loved. With feral cattle and wild stockmen to muster the belligerent beasts, along with bull dust that challenged even the most seasoned of drivers, corrugations in the road that were teeth-shattering, and the infamous min-min lights that scared the bejesus out of most, including himself, the brutal landscape that bled and breathed with life fed his soul. The healing qualities of swagging it in the middle of nowhere, with the dazzling constellations above and a campfire to stare into over a pannikin of billy boiled tea, were exactly what he needed. While some might find station life a lonely existence, he was born and bred for this dusty old country. Once a bond was formed with this timeless land, it could never be broken.

No matter how many times he'd gazed at her rich beauty from the air, he was always in awe of the magnitude of the property his family had called home for generations. Getting stuck out yonder without water and supplies, even as a savvy bushman, would be a death sentence. If it wasn't the dehydration that got you, the wild animals – dingoes, snakes, spiders and scorpions, to name a few – most certainly would. Rosalee undeniably lived up to the reputation that the Australian outback, and the wildlife that lived there, could be deadly.

A startled mob of mickey bulls jogged away from the sound of the Cessna, quickly swallowed up by the red dust they kicked out behind. Strewn with spinifex bushes and riddled with cracks, the ground was an endless sea of red dirt rippling with heat. Barbed-wired fencing stretched into the never-never, keeping their twenty thousand head of cattle in and the neighbouring station's cattle out. He fleetingly saw the glimmer of a dam beneath them, the towering ghost gums surrounding the water's edge so tall Matt felt he could reach out and touch their silvery leaves. He wondered how many red claw were in there, and made a mental note to go and check when he got time – no doubt his dad would have him working to the bone in a bid to keep him away from the lure of the bottle. *Hard work never killed anyone, Matthew, and it most certainly keeps people out of trouble.*

Besides the hard yakka, an eight-hour round trip to grab himself a bottle of the hard stuff from the nearest bottle shop wasn't on his agenda – being out here was going to be his rehab in more ways than one. And if it came down to it, he had the backup of medication to get him through the first few weeks. He'd stuck to his word and made sure to fill the script while waiting in Mount Isa for Stan to pick him up.

The Cessna began to gently drop altitude and Stan took a hard right-hand turn, and then Matt saw it – the very place where everything had changed in a split second. The place he'd hit the bull and rolled the ute. The dagger that was already lodged within his heart twisted and turned, going in that little bit deeper. His breath snagged. Sweat beaded on his forehead. His hands were instantly clammy. He suddenly craved a drink – just a shot to calm his nerves. A little voice in his head screamed, *One wouldn't hurt, would it?* Ashamed, he silently prayed for God to help him through this when out of the corner of his eye, he spotted Stan take a fleeting glance sideways.

'You right, Matt?' Stan's voice was gruff yet compassionate as it crackled through the headphones.

'Yup, right as rain, mate.' Matt gave him a curt nod to back up that he was okay, even though he really wasn't.

As much as he tried to block it out he could still hear Eve's screams as the bull appeared out of nowhere and then Slim's calls as he wrenched the steering wheel sideward and the ute tipped and then rolled. Could still hear the sounds of metal twisting and glass exploding, and Eve's gasping breath when she was thrown through the windscreen. Could still see the blood gush from the wound on her head, and the heart-wrenching feeling of her body as the life drained out of her. Could still hear the anguished screams from Sarah as she'd fallen to her knees beside him. Could still picture his daughter's tiny coffin being lowered to a place a parent should never bear witness to. Could still feel the shooting pain when he'd gone home and punched the wall of the stables until his knuckles had bled, and the feel of the whiskey sliding down his throat and making the ache in his heart ease, as he'd sat in the dark and devoured the entire bottle. Sarah had found him the next morning in a heap on the stable floor. That had been the beginning of the end for them.

Guilt pounded him hard and fast, drawing him deeper into the dark hole he'd fallen down. The shot of alcohol he was craving became an obsession, the only way out of this downward spiral. He squeezed his eyes shut in a bid to stop the tears. He wasn't about to cry in front of Stan. He grit his teeth and forced his thoughts elsewhere – to another time and place where life was good and happy and filled with so much hope. It was a struggle, but he got there. As if it were only yesterday, he recalled the day he and Sarah first shared a kiss, and even now, after almost nine years, it made his heart skip a beat. They'd gone fishing at the dam, where Sarah had out-fished him in legendary style, and the old farm ute had broken down. He'd spent hours trying to fix it, and at the end of the ordeal he was covered in grease. Holding his hands out, he'd playfully threatened to cover her in it too, and she'd taken off like a bull at a gate towards the safety of the water. He'd given chase and leapt in after her, boots and all. Things had intensified between them as they'd played and splashed in the water, but as a man spoken for, he'd fought off every urge to kiss her. Back at the ute and ready to head home, Sarah had tripped over a branch and fallen into his arms, both of them landing in a heap on the ground. Their eyes had locked, and he finally gave in to the desire he'd had since he'd first seen her months before. He'd kissed her, no holds barred, and in that very moment, he knew without a doubt that she was the one for him. But with Brooke, his girlfriend at the time, still in the picture, his conscience had overwhelmed him. The broken-hearted look in Sarah's eyes when he'd pulled away and told her it was a mistake for him to kiss her, had been one he'd promised he would never, *ever* cause again, and yet here he was, doing exactly that. It was no wonder she'd given her ring back – a woman like Sarah deserved so much more than what he'd given her this past year. He had a lot of making up to do.

The glint of the homestead's corrugated-iron roof caught his eye, and he swivelled in his seat just in time to watch the two-storey, red brick house shrink quickly behind them, along with the rustic workers' cottage, the other little cottage he'd be staying in, Georgia and Patrick's new house, and the impressive stables. He could almost see the buildings sighing in the heat. Vivid green surrounded the living quarters, his mother's need to have a flourishing garden worth more to her than diamonds or gold. And his father loved her all the more for it. The pops of vibrant colour from the numerous bougainvillea bushes and flame-red poinciana trees were a sharp contrast to the surrounding arid countryside. Matt admired the resilience and strength his mother and father had shown throughout their years together – Rosalee Station was ruled by his dad, with his mum reigning at his side. The pair of them had personalities bigger than the land they worked, and were a power couple admired by other cattlemen and cattlewomen. They were childhood sweethearts who'd got pregnant, got married, and then had children – in that order. Matt was proud and also envious of their resilient relationship.

If only he could have been the rock for Sarah that he should've been they wouldn't be in this mess. His heart squeezed – as a man, husband and father, he felt an absolute failure.

'In we bloody well go then.' Stan's voice dragged Matt back to the present as the accomplished pilot honed in on the ground. 'Hold on to ya britches, Matthew.'

Matt braced himself for the bumpy landing that was a given with the dirt runway when Rosalee's mailman of the past fifteen-odd years pulled up suddenly. With swift, sure adjustments to both hand and foot controls, Stan pulled the reluctant aircraft back towards the clouds.

'Bloody roos,' Stan sputtered through the headphones. 'Anyone would think the crazy bastards have a death wish.'

Matt stifled a chuckle at Stan's colourful vocabulary.

Stan's bushy grey brows yanked together as he continued to circle while waiting for the 'roo-shoo' to be completed. Both men watched on as someone below on a four-wheeler chased two enormous grey kangaroos off the landing strip. Job done, Slim skidded to a stop and then yanked off his wide-brimmed hat, giving them a wave, which was the all okay for another go at landing.

'Let's bloody well try again, shall we?' Stan muttered.

Laughing, Matt braced.

With a swooping descent almost worthy of mustering cattle, Stan headed for the cracked red earth as if he were a fighter pilot. Skilfully, he eased the Cessna down, the landing wheels hit, and then they roared along the rough surface and bumped to a standstill, a cloud of red dust engulfing them.

Stan cut the engine. 'Hang five until the dust settles before we get out, Matthew. The wife will scream blue bloody murder if I pull up at home with the plane in a shambles. She hates the sight of dust.' He chuckled, shaking his head. 'She wouldn't last a minute out here, would she?'

Grinning, Matt gave him the thumbs up. 'Nope, she bloody well wouldn't, Stan.'

The four-wheeler motorbike drove up quickly and then skidded to a stop. From beneath his tattered dusty hat the familiar stockman/handyman/windmill fixer/mechanic/fencer/ anything else that cropped up out here flashed Matt the kind of smile that would brighten even the gloomiest person's day. The six-foot-five bloke's teeth were stark white against the dust covering every inch of his face – red dust that matched his shock of hair peeking out beneath his hat.

Shoving his door open, the searing heat hit Matt like a slap in the face. He chucked his backpack over his shoulder and stepped out onto the wing and jumped the short distance to the ground, landing with a dusty thud. The fierce heat made him feel like he'd stepped into an oven. 'Hey, mate, long time no see.' Swishing at flies already, he adjusted his Akubra and then stretched out his hand.

'Sure has been, buddy, too long.' Jumping from the bike, Slim's mammoth frame unfolded. Ignoring Matt's hand, he pulled him into a tight man-hug. 'It's bloody well good to see ya, Walshee.' A few swift slaps to the back and Slim released him.

'Cor, Slim, talk about almost crushing me to death.'

Slim tugged his baggy jeans up, a zip tie where his top button should have been. The lack of belt wasn't helping any. 'Gotta give a bloke a warm welcome round these here parts, hey, mate.' He beamed as he tugged his hat off and wiped his brow, his ginger head of hair made brighter by the blazing sun.

Matt gave Slim's belly, or lack of, a pat. 'What's happened to the old beer keg? You're not starving yourself, are ya?'

With a playful grin, Slim straightened up and sucked in what was left of his gut, proudly tapping it. His jeans inched their way down his hips once again, and he quickly yanked them back up. 'The doc said I was heading for an early grave, especially seeing as heart disease runs in the gene pool, so I put meself on a diet. It's working, huh?' He turned this way and that, posing as if he were in front of the cameras.

'It sure is, there's only half of you left.'

'I'll take that as a damn good compliment. And I have to say, it's been a winner winner chicken dinner with the ladies in the Isa. Every time us boys head there for a weekend off, there's always a sheila wanting to give me her number.'

Impressed, Matt gave him the good-on-ya nod. 'True shit, mate.'

'Yup, truest shit there is. I met a keeper last time I was there, too, over a game of pool. I did the gentlemanly thing and bought all her drinks and at the end of the night I gave her a kiss on the cheek and told her how much I liked her.' Slim's face grew redder beneath the film of dust. 'And she said she liked me too. She was a real looker, and so sweet. Hopefully we get to catch up next time I head to the big smoke.'

Shaking his head, Matt grinned at his notoriously larrikin mate now smiling like a man in love. 'Look at you, all loved up. You'll be married with three kids soon.'

'Trust me, I'm working on it. 'Bout time I found me a woman and settled down … I'm not getting any younger.'

With thoughts of Sarah and their failing relationship, Matt's smile faded. He rocked back and forth on the heels of his boots, his hands now shoved in his pockets and Sarah's wedding ring reminding him ever so strongly why he was here. 'True, hey, none of us are.'

A huge parcel satchel in his arms and his face barely poking over the top of it, Stan joined them. With his socks pulled to his knees and his shorts pulled high up on his waist, he reminded Matt of an old school teacher. Stan gave a weary groan and passed it to Matt, who also groaned at the weight of it.

'Holy crap, Stan, you got the kitchen sink in here?'

Stan rolled his eyes. 'Your mum has got right into this internet shopping malarkey of late, almost weighs the plane down with all her parcels. You should have seen it at Christmas time.' He blew air through his lips, rolling his eyes before he turned his attention to Slim. 'So how's things with you, old mate?'

'Yeah, good, Stan, can't complain.' Slim handed him the satchel that Judy had packed with the station's outgoing mail.

'Good, because nobody would bloody well listen anyway.' Stan snorted with loud cackling laughter, making both Slim and Matt exchange amused glances. 'Oh, I crack myself up.' Then as abruptly as he'd laughed out loud, Stan stopped. Looking from one bloke to the other while he re-tucked his shirt into his shorts with his free hand, he grinned. 'Right, no good standing about dilly dallying, better get back to it.'

Slim chuckled. 'You're an eager beaver today, Stan. Not stopping in for a cuppa?'

Stan readjusted his glasses. 'Thanks but no thanks, mate. I got myself two more stations to call into and I want to get home before dark.'

'No worries, why the rush?'

'The footy's on at the pub tonight. Australia versus the All Blacks and I got my money on Australia winning.' Stan rubbed his hands together as if he was about to collect his winnings.

Matt reached out for a handshake. 'Well, enjoy, and thanks for the lift, mate.'

Stan shook it more firmly than a man of his small build should be able to. 'Any time, Matthew.'

'Make sure you say hi to Missus Loot for me, and tell her next time you come out I'd kill for one of her famous passionfruit sponge cakes.'

Stan grinned. 'Will do, you cheeky bugger.'

Matt and Slim stood back. Nimble and deft, Stan climbed back into the Cessna with an ease a seventy-one-year-old man shouldn't have. With a brisk wave, he taxied it away and up into the brilliant blue sky, disappearing in just a few minutes. It would be another week before he was back.

A comforting country silence settling on the airstrip in Stan's wake – the call of cattle and the distant hum of the massive generator that supplied the station with electricity the only sounds. Slim gave Matt a pat on the back. 'Right then, you ready to go get your life back on track, mate?'

As per usual for Slim it was straight to the point, and confronting. Matt went to bite back, his defences rife, but he swallowed his snide remark and his beaten pride – Slim meant well, and always had. He was a mate who always had his and Sarah's best interests at heart. Forcing a smile, Matt pulled his hat down to ward off the glare, and swatted at the damn persistent flies that were now sticking to him like superglue. 'Yup, let's do this.'

Clearly noting Matt's slight change of mood, Slim paused, lifted his sunnies, and placed his hand on his shoulder. 'I know you and Sarah have had a rough year, Walshee, and who wouldn't after what you've both been through. Don't be too hard on yourself, and remember, no matter how hard it is to get off the grog and put all of your broken pieces back together, I got your back, okay?'

'Thanks, Slimbo.' Ashamed, but determined to look his mate in the eyes, Matt lifted his glasses, squinting from the sunshine. 'I can always count on you, can't I?'

'Yup, and you'd do the same for me given the chance.' Slim gave Matt's shoulder a reassuring squeeze. 'After watching my old man go through the same thing when Mum passed away, I know how hard it is, but I also know how hard you can be, Matt – you got this, buddy.'

This time it was Matt who pulled Slim into a firm man-hug. It was the very first time anyone had stood before him and told him he could get through this. It was a welcome change to see not an ounce of doubt in a loved one's eyes. 'Thanks, you have no idea how much that means to me.'

Slim gave him a few firm slaps on the back. 'No wuckers.' He pulled back, sniffling. 'Bloody sinuses are playing up,' he mumbled.

Matt looked away momentarily, giving his mate time to regroup – he'd always been a big softy.

Slim cleared his throat and puffed out his chest. 'Righto, let's head then.'

Bounding on the four-wheeler motorbike, Slim waited for Matt to jump up on the back and then revved it to life. He took off across the red dirt plains like a speeding bullet. With smooth gear changes they were soon in top gear. Matt leant into the rushing wind and tightened his grip as Slim swerved to dodge rocks and bull holes at full throttle. Too often the bike tipped precariously to one side before righting itself, and Matt made sure to hang on for dear life. It was always the same with Slim at the helm – never a dull moment. Avoiding an emu that was tearing across the flat with the speed of the roadrunner, the quad hit a dip in the rocky terrain and all four wheels left the ground. For a few seconds they were airborne and both men yahooed their delight. His hand atop his hat to keep it in place, Matt swept a quick glance to the right, where the far-off cattle yards stood vacant – but not for too much longer. He couldn't wait to get back into the saddle and start mustering.

CHAPTER
9

The clatter of Victory's hooves broke Sarah's dark thoughts, ones where she and Matt never got the chance to be back together. What if he couldn't get over his addiction to the booze, or god forbid, he decided he didn't really love her anymore? What if he and the boys went to Mount Isa, like they usually did on a weekend off, and he got drunk and met a woman who caught his eye? Was this time apart going to be good for them, or the straw that breaks the camel's back? She groaned – irrational fear sucked. As worried as she was about the scenarios her mind had concocted, she knew she needed to focus on the future and not on the past if she and Matt were ever going to make it through this. As if life hadn't been challenging enough.

Taking a deep breath and imagining blowing all her negativity out as she sighed it away, Sarah instead focused outwardly, on the picturesque countryside surrounding her. Considering the circumstances, it had still been an enjoyable kind of day – as it always was when she was riding out in the great yonder. She was glad for her wide-brimmed hat, and not because of bright sunshine but to help shield her eyes from the rain she and Victory were destined to encounter on the way home. The dark clouds were quickly moving in. She'd been riding so long her thighs and butt were beginning to get sore, even though she sat high in the saddle, the creak of it beneath her a comforting sound.

Cantering across the open countryside, she tried not to think about going home to an empty house, or cooking a meal for one. It was only for tonight – tomorrow she was heading to Mareeba. Maybe she needed to look at the positives with Matt now back at Rosalee Station, as hard as that was in her frame of mind. For one, she'd only have herself to worry about, and in a way, that was a refreshing thought. Secondly, she could enjoy a glass of wine or a nice cold beer without hiding away as she did so. Thirdly, her heart wouldn't have to break as she watched Matt sliding down a slippery slope and not being able to do anything about it. And although she'd lost the most precious thing to her, her beautiful Eve, she also had a lot to be thankful for in life – her health, her loving family and friends, human, furry and feathered, and this place she called home, Tranquil Valley.

One ear pricked forward and the other back, Victory awaited her signal to slow. From her seat in the saddle, she smiled tenderly at her horse. It had been months since they'd ridden through this part of the Malanda Falls National Park, but Victory knew they usually stopped for a breather up ahead. She gave him the okay to slow to a trot and then a walk, and he tossed his head in excitement. Veering around a clump of trees, she brought him up beside the creek, beneath a canopy of paperbark trees. The water level was much higher than usual with the recent torrential rain and if it hadn't been such an overcast day, when she knew the water would be like ice, she would have considered going in for a dip in her underwear.

She gave the horse a rub on the neck. 'You want a drink, buddy?' Victory nickered, nodding his head in approval.

'Me too, I'm as dry as a bull's bum going up a hill backwards.' Remembering Slim saying this so often when she was camp cook at Rosalee Station, she chuckled. She missed how her life had been back then, and the fun they all had out mustering; she missed Slim and Patrick and Georgia. Part of her felt a little jealous that Matt would be experiencing all of this, but she reminded herself there was a rhyme to his reason.

She slid out of the saddle, keen to stretch her legs and ease the numbness from her butt. While she did, Victory clomped into the shallows and drank his fill, his coat slick with sweat. The creek bubbled and danced over rocks, meandering towards a rocky cliff where it would fall off the edge in the most spectacular waterfall she'd ever seen. Malanda Falls was famous; a shampoo advertisement filmed there in the nineties had made it so.

Squatting down beside Victory and cupping her hands, she splashed her face and then lifted the crystal clear water to her lips, savouring its icy coolness as it slid down her throat. Stupidly, in her flurry to get into the wide-open spaces, she'd left her water bottle on the tack room bench, along with an apple for Victory and a Vegemite sandwich for herself. Her belly grumbling in protest, although her appetite was usually non-existent, she sat back on her rump. Wrapping her arms around her legs, she brought them to her chest as she watched a dragonfly skim across the water, its red hue vibrant. A duck glided by with eight ducklings in tow. Her heart swelled at the sight of them. A kookaburra laughed somewhere nearby. The trees swayed, the leaves whispering in the wind. Frogs sung from the water's edge, the reverberant song a gravelly basso, the reeds shifting as they bounded amongst them. There was so much life, so much to be awed by, and yet this magical place was far away from the usual human existence of houses and cars and shops and the hustle and bustle of everyday life for many people. As it was Sarah's, this had been one of Eve's favourite spots.

With the thought of Eve, her heart clenched. She rested her chin on her knees, looking to the place Eve used to try to climb across the rocks without slipping into the water. It had been a game she loved and was always accompanied by a massive amount of giggling. 'I love you and miss you, baby, more than all the stars in the sky. I hope you're happy wherever you are, and there's loads of fun stuff to do.' She whispered it, the words drifting on the gentle breeze. A lone tear ran down her cheek, and she wiped it away, smiling through her wretchedness.

Lying back, she took comfort in the softness of the grass. She stared up at the dappled light shining through the leaves. Raising her hands, she played with it, the rays dancing across her fingers. Birds sung from the overhanging branches and crickets chirped as if triumphant – she took pleasure in their melodious song. These were all the sounds she loved, the sounds that spelled security, contentment and home. Soothing and hypnotic, the hum of the running water lulled her. Her body weary and her eyes heavy, she closed them, her intention to do so momentarily. The last shreds of thought swept away, and she was sinking into oblivion with the welcome dark velvet of nothing overcoming her, and she fell into a dream-filled sleep.

❧

It was almost an hour later when Sarah woke to the sensation of someone gently touching her cheek. Words drifted into her consciousness, muted and hazy. And then she heard the sweetness of Eve's voice, although it sounded a million miles away. *'I'm okay, Mummy, stop worrying about me. I love you too.'*

Her eyes wide as saucers, Sarah scrabbled to sitting. 'Eve?' Her heart beat frantically in her throat as she anxiously looked for her daughter, knowing at the same time it was ridiculous to be doing so. She knew she was forever gone. She'd held Eve's cold hand to her heart at the viewing, seen her coffin being lowered into the ground, ached for her every single day since the accident, but the touch had felt so warm, the voice had sounded so real.

She brought her trembling hand to her cheek. 'Eve, if you're here, darling, can you show me a sign, something to let Mummy know it was you and I wasn't dreaming?' She held her breath, waiting, praying.

But there was nothing, no indication of Eve, and no miraculous sign from heaven. Sarah's heart broke that little bit more as her living nightmare returned in blinding clarity. She was being silly. Probably dreaming of Eve, she'd tried to drag her back to the land of the living as she'd woken. It was the only explanation. As she'd learnt this past year, the mind could at times be so callous and cruel.

Still trying to slow her hurried breath, she looked for Victory. He was standing not far from her, his head hung low and his back left leg resting on the tip of his hoof. Unlike Sarah, he was calm and at peace. She truly believed that animals sensed things way beyond what humans did, especially horses, so if Eve had somehow reached out from the other side, surely it would have disturbed Victory's afternoon snooze?

Shaking the sensation off, she pushed to standing and walked over to him. 'Hey, buddy, wakey, wakey.' She said it gently, not wanting to spook him.

Raising his head, Victory sniffed at her hair. She smiled and gave him a kiss on the muzzle. 'We should hit the road.' Slipping her foot in the stirrup, she hoisted herself up.

Waiting patiently for her to get settled, Victory blew ever so slightly, and they meandered off. She kept a loose hold on the reins until they cleared the bushland that surrounded the creek. Then she gave him the cue to go. Victory needed no more of an invitation as his gait widened. The warm smell of horse drifted up, filling her senses, making Sarah smile. He cleared a fallen tree trunk effortlessly, landing gently as they soared onwards. The copper-red clay beneath Victory's hooves lifted in grassy clumps as they cantered across the flat of the valley. A few of the neighbour's Hereford cattle looked up from the grass they were pulling at, their rust-coloured coats matching the volcanic soil.

As they reached the rocky hilltop and horse and rider edged their way over and down it, Sarah heard a low growl of thunder in the distance. Far off in the west, between land and sky, long streaks of grey rain arced towards the ground. The mist began its march forward, slowly rolling towards Tranquil Valley. They didn't have long before the storm hit. Looking up from beneath the rim of her hat, Sarah scanned the sky with the concentration of a woman whose livelihood depended on the weather – forever a fruit farmer's daughter. The menacing black clouds now covered the blue sky. Reaching the bottom of the descent, Victory breathed heavily. Sarah let him stop for a few moments as she leant in and gave him a hug around the neck. But not wanting to waste too much time, she sat back up and gave him a little squeeze. With gentle commands it took only a few seconds for Sarah to urge Victory to adjust his stride so they were galloping across the paddock towards home.

Seeing the old red barn that housed the tractor and a wide array of farm equipment – new, old and ancient – Sarah prompted him to slow down. Just as they reached Tranquil Valley's fence line, thunder cracked and lightning flew across the sky. Leaning over in the saddle, Sarah undid the gate and shoved it open with the toe of her boot. Victory made his way in and then stood so she could close it again. They worked well together, and always had. If only the same could be said for her and Matt. She tried to rid the thought from her mind before she gave it wings.

Full throttle once more they tore across the paddock and as they were about to reach the stall the spots of rain became a downpour, clattering against the roof of the stables with deafening intensity. Sarah was instantly soaked through to the skin, but she didn't care – it wasn't like she was going to shrink if she got wet. As she slid down from the saddle, water dripped from her sodden hat and ran in cold rivulets beneath her collar. In the shelter of the stables she unsaddled Victory and then rubbed him down, his lips quivering the entire time. He always loved a good brush down. Job done, she went to the tin she kept on the workbench and fished out a sugar lump. Victory gently took it from her outstretched hand, licking his lips when he'd finished rolling it around his mouth as if savouring fine champagne.

Smiling, she wrapped her arms around his neck and breathed in his horsey scent. 'You seriously don't know how much I love you, buddy. You've helped me through so much, more than any human has to be honest.'

Victory nickered a response and then tried to take her hat from her head.

Accustomed to his antics, she quickly threw her hand over it to keep it there. 'Oi, you cheeky bugger, get your own.' She could almost swear Victory grinned at her.

Incessant clucking sounded from the doorway and she turned to see Chilli, dripping wet and looking none too happy. With a whicker, Victory stepped past Sarah towards his feathered friend. Dropping his head, he gave Chilli a gentle nudge and Chilli pecked him on the muzzle. Twice. If the chicken had had arms, Sarah could picture her folding them and tapping her pronged foot. Neighing, Victory jumped back, and then holding his head high he strutted past Chilli and out into the misty rain.

'You two are so funny to watch,' Sarah said, walking towards the drenched chook. Warily, she reached down, relieved when Chilli allowed her to pick her up. 'Typical woman, getting in a huff because you're not getting enough attention from your man.' She gave the chook a gentle scratch and Chilli's eyes almost rolled back in her head. 'I better get you into your pen for the night, my girl. I'm guessing, with this weather, your tribe of sheilas will already be hunkering down in there.'

Victory was way over the other side of the paddock, standing under a gum tree with his butt pointing in the direction of the rain, when Sarah stepped outside. 'Catch ya, buddy,' she called out. Now sulking, he didn't acknowledge her. Sarah didn't take it to heart, but instead chuckled at the lovers' quarrel. She'd have to seriously think about bringing Chilli with her to Mareeba for the few weeks she'd be staying with her parents on the farm, worried that Chilli might fret otherwise.

Trudging across the paddock with the chicken tucked under one arm, Sarah admired the brawny build of their stud bulls in the surrounding paddocks. All horns, mystic and menace wrapped in rippling muscle, they were beautiful creatures to be both feared and loved. Most were friendly, a few were cantankerous, with each bull having their own personality. She regarded them almost as her children – from toddlers, to teenagers, right through to when they settled down as sensible bulls. She found it was the extremely difficult ones, the bulls that took longer to train, who were the ones she developed more of a soft spot for. And unlike what some people tend to believe, a bull won't buck unless it wants to. Like anything in life, you're a swimmer or you're not, a runner or you're not – the same went for their bulls. If they didn't want to buck, she and Matt didn't force them to. But regardless of their good or bad attitudes, they were all treated like part of the family. She and Matt had hand raised each and every one with love and care. She was glad they had taken the risk and pushed the envelope when they'd first moved here, adding top genetics to their herd. They'd succeeded in raising top bucking bulls and top producing females, as well as eventually selling the semen of their finest. Some of the bulls' offspring were heavyweights in the rodeo arena, a number of them bucking stars in their own right, while others were bought for breeding, and their sires were often leased out for a breeding season. Their superstar bulls had produced many top females over the years, dams to a few of the present and past Australian champions – both in rodeo and bloodline. With five hundred head all up, sixty of them Matt's own prized bucking bulls, and with three thousand acres of land for the cattle to call home, their bulls lived a good life with plenty of space to roam.

As she walked out she made sure to latch the paddock gate behind her – Victory was renowned for taking advantage of the occasional times Sarah had forgotten to do this, and he would be found grazing on her back lawn. She was relieved the rain had eased to more of a sprinkle, making for an easier trek to the homestead, via a quick detour to the chook pen. With Chilli home safe and sound, and all the other chooks accounted for, along with the rooster, she secured the pen door and made her own way home. Feeling the water squelching inside her boots with every step, she walked quickly down the garden path and up the front steps. Duke met her there, still half asleep and as dry as a concrete path on a hot summer's day. She gave him a loving scratch behind the ears. 'You're not silly like me, are you, boy? This weather's the best to curl up and nap in.'

Kicking her boots off, she peeled off her wet socks and shivered right down to the bone. Suddenly longing for a hot shower, she hung her hat on the horseshoe hook near the door, trying to ignore the empty space where Matt usually slung his, and then dashed down the hallway, with Duke hot on her heels, as always. Skidding to a stop near the laundry door, she tossed her socks towards the open washing machine, punching the air when they landed within, and then ran into the bathroom. Turning the taps on to give the old piping time to carry the water from the gas hot water system out the back, she began stripping off her clothes. Her jeans took some effort, the wet denim sticking like cling wrap to her skin – it was a job she had to do while sitting and squirming on the edge of the claw-foot bathtub, nearly falling backwards into it. Finally naked, she headed through the steam into the hot water while Duke got settled on the bathroom mat. Humming to herself, Sarah grabbed the bar of oatmeal soap and lathered up, and once done, she washed and conditioned her hair. There was something to be said for the healing qualities of a scorching hot shower.

Dried, dressed in her daggiest, comfiest PJs, and her hair wrapped in a towel, she wandered down to the kitchen in search of food. Having not eaten all day, she was beyond ravenous. Duke's nails clip-clopped on the floorboards as he traipsed beside her. The hot shower had warmed her up, but had done nothing to melt the ice encasing her heart. The house was quiet, deafeningly so. Matt was gone, just like Eve. Grabbing hold of this thought, she unwillingly clung to it, annoyed she couldn't shake it. Goddamn it, she didn't want to do this, not after the enjoyable afternoon she'd had. The flickering of the answering machine light caught her eye. She pressed the button to listen, Matt's husky voice making her tumble inside.

'Hey Sarah, it's me, just letting you know I'm here safe and sound. Hope you've had a good day, and you're feeling okay.' There were muffled voices in the background and Georgia's unmistakable laughter. 'The gang said to say hi. They're all here for dinner. Mum's made enough food to feed an army, as usual. Anyway, they're all waiting for me to eat, so I better go.' There was a pause, and then, 'I love you.' His voice broke and he cleared his throat. 'Talk again soon, bye.'

Her eyes filling with tears, Sarah remained staring at the answering machine for a few more seconds, growing increasingly annoyed that he was in the company of loved ones while she was standing here, all alone. He was being cared for while she had to fend for herself. Mentally, she fought hard to try to focus on the reality that he was there to work, and to heal, but at the moment, she was too angry and hurt to be reasonable. This situation they'd found themselves in was truly shitty and the way Matt had gone about it all was even worse. As if sensing her heartache, Duke whined at her feet. Distractedly, she reached down and gave him a reassuring pat, mumbling about giving him some dinner in a second.

Making her way into the kitchen, she looked around, not liking the emptiness or the silence. She had a sudden urge to hurl something across the room, but drew in a deep breath and shook the feeling off. She had to try to keep it together. Snatching Duke's bowl from its place near the back door, she picked up the bag of farm fresh beef offcuts she'd taken out of the freezer that morning and tipped them in. When she placed it down by the door, Duke's tail slapped the floorboards as he patiently waited for her to tell him it was okay to start eating. Slobber drooled from his lips and he licked his chops.

'Come on then, buddy, tuck in.'

Duke scampered over as though he were starving to death, basically inhaling the contents in less than a minute. Leaning up against the bench, watching him, Sarah smiled tenderly and shook her head. 'You truly have no idea of table manners, buddy.' Excited he now had a full belly, Duke skidded to her feet and snuck a lick to her hand. 'And you really should chew your food before you swallow it.' She knelt down. Giving him a hug, she buried her face in his furry coat, thankful to have something warm and living to hold on to.

Kissing him on the nose, then standing, she tugged the fridge open. She eyed the contents – half a bottle of milk, a bowl of farm fresh eggs, butter, a flat bottle of Coke she had kept taking mouthfuls from over the past couple of days and shoving back in (she really should put it in the bin, tomorrow), jars of pickles and chillies and olives, and half a block of cheese. When she slid the veggie drawer out, she found two apples, a bunch of shallots that had seen better days, a couple of potatoes and a lone tomato. Long gone were the days when she loved to cook. She would spend hours in the kitchen preparing meals; it used to be her way of winding down. That was before her entire life had turned to shit. With bread in the freezer, at the very least she had the makings of a toasted cheese and tomato sandwich, or even cheesy scrambled eggs, but she really didn't want to eat alone tonight. Hauling the deep freezer lid open, under the half a side of beef they'd butchered last month, she spotted the two boxes of frozen pizza she'd forgotten she'd bought. She turned to peer out the window at the light spilling from the verandah of the workers' cottage, wondering if the boys would be up for some pizza, if they hadn't eaten already.

A few minutes later, changed out of her PJs and clutching a bottle of red wine, with the two boxes of pizza under her arm, she crossed the lawn of the workers' cottage and walked up the front porch steps. She noticed four pairs of boots near the front door, alongside two pairs of four-wheel-drive thongs – muddy old work ones and going to town ones. She hadn't even raised her hand to knock when the door was flung open. The cheeky smile that greeted her was one she couldn't help but match.

'Howdy there, Sar.' Still in his work clothes – jeans and a Bonds singlet – Liam ruffled his already chaotic hair. Even after fifteen years in Australia, Liam and his brother Patrick still had the lilt of an Irish accent.

'Hey, Liam.' Sarah had a flashback to the day she'd first laid eyes on him, when he'd been walking to the outside shower at Rosalee Station, butt naked. It was a moment Liam had never lived down, a continuing joke between them.

Liam eyed the pizza and wine. 'I see you've arrived bearing glorious gifts.'

'I have. Are you guys still hunting for your dinner?'

'Kinda sort of.' He leant in, clearly intent on whispering. 'Jimmy's hell bent on using up what we've got before we go shopping again over the weekend, so apparently we're having stir-fry canned corned beef and frozen veggies.'

She grimaced, her gag reflexes kicking in.

'My thoughts exactly.' He stepped out of the doorway and waved her in. 'So come into our castle and let us feast on your delectable wares, fine lady.'

'Why, thank you, kind sir.' She matched his shocking attempt at an English accent, and both of them chuckled.

The television blared from atop a set of old drawers, the country music channel on. Jimmy looked up from where he was texting and gave her a smile. His lanky legs were crossed at the ankles and his feet were resting on the coffee table they'd made from an old door, his socks possibly with more holes than yarn. 'Hey, Sarah, how's tricks, matey?'

'Hey, Jimmy, yeah, you know, not the greatest day of my life, but I'll be right.'

'Will you?' Jimmy's concerned gaze held hers.

She shrugged. 'I just have to be.'

Liam wandered past her, taking the boxes of pizza from her arms. 'I'll get dinner started then. You want a glass of rotten grapes poured?'

Grinning, she held the bottle out. 'Yeah, thanks, that'd be nice.'

Jimmy took a swig from his beer. 'Hey, hold ya horses … I thought I was on dinner duty tonight and I was actually looking forward to cooking us a stir-fry.'

Liam gave Sarah a sideways glance. 'Change of plans for supper, Jimmy, we got …' Liam studied the packaging. 'Gourmet mushroom spinach and mozzarella, and good ol' supreme pizza.'

'Cor …' Jimmy grinned and rubbed his stick-thin belly. 'Well, aren't we lucky then, going all gourmet?'

'I take it you're okay about giving up the kitchen duties tonight, then?' Sarah said.

'Oh shit yeah, and hurry it up, would ya …' Jimmy smiled. 'I'm that hungry I could eat the butt out of a low flying duck.'

Passing the back of the couch, Liam gave Jimmy a clip over the ear, his grin spirited. 'Careful, smart arse, or you might find yourself doing just that while Sarah and I eat the pizzas.'

Jimmy pretended to be deeply offended. 'That's a bit harsh; I got feelings, you know.'

Liam rolled his eyes. 'Yeah, whatevs.' He disappeared into the kitchen.

Sarah laughed, shaking her head. 'You two never stop stirring each other.'

'Nope, that's just what we do.' Jimmy patted the cushion beside him. 'Come and sit, and tell me all about your day … only if you want to, of course.'

With an appreciative smile, Sarah joined him on the couch. With both her brothers, Daniel and Peter, living in Mareeba, the comfort she drew from Jimmy and Liam was worth more than gold. Curling her legs up underneath her, she cuddled a cushion to her chest. 'It wasn't easy saying goodbye to him today.' Her throat tightened and she willed away the tears.

Jimmy dropped his feet to the floor and turned so he was facing her. 'Of course it wouldn't have been. You two have basically been joined at the hip since you met each other, so it would kinda feel like you're missing an arm.'

Sarah nodded. 'It sucks, you know, that he has to get away from me to get better. I know it might sound selfish, and stupid, but it makes me feel like he doesn't love me as much as he says he does.'

'Don't think like that, Sar … you're the furthest person from being selfish I've ever met.' Jimmy's lips set in a grim line as he regarded her with so much kindness and understanding she almost wept.

'Thank you, Jimmy, but honestly, what am I meant to think?' She picked at some dirt left beneath her fingernails. 'For the past year he's shut me out, at a time when I needed him the most, and now he's left on some voyage of self-discovery that I couldn't be a part of, even if he wanted me to be – I haven't stepped foot back at Rosalee since …' She stumbled on her words and Jimmy gave her hand a squeeze to let her know it was okay and she didn't need to continue – he got what she meant.

'I'll let you in on something.' He leant in, looking around as if he were about to reveal a massive secret. 'You think you women are bloody complicated. Well, us men are wayyy worse. We laugh when we should cry, we act tough when we're dying on the inside, we think that asking for help is a sign of weakness, and to top it all off, we think the floor is a big clothes basket, and we secretly all think the toilet seat should be left in the upward position.'

Sarah smirked. 'You do?'

Grinning, Jimmy nodded. 'But don't let any other man know I let you in on all of this, okay? It's secret men's business.'

Sarah pretended to zip her lips. 'Your secret is safe with me.'

'Thanks, Sar.' He smiled compassionately, his wind-chapped lips revealing one missing tooth from where he'd been bucked off a bull a few months back. He still hadn't given up his dream of being a bucking bull champion, and Sarah wasn't about to crush his hopes by telling him how dreadful he was at the sport. 'All jokes aside, I know it must be hard, especially after the terrible year you've had, but don't ever question his feelings for you. That bloke is head over boots in love with you.'

Her bottom lip trembling, she bit it in a bid to stop from crying. 'Yeah, I hope you're right, Jimmy, because to be honest, him leaving is making me question so much about our relationship, and it's scaring me.'

'Just try not to think about it too much, Sar, and go with the flow of it, yeah?'

Sarah nodded. It was great advice – but putting it into action wasn't going to be easy. 'Yeah, I'll try to.'

Liam returned with a massive tumbler of wine in his hands, his tongue out as he clearly tried his best not to spill it.

'Holy shit, Liam, you didn't have to pour the entire bottle,' she said playfully.

'Yeah, well, saves getting up for more.' Placing it down on the coffee table, without spilling a drop, he smiled triumphantly. 'Sorry about not using a wine glass; us blokes don't really have the need for them.'

'All good, still tastes the same.' Leaning forwards, Sarah slurped a sip before she dared try to pick it up.

'True that.' Liam spun on his heel. 'I'm going to grab myself a cold one and then I'll join yas.'

'While you're there, buddy ...' Jimmy held up his empty beer bottle and grinned.

'Yeah, righto.' He looked to Sarah and thumbed to Jimmy. 'Anyone would think I'm his bloody missus, the way he bosses me about.'

Smiling at the banter, for the first time in a long time Sarah felt a sense of family, of belonging. And it felt damn good.

CHAPTER
10

Rosalee Station, Central Australia

Just like the homestead at Tranquil Valley, Eve's memory was etched everywhere here. If he allowed himself to, Matt knew he'd still hear the pitter patter of her feet racing down the hallway the very last Christmas morning they'd shared, her laughter and excitement as she'd opened her presents, the tight hug she'd given him when she'd got her wish – her very own pony – and the hundreds of kisses she'd planted on his cheeks. She'd been his and Sarah's world, their everything. And now, because of his stupid mistake, she was gone. Forever.

He wanted to run, cry out, have a round on the boxing bag hanging in the shed – anything but have to sit still and remember all the good times they'd shared as a family under this roof. It hurt too much. The ceaseless inner voice nagged at him. Reminded him over and over that it was time for a drink. Lured him with the promise of deadening the heartache for a little while. As much as he tried to block it out, he felt as if it were growing louder and more insistent, until he wanted to scream at it to stop. If he were alone, he might have done just that. As he knew it would, coming back here had dragged up all the painful memories, all the buried emotions, and compounded his guilt and shame. He knew it was going to be hard facing his fears head on, but this was going to be way tougher than he'd first thought.

Fidgeting in his seat, he tried to focus. It was taking every bit of his willpower to keep his attention on the conversation at the table. He knew it was the lack of alcohol playing with his mind, making him jittery. It came with the territory of giving it up cold turkey. Doctor Lawson had covered all angles of the recovery process, so Matt knew what he was in for. And to top it all off, if it wasn't hard enough already, it didn't feel right being here without Sarah. His heart yearned to be near her, to be able to click his fingers and change back into the man she needed him to be, that he wanted to be. Then he would run home to her and tell her everything was better, that they would be okay. His face ached from the smile he'd plastered there the past couple of hours. His family were acting like nothing was out of the ordinary, while skilfully avoiding the elephant in the room. Everything felt too cheery, too upbeat, when his world was in tatters. They usually drank wine or beer with dinner, and his dad and brother-in-law and himself would have a glass of scotch over dessert – so the glasses of juice looked weird amongst the empty plates. He realised he needed to be thankful for their company and their understanding of his request not to be grilled about it all, but with every nerve on edge, everything was annoying him.

'You okay, bro?' Georgia's lowered voice snapped him out of his internal natter.

He looked to her eight-month pregnant belly lightly pressed into the table, and smiled. 'Yeah, sis, all good.'

Her hand going to rest upon her belly button poking up under her top, his younger sister gave him a look to let him know she didn't believe a word. 'You don't look all-good to me.'

He rubbed his face and sighed. 'Just tired, that's all. It's been a really long arse day.'

'More like a really long arse year.' She smiled sadly, compassionately.

'You bloody well got that right.'

Seated beside him, she dropped her hand from her belly and placed it on his bouncing leg beneath the table, gently urging him to stop. She leant in closer, the chitchat drowning out her voice so only he could hear her. 'You don't need to go this alone, hey. I know you're not one to talk about it all, but remember, we're all here when you need us. Okay?'

'Yeah, I know, thanks, sis.' He looked at her with a confidence he was far from feeling. 'Don't worry so much, I'll be right. You just focus on that little rascal in there.' He pointed to her belly.

Georgia silently gazed at him, her brows rising.

He shrugged. 'What?'

'You're a master of diversion tactics and possibly even more stubborn than me.'

'Hmmm, I don't know about that.' His smile widened of its own accord. This banter was exactly what he needed – it gave him a distraction from his thoughts, and from his addiction. 'I beg to differ.'

'Of course you would. You stubborn old mule.'

'Hey, what do you mean by old?'

'Well, you're older than me.'

Matt gave her the finger.

She gave him one back, grinning. 'I've missed you.'

'I've missed you too, sis …' He shrugged. 'And while we're on the subject, I've missed me as well.'

'Matthew and Georgia, please refrain from using such rude actions at the table. We may be rough around the edges, but try to have some class, won't you?' Judy said, grinning.

A playful glint in his eyes, Steve threw his two bobs worth in. 'Listen to your mother, you pair.'

Both smiling, Matt and Georgia apologised, and Judy shook her head and chuckled.

'I'll help you clear the dessert dishes before we hit the sack, Mum. Patrick and I have to be up at sparrow's fart to get on the road for the airport.'

'Oh, okay, thanks, love.'

The two women stood and collected the plates, chatting as they carried them to the sink, rinsed them off and stacked them in the dishwasher. Matt looked on admiringly. He'd missed this – this sense of family. And he was glad Sarah was going to spend a few weeks with her family in Mareeba. It was what they both needed to get them out of the ruts they were in and back into the living world where life went on, as hard and cruel as that was.

Turning back to the table, he pretended to be engrossed in his father and Patrick's debate over whether John Deere or Husqvarna ride-on mowers were more reliable. The whole time something felt as if it were scratching his soul, as if darkness was trying to climb out from inside him. He gritted his teeth as a wave of nausea washed over him. A craving, so deep and intense, to feel the burn of alcohol sliding down his throat, claimed him. Knowing it would quieten the endless ache and guilt in his heart, it was all he could do to stop himself from sculling any drink he could get his hands on. He stared across the room at the liquor cabinet and spotted a bottle of red wine – not his preferred drop but at the moment he was desperate for anything to take away the edginess he felt in the pit of his stomach. When Judy and Georgia joined them back at the table, he caught his mum following his eyes and then turning to him; the look of dread on her face was one he was very familiar with – he'd seen it in Sarah's eyes way too many times to keep count.

Steve Walsh looked over at Matt, completely oblivious to the tension straining between mother and son. 'You should take tomorrow to settle in, Matt, and then maybe get to work on Monday, when the boys head off for the muster. Sound good?'

'Yup, as long as that suits you, Dad.'

Steve nodded, stifling a yawn. 'Of course.'

Staring down at the tablecloth now, Judy smoothed out a few crinkles.

Stella, his mum's nine-year-old staffy, nudged his hands from under the table. Matt gave her a quick scratch behind the ears, glad for the distraction. His head smashed as if a jackhammer were working away inside it, and although the air-conditioner was on, sweat beaded on his forehead. All he could think of was pouring a stiff drink, and sculling it in one mouthful, followed by another and another.

Patrick yawned, making Georgia yawn too.

The old grandfather clock ticking in the corner of the room reminded him of the many generations of the Walsh family that had lived, and died, here. Eve was one of them. The thought struck him like a thunderbolt to the heart. 'Anyways, I'll be off, let you lot get to bed.' Not wanting his family to see his trembling hands, Matt quickly shoved them in his pockets as he stood. Having put it in there for safekeeping during his travels, Sarah's ring poked into his fingertip and he cursed beneath his breath. He needed to put it somewhere other than in his jeans pocket. Not only because he'd possibly lose it, but because he didn't want to be constantly reminded that she was not wearing it.

His father nodded. 'Yup, goodo, I'll catch you tomorrow sometime, mate.'

Georgia reached out. 'Come and give me a hug, bro. I'm not sure we'll catch you in the morning seeing as we're leaving before dawn. We've got to get to the airport stupidly early as some boofhead booked us on the first flight.'

'Oi, I'm sitting right here, hey,' Patrick said with a playful grin.

Chuckling, Matt leant in and wrapped his arms around her. 'Can't wait to meet my nephew.' He straightened. 'Happy travels and let us know when you're there, hey.'

Georgia smiled. 'We most certainly will.'

'I might drop in on the way past for a b ...' Patrick skidded to a stop. Judy, Steve and Georgia all stared at him with wide eyes.

'Shit, sorry.'

'Don't apologise, mate – easy mistake.' Matt turned to walk away but thinking better of it, turned back to them. 'Will everyone just calm their farms. You don't have to be so weird around me. Okay?'

Four heads nodded.

'Good, that's settled then, night all.'

'Night,' Steve, Patrick and Georgia replied.

Judy stood. 'I'll walk you out, love.' Stella scuttled from beneath the table and to her side.

A minute later, standing by the back door with his backpack in his hand, Matt gave his mum a peck on the cheek. 'Thanks for a beautiful dinner, Mum, as always.'

'You're welcome, love, it's the very least I could do.' The lines etched at the corners of her eyes, from both the years and the many hard times on the land, deepened as she smiled tenderly.

'What do you mean, it's the least you could do?'

Blinking faster, Judy wrung her hands, shaking her head. 'I've felt so damn helpless here, with you going through the toughest time of your life. I wanted to be there for you, and for Sarah, but your father needed me here too, and I can't be in two places at once, I'm afraid.'

Usually a strong country woman, shaped by the years of resilience it took to survive in an unforgiving land, Judy looked at him with such deep vulnerability and sadness it stole his breath away. 'Mum, please don't cry. You've been there for Sarah and me the entire way.'

His mum quickly dabbed her tears with a tissue she pulled from her pocket. 'Sorry, I don't want to blabber like an old fool. It's just, I'm so worried about you.'

Pulling her into a tight hug, Matt rubbed her back. 'Worrying isn't going to make things any better, Mum.'

'I know, but I'm your mum, so I can't help worrying. It's my job.' Stepping away from his hug, she smiled down at Stella, who'd made herself comfortable right on top of her feet. 'Sarah sounded terrible on the phone when I spoke with her yesterday, and she's not saying much about you coming out here, avoiding the topic like the plague actually.' She brought her gaze back to Matt's. 'How's she coping with you leaving?'

'Not great, and I feel terrible for that, but it's what has to happen, and not only because of my drinking.' He shrugged, his heart heavy. 'Otherwise we may as well kiss our marriage goodbye right now.'

'Things are that bad, huh?'

'Pretty much.'

'I thought so, but neither of you were opening up to me and I didn't want to pry.' She sighed. 'Well, as hard as it must be for both of you, you're doing the right thing.'

'I'm glad you think so, Mum.'

'Trust me, I know so.'

'How come you're so certain?'

'I'll explain another time. You get yourself off to bed now.' She placed a hand on his cheek. 'You look absolutely exhausted.'

'I am. Night, Mum, sleep well.'

'You too, love.' She gave his arm a pat. 'I've stocked the fridge for you, there's a fresh loaf of bread in the freezer and I've put some essentials in the pantry.'

'Geez, thanks, Mum. What would I do without you?'

She waved her hand through the air. 'It was nothing. Now off you go.'

He stepped out of the homestead and into the comforting darkness of night. Wandering towards the cottage, the laundry light faded behind him and he heard the click of the back door. With the sense he was finally alone, he released the breath he felt as if he'd been holding the entire night. He really wasn't feeling crash hot. Nausea swirled, and for a second he thought he was about to throw up, but as quickly as the sensation hit him, it died down. For a brief moment, he considered wandering over to the workers' cottage, to see what Slim and the other stockmen were up to, but then he thought better of it. With an early start, the blokes wouldn't be far off from hitting the sack, and if any of them were still up, they'd be yarning over icy cold beers. He needed to stay away from all temptation.

Approaching the patio, he watched a possum scurry out from under a cane chair, across the front lawn, and then dart up the trunk of the paperbark tree Sarah loved so much. Hardy hibiscus and bougainvillea bushes covered the front of the cottage. Insects buzzed around the light his mother had left on for him and geckos darted to catch their dinner – it was an outback buffet like no other. Kicking off his boots, he tugged open the flyscreen door and stepped inside. The door creaked closed behind him. The smell of furniture polish and potpourri lingered – his mother had been hard at work sprucing the place up for him. She really was the best. Dropping his bag, he tossed the keys his mum had given him on the hall table and flicked the lights on. The open-plan living, dining and kitchen area lit up. Rocking back and forth on his heels, he surveyed his home away from home, the very one he'd lived in with his ex and had left behind to be with Sarah all those years ago. As much as it was familiar, it felt foreign standing here. A kind of dread settled inside him. Never would he have believed he'd be back here again for more than just a leisurely holiday, alone, and their marriage in tatters. The place felt empty, just like him. They'd be good for one another.

Desperate for a drink, to the point where he could no longer think of anything else, he made a beeline for the kitchen. Grabbing a glass, he turned the tap on and filled it to the brim,

sculling it. He quickly refilled it and drank deeply. His yearning
not sated, he decided to have a long, hot shower. He knew that
distraction would be his biggest weapon. He opened the door
to his bedroom, briefly admiring the thick doona and plump
pillows, and then undid his backpack, took out a pair of boxer
shorts and his bathroom bag, and headed into the bathroom.

Stripping his clothes off and busting for a pee, he made a quick
pit stop at the loo. A bright green tree frog sat on the cistern,
eyeing him cautiously. It croaked. He said, 'Hi.' Job done, he slid
open the shower door. Turning the taps, he stood back and waited
for the hot water to come through. Then, stepping beneath the
stream of water, he rested his head against the coolness of the
tiles while the scorching water helped ease his throbbing lower
back – a part of life given his years in the saddle and on the backs
of bucking bulls. He hoped he was going to be able to sleep, so
he'd at least get a bit of a reprieve from the ache to have a drink.

Balancing three plates, a few coffee mugs she'd retrieved from
around the lounge room, one of them with the mouldy remains
of something she didn't care to know about, a couple of empty
beer bottles, a tomato sauce bottle that had seen better days,
and her empty glass, Sarah made her way into the kitchen. The
country music channel had boot scooting hoedown music on,
and Liam had turned it up full blast. Placing everything down
on the counter, and then popping the tomato sauce bottle back
in the fridge (she couldn't believe Liam liked it on his pizza, but
each to their own), Sarah shifted from foot to foot, swaying her
hips in time to the upbeat tempo as she hummed to herself.

The blokes' riotous laughter carried into the kitchen while she tidied up, making her smile from the inside out. The atmosphere of the cottage reminded her of the good ol' days back at Rosalee Station, when she'd thrown caution to the wind and taken the job as camp cook – a position offered to her by her then boyfriend, and the station's chopper pilot, Bradley Williams. She'd never forget the horror of the chopper accident that had nearly taken his life at Rosalee. It had changed the course of both their lives.

With Brad Paisley's voice fading away and Adam Brand's hot and husky version of 'Cigarettes and Whiskey' starting, Sarah jiggled excitedly on the spot. She loved this song and had danced to it many a time – at B&S balls, on tables, around the house in her underwear, on the bonnet of Lily's old ute, and at a couple of Adam's gigs, to name a few. The legendary Australian country singer and all-round nice guy had to be her very favourite, swiftly followed by Johnny Cash and Waylon Jennings. Hands in the air, she twirled in circles, singing the lyrics out loud, the boys not able to hear her as they were doing the same. Killer howled along with them, the dog notorious for his love of canine singing. Duke bolted into the kitchen and flopped down at her feet, his paws going over his head as if to say she, Liam, Jimmy and Killer were all rotten singers. She had to agree with him. Laughing, she bent and gave him a ruffle behind the ears, and he glanced up at her. She'd really missed this, the uplifting feeling of a happy household. The company of jovial people had been exactly what she'd needed tonight.

Still bopping, she picked up the dishcloth and went to wipe the counter down, but instead of tackling the task she leant against the bench and rocked from foot to foot. With her gaze snagging on the sun catcher Eve had made Jimmy for his birthday, she paused for a few moments to remember carefully popping all the little crystals into the mould with her. The glee on Eve's face when they'd melted into a multi-coloured masterpiece in the oven had been priceless. Reaching out, she brushed her fingers over it, smiling fondly – Eve had always loved art and craft. Tears threatened, but she quickly blinked them away. She wanted to smile when she thought of Eve, because that's what her daughter would want, for the people she loved to be happy. So, she looked beyond the sun-catching unicorn and out the window, trying her best to turn her thoughts to happier ones.

A bubble of positive emotions surfaced, as did a smidgen of optimism for the future. Coming here tonight had somehow helped her to apply the brakes, to see her life in a different light, and it felt damn good. Life had passed her by in a blur of hurt and heartache this past year, and she really wanted to learn to stop and smell the roses again, like she used to, instead of focusing on all the thorns in her side. Easier said than done, but she could, at the very least, try. Matt wasn't the only one that needed to work on himself for the sake of their marriage. She knew she'd played a part in their problems too. It always took two to tango. She hoped they'd find a way to get back to being the people they were before Eve left this earth; otherwise she wasn't sure they'd ever work it out. And as much as it broke her heart to think such a thing, it was a possibility, and one she had to acknowledge.

Sighing softly, she propped her elbows on the sink and rested her chin in her hands. The night vista was simply beautiful – Mother Nature at her finest. Rolling countryside lit up beneath the silvery full moon, and the silhouettes of the horses stood out against the soaring mountains off in the distance. The millions of stars sparkled like diamonds against the velvet black of night, their brilliance captivating. Fiddling with her half-moon pendant, she couldn't help but smile as she imagined the brightest of the stars was her darling Eve, her spirit filling her with Eve's love. She blew a kiss towards the heavens, hoping that wherever Eve was, she would catch it like she always had, and be reminded just how much she was loved here on earth.

Straightening, she looked at the bottle of wine on the sink and considered a top-up. The two glasses she'd already enjoyed over the past couple of hours had gone to her legs, but in a good way. She didn't feel drunk, but she did feel tipsy, her mental and emotional load lightened just enough to allow her some breathing space. At first she'd felt guilty, enjoying a few drinks when Matt was fighting his battle with the bottle, but the difference was she knew when to stop; he didn't. She wasn't dependent on it for a way out of reality, whereas he was.

'You ever coming back to join us, Sar?'

She turned to see Jimmy standing at the doorway, his face as red as a beetroot. 'Yup, sorry, got a bit sidetracked.'

'Well, hurry it up, would ya. I need some backup.' He thumbed over his shoulder; the expression on his face was hilarious. 'Shit's getting real in there.'

Sarah chuckled. 'What's going on?'

'Liam's trying to get me to line dance with him, and he won't take no for an answer.' He rolled his eyes. 'I really think he needs to get out more.'

'Righto, well I'll only be a sec, and then I'll come pull him into line … or line dance with him, whichever works.' She said it playfully and Jimmy laughed as he disappeared out the doorway.

Placing the three plates into the dishwasher, a half-guilty smile tugged at Sarah's lips. She felt like an absolute rebel, not rinsing them first. She turned it on then stood up straight and stared at the machine. If putting un-rinsed dishes into a dishwasher was the most wayward thing she'd done for as long as she could remember, she really needed to inject a little fun back into her life. As much as she felt she didn't deserve to enjoy living, because Eve no longer could, and because Matt was at rock bottom, she really had to find a way to allow her inner child to rejoice before she let any more of her life pass her by.

Tonight had been a good start; the cheery atmosphere was exactly what she'd needed, and had needed for a long time. The pizzas had been a hit. 'Ahh McCain you've done it again,' she said to herself, chuckling. They had been devoured over a few drinks and infectious belly laughs while the three of them had reminisced about times gone by, and her face hurt from smiling so much. They'd shared many a memorable moment, both here and while working at Rosalee Station, and the friendship they'd forged from going through all life's ups and downs together was unbreakable. If only Matt was here, and Slim, and Georgia and Patrick, and Stumpy – God rest his soul – then they could all enjoy the night together. Now that would be the absolute best.

Walking back from the kitchen with her third glass of wine for the night – the bottle now finished – Sarah ducked the cushion just in time, yahooing when she succeeded in not spilling a drop. 'Righto, which one of you cheeky buggers threw that?' She carefully placed her glass down on the coffee table.

Liam pretended to be engrossed in the country music clip playing on the telly and Jimmy whistled while gazing upwards at the ceiling. Both of them looked guilty as hell, and both of them were stifling laughs.

Folding her arms, she looked at them – letting them know in no uncertain terms that the challenge was on. Tapping her foot, she waited for an admission she clearly wasn't going to get – each man was now pointing to the other.

Unable to keep a straight face any longer, Liam buckled over in laughter. The guilty look on Jimmy's face as he begged her to believe it wasn't him was priceless.

'I hope you know this means war, Jimmy Hercules Turner,' Sarah said.

Momentarily speechless, Jimmy looked mortified at the mention of his full name.

Laughing even harder now, Liam fell to the floor, clutching at his side. 'Hercules? Are you fucking kidding me?' He averted licks to the face from both dogs by waving his arms around.

Jimmy gave his mate a playful slap over the head. 'Shut up, you. I can't help it that my dad is a fan of the movie.' He turned his attention back to Sarah, the slight curl of his lips amiable. 'And how do you know my middle name, Sarah Margaret Clarke Walsh?'

'Adding my maiden name doesn't make it sound anywhere near as outlandish as yours, Jimmy.' Sarah grinned. 'I'm officially your boss, and you had to fill out a tax file number declaration when you first started, remember?'

'Oh yeah, that's right. Forgot about that minor detail.' He flashed her a gappy grin as he pulled his jeans up to sit on his bony hips. Then his eyes narrowed and he mocked her stance, folding his arms and widening his gait, as though preparing for a gun-slinging match. 'Hang on a minute, how do you know it was me that chucked the offending pillow?'

'Because it's written all over your face.'

Jimmy eyed her suspiciously, and then nodded. 'Very good observation.' He smirked. 'You haven't got the balls to pillow battle with me, Mrs Walsh.'

'You wanna make a bet?' Taking three steps forwards, Sarah armed herself with two cushions. Feet wide apart and firmly on the ground, she exuded fierceness while eyeing her opponent, at the same time trying desperately to appear serious.

'Oh, you're on, missy.' Somersaulting across the lounge, Jimmy leapt to his feet just shy of her, ready for battle, now also with a cushion in either hand. He narrowed his gaze, reminding her of a very Aussie Jackie Chan as he lifted his leg and poised to strike Kung Fu style, even making the little sound they do.

Sarah stifled a chuckle. Lashing out before he got a hit in, she struck him, sending him stumbling sideways.

Barely dodging the missile that was all six feet of Jimmy, Liam jumped up and disappeared down the hall, the two dogs running at his feet. 'I'm not missing out on this,' he called out in between snorts of laughter.

Jimmy returned from where he'd landed, cushions blazing. Sarah did the same, the pair of them laughing so hard she was afraid she might actually pee herself. Cushions met with targets in riotous gasps and mock cries of hurt as they battled each other over and around the couch, into the kitchen, down the hallway, and then back into the lounge again.

Then, with an entrance that would outdo Tom Cruise's infamous scene in *Risky Business*, Liam slid down the hall and into the lounge room in his woollen socks, two massive European-style pillows at the ready.

'Hey, no way … that's cheating.' Sarah hesitated for a brief second while she stared at the mammoth pillows in Liam's hands, and found herself sideswiped across the head by Jimmy.

'Yeah, Liam … no fair,' Jimmy said, skilfully ducking a double whammy payback from Sarah.

Wriggling his brows and gesturing to Jimmy with an evil glint in his eyes, Liam silently let Sarah know they both needed to gang up on him.

'Oh hell yes.' Sarah and Liam went in for the kill, cushions going left, right and centre.

Outnumbered, Jimmy crouched to the floor and covered his head, begging for mercy amidst his riotous laughter.

Duke and Killer had joined in on the action, the dogs barking excitedly as they ran around in circles. Jimmy was now in the foetal position on the floor, tears running down his face from laughing so hard. Sarah's face and sides hurt as she cackled along with the two guys. Giving up the fight, she and Liam tumbled to the floor, all three of them now trying to avert slobbery licks from the over-excited dogs as they all tried to catch their breaths. Just like the old times, this was absolute spontaneous chaos at its finest, and Sarah silently admitted to herself that although she missed Matt, she felt better than she had in a very long time.

CHAPTER
11

Rosalee Station, Central Australia

The wind blew through the verandah gauze, just strong enough to make the back door bang over and over. He must have left it ajar. Groaning, Matt kicked the blanket off, cursing beneath his breath. He was balancing dangerously on the edge, coming apart at the seams, thread by agonising thread. The headache he'd felt coming on over dinner was gearing up to turn into a full-blown migraine, getting ready to assault him. His head smashing unbearably, he climbed from his tousled bed and tramped down the dark hallway for what felt like the hundredth time. Not caring to turn any lights on, he fumbled around in the dark. Any form of brightness would be as excruciating as pushing needles into his eyes. The time had come for him to do what Doctor Lawson had begged him to. Popping two Valium from the packet he retrieved from his backpack, he chucked them in his mouth and sculled from the half-empty bottle of water beside his bag. And then he paused, wondering what to do next. Go back to bed or try and walk it off? Get some fresh air, or bang his head against a wall in frustration?

Throbbing pain answered every beat of his heart, and struck at his temples like fists. His body ached, his heart felt like lead, and his eye sockets could have been full of sand. It was just past two in the morning and he was so close to his breaking point he felt he could reach out and touch it, the bastard of a thing. If there'd been any chance of getting his hands on a drink, he knew he'd have caved right this very second. And that's exactly why he was out here, hours and miles away from a pub or bottle shop. There *was* the booze cupboard at his mum and dad's, and by Christ he'd considered raiding it the past couple of hours, obsessed with the thought, but that wasn't an option. He wasn't about to get busted with his hand in the cookie jar, so to speak – especially on his first night here. He had a point to prove to himself, to Sarah, and everyone else who doubted him, that he could do this, and he was going to damn well prove it, even if it damn near killed him. But right now he felt as if he could curl up and die; the nausea and shakes were worse than he'd ever imagined them to be.

With the flyscreen door squeaking shut behind him, he stepped into the soothing dark of night and leant against the verandah railing, drawing in deep lungfuls of air. The familiar smells of Rosalee Station – cattle, dung, dust, horses, and what could only be described as pure, clean air – helped to calm him, although nothing could ease the migraine. He licked his parched lips. He so wanted a drink, ached for a drink, and not the kind to quench a thirst. It was the last thing he needed, but the only thing he could think about. The word *alcoholic* ran amok in his head, making the throb more painful, more incessant. Never would he have believed such a word would apply to him.

A gust of wind picked up, and his skin bristled from the cool flurry that sent dry leaves scattering across the verandah floorboards and over his bare feet. Abruptly, icy pain squeezed his brain. His legs trembled, barely holding him upright. He gritted his teeth. A heavy layer of sweat broke out on his forehead. His mouth went dry and he struggled to swallow. His vision blurred. A wave of dizziness hit him and he clutched the banister, instantly feeling the need to retch. Throwing up what he'd been able to eat of his dinner, he retched until he was dry heaving. There went most of the Valium. Still holding tight to the balustrade, he waited for the world to stop spinning, and slowly, gradually, thankfully, it did. Feeling every ounce of energy drain from his body, he sank down along the outside wall of the cottage and placed a hand against his clammy forehead. The pounding in his head still echoed in his ears, but at the very least the nausea had waned. For now. How the fuck was he going to get through this?

Keep it together ... he silently told himself, over and over.

He stood up, took a few steps and flopped into the hammock and tried to relax, even though he believed he had Buckley's of doing so. Not when his adrenal glands were firing as if ready for battle, and tension strummed on every one of his nerve endings. It was his first night being sober in a little over twelve months, and he was feeling everything as if it were magnified, intensified. With no liquor to dull the heartache, to take the edge off the shame and guilt, or to stop the distressing thoughts that tortured his every waking moment, it had been impossible for him to drift off to sleep. Then things had gone from bad to worse – his mind terrorising him with memories he'd rather forget.

The hammock not the most comfortable for his six-foot frame, he considered heading back to bed, but tired of tossing and turning and pacing the hallway as he begged the powers that be for even an hour of shut eye, he rolled onto his side and stared out at the expanse of nothingness. Maybe this was what he had to do, to heal and get back to the man he once was – face up to things, remember everything in vivid detail, and really, truly feel the agony of it, without pouring himself something to numb his senses. So, he allowed his thoughts to manifest at their will … he was too tired, and in too much pain, to fight it any longer.

Mentally dragged back to Eve's funeral, he shivered and squeezed his eyes shut, as if that would somehow help to block it out. The strength of having to say goodbye as he was standing by her tiny grave, while at the same time staying in control of his emotions so he could remain The Rock of Gibraltar for Sarah, Maggie and his own mum, was one he never knew he'd possessed. As he'd watched the coffin being lowered, he'd felt every inch of his heart and soul going with it. If only he could stop reliving each second as if he were back there, but it was a moment in time that was etched into his heart, burnt there for an eternity, the pain as excruciating now as it had been that day. His history was inescapable, that he was acutely aware of, but his future, now that was totally within his hands. If only he could take hold of it and heave himself forwards instead of forever looking back.

Opening his eyes in a bid to escape the haunting images, Matt gazed at the shadows stretching across the yard. He breathed in deeply, trying to draw strength from the brutal yet beautiful landscape surrounding him by tuning every one of his senses into it. The night was quiet, save for the gentle breeze. A big old gum hugged the side of the cottage, and the slight wind ruffled its leaves and scraped a branch along the edge of the tin roof. Silvery light shifted and changed as the full moon went in and out of hiding among the scattered clouds. As if diamond encrusted, the sky shimmered with hundreds upon thousands of stars, the black sheath of night stretching on into the never-never. Without question, a country night sky was all it was cracked up to be, and then some. It was no wonder tourists flocked here from all four corners of the world to witness it.

The migraine started to loosen its grip, just enough to allow him to sink a little further into the hammock. Maybe he hadn't heaved up the Valium after all. Close to three o'clock, the night had cooled down. Dressed only in his cotton boxers, he was glad for the blanket his mum had left hanging over the rope that tied the hammock to the post – just like Sarah, she always thought of everything. Sarah had so many characteristics in common with his mum – strong, kind, loving, thoughtful, funny … to name a few. Pulling the blanket over himself, he half smiled. They say a woman always went for a man like her father, and if that were the case he'd be proud to be half the man Jack Clarke was. Although, Matt knew he'd done a pretty shit job of it this past year. Remembering the pitiful look in Jack's eyes when he'd lost it on Christmas Day and Jack had dragged him almost by the ear to the man-shed out back for a talking to had been enough to break a proud man in two.

Pushing the post with his toes, he sighed. His thoughts slowing, thankfully, he enjoyed the to and fro of the hammock as he gazed up at the sky. So much for getting any sleep; he was going to be dog-tired for his first day back here, but then again, he was always dog-tired. Being depressed and guilt ridden took a lot out of a person. It had been a great suggestion of his dad's to use the time to settle in – an entire day in the saddle mustering in the heat would probably have done him in. What a lightweight. For Christ's sake, where was the indomitable, optimistic man he once was? It was no wonder Sarah was having a hard time loving him, with the state he was in. How could she, or anyone else for that matter, be expected to love him when he didn't even *like* himself?

Sighing, he ran his fingers through his hair, making a mental note to get a damn haircut, and then massaged his temples, trying to ignore the humming in his veins and the rhythmic throb lingering behind his eyes, the migraine threatening to return if he didn't remain calm. The longing for a beer, or rum, or whiskey – anything he could get his hands on – was growing stronger and more menacing as the hours ticked on by. It was to be expected, so he held on to the hope that he would eventually reach the peak of desperation and then, if he stood his ground and didn't cave in to the addiction, he'd be on the mend, aiming for the sliver of light at the end of the dark tunnel he was in right now. Trying to find some positive focus, he recalled Doctor Lawson's advice – *distraction, determination and direction*.

Grabbing tight on the reins of his thoughts, he went back to happier days, as a young lad, out riding the station with Georgia galloping at his side. They'd always had so much fun, and had got up to loads of mischief. In the Australian outback fun was what you made it, and didn't involve being glued to iPads and iPhones and televisions. Unless it was bucketing down, which was a rare event, they were always in the great outdoors. His little sister had been his shadow, his partner in crime, occasionally the thorn in his side, and always his confidante when things went sour. When Matt and Georgia were young kids, their two horses had been extremely competitive, so when Georgia's horse bolted past him with no sign of his sister on its back one day, he knew he was in big trouble. After trying, unsuccessfully, to pull his stubborn old mule of a horse up – one his father had warned him not to ride because of its pig-headedness, which made Matt even more determined to ride it without coming off – he'd abandoned ship and leapt out of the saddle. The wind knocked out of him, he'd tumbled and rolled through the red dirt, coming to a stop at the toes of Georgia's boots. With her shirt torn, her hair in complete disarray and smudges of dirt all over her face, she looked as devilish as he felt. At first they'd just stared at each other, but once the initial shock waned they both started laughing, a little hysterically, as they watched their horses run off into the distance, but thankfully towards the homestead. God would have had no help for them if they'd lost their father's good mustering horses. It had taken them a few minutes to pull themselves together after their fit of mirth before they were able to start the long walk back home. Thank goodness they'd been wearing their wide-brimmed hats and boots. Arriving back three hours later, their distraught mother had tended to their grit-filled wounds while their father had lectured them about taking horses without asking. It had been a lesson learnt – one of many hard ones over the years. Matt had always had to learn things the hardest way possible – looks like things never changed in his life.

Feeling more at peace than when he'd wandered out here, Matt decided he would give going to bed another try. Even if he could get a couple of hours' sleep before daylight, it would be better than nothing. Peeling himself out of the hammock, he then folded the blanket, placed it back where he'd found it and stretched his arms high, yawning. Walking in, he navigated through the dark and once in the kitchen made his way towards the tap, glancing at the glowing clock on the microwave. It was 3.23 am – only two and a half hours until dawn. His glass now refilled for what felt like the umpteenth time that night, he traipsed down the pitch-black hallway. Heading into his room, he turned the fan to top speed, slumped down on the bed, took a huge glug of water, and then flopped backwards. Getting as comfy as he could on the pillow higher than Mount Everest, he tugged the doona up and over himself. Just as he was about to close his eyes, something scurried across the ceiling. He followed the noise with his eyes. He had no doubt it would be the possum he'd spotted climbing the paperbark tree earlier. A bit of scratching and then it quietened. A scattering of leaves fluttered across the corrugated-iron roof, and a branch gently scraped along the outside wall of his bedroom. The sounds strangely comforted him. Finally feeling his body sinking into the mattress, he sighed and gave way to sleep. His mind swirling with indecipherable images, it then went into freefall – it was a sweet release. The numbness was a welcome reprieve from the incessant sensation of every single one of his nerve endings dangling in water. Momentarily, he floated, blissfully weightless, and somehow worry-free, before sinking into the depths of a dreamless sleep he hadn't fallen into for a very long time.

Sunlight streamed in between the bedroom curtains, and dust particles floated on the brilliant sunbeam that bounced off the mirror, hitting Matt's face. He woke shivering, despite the warmth of the room and the doona over him. Momentarily lost in his surroundings, he kicked the covers off, wiping at the sweat beading on his chest and stomach. As if it had been hobbled and broken, his mind finally kicked into action, and realising where he was his breathing slowed, but only a little. Feeling as if the room was spinning, he sat on the side of the bed and then stood on shaky legs. Movement made him feel worse, but he had to do something, anything, rather than sit still. He had to keep his mind busy, distracted. Unsteady, he used the wall for balance, waiting for a wave of nausea to pass, while ready to dive towards the wastepaper bin in the corner of the room if the need arose. But then the seasick sensation eased a little, although the dizziness stayed and kicked into full force. Licking his dry lips, he wiped the sweat from his forehead. He squeezed his eyes shut and took a few deep breaths. Although it was his first day waking up without a hangover, this was way worse. He felt as though he'd been run over by a bus, and then it had reversed back over him for good measure. The horrible sensations coursing through him would only stop with the help of a stiff drink, but come hell or high water, he was going to push through it stone cold fucking sober.

Shuffling down the hallway as he tugged on the singlet he'd retrieved from the floor, he then headed into the bathroom to toss some water onto his face and brush his teeth. Then, feeling a little more human, he padded into the kitchen, squinting as golden light flooded every surface. Standing at the fridge, he pulled the door open and tried to conjure up an appetite. Food would be his saviour right now, but he was afraid that if he ate, he would have something in his stomach to throw up. Seeing the bowl of fresh eggs, he grabbed it and placed it on the bench, along with the carton of long-life milk. He'd make some scrambled eggs.

Flicking on the jug, he took a mug from the cupboard and got to making himself a stand-his-spoon-up kind of coffee when the familiar pounding of a kangaroo caught his attention. Dropping the second spoonful of sugar in his cup, he stared out the kitchen window in time to see a huge red roo bound past, with a female and joey in tow. In the shady gums lining the back fence, dazzling lime and yellow rainbow lorikeets darted between the branches, and his mum's prized chickens pecked beneath, getting their fill of worms and insects. The scene brought a much-needed smile to his face and helped to centre him. The vastness of Rosalee Station seemed impenetrable, and yet it was so fascinating, with its large, uninhabited stretches of scorched land. He suddenly felt the pull to be out there. A trip to the dam for some fishing and to drop in some red claw pots was exactly what he needed to be doing, after he tried to eat some breakfast.

Fifteen minutes later, after tossing half the scrambled eggs in the bin but also succeeding in keeping the other half down, for now, Matt lifted the latch on the weather-beaten gate and stepped through it. Making sure it was shut behind him, he headed down the path and towards the back door of the homestead. Stella skidded to his side, barking excitedly as she ran around in circles. Chuckling, he sat on his heels and gave her a scratch behind the ears, while avoiding any licks to his face. Passing the Hills hoist, Matt saw the usual line-up of jeans, work shirts, singlets, socks and then jocks, in that order and all pegged up carefully, flapping in the balmy breeze.

Up the back steps and opening the flyscreen door, he stepped inside, his eyes taking a few moments to adjust to the difference in light. He followed his nose into the kitchen – the place his mother could almost always be found. Looking up from where she ladled fat over sizzling eggs, Judy smiled. 'Morning, love, how'd you sleep?'

'Not bad, but not great either.' He leant against the bench and rubbed the place where his belly ached.

'Oh, that's not good, love.' Frypan in hand, Judy bustled over to him, and on her tippy toes brushed a kiss over his cheek. 'Make sure you rest up a bit today, hey? It's been a big twenty-four hours for you.'

'Yup, will do. I think I'll saddle up one of the horses and head down to the dam for a while.'

Judy moved along the bench, sliding eggs onto already lined up slices of buttered toast, the tops of the sandwiches lined up above them with a decent squirt of tomato sauce on each one. 'Sounds like a plan, love.' Walking over to the stove, she popped her oven mitts on, pulled a plate from the oven, and then placed crispy pieces of bacon atop each egg. 'Have you eaten breakfast?'

'I have … scrambled eggs. And they were pretty damn tasty if I do say so myself. ' He smiled proudly.

'Good on you.' Alfoil in hand, Judy ripped off sheets and began wrapping up the sandwiches. 'I'm going down to drop off the boys' morning tea, and then I'm going over to Geraldine's house for a game of bingo.'

Matt chuckled to himself. It sounded like his mum was just popping next door, when in reality she was going to drive almost forty-five minutes to one of the neighbours' places. 'Bingo, huh … you girls are party animals, aren't you?'

'I know, tell me about it.' She grinned. 'You're very welcome to join, if you like … but I'm not sure you'll be able to keep up with us wild CWA women.'

'Too right, you lot are like a pack of chooks when you get together … a man can't get a word in edgeways.' Stealing a spare piece of bacon while avoiding a playful slap on the hand, he surprised himself by taking a bite and thoroughly enjoying it. 'I think I'll leave you to it while I do my hunting and gathering down at the dam.'

'Goodo.' Going a hundred miles an hour, as she usually did, Judy ripped her apron off and hung it from the hook on the wall. She glanced at her watch. 'Oh no, where's the time gone? I better get a move on or I'm going to miss out on morning tea with the girls.'

'Righto, Mum, have fun, and say hi to Geraldine and the others for me.'

'Will do.' Judy paused, her smile fading. She cupped his cheeks and held his gaze with eyes that matched his own. 'Please don't think I don't know what you're going through right now, because I googled it and I completely understand how hard this is for you, giving up drinking.'

'You did? But you hate computers.' Matt's eyes were as wide as saucers.

'Yes, I do, but I love you and I needed to know what you were in for.'

'So that's what you meant last night, about me doing the right thing by coming here.'

'Yes, it was. As much as Sarah loves you, and you her, I think you both need this space to find yourselves again. And so you know, I'm going to try my best by keeping things normal around here for you, as I think that will keep you grounded and be more help than me harping on at you all the time about how you're coping. You're your father's son, and just as he doesn't like talking about stuff, I know you're the same.'

Matt placed his hands over hers, noticing how frail they felt. She was getting older, as they all were. 'Thanks, Mum, I appreciate you keeping things running as usual, because that's exactly what I need.'

She sniffled and blinked faster, stopping the tears in her eyes from falling. 'That's my boy.'

'Love you, Mum.'

'Love you too, son.' She pulled him into a hug. 'No matter how old you get, you'll always be my little boy. I'm here, anytime you need me, day or night, okay?'

Matt stood back from her and smiled. 'Yup, I know.' He looked to the phone sitting on the bench. 'Do you mind if I give Sarah a quick call? I couldn't be bothered walking all the way back to the cottage to use the phone there.'

'Matt, don't ask, just do. Of course I don't mind.' Judy picked up the handset and passed it to him. 'Say hi from me.' She picked up the box of toasted sandwiches. 'Righto, I'm off, catch you this arvo.'

'You will.'

Judy retrieved her car keys from the bowl on the bench. 'You going to join us for dinner?'

'If it's okay, I might eat in tonight.'

'No worries, whatever makes you happy makes me happy.'

'Thanks, Mum.'

Waiting until the sound of his mother's footfalls had faded, Matt then dialled his home number. Drumming his fingers on the bench, he waited for Sarah to pick up. But to his dismay, it went to message bank. He decided not to leave a message this time round – it was her turn to call him. Maybe she'd left for her parents' place already anyway, so it was no use leaving a message. He considered ringing her mobile, but then thought better of it. They needed space, so calling all the time wasn't going to help, although it would be nice to hear her voice.

Out in the paddock, he caught one of his father's older horses, Bonfire, a steadfast gelding he'd ridden many times before, and got him ready for the day ahead. He'd barely swung himself into the saddle when he had Bonfire cantering across the flats. He leant in close to the horse's neck, like a jockey in a race, and galloped at break-neck speed. It made him feel more alive than he had in a very long time. Dust rose in clouds and drifted high into the sky. He clamped his mouth shut so he didn't breathe in half the countryside. The wind tearing past him was hot and dry, and it cut at his lips like spikes of steel. Overhead, a flock of grey and pink galahs squawked as they made their way to the same place he was – the closest watering hole. It was a sight to behold, seeing hundreds of birds so colourful against the blue sky.

Twenty minutes later they were nearing the closest dam to the homestead. Slowing Bonfire to a walk, Matt held the reins lightly in one hand, while with the other he tugged at his Akubra, pulling it low over his eyes for protection from the savage brilliance of the mid-morning sun. Up ahead, a line of eucalypts thickened into a clump at the base of a small rocky outcrop. That was where the water was. An oasis in an arid landscape, this was a hidden luxury, treasured and protected. As beautiful as this spot was, though, he preferred the next dam on, about another twenty minutes away on horseback, but to get there would mean having to ride right past where the accident had happened, and he didn't have the strength for that today.

Reaching the water's edge, he slid from the horse and tethered him to a tree, close enough for Bonfire to have a drink. He stretched out on a grassy spot in the shade, his palms pressing into the rocky ground for support. He stared into the water, the smell of cattle and gum trees and hard-baked earth lingering on the humid breeze. A red claw fleetingly broke the surface, and ripples spanned out, clear in the sunlight. In a few minutes, he would undo the pots from where he'd tied them to the saddlebag and pop them in, along with the socks already filled with dried dog food (his secret lure to catch mounds of red claw). But for now, he just wanted to chill in the moment.

Picking up a smooth stone from beside him, he tried to skim it across the surface. Instead, it plopped into the depths of the water. He tried again, and the same thing happened. He groaned, increasingly frustrated. Usually a master of rock skimming, he wasn't giving up. He did it another three times, and each time the rock would hit the water and sink to the murky depths. With each unsuccessful attempt he felt emptier, and angrier, at everything and everyone. He picked up another stone, and instead of trying to skim it, he hurled it across the water, crying out as he did, 'Fuck it all, fuck everything, and fuck everyone.'

The anger increased to a red rage.

They'd been so happy.

They'd had so much to look forward to.

He and Sarah were talking about having another baby, a sibling for Eve.

Eve had her whole life ahead of her.

And then one split second, one bad decision, had changed everything …

Then it all hit him like a freight train. Clutching his head, he begged the whirring thoughts to stop. But they didn't. He recalled the impact, the screams, and the nauseating thud of Eve's body slamming into the windscreen. He remembered saying '*No, no, no!*' and the paralysing fear that swept over him as she lay lifeless. The seconds had felt like hours as he'd held Eve in his arms. He'd wiped the bloodied hair from her face, and tried to clean it from her eyes. It had all felt surreal, as though it wasn't really happening. And then, clutching her body while begging God to save her, to take him instead, he'd watched her die. He'd witnessed his beautiful, darling little girl take her very last breath. Then the world had spun, rocked, shaken beneath his feet. His soul had squeezed tight and his heart had exploded in his chest, so for seconds he couldn't breathe. He'd collapsed, unable to take in what was happening around him. People were shouting, shrieking, crying. Sarah was huddled over her baby, sobbing, screaming; her painful cries for help unfathomable. He'd looked at his hands, covered in blood, Eve's blood. Then time had sped up, paused, rewound, fast-forwarded, to the point he didn't know where he was. Back at the homestead, the police had hit him with their cold questions, and a request for him to do a drug and alcohol test – so they could confirm his statement of being stone cold sober. Which he had been, one hundred percent. Then there was the trial of going home, back to Tranquil Valley, without Eve. There was the very first walk through the door without her, her toys still scattered on the lounge room floor, her clothes in the laundry basket, her drawings held onto the fridge with alphabet magnets. Her fingerprints were still on the glass doors, and the dishwasher, and the bathroom mirror, her lunchbox, her backpack, her bedroom, her everything, everywhere. Then there were the *what ifs*, marching in, one by one, in an incessant cry in his head. What if he hadn't gone fishing? What if he'd seen the bull sooner? What would have happened if he'd swerved the other way? It all replayed, over and over and over, as it always did when he hadn't had a drink.

Crying out, he smacked his head, once, twice, three times, trying to make it stop. But like a cruel assassin, the painful memories continued torturing him, hunting him down. He jumped to standing, began to pace, anything but sit still. No matter how often people told him that time would heal, he knew damn well it wouldn't. He'd have to learn to live with the pain, learn to live with the guilt, and somehow learn to survive without Eve in this world – all without the shelter of alcohol. It was an impossible task to erase the footprints a child had left on a person's heart, but it was one he had to master if he wanted his marriage to work. Which he did, without a doubt. Exhausted, physically and mentally, he dropped to his knees and buckled over, and for the very first time since his baby girl had left this earth, he sobbed and sobbed until he had no tears left.

CHAPTER
12

Tranquil Valley, Malanda, Far North Queensland

Wanting to do anything she could to feel like her old self, and also needing her furry companion to ride beside her, Sarah ditched the idea of taking their two-year-old Toyota Prado for the drive over to her parents' place, and instead opted for the beloved tray-back LandCruiser she'd inherited from her grandfather. It might not be as comfortable, but the old girl certainly had character. With Victory not keen on leaving his paddock, it had taken a bit of effort, way too much for how she was feeling, but she had eventually got him on board. Sarah had grumbled at him as she shut the back of the horse float, and with his bum to her and ears flat, Victory nickered back, clearly grumpy at being confined. As he'd grown older he'd become more set in his ways and hated travelling. Sarah huffed and threw her hands in the air. So they were both in the same mood, go figure. Taking a second to catch her breath, she gazed out at the lush green paddocks scattered with wildflowers, and admired how healthy their stud bulls looked. They were like her children, as stubborn and determined as they could be, and although she knew the boys would take super good care of them, she still worried. It was going to be hard, being away for a few weeks, but she had to be thankful it wasn't yet another goodbye.

Groaning, she stretched out her aching neck. Face-planting her bed at two this morning, she'd fallen asleep at an awkward angle. Not able to party the way she used to, she felt like death warmed up now, but she knew she didn't deserve any sympathy. It was all self-inflicted. The dull ache across her temples from the lack of sleep coupled with the sick feeling in the pit of her stomach from the bottle of wine she'd demolished made her wonder how Matt could handle constantly feeling hungover. Once in a blue moon was still way too often for her liking, and when she did lash out and have a few drinks, she always swore black and blue she'd never drink again – which she had sworn again this morning, several times. As fun as it had been at the time, she wasn't keen on the aftermath. Her mind on Matt, she thought she better try to give him a call, so he didn't think she was ignoring him. Which she kind of was in a way; her hurt that he just up and left instead of trying to work through things together was weighing heavily upon her. Even though she desperately tried to understand it, and could see why he wanted to do it, it didn't ease her hurt or erase her anger at the unfairness of it all.

Plucking her mobile phone from her jeans pocket, she punched in the cottage's phone number and waited. It would be a fluke to catch him at home this time of the day, of that she was sure, but at the very least she could leave a message, seeing as he'd left her one last night. Four rings and it went to the answering machine.

'Hey, Matt, it's Sarah. Just calling to say I got your message and I'm glad you're there safe and sound. I'm about to head over to Mum and Dad's now, so I'll maybe give you a call tomorrow after dinner, see if you're about so we can catch up for a quick chat.' She went to hang up but put the phone back to her ear. 'I love you.'

Biting her lip, she fought off tears – the damn hangover was making her emotional. Heading towards where she knew Chilli would be hanging with her feathered girlfriends, the pet chicken having legged it when Sarah and Victory had found themselves at a stand-off in the middle of the paddock, she tried to focus on her few weeks' holiday over at her parents' place. It was going to be nice to catch up with her best mate and sister-in-law, Lily. Literally joined at the hip as they'd grown up, and even as young women, Sarah missed her terribly. They hadn't had much quality time together lately as they lived so far away from each other. And it would be equally wonderful to spend some time with her family.

With Chilli finally safely tucked away in a pet carrier on the front verandah, Sarah walked from room to room, closing curtains and double-checking she'd switched off all the electrical appliances, except the fridge and freezer. She'd accidentally done that once, when she, Matt and Eve had gone camping, and it had been a very smelly, and expensive, lesson learnt. Pausing at what was once the matrimonial bedroom, but now more or less her own, her heart squeezed painfully. Memories of a happier past danced through her head. She pictured Matt holding her close, kissing her like he used to, so passionately it would lead into one of those nights where they'd still be up to see the sunrise. Then she saw the two of them cuddled up, Matt whispering in her ear how much he loved her as he rubbed her eight-month pregnant belly and spoke to Eve through her belly button. Then two became three and Eve would quite often be cuddled up between them, all three of them telling each other how much they loved and adored each other. There had been so much love, so much happiness. So. Much. Her arms came to wrap around herself, as if unconsciously trying to keep herself together.

Were she and Matt doing the right thing, or were they closing the door on their marriage? The unknown was terrifying. As tough as it was right now, this life she was living was all she knew, all she was used to, the one she thought she would have always. And yet, the past year had taught her that nothing was a given, nothing was promised, and nothing lasted forever. In a split second, just when everything seemed perfect, a life could be turned upside down and inside out. What had she done so wrong to deserve everything that was happening? Her heavy sadness was replaced with a wave of anger. She pulled the door shut with a thud. Only time was going to tell if they'd make it through this.

Next was Eve's room, and as a coping mechanism, she'd grown accustomed to stepping into it with blinkers on. Hell, she even sometimes held her breath in here, as if waiting for Eve to suddenly jump out from under the bed or from the cupboard, to surprise her and tell her it had all been a really bad joke. And how tight she would cuddle her and the hundreds of kisses she would place on her little girl's cheeks if that were only so. Smoothing the princess doona, as she did every time she stepped in here, she picked up the oversized teddy from where it was propped on the pillow and gave it a hug. Daring a look to the dressing table, where Eve's pretty things still sat, her eyes began to burn and her insides twisted with knots, making it hard to breathe. Her vision becoming unclear, she quickly put the teddy back and marched towards the doorway, daring not blink because the tears would come and then she'd fall to pieces. Slowly, she pulled the door shut, running a hand softly down it when she did. One day, she would have to find the courage to pack up Eve's room, but not yet – she simply wasn't ready for such finality.

Heading down the staircase, two steps at a time, she took her wide-brimmed hat from the hook at the front door while trying to ignore the dagger in her heart when she looked to where Matt's Akubra would usually be, tugged her boots on, and then found the house keys beneath batteries, bullet casings, rubber bands, hair ties, bobby pins, odd bolts and screws, in what she liked to call 'the bitza bowl'. It was the place where things went that didn't really have a place, and where Matt would quite often empty his pockets as he came through the door. She'd leave the keys with Liam and Jimmy while she was away, so they could get in if need be.

Satisfied that the house was safe and sound and she'd packed everything she needed for the next couple of weeks, including her going-to-town boots just in case she went anywhere special with her parents, she stepped out onto the verandah and pulled the timber door closed behind her. She glanced at her watch. It was nearing eleven o'clock. When planning the day she had thought it would take her till after lunchtime to pack and get ready, so she mentally gave herself a pat on the back. The process hadn't taken too long considering it included an obstinate horse, an overly excited pooch – Duke always loved a road trip and could sniff one out a mile away – and a very startled chicken. Chilli had only been in a pet carrier once before, and that was when Sarah had saved her from the tiny cage at the battery-egg shed down the road, along with fifteen other chooks – half of which were now living at the farm in Mareeba.

Slipping a clucking Chilli, who was huddled into the corner of her travel crate, onto the front passenger seat of the old LandCruiser, Sarah walked over to the stable door and had one last look-see to make sure she'd left nothing behind. Then she headed over to the workers' cottage and left the keys where she said she would, under the pot plant near the front door. She'd have to ring and remind the boys they were there once they were home from their day's work out repairing one of the fence lines and cleaning out the dam. Ready to hit the road, she whistled to Duke who was lying in the shade of the tractor with Killer. Dashing through the old blue gum stockyards, he was at her side in seconds, bringing with him the stench of something that had been dead for a few days. Killer didn't move a muscle as he watched them from sleep-heavy eyes.

Sarah swiped at the air. 'Oh boy, what the heck have you gone and rolled in?' she moaned, shaking a finger at him. 'You're naughty going and doing that just before we head off. It's going to be real pleasant driving over to Mareeba with you stinking up the cab now, isn't it? We're going to have to have the windows down the entire way.'

Squinting into the sunshine, she did her best to ignore the splitting headache pounding her skull. The two paracetamol she took half an hour ago weren't doing a damn thing. Leaning into her four-wheel drive, she searched high and low for her sunnies, cursing when she couldn't find then. Hands on hips, she threw her head back and groaned. Damn it. She must have left them in the house. Contemplating having to go and hunt for them, she ran her hands through her hair, discovering her sunglasses right where she'd left them. She rolled her eyes. Blonde moment if she'd ever had one.

She glanced down at Duke who was now sitting on her boots, looking up at her through kind eyes. How could she be mad at him? 'You right there, buddy?' Duke pawed her leg and she cracked a broad smile. 'Seeing as we're taking the old beast, you know you're riding shotgun, don't you, even though you stink like a garbage dump?'

Duke barked a short sharp response and then nudged her hand for the kind of attention she wasn't about to give … there was no way she would give him a cuddle with him reeking so badly. She quickly ruffled his head. 'Well, sorry to say I'm afraid you're gonna have to share a seat with Chilli today, buddy.' She tugged the driver's door wide open, gesturing for Duke to get in. Lithe on his paws, the stinky pooch did as he was told, skidding across the seat and banging into the travel carrier. Chilli squawked, startled by the intruder. Duke retreated to the driver's seat, his eyes as wide as saucers.

'Oh come on, you big chicken, move on over, will ya.' Sarah gave him a playful shove as she climbed in. 'There's nothing to be afraid of. It's just Chilli.' She popped the lid slightly ajar so Duke could peer in. He did so, cautiously. Chilli tried to nip his muzzle, but he stealthily avoided her – accustomed to her ways after chasing her countless times and getting told in no uncertain terms by the stout chicken that it wasn't very gentlemanly of him. Then, his tail slapping excitedly, Duke clambered around the small cage, so he was flush up against the door. His tongue hanging out the side of his mouth, he placed a paw on the doorframe and looked out at Sarah, whining, as if to say hurry the hell up. Drool hung from his lips, what was left of a cobweb clung to the tip of his ear, and he had twigs stuck to parts of his coat. He'd very clearly been out on an adventure this morning while she was packing.

'Yeah, yeah, hold ya britches, I'm getting there.' Sarah got in, tugged her seatbelt on and revved the old girl to life, proud of the fact she still had, and still loved, her grandfather's timeworn but partly restored LandCruiser. It was a relic she'd never, ever, part with. Many people had offered to buy it, but not even a million dollars would persuade her. Then, remembering she was going to call her mum when she was leaving, she grabbed her mobile from the dash and sent her a quick text.

About to hit the road, see you all soon. Love you a million. Xo

Seconds later, as if her mum had been sitting on her phone, a reply appeared.

See you soon love ☺ we can't wait to give you a big hug!

Feeling loved and wanted, Sarah smiled as she plonked her mobile back on the dash. Heading down the gravel driveway, she moved through the gears, in no rush – *smelling the roses* was her new motto and she was going to try damn hard to live by it. While she decelerated at the front gate to cross the second cattle grid, Duke did his usual trick of barking hysterically, and then they were off. Paddocks, livestock, orchards, and the occasional house rushed past in a kaleidoscope of earthy colours. She kept waiting for an overwhelming feeling of sadness to claim her, but strangely, the more distance she put between herself and her home, the more weight seemed to lift from her shoulders, and she felt, for the first time in what seemed like forever, she could draw a decent breath. And then she realised that as emotional as she was about her and Matt needing a trial separation, she was actually excited about the time away from the rut they'd dug themselves into. She smiled. Maybe this wasn't such a bad idea after all.

❦

Driving down the main street of Malanda, Sarah waved to almost every Tom, Dick and Harry, and Duke bared his teeth in a doggy grin to passers-by. Being a local in a small town certainly had its pluses, but it could also be a pain in the butt when wanting to dash into town for some milk or bread without being cornered by somebody who felt like an hour's chinwag. At least today she wasn't making any pit stops. She really wasn't in the mood for small talk about the weather or the price of beef, or how someone's cousin's mother's brother was in trouble for cheating on their spouse.

Totally engrossed in the passing scenery, the next half an hour passed for her in the blink of an eye. Just outside of Atherton, the roadworks that had been going on for the past five months, and looking as if work hadn't progressed since the last time she came through here, stopped Sarah in her tracks. Drumming her fingers on the steering wheel, she groaned as she waited for the bored looking bloke to turn the *Stop* sign around. On one side of her a potato farm stretched into the distance and on the other were rows of sugar cane topped with pretty pink flowers that reminded her of fairy floss. The minutes ticked on and she started to get fidgety. Duke whined. Chilli scratched at the floor of her cage. Without a breeze being whipped around the cab now they were stationary she could smell whatever Duke had rolled in as if it were right under her nose. Glancing up at the rear-view mirror, she watched Victory shifting about in the float. Another godawful advertisement came over the radio, announcing the closing-down sale of the rug shop that had been closing down for the past three years. Did they ever play songs anymore? It was the fifth or sixth advertisement in a row. She stabbed her finger on the radio's control button, cutting off the presenter's annoyingly shrill voice. Just as she was about to reach for her CD binder, the bloke holding the *Stop* sign responded to someone on his walkie-talkie. Nodding, he flipped the sign from *Stop* to *Drive Slowly* like it was the most amazing thing to do, smiled broadly, and then waved her forwards and into the opposite lane. She said a quick g'day in passing, and liked the fact he responded. It didn't take much to be courteous.

A few kilometres down the highway stormy darkness quickly descended. The sky boomed and crackled, as if splitting down the middle, and within seconds it opened up and heavy raindrops hammered the roof of the four-wheel drive. She quickly wound her window up, at the same time stealing a sideways glance at Duke. He was still hanging out the window, blinking fast, the water pummelling his face while he tried to lick the raindrops from the air. She shook her head, grinning at the sight of him. Her animals gave so much pleasure. Needing to wind his window up before he got completely drenched and poor Chilli found herself swimming in her cage, Sarah pulled over to the side of the road. Leaning across the seat, at the same time trying to avoid Duke's slobbery kisses while holding her breath, she sighed with relief when the window finally screeched to the top. Straightening, she used the pit stop to pop one of her favourite

CDs of all time into the stereo – *Trio* with Linda Ronstadt, Dolly Parton and Emmylou Harris. Give her seventies music and good old-fashioned country like Johnny and Waylon and these three legendary artists over the new stuff any day. There was something to be said for the lyrics in the old-time country, the songs filled with love and heartache and more love, whereas most of the new stuff was all about tractors and whiskey and women.

Flicking the widescreen wipers to warp speed, she waited for a road train filled with cattle to pass, while wishing she could stick her head out the window to breathe in the scent most people disliked before she pulled back onto the highway. The road wet and slippery, she drove cautiously, and with towing Victory's float she wasn't taking any chances. There wasn't a fire, they had nowhere to be at a given time – they were in no rush. *Smell the roses.* Humming away to 'Silver Threads and Golden Needles', she watched raindrops slide down the windscreen and blow away in the wind. Soon the deluge was so heavy she was having trouble seeing a metre in front of her. Tropical North Queensland – sunny one minute and bucketing down the next. This was monsoonal weather at its finest. The scent of rain was heavy as it filtered through the air-conditioning vent, as too was Duke's pong and the unmistakable smell of chicken poop. *Oh the joys of country life*, she thought happily.

To see through the rain she clutched the steering wheel and leant forward like an eighty-year-old when a memory claimed her mind. A wayward smile tugged at her lips as she remembered the very first time she'd hit a patch of bull dust on her way out to Rosalee Station for her cook's job. In a panic, she'd gone to slam on the brakes, but thankfully, Daniel had been in the car and he'd talked her through it. It had been one of many lessons she'd learnt about the treacheries of outback Australia. With the most venomous snakes in the world, remorseless flies that put the city flies to shame, min-min lights, and kangaroos that would beat a world-champion fighter in a boxing match, it wasn't a place for the faint of heart. And she'd proudly proven to Matt and his parents that she was cut out for the dusty old country within a week of getting there as an eager twenty-three-year-old. It was only eight years gone, but it felt like a lifetime ago. Her mind then turned to Matt and to how they fell in love that mustering season – it had been such a sweet journey. They'd had many obstacles, but they'd climbed and battled every one of them to be together, and now here they were, unable to be under the same roof. So very sad, how things had worked out. She wondered how he was doing, and if he missed her. It felt so strange, going a day without seeing him. Would this be something she'd have to get used to? She really didn't want to give much thought to that right now.

The windscreen was fogging up, so she alternated the air to come up the dash vents. 'Far out, you're doing some heavy breathing over there, buddy, because it sure as hell ain't Chilli.'

Resting his head on the top of the pet crate, Duke eyed her dotingly.

'Awww, love you too, buddy.' His pong assaulting her nostrils, Sarah clamped them shut with her fingers. 'But I am not liking that stink. Cor, Dukey boy, you're in desperate need of a bath.'

Pulling the forest-scented air freshener from the door pocket, she squirted it left, right and centre. Hating anything that smelt half decent, Duke wiggled down to the floor and put his paws over his head.

Listening to the intermittent thump of the windshield wipers, Sarah turned the stereo up, the country love song a favourite. And then, thankfully, as quickly as the downpour had arrived, the clouds began to disperse and rays of sunshine shot through the gaps like golden spears.

Passing the drive-in, and then the sign that read 'Welcome to Mareeba 300 sunny days a year', she wound her window down and took a much-needed deep breath. She loved the scent of wet leaves and damp earth; something about it was so invigorating.

Duke jumped back up on his seat and pawed at the window.

'Sorry, buddy, but there's nowhere for me to pull over here. You can just wait until we get to Mum and Dad's now.'

Passing the laundromat that also housed the local Thai takeaway, followed by the top pub, the middle pub and the bottom pub, then a servo and one of the two newsagencies, she felt a sense of familiarity catch hold of her heart. Without a set of traffic lights in sight and only roundabouts to keep the traffic flowing, this was the epitome of country-town driving. And then they were out the other side of town and on the home stretch. Butterflies flurried in her belly. It had been a long time coming, visiting her family and the farm. Crossing the railway tracks that marked the outskirts of town, only used in the sugar-cane season, she felt something deep inside of her ease a little. She was almost home, almost back to the people who loved her unconditionally. Normal people. Well, as normal as her family could get, she thought with a playful smile.

Her mobile phone buzzed from the dash, and she tossed it into her lap, pressing the speaker button. 'Hey, Mum.'

'Hi, love, how's the drive over going?'

'Yeah, good, I'm not far off.' She glanced out her window at the rodeo grounds, many happy memories flooding her in an instant. Only a week to go and the sleeping giant would be flooded with show rides, saddle-bronc horses and bucking bulls, fairy floss and dagwood dogs, and cowgirls and cowboys – it was the event of the year for Mareeba.

'Whereabouts are you?'

'I'm about to turn down Brookes Road.'

'Oh, wonderful, I'll pop the kettle on then, and I've made your favourite.'

'Lemon meringue pie?'

'Yup.'

'Oh, Mum, you're the bloody best, I tell ya.'

'Yes, I am, and don't you forget it.'

Sarah chuckled. 'I don't think you'd ever let me.'

'You sound more and more like your father every day.'

'Oi,' Jack Clarke piped up in the background.

Sarah laughed, her parents' banter was a given, and she loved listening to them as much as they loved winding each other up. 'See you both in a jiffy.'

Turning off the rain-slicked highway, she headed down the familiar dirt road, barely wider than the four-wheel drive and horse float, slowing at each corner to look for oncoming traffic. Courtesy was the way of the road here. The driver of the bigger and more bush worthy vehicle, one more capable of ploughing through the anthills and potholes that were common round these parts, was always the one to move over to let the oncoming car pass. Duke jumped around like a frog in a sock on the passenger seat, whining excitedly, reflecting how Sarah felt.

The nets that kept the fruit trees safe from the bats and birds came into view, and then Sarah saw the family's two-storey Queenslander, the recent paint job on the weatherboards not taking away from the old charm of the place. She slowed and pulled into the drive. The big verandahs that wrapped around the house were, as always, filled with pots of flowering plants, thanks to her mum's amazing green thumb. She couldn't help but smile as she admired the mango-wood sign she and her brothers had bought her dad eight years ago that read 'Clarkes' Farm', and just beyond it, settled among a flourish of blooming rose bushes, was the little windmill her best mate, Lily, had given her parents ten years back. She hadn't even switched the ignition off when her mum and dad appeared, Jack with his customary wild hair and Maggie with her floral apron tied to her wide hips.

'Mum, Dad,' Sarah squealed as she all but jumped from the four-wheel drive and fell into her mum's open arms.

'Oh, my beautiful girl, it's so good to see you.' Maggie tightened her hold.

Jack stood patiently behind, and when they untangled, he pulled Sarah into a big bear hug. 'Hey, love, it's so good to see you.' He kissed her forehead, like he had since she was a young child. 'And I see you brought the beast for a bit of a wander.'

'Of course I brought Duke, and the horse, oh, and a chicken.' She grinned.

On cue, Duke leapt from the driver's side, his tail going like the clappers and his bum swaying in time with it. He skidded to their feet, doggy grinning, and baring his teeth so it almost looked like he was snarling.

'Hey, Dukey.' Jack gave him a quick pat. 'No, love, I meant Dad's four-wheel drive.'

'Ahhh, yup, thought she needed a bit of the dust cleared from the old exhaust pipes.' She glanced to the heavens. 'Grandad will be proud the old girl's still hitting the dusty tracks.'

'He will be, God love him.' Jack smiled. 'She goes well still?'

'She sure does … never skips a beat.'

Maggie knelt down and went to give Duke a cuddle, but quickly stood up again, patting his head instead. 'Good Lord, you stink to high heavens.'

'Yeah, sorry, Mum, he's in desperate need of a wash down.'

Maggie chuckled. 'I reckon he's in more need of a spray with a high-pressure hose by the smell of things.' Hands on hips, she tutted at him. 'What the hell have you been rolling in? I'll get a bar of soap onto you later, boy, before you step foot in the house.'

'Ha-ha, good luck with that, Mum, you know how much he hates being washed.'

'Trust me when I say your mother will pin him down if need be … she won't let him in the house stinking like that. She bloody well hoses me down before I step through the door if I'm too smelly and grotty.' Jack gave his wife a playful sideways glance.

'Oh rubbish, I do not, you old pot stirrer, you.' Maggie slapped him gently on the arm in fun. 'I reckon I might buy you a wooden spoon next Christmas.'

'Oh come on, darl, you love it.' Jack chuckled and brushed a kiss over Maggie's cheek. 'I'll go and get Victory settled in his paddock, Sarah, while you and your mum catch up, if you like.'

Sarah nodded, knowing full well it was her dad's cryptic way of saying, 'I'm going to leave you two women to it and I'll be back once things have quietened down a bit and I can get a word in edgeways.' She watched him go over to the float and check on

Victory. 'Chilli's on the front seat, Dad. She's pretty social but maybe shut her in the chook pen for now, so she can settle in, and we'll let her out to forage tomorrow. I'll get all my stuff out later.'

Jack gave her the thumbs up. 'Sounds like a plan, Stan.' He gestured to Duke to join him and the overexcited pooch didn't need any more of an invitation. 'You better come with me, buddy, because there'll be no going inside for you just yet.'

Maggie put her arm around Sarah's waist and gave her a gentle squeeze. 'Come on inside then, love, we've got some catching up to do … and some lemon meringue pie to eat.'

Smiling from the inside out, Sarah slid her arm around her mum's shoulder, feeling stronger just by being near her. 'We sure do.'

Cookie, the kookaburra, laughed from his perch on one of the clothesline's posts – a pet, of sorts, Cookie had been a part of the Clarke family for twelve years now. Beside him sat a female kookaburra and two babies. In her turmoil of the past year, Sarah had forgotten all about him. 'Oh my god, Cookie, you devil. You've gone and got yourself a little family.' Cookie eyeballed her and then laughed again. The bowl her mum always used to put mince in for him was empty and upended on the ground.

Once in the kitchen, Maggie pulled the most decadent looking lemon meringue from the fridge. 'Tah-dah.'

Sarah's mouth watered instantly. 'Oh wow, Mum, that looks amazing.'

Placing it on the table, beside a little jug of cream, Maggie grinned. 'I think it's one of my best yet.'

'Only tasting it will tell us that.'

Sarah flinched when she felt the electric jug and it was red-hot. Her mother wasn't beating around the bush when she said she would put the kettle on. 'Should I make enough tea for Dad too?'

'Probably not … it'll be cold by the time he gets back. Lord knows what that man does, but a job that should take half an hour tends to take him hours. He's a side-tracker if I've ever seen one.' Maggie rolled her eyes to the heavens.

Sarah chuckled as she recalled how long it used to take her dad to fix anything in the house – outside was a different story. 'You got that right, Mum.' Picking up the teapot that matched the cups that were already set out on the dining table, alongside the good china plates, Sarah felt very special. She put in two heaped teaspoons of tea-leaves and then poured the hot water in. Job done, both women got themselves comfortable at the table.

'So, love, tell me, how are you coping?'

Her mother's eyes were so kind, so compassionate, Sarah had to choke back a sob. 'I'm managing, and pushing through day by day, because that's what I have to do.' She shrugged. 'If I want to have any kind of life, what other choice do I have but to soldier on and hope for the best?'

'Very true, but make sure you allow yourself time to get to the bottom of how you're feeling too, won't you? This time apart is very important for you and Matt.'

'I will, which is why, as well as wanting to see all you guys of course, I've come over for a couple of weeks. I need time to stop and find myself again.'

Placing her hand over her daughter's, Maggie sniffled. 'I'm sorry you're going through all this, love. I wish there was something your father and I could do to make things better.'

'Just by being here for me makes things better, Mum.' Needing to do something, anything but stare into her mother's soulful eyes, Sarah picked up the teapot and started pouring. She didn't want to wallow in self-pity; instead she wanted to try to focus on the good things. 'I admire you and Dad, sticking together and still being so in love after all these years.'

Maggie put a teaspoon of sugar in her tea. 'Thanks, love, but trust me when I say it hasn't always been smooth sailing for your father and me.'

'It hasn't?'

'No, far from it actually.' Picking up the knife, Maggie started slicing the pie. 'Like you and Matt, we've had our fair share of struggles in our marriage over the years.' She passed a piece to Sarah, who was holding out her plate in eager readiness.

'You have?' Unable to hold off any longer, Sarah picked up her fork and took a mouthful. Her eyes almost rolled back in her head in culinary pleasure.

'We're only human, your dad and I, and I look at a marriage as always being a work in progress,' Maggie said.

'That's a really good way to look at it,' Sarah mumbled through another delicious mouthful.

'I like to say that when the going gets tough, we don't get going … unlike too many young people these days. I truly believe that if you stick it out, most of the time you will work it out and live a happy life … apart from the few times when you may want to poke your better half with a fork.'

Sarah chuckled. Wiping her mouth with a paper napkin, she considered having another piece, but thought she'd sit on her tea for now.

As though measuring her words, Maggie paused, then said, 'I want to let you in on a little secret, and only because it might help you feel a bit better about what you're going through.'

'Okay, go on ...' Completely intrigued, Sarah cradled her cup and sat back. 'I'm all ears.'

'Your father and I have been through a trial separation too.'

'Holy crap, really?'

'Yes, really.'

'When?'

'Let's see.' Maggie mumbled to herself, while counting her fingers. 'About twenty-five years ago now.'

'What happened?'

'Life did, I suppose.' She shrugged. 'The farm was struggling after your dad had been in jail because of his stupid decision to try growing pot, and we were having trouble paying the bills. Also, we had to give all our time to two young children. So at the end of the day we were too exhausted to have time for each other, and that eventually grew into resentment, from both sides. We were arguing a lot, mostly over silly things, to the point where I thought it would be better for you and me and Daniel to move in with my parents for a while.'

'Wow, Mum, I never had the slightest idea you and Dad had been through the same thing.'

'Well, it's not really something you openly tell your kids.'

'Did it help?'

'Not at first. Your father was so hurt at me leaving, I thought I'd gone and ruined it. But then as time went on, and we would meet up for a coffee or some dinner, we really started to see each other again, you know, like really see inside of one another, past all the fog of life, and we realised we were still so very much in love … probably more in love than we'd ever been.'

'That's a very beautiful story, Mum. I'm glad you and Dad made it through because you two are made for each other.'

'That we are, love. And I truly believe you and Matt are made for each other too. He needs to sort his drinking out, and you need time to find yourself again, and everything will work out, you'll see.'

'I really hope you're right, Mum.'

'I'm always right.' Maggie grinned and glanced at the clock above the stove. 'See, almost an hour now and he's still not back.'

Uncannily, the back door squeaked open and Jack wandered in with a freshly scented and damp looking Duke following him.

Maggie looked to her husband of forty-eight years. 'Speak of the devil.'

Jack grinned sheepishly. 'I thought my ears were burning.'

'Holy crap, you actually pinned him down long enough to bath him.'

'Sort of … I threw a stick in the dam, got him wet, and then when he brought it back to me I tipped a heap of horse shampoo over him, and wallah, Bob's ya mother's brother.'

Duke curled up in the corner of the room and was asleep in seconds.

'Good thinking, Ninety-nine.'

'See, I'm not just a pretty face, ladies.' He headed over to the sink with a smug smile and washed his hands. 'Victory is all settled with his old mate, and Chilli is sashaying around the chook pen like her poo doesn't stink … so all in all, all the critters are happy.'

'Grooviness, thanks, Dad … you're the best.'

'I'm the grooviest groover that's ever grooved.' Giving Sarah a gentle poke in the ribs, he joined them at the table, slicing the biggest piece of pie.

Sarah smirked. 'You got enough there, Dad?'

'Not sure yet.' His tongue curled to the side of his lip as he balanced the piece precariously on the knife and then ceremoniously plonked it down on his plate – clearly happy he'd succeeded in not dropping it. Then grabbing the jug of cream, he poured a heap over the top; so much that the pie could barely be seen.

Maggie tutted. 'Good Lord, you're going to give yourself a bloody heart attack one of these days, Jack.'

'If it's while I have a spoonful of your lemon meringue in my mouth, Maggie, I'll die a very happy man.'

'Oh, you old charmer, you.'

Leaving her parents to their banter, Sarah went over to the electric jug and made her dad a fresh pot of tea and pushed the cup in front of him. Jack took a sip, wincing at the heat. 'So, kiddo, how you holding up?'

'Yeah, all right.' She picked at some fluff on her jeans. 'Just gotta roll with the punches.'

Jack gave her a tender pat on the back. 'That's my girl … the Clarkes never quit when the going gets tough.'

'So I've heard,' Sarah mumbled.

'Pardon?' he garbled through a mouthful of pie – like father like daughter.

Her mum kicked her beneath the table, and Sarah winced. 'Oh, sorry, nothing … just talking to myself.'

'Fair enough, I do that too.'

Then the three of them sat and chatted about anything and everything. Eve's name was mentioned quite a few times as they retrieved memories and relived them. And although it tugged at her heartstrings, and sometimes brought tears to her eyes, as it did her mum and dad's, Sarah smiled through it all. It felt so damn good to finally be able to speak about her beautiful daughter and rejoice in her life, instead of focusing only on her death. *Smelling the roses*, that's what she was doing, instead of pricking her fingers on the thorns.

CHAPTER

13

Rosalee Station, Central Australia

It was three days into the weeklong muster. The last of the men to enjoy a bush-bath, Matt stood in the dark, stark naked, the sweat and dirt of the day now washed from his skin. The doughy aroma of coal-baked damper and rich stew drifted on the gentle breeze, making his belly rumble. Having washed as best he could with a bar of soap and a bucket of water pinched from the cattle trough, he dried himself off, tugged on a fresh pair of jeans and a singlet, and then slipped his bare feet into his four-wheel-drive style thongs. Heading back to camp, he hung his towel among the others on a branch, dished himself up some dinner and then traipsed back towards the glow of the fire. Humming to the Slim Dusty tune 'Lights on the Hill' playing from the stereo in the cook's ute, he sat down on a log beside Whisper, the head stockman, who was staring into the glowing coals, the almost mandatory pannikin of tea in his hands and a half-smoked rolly hanging from his lips. An empty bowl sat on the ground beside him. A spitting image of the actor Sam Elliott, he looked like a man that should be starring in a wild west movie.

Huddled around the campfire, the weary group of dishevelled blokes sat in companionable silence, the scraping of plates and the crackle of burning logs the only noises in competition with the gentle bellows of the mustered cattle and the occasional call of a nocturnal bird or cricket. Enjoying his first taste of the melt-in-the-mouth beef stew, Matt squinted from the smoke curling into his eyes, both from the cigarette and the fire. Give him smoke from a campfire any day but he hated the stench of cigarettes, although he wasn't about to complain when he and Slim were the only ones in the bunch who didn't smoke. A boobook owl hooted above them, to be echoed by its mate across the way; the sound was one of the most common in the Australian outback at night. He looked up, trying to spot it, but with the bird's clever camouflage it was virtually impossible.

The air had cooled tenfold after the scorching heat of the day, and thankfully so. The high temperature and long hours in the saddle were making every man dog-tired – muster-lethargy had definitely set in. Yawning, Matt tried to stretch out the chinks in his neck, as well as in his aching lower back. He couldn't wait to climb into his swag and shut his grit-stabbed eyes. The physical and mental exhaustion was proving invaluable for his recovery, and the occasional dose of Valium was helping too, as much as he hated to admit it. The day in the saddle allowed his mind to go where it willed, and he spent most of the time thinking about Sarah and Eve and how much he'd failed them. On rare occasions his thoughts were happy, but usually he found himself fighting back tears. He would never break down in front of the men the way he did back at the dam when he was on his own, even though it had been a massive step in his healing. He'd been amazed at how he'd felt cleansed after weeping for hours, and since then had allowed himself, when he was on his own, to cry if he needed to. He knew that would help him step closer and closer to achieving his goal of becoming the man he once was.

As each of the stockmen finished their mountains of moreish beef stew, coal-baked potatoes and buttered slabs of lip-smackingly delicious damper, most of them having gone for seconds, groans and moans were a given. One by one, they stretched their saddle-bent backs and wandered towards the makeshift camp kitchen, lit up by two gas lanterns surrounded by flying insects. Rinsing their plates and cutlery in a bowl of soapy water while dodging kamikaze moths, they then left their dishes on a tea towel to dry. At last, each man made himself a billy tea, then joined the group back at the centre of gravity – the fire.

His appetite not as big as that of his fellow stockmen, although it was getting there, Matt did his best to eat every morsel of food on his plate. Drinking in the untainted views lit up beneath the diamond-encrusted sky, he smiled, and sighed. The cattle had been yarded just before sunset and were milling around peacefully. An endless volume of dust hovered above them, as if it had an inherent right to be there. Two horses were saddled up and at the ready, in case the cattle took fright in the middle of the night and knocked down the yards. The fences were strong enough to hold a thousand head, but wouldn't stand a hope in hell if all the cattle spooked. He and the boys couldn't afford to lose them. It would mean they'd have to muster the mob again – and that would mean at least an entire day lost and another day of wages to be paid out. His father would be pissed off, and the boys were working super hard so they could finish in time to spend the weekend at the legendary Mount Isa pub. The lure of icy cold beer and pretty, cowboy-seeking women made the men work harder and faster as the days wore on. But Matt couldn't think of anything worse right now. The pub was the last place on earth he wanted to be; women and drinking were no longer part of his vocabulary. His plan was to hang back at the station and do some fishing, as well as catch up on some much needed sleep.

Taking a bite of damper, his eyes rolled back in pleasure – there was something to be said about the Australian campfire classic, smothered in butter for stews and for dessert topped off with golden syrup. As difficult as the alcohol withdrawals and his cravings for a drink were, he was enjoying every second of the muster – the good, the bad and the ugly. He eyed the flame-lit faces of the guys sitting round the fire. It was nothing out of the ordinary that the stockmen were a rough looking lot, and all notable characters, each in their own right – and as per usual for the Aussie outback they each had nicknames to boot. The newest addition to the bunch was the cook, AKA 'Pothole', because he always seemed to be in the road. 'Fifty-four years young,' he liked to say when asked his age, Pothole had a laugh like a hyena and chaotic salt-and-pepper hair that reminded Matt of Albert Einstein.

Then there was Hasselhoof (not Hasselhoff), labelled so *not* because he looked like the guy from *Baywatch*, but because everything was a hassle for him. He complained non-stop about everything from the weather, to the price of beer, to the flies, to the fact there was no iodised salt to put on his food at camp. But when he did rarely smile he had a joker's grin, so upturned at either end that it looked like a horse's hoof. Even though he was a grump, he was a very likeable old bloke; just not someone Matt would choose to spend much time with outside of work. Then there was Showbags, a twenty-something, sandy-haired, freckle-faced tower of lanky limbs, aptly named because he was so full of shit half the time, and he owned the fact with the kind of hilarious wit that could almost send Matt falling from his saddle with laughter.

The head stockman and the oldest of the bunch was Whisper, a no-nonsense kind of bloke and very down to earth. He had earned his nickname from not ever having shouted a round of drinks in his sixty-six years. Matt hadn't believed it at first, but Slim had sworn black and blue that it was true – Whisper was a diehard, tight-arse bastard, especially at the pub. What was even more outrageous was that Whisper gloated about the fact – grinning like the cat that had got the cream each and every time he made mention of it. But tight-arse aside, the men all held him in high regard because fire, flood, drought or stampeding cattle rush, Whisper took it all in his stride, remained cool, calm and collected, and always got the job done no matter what, albeit cussing a more colourful language than Matt had ever heard, and he'd heard a lot of foul mouths over the years spent on the station. Finally, there was the youngest of the cluster of men, Tumbles, aptly named because he rarely made it through a day without tripping over his own feet or, god forbid, thin air. He'd already fallen out of the saddle more times than Matt could count and had face-planted the dirt on numerous occasions when there'd been absolutely nothing to fall over, and yet he would always get to his feet with a wide smile. All in all, they were a mixed-up, muddled-up group, but one Matt felt very at home with. These were his kind of people.

His second plate of dinner finished, Slim burped loud enough to rattle a window. He quickly pardoned himself, chuckling. 'Pothole, mate, that was so bloody awesome, as usual. Talk about driving a man to eat, I'm going to undo all the hard work I put into losing my beer keg this past year.' He patted his slightly protruding belly for effect as he wandered towards the washing-up bowl.

'I've been slaving over the hot coals all day, so cheers, Slim,' Pothole said with a proud smile.

The rest of the group chimed in, assuring Pothole they all appreciated his efforts, because not only did he cook, he also gathered firewood, kept the camp clean, and packed and unpacked a new camp each and every day while the men were out mustering.

Still laughing at Slim's lack of table manners – not that they were needed, or expected, out here – Matt pointed at him with his fork. 'You're a bloody charmer if I've ever seen one, Slimbo.'

'There's always one in the crowd that you can't take anywhere,' Whisper said with a hearty chuckle before blowing a smoke ring into the air.

'Yeah, I can't believe you're not married yet, you stud,' Showbags chimed in, his grin rebellious. 'You're a bloody catch and a half.'

Wiping his hands on a tea towel, Slim looked from one bloke to the other, his mischievous grin getting wider and wider by the second. He clearly loved the banter. A top contender in being able to dish it out, big time, Slim was also good for taking it on the chin, nothing ever really fazing him. Piss him off though, and look out.

Hasselhoof grunted, catching everyone's attention. 'Count your lucky stars it's not coming out the other end, boys, because believe me when I say I've smelt Slim's farts on a down wind and they're enough to choke a damn cat.' Hasselhoof grimaced and then burst out laughing.

'Fair crack of the bloody whip, you lot. I'll have you know that it's better out than in. Otherwise I could spontaneously combust, and that could be messy.' Slim tried to keep a straight face but failed miserably.

Resounding gravelly laughter followed.

Now settled back on his log, Slim wiped mirth-filled tears from his eyes. 'You want a cuppa, Walshee.'

'Yeah, wouldn't mind one thanks, bro.'

'Ripper, can you make me one while you're at it? I forgot to get one when I was up and you're younger than me.'

'Only by five months, boofhead.'

Slim nodded. 'Exactly, like I said, you're the youngest.' He folded his arms, stretched his legs out and crossed them at the ankles. 'So, respect your elders, buddy.'

Matt gave him the finger. 'The bloody cheek of ya.'

'Me? Cheeky?' Slim bared his teeth in an all-out wicked grin. 'Who would of thunk it?'

'Yeah, righto, but it's your job tomorrow night, and you can wash my plate while you're at it too.'

Slim gave the thumbs up. 'It's a deal, Walshee.'

His plate finally empty, Matt stood, making sure to thank Pothole for the feast again before heading to the camp kitchen. The man liked to be reassured and the number-one rule in a stock camp was to keep the cook happy, otherwise Lord knew what you'd get for grub, if anything at all. Moving away from the friendly glow of the campfire and the talk about the day, Matt busied himself making two pannikins of tea, occasionally glancing up at the holding yards to make sure the cattle and horses were happy. The freshly broken geldings were doing well, each of them getting enough of a workout to keep them in tune, as were the two new stockmen his father had hired this year – Showbags and Hasselhoof. The other blokes had been here for five years running and had proved their worth time and time again on the musters.

Tea in hand, he wandered back and held one out to Slim. 'Here you go, old mate.'

Yawning so wide his jaw neared dislocation, Slim garbled a thank you.

Matt chuckled, totally understanding his exhaustion. 'No probs, buddy.' It had been another long, sweaty, dusty day in the saddle – he was looking forward to a decent hot shower. Four more days and he'd be able to enjoy one. Wanting to stand for now, he moved closer to the fire.

'You sure you aren't crook, Tumbles? You look like you've eaten a dog bait,' Pothole piped up, a hint of a smile shining through his wrinkly, stubbled face.

'Yeah, well, being stung by a hive of bees while at the same time being thrown from the saddle will do that to a bloke.' Tumbles grinned a gappy smile. He'd lost a front tooth today when he'd hit the deck while trying to raid a beehive they'd spotted in a boab tree. It had been a fruitless mission, the bees getting the upper hand from the get go and sending every bloke and his horse galloping like bats outta hell. He rubbed the crotch of his jeans, wincing. 'I thought I was a goner when they started stinging me on the jatz crackers; they're the size of bloody golf balls right now.'

Another round of deep, throaty laughter followed – the expedition would have been priceless if caught on camera. It was a story that would be retold for years to come, eventually taking on details that would alter it almost completely – a bush yarn at its finest.

After pouring his second cuppa, Whisper joined them back at the fire. 'Sweet baby Jesus. Where's ya bloody teeth gone, Hasselhoof?'

Mid-laugh, Hasselhoof frowned as though it was the most ridiculous question in the world. 'Where they should be, boss ...' Hasselhoof thumbed over his shoulder. 'Wrapped up in my handkerchief and back in my saddlebag.'

Clearly speechless, Whisper shook his head and then focused on his pannikin of tea, taking small sips and sighing with pleasure each and every time he did.

Returning from a quick exit to the bushes for the call of nature, Showbags stood close to the fire and rocked back and forth on the heels of his bare feet. 'You look like a ridgy-didge gummy shark without any fangs in, Hasselhoof.'

'Yeah, well, I don't have any private health so those fangs cost me an arm and a leg. I don't want to wear the bastards out too quick because I don't reckon I'll be able to afford another pair in my lifetime. I only put them in to eat, or for special occasions like going to town when I want to impress the sheilas.' He stood up from the log and turned to warm his rump by the fire, his threadbare pair of jeans he'd worn for three days straight revealing patches of his red jocks beneath. 'I have no bastard to impress out here in bloody Timbuktu.'

Whisper gazed into the fire contemplatively. 'That's a real place, you know.'

Hasselhoof shifted from foot to foot, rubbing his lower back. 'What is?'

'Timbuktu.'

Hasselhoof's bushy grey brows creased together. 'Is not.'

Whisper shrugged indifferently, smirking as if to say, 'I'm not getting into a debate about it.'

'Is too,' piped in Showbags. 'It's a city in Mali, north-east of Bamako … It was a huge trading place for gold and salt in the eleventh century.'

Not usually a walking encyclopaedia, Showbags stunned them, and every man stared at him in shock.

'Cor, witty *and* bloody clever … you're the bloody catch round here by the sounds of it, Showbags,' Slim chimed in.

Showbags puffed his chest out as he pretended to blow smoke from his fingertips. 'Yup, and that's why the ladies flock to me like bees to honey.' His lopsided grin said otherwise.

'Stop! Please don't talk about bees and honey right now.' Tumbles grimaced as he touched a huge red welt on his cheek.

'As if I'd believe anything that came out of your mouth.' Hasselhoof glared at Showbags, his eyes slits and nostrils flared – he wasn't one to take anything on the chin.

But Showbags clearly didn't care as he kept going. 'Fair play, you old bugger. It's for real. Didn't you ever get proper edumacated?'

Hasselhoof's frown deepened. His body stiffened. 'What bloody language are you speaking, Showbags?'

'Proper Aussie slang.' Showbags wriggled his brows; his infectious laughter had Matt stifling a grin.

Hands now on his hips and his gait wide, a crimson-faced Hasselhoof was at a standoff. This could go one of two ways. A few moments passed until he chuckled, shaking his head. 'You're full of shit.'

'Most of the time, yes I surely am, but not this time.'

'Smart arse,' Hasselhoof grumbled.

Showbags had baited and was reeling in his catch. 'Yes, I am that too.'

Hasselhoof turned his back to them all and stared at the fire. 'Get stuffed, Showbags.'

Showbags rubbed his belly and grinned like an unruly kid. 'I'm already stuffed like an olive, but thanks for the suggestion.'

Collective chuckles followed.

Hasselhoof grunted.

Matt looked at Showbags as if to say, 'Stop now, before shit gets real.'

Showbags' grin widened.

Stretching his arms in the air, Whisper groaned. 'Righto, you lot, I'm hitting the hay. Catch you all bright and early for yet another round of *Who can find the mickey bulls?*'

Whisper's movement caused a ripple effect – Showbags, Tumbles, Pothole and Hasselhoof all followed. They mumbled their goodnights as they rinsed out their pannikins and then shuffled over to their swags, where snoring commenced within minutes.

Sitting on an empty fuel drum, his pannikin of tea in hand, Slim flashed Matt a toothy smile. 'This is the life, hey, Walshee?'

'It sure is.' Matt felt a surge of gratitude with the acknowledgement. 'So peaceful, huh.'

An explosive fart erupted from Slim's direction. 'Oops, sorry 'bout that.' He grinned. 'Think I might need the little boys' room.' He jumped up and dashed for the bushes.

Not ready to hit the sack just yet, and wanting to take advantage of the rare time to himself, Matt settled back on a log in front of the fire. Three days in and he'd loved every single second of it so far, the distraction helping to keep his mind off the drink. It was not that he didn't still crave it; he just didn't have time to obsess about it, and had Buckley's of getting hold of anything alcoholic out here. Now four and a half days into going cold turkey and his initial withdrawal symptoms were beginning to ease, although the shakes were still there. It made it a little tough to hold the reins at times, but he gritted his teeth and bore it. Breaking down at the dam had certainly helped him to release a fair bit of pent-up emotions, but he still had a lot of healing to do. At the very least he was on his way, and on track. If only he could pick up the phone and call Sarah, tell her how well he was doing and how much he missed and loved her, but that was impossible out here with no phone reception.

The boobook owl caught his attention once more with its distinctive call, and he tried to turn his focus outwards. It had never ceased to amaze him how the weather could go from blistering hot to freezing cold at night – but that was the way of the outback, from one extreme to the next. A person just had to flow with it – a great lesson in life. He heard the wind rustling the leaves of the scribbly gums surrounding the camp as he poked the glowing embers with a stick. Once again he found himself captivated by the flickering red flames, dancing and twirling around each other like lovers in the night. Back in the day, he and Sarah used to cuddle up around the campfire at the end of the day when they went mustering. God, he missed her like crazy. He couldn't wait to get back to the homestead so he could call her and hear her voice. Leaning in, he added kindling and the fire crackled and popped, bursts of sparks twirled upwards in the spiral of smoke, towards the star-studded, velvet black sky. Scuffling noises and the movement of the bushes behind him dragged his gaze over his shoulder. It was most probably Slim, but even so, his hand went to the shotgun leaning on the log at his side – hungry dingoes were rife on the station. But then Slim appeared, his teeth bared and hands gnarled, pretending to be a bear and making an absolute fool of himself, as usual.

Cracking up, Matt tried to keep his chuckles low, as did Slim – neither of them wanting to disturb the sleeping stockmen. Their laughter subsiding, Slim sat down beside Matt, groaning like an eighty-year-old as he did. Silence settled momentarily, and then Slim whistled through his teeth – something Matt knew he did when weighing up what to say.

'What is it, Slimbo?'

'Just wondering how you're going with the DTs, buddy?' Slim kept his voice low. 'I know from watching Dad go through it, it ain't pretty.'

Matt sighed and offered a lacklustre smile. 'Yeah, all right, I suppose. It's getting easier as the days go on, but a lot of the time I still crave a drink like my life depends on it.'

'That's to be expected, so don't be too hard on yourself, hey.' Slim smiled compassionately. 'You taking any of the drugs the doc gave you?'

'Yeah, I'm taking a Valium now and then, to take the edge off so I can deal with the side effects.' He shrugged. 'Not sure if it's doing too much, or if it's the lack of a constant hangover, but I'm feeling a lot calmer than I was when I first got here.'

'That's good to hear. And if you want my opinion, which you know you'll get regardless, I reckon you're going great guns.'

'That means a lot, thanks, mate.' Not used to compliments of any kind when it came to his drinking problem, he half laughed off the praise.

'Seriously, Walshee, you should be proud of yourself, mate. It takes a lot of strength, grit and guts to give up the drink.' Slim's face turned solemn. 'My father tried countless times and never had the strength to do what you have. If he had, he'd probably still be here today, instead of six foot under.'

'I'm real sorry about your dad, mate. It must have been tough, as a teenager, to see him going through it, especially after already losing your mum.'

'Yeah, it was. It sucked having to pick him up from the floor and then get down on my hands and knees to clean up his vomit, and even worse copping his abuse when he was in one of his stormy moods because he was coming down from a binge. He was a changed man after losing Mum, and not for the better. Sad really, watching someone you love fall to pieces and there's nothing you can do about it.'

'Oh shit, mate.' Matt gave him a gentle slap on the back; at the same time his thoughts went to Sarah and what he'd put her through. It was exactly the same as what Slim had gone through with his father. 'I really wish I'd known you back then so I could have helped you through it. So sorry, buddy.'

'Not your fault my dad was a drunk.' Slim slumped forwards, holding his hands up to the fire to warm them. 'For a while there, I actually hated him and wished he'd die, so I could get some reprieve from his bullshit. But then he did go and die, and it damn near killed me.' Leaning back again he shrugged, his forehead puckering as he folded his arms. 'Outside of all the drama, I loved the old bugger, more than words can say. I wish he was here today for me to tell him so.'

Matt's heart ached. 'Damn, Slimbo, how come you've never told me about all this before now?'

'To tell you the truth, I don't like talking about it, and I suppose I didn't feel the need to.' Then pulling a toothpick from his top pocket, Slim started picking at his teeth. 'But now I reckon it might help you some.'

Matt nodded. Clasping his hands together he squeezed them so tight his fingers hurt, and it was all he could do to stop from crying. This all felt so close to home. Slim was sharing his story to try to reach out to him in a roundabout kind of way, and by Christ it was working. It gave him a new perspective, seeing things through Slim's eyes. Poor Sarah – he'd done everything Slim's father had done. It made him sick to the stomach, and even more determined to never, ever, drink again.

Yawning for all of Australia, Slim pushed himself to standing. 'Righto, Walshee, I'm going to hit the sack too, before I fall asleep sitting up.' He chuckled, shaking his head. 'And trust me when I say it's happened many times before.'

'I know, I've been a witness, Slimbo.' Yawns always addictive, Matt stifled one of his own. 'I'm not far behind you, buddy.'

Slim rinsed his pannikin in the bowl of soapy water and upended it on the drainer. 'Catch you at sparrow's fart.'

'You most certainly will.'

After turning off the two gas lanterns, Matt carefully stepped around the sleeping bodies in their swags. The howling of dingoes carried on the night breeze, as did the bellows of the cattle in the holding yard. Bone-weary, he hunkered down in his swag, making sure the shotgun was close by. The dingoes could be ballsy buggers and he was taking no chances. A rock poked into his hip and he turned the other way, only to find himself in the same predicament, but he didn't let it get to him. There was something so freeing and so real about sleeping on the ground. Like a hippy walking barefoot, it was his way of earthing himself. The spiralling smoke and crackle of the smouldering campfire, the thick blanket of stars above, and the feel of the earth beneath him, all contributed to a feeling of peace he wasn't used to of late. And grateful the shackles that had bound his heart and soul had loosened that little bit more, allowing him to take an even deeper breath, Matt closed his eyes, and tumbled into a deep sleep within minutes.

CHAPTER
14

Clarkes' Fruit Farm, Mareeba, Far North Queensland

It was a scorching, melt-into-your-boots, thirty-five degree day, but unlike the past five days spent out picking and packing fruit, tending to the horses, and helping her dad fix some fencing, it wasn't bothering Sarah in the slightest. With her stash of old movies recovered from the storage room, the heavy curtains pulled closed, comfort food in surplus, her feather pillows plumped up for lounging, and too many scatter cushions to count, it was a movie marathon like no other. The air-conditioning was set at a chilly eighteen degrees and the ceiling fan spun at a dizzying speed, as wonky as the day it had been put in by the family's good friend and electrician of the past twenty-odd years. Stroking Harry, her mum's seventeen-year-old cat, who she'd peeled from his usual place smack bang in the middle of the staircase after worrying he might suffer from heat stroke, Sarah giggled at the predicament the characters on the telly had got into. Having been on an emotional rollercoaster the past few days, going from sad, to happy, to disappointed, to angry with the world, to loving Matt, to hating him, and then back full circle again, so many times she'd lost count, this was exactly what she needed. So occupied with the television, she didn't hear the creak of her bedroom door.

Easing open the door and then quietly standing in the doorway of Sarah's bedroom, Lily eyed the empty packet of salt-and-vinegar chips on the dresser, the opened packet of Cheezels on the bed, and the almost demolished packet of Monte Carlos in Sarah's lap. Duke had leapt from his bed at the corner of the room and was now standing at her side, his tail slapping her leg while she gave him a scratch behind the ears. 'Wow, are you trying to commit carboside, girlfriend?'

Completely immersed in *Bridget Jones: The Edge of Reason*, Sarah jumped in fright. 'Hey, Lily.' She clutched where her heart beat frantically, smiling from ear to ear. 'Holy crap, Batman, you scared the bejesus out of me.'

'Sorry not sorry.' Lily grinned her trademark cheeky smile.

'You're a horrible sister-in-law, Lily Clarke,' Sarah said playfully as she found the remote and paused the DVD. 'And in answer to your carboside question, hell no, I'm just living it up while the oldies are away for the night. I've been helping them around here every day since I arrived, which has been really good, but I'm knackered and was in need of a do-nothing-kind-of-day, so I'm doing it and not feeling bad about it for a single second.'

'Good on you, hun, everyone needs some down time in their lives. Where'd the old folks go?'

'To some bigwig fruit conference down in Cairns … they're apparently staying at the casino and having dinner along the esplanade. Living it up and reliving their youth and all that.' Sarah screwed her face up. 'Mum said something about taking her good lingerie, and I was like, *la la la, I can't hear you.*'

Lily grimaced and held up her hands. 'I really don't want any more information, please. Picturing my in-laws getting jiggy-with-it is way too much for this sex-deprived woman to bear.'

'Oh yuck, Lily, now I'm thinking about my mum and dad getting it on, and you and my brother.' Mortified, Sarah tapped the side of her head. 'I need to get the images out of my head, they're disgusting.'

'Ha-ha, sorry … there's been no hanky panky for me and Daniel with him laid up and recovering.'

Sarah covered her ears. 'Stop!'

Lily poked her tongue out.

Still dressed in her pyjamas even though it was almost three in the afternoon, and with her hair resembling a bird's nest, Sarah grinned at her best mate. She patted the tousled bed beside her. 'Come join me for some cheesy romantic comedies.' She wriggled her brows. 'I even have cookies and cream ice-cream, popcorn, and a bottle of red for later.'

'I thought you'd never ask. You're on, sister.' Needing no more of an invitation, Lily dived towards the bed as if going for a goal, connecting with Sarah in an all-out tackle. Duke took it upon himself to jump up and join in the fun too.

With Sarah bowled over and trying to save herself from rolling off the side of the bed, both women giggled like a pair of teenagers as time was erased and they were back being young girls without a care in the world. Sitting up again, Sarah gruffly reminded Duke he wasn't allowed on the bed. Quickly obeying, he went back to his bed on the floor.

Lily wiped happy tears from the corner of her eyes. 'It feels so good to laugh like that.'

'It sure does, Lil.' Propping a pillow behind Lily's back, Sarah helped her to get comfy before wriggling herself into a cosy position within her favourite boomerang pillow. 'So what's my annoying little brother up to today?'

'He's got a few of the guys coming around to watch the Ashes this arvo, and you know how much I'd rather watch paint dry or poke my eyes out with a blunt knife than watch cricket, so I thought I'd jump ship and come and annoy you instead.'

With cricket on the bottom of her sport-loving list, and bull riding at the top, Sarah nodded. 'Good move, otherwise you might have found yourself serving beer and making them food.'

Lily's eyes widened to saucers. 'Like bloody hell I would have. I ain't nobody's kitchen bitch, girlfriend.' She snapped her fingers and shook her head. 'Nah ah.'

Sarah laughed out loud. 'God, I've missed you so much.'

Wrapping her arms around Sarah's shoulders, Lily gave her a squeeze. 'Ditto, my beautiful friend.' Unravelling and settling back for a movie marathon, she took a handful of Cheezels, popping each of them on her fingertips in readiness for devouring, while Sarah got the movie back on a roll. 'So how are you coping, being away from Matt?'

Sarah grabbed some of the moreish cheesy rings too, and then did the same as Lily (a mannerism they'd shared as kids – Cheezels always tasted better when eaten off one's finger). Her gaze was fixed on Renee Zellweger (AKA Bridget Jones) realising she was pregnant before precariously sliding down a ski slope sideways.

'Hmmm, I'm missing him, Lil, don't get me wrong, but I'm also enjoying this time to myself. I really didn't know how much I needed to get away from the farm, and him, to come to grips with everything that's happened this past year. It's kind of like the smoke has cleared and I can see clearly for the first time since it all happened.' Casting Lily a sideways glance, she smiled softly. 'Even though it still hurts me like nothing else, knowing I'm never going to get to hold my little girl again, or get to see her grow up …' She paused, trying to keep her emotions in check, her vision blurring. 'I can actually think about Eve with a smile on my face, even if I am shedding a tear, instead of wanting to break into a million little pieces.' She smiled sadly. 'Most of the time, that is … one step at a time.'

Lily wrapped her arm around Sarah and shuffled closer. 'Aw, Sar, it makes me so happy to know everything's coming into focus for you, and your grief is easing little by little. Even though I've been by your side the entire way, sometimes in spirit because of the distance, I can't even begin to comprehend the heartache you've suffered.' She sniffled, blinking back tears. 'I miss her too, so much.'

Sarah tapped Lily's hand that was slung over her shoulder. 'Oh, hun, please don't cry or you'll get me going too. And trust me, once I start, it's kind of hard to stop.'

Lily half laughed. 'I'm sorry.' Wiping a few tears that had escaped down her cheeks, she tipped her head to the side, a moment passing between her and Sarah that only lifetime friends would understand. 'I hate knowing I can't do anything to ease all this heartache for you.'

'You've been here for me, day and night, and that's helped beyond words.' Sarah squeezed her eyes shut, sighing. 'Sadly, this is something Matt and I have to work through on our own. There's nothing anyone can do or say to make it any different. I've spent the last year worrying about him every waking second, wondering if I'd eventually find him having drunk himself to death. I'd convinced myself I could live with the way he was, that if I could somehow find a way to love him more, I could change him … but clearly that wasn't the case.'

Lily bit her bottom lip. 'Do you still love him?' She grimaced as if afraid to hear the answer.

Sarah didn't miss a beat. 'Yes, of course I do.' She exhaled a weary breath and shrugged. 'But is that enough to be able to grow old together? I'm really not sure. I honestly don't know if we're going to ever be the same again, and that scares the crap out of me.'

Lily looked as sad as Sarah felt. 'I'm sure it will all work itself out, Sar.'

'I hope so, because as much as I love him I can't go back to what we were, Lily. I just can't.' She took a moment to gather her thoughts. 'I feel like such a bitch, saying all this, but I'm not going to lie and say it's all going to be hunky dory, because I truly think it could go either way.' Saying it out loud hurt like hell, but it was the cold, hard truth. Tears welled but she quickly blinked them away. She was so sick of crying.

Lily took both her hands and gave them a squeeze. 'Oh, hun, it's okay to feel like you do. As much as I adore Matt and understand how much he's beaten himself up over the accident, he's dragged you through hell and back this past year with his drinking and toxic moods. Christmas Day was a huge eye opener, for all of us, with what he was putting you through. He really hasn't been there for you through one of the hardest times of your life, and you're entitled to feel angry about that,' she said. 'To be honest, as much as I love Daniel, I don't know if I could've stayed as long as you have if he behaved like Matt did, especially after losing a child. You're a very strong woman, Sarah.'

'Thank you, Lil, I love you heaps, mate.'

'Love you too, bugalugs.' Lily grinned. 'I'm so sorry to turn up here and upset you, that's not what I came here to do.' She slapped her forehead. 'I'm such a shitty friend.'

'You're not a shitty friend.' Sarah pulled her into a hug. 'You're the bestest friend, and sister-in-law I might add, any gal could ask for. I appreciate you asking the hard questions and caring so much about how I'm feeling. Apart from Mum, and sometimes the old man, everyone else likes to sidestep the hard stuff.'

'Thanks, Sar.' Untangling, Lily smacked her hands together, making Duke startle. 'Righto, no more being negos, let's have some reckless fun and get this girly movie marathon underway.'

Sarah smiled through her wretchedness. 'I like your way of thinking.'

'They say great minds think alike, don't they?'

'Uh-huh.' Sarah pressed play and they both sat in contemplative silence for a few moments, laughing at Bridget Jones trying to ask for a pregnancy test in German, with overzealous actions to boot.

'I can't believe it's your birthday in a few days' time, and you're going to be here to celebrate it.' Lily licked the last of the Cheezels off her fingertips.

Sarah rolled her eyes to the heavens. 'Please don't remind me about my birthday, Lil.'

'Oh come on, you're still a spring chicken at thirty-five, Sarah.'

Eyes wide and mouth agape, Sarah sideswiped Lily with a cushion. 'Oi, you … I'm only thirty-one.'

'I know, I know, just stirring.' Avoiding another wallop from Sarah, she grinned. 'I love how you're so damn easy to stir … like your brother.'

Sarah gave her the finger before retrieving the packets of biscuits that had rolled onto the floor in their earlier tussle. 'Like I said, what a horrible woman you are!' Riffling to the bottom of the packet, she bit down on the second last cream biscuit while offering the last one to Lily.

'Thanks, but no thanks … watching the waistline so I can look sexy in my kinis on the Bali trip next month.' Lily tapped her ripped stomach. 'I'm not sweating my arse off at the gym every morning just to eat the calories I burnt off.'

'Argh, blah blah blah … you're sooo boring.'

'Am not.'

'Are too.'

Lily eyed her challengingly. 'Am not.'

Sarah shoved the biscuit in Lily's face. 'Prove it and eat the damn cookie.'

Groaning, Lily took it and shoved it in her mouth, shuddering with every chew. 'Oh my god, it's so sickly sweet.'

'That's because you don't eat anything with flavour anymore.'

'What do you mean? Kale and quinoa have flavour.'

Sarah pretended to gag. 'Like I said, boring.'

Grabbing Sarah's glass of water from the bedside table, Lily gulped it down. 'So are we going to celebrate your birthday at the Mareeba rodeo this year?'

'Oh, I don't know, Lil. I'm getting too old for all of that.'

'For all of what?'

'Drinking shots and dancing till sunup.'

'Argh, you're sooo boring.'

'Get stuffed.'

'Oh, come on, Sarah, it'll be like the good ol' days. And I reckon that's exactly what you need right now.' Lily eyed her pleadingly. 'I could really do with a girls' night out, and a catch-up with everyone. It's been yonks since we've been out together. Like probably four years, or more.' She put her hands together as if in prayer and looked at her. 'Pretty please with strawberries and cream and hundreds and thousands on top.'

Sarah huffed and rolled her eyes to the heavens. 'All right, all right, but only if you promise we'll be home by midnight. I'm not really up for partying until stupid o'clock, or enduring the hangover the next morning.'

Lily marked a cross over her heart. 'Promise we'll get you home by midnight so you don't turn into a pumpkin. Deal?' She paused, her perfectly shaped brows furrowed as she waited for Sarah's answer.

An excited rush gave Sarah goosebumps as she thought about watching the bull riders buck it out. Maybe this wasn't such a bad idea after all. And she had packed her going-to-town boots too ... 'Okay then, it's a date, girlfriend.'

'Yay!' Lily said as she raised her hand and they high-fived.

But then Sarah's elevated mood quickly deflated. She groaned and rubbed her face.

Lily placed her hand on her back. 'What is it?'

'It's just, well, I can't help but wonder how Matt will feel about me going?'

Lily couldn't hide her shock. 'He'll mind?'

'Yeah, probably. He's been really funny about me going anywhere without him, like he doesn't trust me, and the rodeo ...' Sarah thought for a moment. 'He knows how much of a party night it is for all of us, and with him going cold turkey and being stuck out at the station while I'm enjoying myself, it's not really fair, is it? Maybe I shouldn't go.'

Lily slapped her fair and square on the arm.

'Ouch, what was that for?' Sarah rubbed the red spot.

'Sorry, but I had to snap you out of it.'

'Out of what?'

'I know he's your husband and he's doing a really tough thing at the moment, but he's a big boy and he has Slim there, and his entire family, to support him through it. So stop worrying about him so much and for once in your life be selfish and think of you, please.' She took Sarah's hands and shook them. 'Trust me, this will be good for you. So if he doesn't like it, he'll just have to suck it up. You're allowed to have a life outside of him.'

Sarah chewed on her bottom lip. 'Yeah, you're right. I think he's back from the muster tomorrow or the next day, so I'll make sure to let him know I'm going, and if he doesn't like it I'm going to have to gently tell him he has to deal with it.'

Lily grinned and clapped her hands. 'That's my girl.'

CHAPTER
15

Rosalee Station, Central Australia

A rhythmic thumping woke Matt from a deep sleep. His heart beating in his throat, he slowly uncurled from the confines of his swag, shotgun at the ready. His eyes took a few moments to adjust. The glowing red coals of the fire provided little light, but just enough for him to make out the shape of a hefty grey kangaroo. Not ideal, but not deadly either. With a relieved sigh, he lowered the weapon. The greedy bugger was sniffing around for food. He considered shooing it away, but then thought better of it. Not only would it wake everyone up, if it hadn't already, but he'd also risk getting kicked in the kerfuffle, and from experience as a teenage boy thinking he could outwit one of the large Aussie legends, he knew it did more than tickle.

If a roo scrounging through their camp wasn't crazy enough, it then stuck its head in an empty soup can and reared up on its hind legs, the can now stuck fast to its snout. Snoring ceased and garbled mumbles soon came from every corner of the camp. Not wanting to be trodden on, Matt shot to standing. Then it was on for young and old as the kangaroo bounded erratically, knocking everything over in its path and sending all the blokes flying from their swags still half asleep. Just as quickly as it had got stuck, the can plonked off and clattered to the ground. For a second there was a standoff, and then the roo took off like a bull at a gate. Chaos averted, mumbled curses and incomprehensible words were muttered as each bloke climbed back into his swag. Matt got comfy and folded his hands beneath his head, while still chuckling at the spontaneity of the bush – it was always full of surprises. The sky ablaze with billions of stars, he felt as if he could reach right out and stroke the Milky Way. Close to two in the morning, he didn't think he'd find sleep again, but surprisingly, within minutes, he was snoozing.

The same as every other morning while on the muster, he was wide awake before dawn. With his boots on, swag rolled and packed into the cook's four-wheel drive, and a breakfast of canned corned beef fried up with onions and eggs done and dusted, he was ready to hit the trail. Unlike his bedding, the rest of the swags had been rolled with each of the men's good going-to-town clothes buried inside them. It was the last day of this muster and that meant tonight the stockmen would all be heading into Mount Isa to kick up their heels and have a good time at the pub before having to do this all over again – it was the done thing after endless days in the saddle. So, the excitement in the camp was palpable.

Heading over to his horse now hitched to a rustic timber railing, Matt surveyed the cattle huddling in the holding pen, most of them not having seen a human in their lives. Located on the highest point of the station, surrounded by gidgee scrub and with open country on either side, it was his favourite spot to camp. Had been since he was an ankle-biter, close by his dad's side. Saddling up his horse, he eyed the windmill turning lazily in the soft breeze. It was doing its job, pumping water in the corrugated-iron tank high up on a platform. Red kangaroos, as large as horses, bounded across the rocky landscape, their silhouettes lit up by the rising sun. The scent of campfire and cow dung hung on the air. With so many special sights and sounds that only belonged in such a scene, dawn in a stock camp was a spectacular time, and he felt blessed to be here, witnessing it all in its jaw-dropping glory. This was exactly why people from the cities and overseas came to the outback, and why many money-strapped cattle stations were now taking advantage of the fact and offering camp stays and real-life muster experiences.

Tightening the girth strap after his horse finally decided to let out his belly full of air, the stubborn bugger did it every day, Matt headed back to where the men were helping pack up the last of the camp kitchen. He looked to the sky – they had time for one more cuppa before climbing up into the saddle. The light was increasing, the sky now awash with delicate pinks and gold – twenty minutes more and they'd have the sun belting down on their backs as they rode out of camp. The fire hissing and crackling thanks to Slim's handiwork, Matt plucked the billy from its hook and tossed tea-leaves into the bubbling water. Then, picking up the handle of the tin can with his wide-brimmed hat, he swung it around vigorously – an old bushman's trick his grandad had taught him as a young lad. One that had taken him a few months, and quite a few painful burns, to master.

Clearly impressed, as he always was because he couldn't get the knack of the swing and had given up trying after upending boiling water over his head a few years back, Slim ran a currycomb through his hair, making the wiriness of it even more shocking. 'Some bloody crazy arse shit that was at two this morning, hey, Walshee? Last time it was emus stampeding our camp, now it's a bloody hungry roo. What the hell is next, dare I bloody well ask?' He tugged his jeans up and sat on his heels by the fire.

Matt plonked the billycan on a plank of timber. 'Heck yeah, scared the shit outta me.'

'Tell me about it. I almost shit my daks.' Slim chuckled, half snorting. 'And I don't have any clean ones left so that would have been a really shitty situation.'

Matt couldn't help but laugh as he made seven pannikins of strong black tea – the men could add sugar and UHT milk themselves. Thanks were mumbled and teaspoons clanked, then as if it were cool water, the blokes drank their last hot drink for the morning, rinsed their cups and tossed the pannikins in a crate in the back of the ute, while Matt and Slim got to putting the fire out and covering the coals. The sound of chopper blades slicing through the air came overhead. It approached quickly, and then hovered, stirring up a massive dust cloud. Steve gave them the thumbs up from the cockpit.

Whisper returned from doing his business in the bushes, his stockwhip cradled in the crook of his elbow. 'Righto, you lot, that's enough dilly-dallying … time to hit it. We have some cutting up first and then we got to take the cattle in a couple of different directions, depending on whether they're going to the saleyards or staying here to fatten up.' He waddled away, his gait wide and hobbled from all his years in the saddle, but then paused and glanced back at the men. 'Oh, and Tumbles, do me a favour and try to stick to the saddle today, buddy. We don't want to see you tossed on your head again like yesterday. And probably best to leave the bee hives alone too, I reckon.'

The men cracked up at Tumbles' expense. Flashing a grin, Tumbles gave Whisper the forks. Whisper laughed from deep down in his belly as he made his way over to his horse.

Less than twenty minutes later, all joking had been pushed aside as the men did what they did best. Matt tugged the rim of his Akubra down lower as he clung to the left of the mob. The dependable coacher cattle – the quiet cattle from the home yard – were let out of the yards first and then the rest of the fourteen hundred head followed. Essential to a good muster, the coacher cattle lured the wild cattle to join them and follow calmly. Although, Matt knew from his many years of experience that the wild bulls were a hard mob to convince. He kept a firm eye on the ringleader – a colossal, muscular bull with a bad attitude and lethal horns. Already antsy, he was disturbing the meandering cattle like a naughty child in the playground. Guiding his stockhorse in closer, Matt worked with the other men as they put the pressure on from all sides, held it for a few minutes and then moved back, allowing the mob to spread out a bit. They repeated this a couple of times, trying to create order. Walking the livestock into the wind was a godsend because they could smell what was ahead and stay settled. Cattle always hated the wind on their butts; it put them on edge.

The land stretched out wide, looking as if it had been ironed flat, the clumps of trees few and far between. Beads of sweat rolled down Matt's face and back, and the flies clung to him like super glue. He'd given up trying to swat them from his face days ago. Dust stirred and hovered in clouds as they did their best to keep the cattle moving in the right direction, while at the same time trying to keep the few head of unruly bulls in line. There were always some in a mob. It was almost impossible to see anything through the vivid sunshine and the immense plumes of dust the hundreds of hooves were kicking up.

The two-way he'd hooked to his saddlebag crackled to life. 'Just spotted a small mob hiding off to the east. I'll go get the sneaky buggers.'

'On ya, boss,' Slim's voice crackled through.

Matt tipped his head to the sky.

With a flash of rotating blades the Robinson chopper lurched to the side, whooshed up a sharp embankment and then dropped from the sky as if the motor had been cut. With a roar it shot back up, then as swiftly as it rose, it nosedived again in a gut-turning display of mid-air gymnastics. Turning his horse on a threepenny bit, Matt admired his father's expertise behind the controls. Chopper mustering could be a deadly job and not one to be taken lightly. A group of reluctant Brahman shot out from behind a line of eucalyptus trees and lumbered towards the mob, all thanks to his dad's airborne acrobatics – it was always safety in numbers for cattle. Within seconds, the chopper was back in place, dancing overhead of the herd, disappearing every now and then to bring more stray cattle into the ever-growing mob with the help of whichever stockman was closest.

Before Matt knew it, it was their lunch break, just enough time to answer the call of nature, scull a pannikin of tea – two if you were lucky – and shove down a sandwich of corned beef and pickles. While he was getting back into the saddle, a large red kangaroo leapt from the embankment of the water hole they'd stopped at, startling the horses. A horse reared and a stockman fell. After being unceremoniously dumped for the second time that morning, Tumbles stood and swiped at the dirt on his arms. 'Fucking thing.' He gave the horse the death stare as he climbed back up. 'You're not a buckjumper, ya bastard.'

Stifled chuckles were a given, as they had been the first time he'd fallen. Tumbles had a laugh at his own expense as he bashed his dusty hat on the leg of his jeans.

For the next hour the cattle meandered calmly, only the occasional wayward bull breaking the monotony by trying to make a mad dash for freedom. Each time Matt or one of the other skilful stockmen quickly mustered it back into place. That was, until the biggest and meanest of the mob decided he was going to make a break for it – and look out any bugger that tried to stop him. The bull had horns and he was keen to use them. In the blink of an eye, the casual ride was over as all hell broke loose. Shaken abruptly, cattle scampered in different directions. Calves lost their mothers. Expert mustering horses were cued into action. Panicked bellows resounded, chopper blades whooped, two-ways crackled, stockmen hollered above the noise, and thousands of hooves thundered. The atmosphere was beyond electric and it gave Matt a rush of absolute pride for home, his country and his fellow stockmen. This, right here, was what made his spirit fly – it was all the medication he needed to help get his life back on track.

Booming snaps reverberated across the flats as Whisper and Showbags cracked their stockwhips on either side of the mob. As if watching it all unfold in slow motion, Matt swore beneath his breath, his heart leaping into his throat. Adrenaline filling him, his horse took his cue and they were off in a wild gallop, the rumble of other stockhorses and the chopper not far behind him. With the ringleader having gained the upper hand, pandemonium erupted as the one-tonne boulder of muscle barged towards the taste of wild freedom. Charging across the flat, it headed straight for a thicket of rubber vines. The clever bastard knew exactly what to do to make the task of catching him close to impossible. Hot on the heels of the mickey bull, Matt spurred his horse on, harder and faster, his mouth now not just dry from the dust. He chased the animal at breakneck speed until the bull was visibly spent – they always tired more quickly than a horse. Finally pulling up a hundred yards from where it was headed, it spun around and faced him, ready to defend its ground. Nostrils flaring, foam dripped from its mouth. It pawed the ground while battle bellowing, its body language warning Matt to keep his distance. Matt smirked – he loved this part of a muster. There wasn't a hope in hell he was about to back up … the battle of man versus beast was on.

Challenge accepted with vigour, he flew out of the saddle and ran towards the bull. Lithe on his feet, he sidestepped a head buck and then with a little bit of rodeo clowning he grabbed hold of its tail. He tried to pull it over, but with no success. Seemingly out of nowhere, Tumbles and Showbags appeared at his side. Tumbles had dirt covering him from head to toe, and blood dripped from his top lip and forehead. He'd obviously been thrown from the saddle. Again. Matt didn't have time to ask his mate if he was all right – he was conscious and smiling, so that was a good start. More irritated than ever, the bull charged and all three blokes dashed behind the only tree to avoid being horned. Collective F words ensued. Repeatedly. The mickey was relentless, doing its very best to get hold of them; the only thing keeping the men safe was a stumpy old tree. Matt finally managed to get to the arse end of the bull and caught hold of the tail. Tumbles and Showbags leapt to action and the three men wrestled it to the ground, landing on top of it in a panting heap. Stripping off his belt, Matt wrapped it around the bull's hind legs; they'd need a back-up vehicle to transport the brute to the homestead. Luckily they weren't far away now. Hobbling back towards the now inquisitive but calm mob, the three blokes whistled for their mounts. Matt and Showbags succeeded in rustling up their horses, and hopped back in the saddle. Tumbles was left scratching his head, until the two-way crackled to life and Matt's dad let them know the horse had bolted back towards the homestead paddocks.

'Oh, for Christ's sake.' A smashed pair of sunglasses atop his dusty, weather-beaten hat, Tumbles squinted into the sunshine. 'Your horse double by any chance, Walshee?'

Matt couldn't hide his smirk. 'I dunno, Tumbles, but we can give it a shot.'

'That'd be beaut, thanks, buddy.'

'Just don't pull me down with you if you fall, will ya?'

'Oh hardy ha-ha, Walshee.'

Tumbles held his arm up and Matt helped him hoist himself up and onto the back of the saddle. His ride didn't blink an eyelid as they cantered back to join the men on the home stretch. Three hours to go and they'd be right back where they started a week ago. Covered in dirt and with dust in places the average person would never experience, Matt didn't care that every one of his muscles ached – instead he felt an absolute sense of accomplishment. The man he used to be had surfaced and, damn, it felt good.

As the mid-afternoon sun belted down everything it had, he paused to wipe the beading sweat from his eyes. Reaching down, he grabbed his water bottle from the hitch on his saddlebag. Squashed up behind him, although doing his utmost to keep a respectable, manly distance, Tumbles took the water bottle Matt offered him and had a swig. They'd been tracking a group of clean skins for the past two hours and gaining on them steadily, the cattle's tracks leading into the dimness of the gorge up ahead. Slender ghost gums flourished on both sides of the swampy water that was coloured a lime green. Half a dozen roos drank at the edges. Docile and quiet most of the time, Matt's horse was also known to throw a rider from the saddle if he wasn't in the mood to be ridden, and with two men on his back and exhaustion setting in for both stockhorse and men, Matt stayed on the alert. He slowed his mount to a walk and tugged his Akubra down further, his trained eye taking in every single detail. He knew the cattle were tiring, too, by the loose, liquid droppings they were leaving behind and by the slobber from their mouths left on the ground.

And then he spotted the stealth cattle, over wayside of the swampy water, near a ravine. Right where he'd rolled the ute, and cradled his dying daughter. His heart skidded to a stop and panic fuelled his adrenaline into action to restart it. He and Tumbles were the closest to them – he had no other option but to go there. Whisper gave them the nod from his post up the front of the mob, a silent gesture to let Matt know he and the other blokes could manage things here while they gathered the strays from yonder. There was no option to back out – he had to do this. His dad got down to business from the sky, bringing the chopper so close to the ground he almost touched it as he pushed the cattle forwards, towards Matt.

'Hold on to ya britches, Tumbles.' His hitchhiking passenger did as he was told as Matt's horse turned on its hind legs. '*Yaaaaa! Yaaaaa!*' he roared, and the horse was off like a speeding bullet, with both men clinging to its back, and their hats.

Galloping right over the spot where Matt agonisingly remembered dropping to his knees with Eve wrapped in his arms, he felt a surge of emotion … anger, sadness, shame, utter heartache, and then … a descending blanket of peace. It shocked him so much he almost slipped out of the saddle. His stare firmly on the cattle up ahead, Eve's smiling face flashed through his mind, and she smiled. Her lips moved, and she said, '*I'm okay, Daddy, please stop blaming yourself. I love you.*' Tears filled his eyes, and he felt one roll down his cheek as his horse neared the mob and got to work. And for the very first time, he didn't care if any man saw him cry, because his tears were for his daughter, and to hell with anyone who didn't understand that.

He soldiered on through blurry vision. Seamlessly, between the men and their steadfast horses and Steve's dipping and diving in the chopper, the stray cattle joined the mob and they were off once more, hopefully without the need for any more pit stops. His horse going back to a walk, Matt sniffled and quickly wiped at the tears on his face, and Tumbles gave him a supportive slap on the back to say, 'I understand, mate, and it's all good.' Slim, along with the rest of the stockmen, all took their hats off and nodded to him, their faces earnest.

The two-way crackled to life and his dad's voice resounded through. 'Good on ya, son, you did it. Love ya, buddy.'

Looking to the sky, Matt gave his dad the thumbs up, and his father poked his arm out the door of the chopper and did the same. It was all Matt could do not to break down and weep.

These strong, country-blooded men showing their support in their very own way was all the reassurance he needed to feel okay about revealing his heartache. If only he'd done this right back at the start and drawn comfort from those he loved instead of thinking he had to bottle everything up and soldier through it. But there was no room for hindsight, or regrets, he had to keep moving forwards.

Now so close to home, Matt was keen to get back to base so he could have a decent hot shower and sink into the comfort of his plush bed, but first things first, he craved to hear Sarah's voice. He was missing her like crazy and couldn't wait to tell her how well he was doing. Rumbling across the flat with Tumbles surprisingly still clinging to the saddle, the shiny corrugated-iron roof of the homestead finally came into view. Like a well-oiled machine, the men got to work and it wasn't long before the cattle were mustered into their final holding yard – the transport truck that would take the cattle to the saleyards was due in at first light.

Matt waited for Slim to shut the gate before he climbed down from the saddle. His back was sore as buggery after mustering for seven days straight, and the confrontation with the wayward bull hadn't helped any. But he'd faced his biggest fear by going back to the place it had all happened, and with the support of the blokes, got through it unscathed. With the last gate closed, every man breathed a sigh of relief. The horizon was turning shades of indigo, the sun quickly descending in a haze of orange and apricot – very soon and Rosalee Station would be shrouded in blackness. Matt smiled to himself. They were home. He'd made it. On a high, he silently cheered for the fact he was well on his way to becoming the man he once was. Sarah was going to be over the moon.

CHAPTER
16

Having said his goodbyes to the rowdy group of pub-bound stockmen, while repeatedly having to knock back their offers to join them for their party weekend in Mount Isa, then a quick detour to the homestead to say g'day to his mum and to pinch some fresh milk and a couple of eggs, Matt cleared his front steps two at a time. He grinned like a lovesick teenager just with the thought of calling Sarah. He couldn't wait to tell her he'd got past the hardest part of giving up the drink. There was a spring in his step that hadn't been there a week ago, and it felt damn good to feel so alive. Without even taking his boots off, a complete and utter sin in his mother's eyes and Sarah's too, for that matter, he tore inside, keen to see if she'd rung while he was away. He couldn't wait to hear her beautiful voice.

Depositing the milk and eggs in the fridge, he skidded over to the answering machine. With the little red light flashing, his spirits soared. It had to be Sarah; nobody else had a reason to call the cottage. He wondered how many times she'd rung just to leave him a sweet message, like she always had when he was out here visiting and she'd chosen to stay back at Tranquil Valley, *to hold the fort*, as she'd say. If the shoe had been on the other foot, and he'd had access to a phone while she'd been out mustering, he most probably would have rung and left a little message for her every day, so when she got home she knew just how much he loved her and missed her.

He pressed play and leant back against the kitchen bench, smiling before he'd even heard her voice. The machine told him he had one new message. Only one? His soaring spirits took a nosedive. His smile all but disappeared as he listened to Sarah's message from almost a week ago. It was a little cold, and her *love you* sounded as if it were an afterthought. So many days on the muster and all he'd done was think about her, pine for her, miss her. He grabbed the cordless receiver, but not ready to dial her mobile number yet, he stormed back out to the verandah to do what he should have done in the first place. Take his goddamn boots off.

Stomping outside, the screen door smacking shut behind him, Matt leant on the verandah railing, his mind in a tailspin. How quickly he'd gone from a high to a low. And although, deep down, he knew he was being unreasonable, ridiculous even, he couldn't help it. Pushing the balls of his hands into his eyes, he tried to calm himself, and fought to think rationally. In reality, why would she call when she knew he wasn't home? But before he could get a firm hold on the notion, his mind laughed at him and reminded him that if she truly loved him and missed him, she would have made more of an effort to make sure he knew it when he got back to the cottage. Maybe she'd come to the conclusion she *was* better off without him. Maybe she didn't miss him at all. And then, like a merry-go-round with no off switch, his mind swirled from one notion to another, all the while with him trying to get a grip.

Straightening up and ramming his hands in his pockets, he sucked in a deep breath. He squeezed his eyes shut and rubbed his now throbbing temples. Didn't she miss him as much as he was missing her? Wasn't she worried about their marriage becoming a divorce? He knew he was being silly, but it kind of felt like now he wasn't with her, he was out of sight, out of mind. And thinking that put him even more on edge than he already was. Feeling like less of a man was bad enough, but now insecurity was raising its ugly head. Sarah was a stunner and had an addictive personality to boot. She would have no trouble replacing him. Knowing she was back in Mareeba made things ten times worse. She knew half the town and there were so many eligible men who'd give their right arm to fill his shoes. Damn it. What had he gone and done, coming out here? He wished he could snap his fingers and be with her again.

Pacing back and forth with the expanse of Rosalee Station sprawled out before him, he pulled the cordless phone from his back pocket and tried dialling her mobile number. His foot tapped in static rhythm as he prayed for her to pick up. But after five rings it went to message bank. He tried again, holding his breath, but once again there was no answer. Wasn't she there or was she choosing to ignore him?

He suddenly craved a really strong drink.

He shook his head as if trying to shake the idea away.

One wouldn't hurt, a little voice said.

He paced faster and faster. The little voice continued, egging him on. 'Stop it, man. Get a fucking grip,' he mumbled.

The phone rang. He jumped so high he almost hit the roof. Before answering he looked at the caller ID. It was Sarah. He released his pent-up breath.

'Hey, babe.' With his heart racing, he fought to keep his voice steady.

'Matt, you're back.'

'Yeah, you sound surprised?'

'Oh, I thought you still had a couple more days to go, that's all.'

'Nope. I told you I'd be home today, so we're actually right on schedule.' How could she not remember the day he said he'd be back? She clearly didn't care. Her voice sounding so blasé, he felt his irritation with her rise a few notches. He cleared his throat. The silence hung heavily.

'So how was it?'

Even though she couldn't see him, he forced a smile. 'Really good. It was just what I needed.' *Tell her how good you're doing …* but he couldn't. He was too worked up to play niceties. 'The blokes were all really supportive.'

'That's good to hear, and I'm glad you enjoyed it. Have you had anything to drink?'

'Nope.'

'Not one?'

'Nope.' Her relieved breath reached inside him and scratched at his soul.

'That's wonderful news, Matt. It makes me very happy to hear.'

And she did sound happy. Very happy. 'Well, it's only the start but at least I'm on the right track.'

'That's right, and yes, by the sounds of it, you are. Good job.'

'Yup, thanks.'

Silence reigned once more. He felt like slapping himself for being so, whatever he was being. What the fuck was wrong with him?

'So, Lily has asked me to go to the rodeo for my birthday and I've said yes. I hope that's okay with you?'

A wave of panic washed over him and he grabbed hold of the railing to steady himself. 'Yup, of course. Why wouldn't it be?'

'Oh, I just thought ...' She laughed a little uncomfortably. 'Don't worry, I'm being silly.'

'Yeah, you are ... being silly.' He tipped his head back and looked to the twilight sky. 'Have a good time. I'm really sorry I can't be there to celebrate with you.'

'Thanks, I will.'

Snap the fuck out of it, Walshee ... 'I miss you, Sarah.'

There was a second's hesitation at the other end of the line. 'I miss you too.'

He didn't believe her. 'Well, I gotta run.'

'Okay, yup. We'll talk again soon?'

'Yeah, sure ... give me a call and tell me all about the rodeo.'

'Okay, yeah, I will.' And there was that godawful silence again. 'I love you, Matt.'

It sounded forced. 'Love you too, Sarah.'

'Night then.'

'Night.'

And she was gone. And tomorrow she'd be off to the country shindig of the year, the Mareeba rodeo. Where every man and his dog went.

He needed that fucking drink.

Now.

Bit hard when he didn't have any alcohol in the place.

Defeated, he slumped down in the hammock. And then, a thought struck him like a smack to the head.

Leaping up, he stomped back inside. Tossing the phone on the kitchen bench, it slid across the counter top and landed over the other side, the batteries coming loose. He went to retrieve it but then thought, *Stuff it*. Who cared if it wasn't working? It wasn't like anyone would be calling him. He took a glass out of the cupboard. Then, a man on a mission, he stormed into the laundry and yanked open the cupboard door. Reaching into the far back corner, behind bottles of laundry liquid and softener and every cleaning product imaginable thanks to his OCD mum, he searched for the bottle of twelve-year-old scotch he'd left there two years back. A gift from his father for his thirtieth, he'd stowed it away for a special occasion – Eve's eighteenth had been his plan. So much for that now.

His heart sinking, he tussled with his mind. He'd made a promise to get sober out here, and so far so good – so this was Sarah's fault, making him feel so worthless. What did she expect, acting like she was free and single? One shot, that's all he'd have. He just needed something to take the edge off. To allow him to think rationally. To get into a mindset where he could talk some sense into himself.

He stomped back to the kitchen and pulled open the freezer. Tossing a few ice cubes into the glass, he poured a nip, deliberately screwed the cap back on, as tight as he could, strode back to the laundry and then shoved the bottle back. Just like him, it was now out of sight, out of mind – and not easy to reach for a second helping. He waved the glass beneath his nose. The alcohol smelt so damn good his mouth watered as if it were a roast dinner. Striding into the lounge room, he collapsed onto the three-seater lounge, his socked feet coming to rest on the arm of it as he stretched out. He really should have showered before plonking himself here, but stuff it. He paused, sniffed the contents of the glass again and thought about putting it down. But then he thought, *Fuck it, why not?* He took a sip from the amber liquid, allowing the slow burn to slide down his throat, and loving every second of it. The familiarity of it was oh so comforting. Sighing, he eased his head back against the cushion. Staring at the ceiling fan, he considered getting up to turn it on but he couldn't be bothered. He couldn't help but think about the look on Sarah's face as she shoved her wedding ring towards him, the ring that was now in the drawer of his bedside table. It had been an expression of complete and utter loathing. He hadn't seen that coming. She may as well have taken a dagger and stabbed him right in the heart. His guilt and remorse ate away at him every single minute of every single day. Every time he looked at her pretty face it reminded him of their child that he'd killed – didn't she understand that?

Selfish woman ...

He took another sip, and then a gulp.

An induced calmness settled.

Just this one drink and he'd be right.

Drawing in a deep breath, he tried to think of Sarah with love instead of hatred. There was a fine line between the two – and he'd crossed it out of insecurity. Although mad and badly hurt, he had to agree she deserved better than he'd been able to give her this past year. She deserved a man who was solid, and unscarred, a man who would stand up and be her rock no matter what. Maybe he should spare her a miserable life with him and stay out here. But the idea of her with anyone else hit him like a sucker punch. He ran what she'd said over in his mind … *if the man I fell in love with is still inside there somewhere, come back to me.* Could he ever be that man again? He looked to the drink in his hand.

Probably not.

Old patterns were hard to break.

A leopard didn't change its spots – he was doing a damn good job of proving the theory right.

In one fierce gulp he swallowed the scotch and then placed the glass down on the coffee table, the urge to pour another already coursing through him. He folded his hands on his chest in a bid to stop himself, but the temptation was there to drink himself into a stupor. With all his willpower he rolled onto his side, picked up the remote and flicked the telly on. It would be a good distraction. Or so he thought. He flicked from one channel to the next, nothing taking his fancy.

Just one more …

Standing, he stormed back into the laundry and tugged the door open. Staring at the bottle right up the back, he clenched and unclenched his fists. Goddamn it. Reaching in and pulling it out, he poured another, this time straight up, no ice. Like a beast fighting its instinct to spring on its prey, he was at war with himself. And he was clearly fighting a losing battle. Swigging it down quickly, he kept telling himself that this was it, no more after this one. He walked inside, stopped and then hurled the glass across the kitchen and watched it smash into tiny pieces against the wall. There, the glass was gone. Not as easy to have a drink now. He almost smirked at his ingenuity. But then, as if his mind was taking on a life of its own, his hand reached for the bottle. A little voice reminded him what a weak fool he was. *Fuck you!* he silently roared. He wrapped his fingers around the neck of the bottle and took a swig, winced against the burn, and then wiped his mouth with the back of his hand. Taking it with him without a second thought, he made his way back to the couch. Sitting, he threw his feet up on the coffee table and settled in for the long haul. One glug after the other, he swallowed it down, and before he knew it, he'd demolished over half the bottle. The room spinning and his eyelids as heavy as lead weights, they slammed shut, and he drifted into weird and unknown places. And then, as if dropping off the edge of the earth, he fell, swooped and was gone, in a deeply unsatisfying slumber.

Heavy knocks at the door and a familiar voice calling out his name coiled into his unconscious. Still out of it, he sat up; the half-empty bottle was clutched tightly in his hand as if his life depended on it. The alcohol had done nothing to numb his senses, and had only left him with a mother of all headaches. The pain, the heartache, and the sense of utter failure on every level were all still there. After an entire week of not touching a drop he'd certainly gone and made up for it. He'd not only failed Sarah, he'd failed himself, like he'd failed Eve. He didn't deserve a beautiful woman like Sarah. And she deserved a man who could give her the world. He couldn't go back. Wouldn't go back. She needed him to do this, to finally cut the cord that bound them, for her own happiness. She was too kind-hearted to make this break, so he would save her the trouble. This was it. There was no turning back. He was done – for her sake. And he wouldn't go through the motions of trying to take his share of their finances and the property; she could have it all. The reality hit him like a thunderbolt to the chest. His incredible sense of loss collided in his heart and soul.

Heavy footfalls approached. The familiar voice caught his wavering attention. His blurry vision slowly cleared as Slim pulled up a chair and leant forwards, his elbows propped on his knees and his hands folded beneath his chin. The worry and disappointment written all over his mate's face was devastating. He'd done it again; he'd let down those he cared about.

There was a weighty sigh. 'Where'd you get that bottle of scotch from, Walshee?'

Matt took a few more hazy moments to come to full attention. Slim was meant to be on his way to Mount Isa. So was he really here, or was Matt hallucinating? Speechless, he shook his head, as if it were going to magically sober him.

'Lucky I decided to wait until tomorrow to head off.'

So he was really here. Matt still found it impossible to speak.

Slim remained silent for a couple of breaths, before exhaling hard. He held out his hand. 'Give me the bloody bottle, would ya?'

Without a second thought, Matt handed it over and then dropping his head in his hands he broke down and wept. 'I'm so sorry, mate. I'm a fucking failure, Slimbo,' he mumbled through his sobs.

Walking over to the sink, Slim tipped the last of the liquid out and then tossed the bottle in the bin. Returning, he sat down beside him. His hand came down on Matt's back, firm but reassuring. 'Mate, you're not a failure. You're a human being who's gone through one of the toughest things any parent could go through.' He gave Matt a firm sideways hug. 'The first step to giving up the grog is not physically doing it, it's learning to stop being so hard on yourself.'

Screwing his face up, Matt shook his head. 'How in the hell am I meant to do that?'

Slim shrugged. 'Like breathing, you just do it.'

Matt felt a rush of irritation, but he bit it back. 'That simple, hey?' His tone was still laced with frustration.

'Yup, that simple.' Slim tapped his head. 'This thing right here is a bloody powerful tool, and if you learn to use it right, you can talk yourself into thinking anything, even good stuff, believe it or not.'

'I killed her, Slimbo. I killed my baby girl, so how am I ever meant to stop being so hard on myself? It's not that fucking easy.' He offered a lacklustre smile. 'You just don't get it.'

'Oh, yes I bloody well do.' Slim held his stare. 'You were the best damn father to Eve, and she knew how much you loved her. I was right there in the ute with you, remember? I saw everything. It was an accident, Matt. Damn it, even the police said so. You have to find a way to forgive yourself so you can move on. Sarah needs you in one piece, not a broken man like you are right now.'

'You're wrong, Slimbo, she doesn't need me. She's better off on her own.'

Slim's forehead puckered and his gaze turned fierce. 'Stop talking bloody dribble, Walshee, because I ain't in the mood to bloody well listen to your melancholy ramblings.'

Slim's harsh tone made Matt sit up and take notice. 'Righto, sorry.'

'I'm here for you, Walshee, like I've always been, but not if you're going to continue to wallow in self-pity and self-doubt. I'm not going to sit by and listen to it anymore. Enough is enough. You're never going to make it through this if you keep beating yourself up. You have to stand up, get a grip on your thoughts, take hold of the reins, and start believing in yourself again.' Reaching out, he squeezed Matt's shoulders. 'You're a damn good man, Matthew Walsh, with strong morals, a top-notch work ethic, and a fucking heart of gold. So start walking with your head held high and that cocky confidence you used to have, because underneath all the shit, in here …' he smacked his hand down on Matt's chest, 'that's who you really are, and that's why Sarah has stuck by your side through thick and thin. She fucking loves you, and she always will. You two are soulmates. Don't go ruining it because deep down you think you deserve more punishment. Because you damn well don't.'

With his throat tight and words evading him, all Matt could do was nod in agreement. Tears welled once more but this time he sat up straighter and sucked them back. Slim was right. He needed to man up, take control of his life, and make it work … before it was too late.

'You good, Walshee?'

'Yeah, thanks for the pep talk, mate. I needed it.'

'Yeah, you did.' Slim smiled. 'You're bloody lucky I didn't slap you over the head instead.'

'Ha-ha, I deserved it.' A hangover kicking into full force, Matt slumped back, groaning. 'Why's life got to be so fucking hard?'

Slim slumped back too, and propped his bare feet on the coffee table. 'Because if it was easy, we'd all get bored.'

Matt stared up at the ceiling fan. 'Yeah, maybe.'

'Now how 'bout tomorrow, you and I head to Mount Isa together, and we have ourselves some man time?'

'Are you fucking crazy, Slimbo?' Panic sent Matt's pulse into a gallop. 'There'll be alcohol everywhere.'

'Exactly, and you're going to prove to yourself you don't need a drop of it to have a good time.' Slim flashed him a sideways glance, his grin lopsided. 'And in response to your other comment, yes, I can be a little bat shit crazy at times, but it's all in good fun.'

'I'll raise a glass to that,' Matt said, before he'd even thought about his bad choice of words.

'Not on my watch, you won't.' Slim shook his head, chuckling. 'You're a fucking handful, Walshee, but don't worry, if anybody can handle ya, it's me. I'll whip you into line in no time, don't you worry.'

'I'm fucking scared.'

'You should be.'

Both men laughed.

'Damn, it's like an oven in here.' Slim wiped beading sweat from his brow as he looked to the ceiling. 'Why in the hell haven't you got the fan on, ya weirdo?'

Clarkes' Fruit Farm, Mareeba, Far North Queensland

Sarah slept fitfully, tortured by unwelcome dreams, swirling pictures of Matt living happily with another woman and a skeletal, black-eyed Eve calling her from the grave. She woke with a whimper, clawing herself to consciousness past the now foggy images. Her face was damp with tears and her body covered in sweat. It took a few moments for her eyes to completely open as she kicked off the sheet. Sunshine, filtered by the curtains, was filling the room and she saw from the bedside clock that it was almost seven-thirty. She'd slept in, but only because it had been two this morning before she'd been able to drift off. She flipped onto her back, trying to summon up the motivation to get out of bed. It was going to be a long day with the rodeo on tonight. Her parents would be home later today and she wanted to make sure she had all the jobs done, inside and outside, and a slow cooker filled with her famous curried sausages on the go, before they arrived. Not because she had to, but because she wanted to do something special for them. She didn't know where she'd be without their unwavering support this past year.

She checked her mobile for any missed calls from Matt, and felt downhearted when she saw there were none. After the way he'd been with her, she'd hoped he'd have at least rung to apologise. Actions, in her opinion, always spoke louder than words. And it felt like he didn't give two shits about her, his short responses and sharp tone speaking volumes yesterday. Although she was enjoying the time to herself, she did miss him and was worried about him. It would have been nice to have a half-decent conversation, not one where she'd felt the need to fill the silences. The mention of her going to the rodeo had gone just as she'd suspected. Bad. Although he'd said it was fine, she could tell by the tone in his voice that he wasn't too keen on the idea. And as much as she tried to see his side, that had pissed her off, so much so she'd gone to bed at nine last night only to roll around for hours cursing his name. On the plus side, he hadn't had a drink, or so he told her. Sadly, after the year she'd had with him, she needed to see it to believe it.

Peeling herself from the tousled bed she wandered over to the window and pulled the curtains open. She spotted the four-wheeler heading down to the paddock with Duke tearing behind it – good lord, she'd forgotten to call him back in after she'd let him out last night for his toilet duties. Johnny Marsh, the family's farm hand and seasonal paddock manager of the past ten years, was at the helm of the quad, heading off to ride up and down each row of fruit trees so he could unblock any of the sprinklers and fix any breaks. It was the usual thing to do on the weekends – unless they'd had plenty of rain and the ground was soaked. Her smile widened when she turned her gaze to the front paddock, where Chilli was foraging for her breakfast right beside Victory. The most mismatched pair, yet such wonderful friends.

She walked into the bathroom and flicked on the light. As her focus rested on the mirror above the sink, her already low mood took an even bigger nosedive. Looking like she'd been dragged through something backwards, she grimaced. With angry rubs, she splashed soap and water onto her face in a bid to get rid of the sleep-deprived puffiness. Keeping her eyes shut, she patted around the basin in search of a handtowel but only succeeded in finding a roll of toilet paper. Ripping off a wad big enough to dry her face, she heard it thump to the floor when she missed placing it back on the basin. She bent to rescue the runaway roll, knocking her head on the edge of the sink on the way up. A glass clattered to the floor, smashing on impact, her toothbrush landing with it.

Shit!

Her left eye stinging from a bit of soap that had snuck its way in, she tried to clean up the mess, only to cut her finger. Shoving it in her mouth, she sucked the blood and then assessed it. Nothing a bandaid wouldn't fix. Sighing, she went to retrieve the dustpan and brush from downstairs, stepping over a snoozing cat on the way.

'Dang you've got the life, Harry. If I'm reincarnated, I want to come back as a cat.'

Rolling onto his side, Harry replied with a drawn-out meow as he clawed the already threadbare patch of carpet he called home. Accidentally tread on him, and Sarah knew that his claws would be embedded in your skin faster than you could say sorry.

Dustpan in hand, she paused at the bottom of the stairs when her gaze caught the crucifix her mum had hanging above the front door. Her parents had always been devout Catholics, and she'd been raised with a strong religious backbone. One that had snapped in two the day she'd lost Eve. She suddenly knew what she wanted to do after she'd caught up on everything around here. Something she hadn't done since the day of Eve's funeral. Visit the local church.

When Eve had been born, and wanting to meet more people in Malanda with kids, they'd gone as a family once a month to the Sunday morning sermon, and afterwards they'd all enjoy a BBQ lunch on the church's back lawn, with the priest in charge of cooking the steak and snags and the women fussing over their plates of salads and desserts. A grog-free event, the men had stood around with cans of soft drink in hand, chatting about the state of farming, the fish they'd caught lately and just men's talk in general. It had been a nice way to spend a Sunday. But then, losing Eve so tragically, Sarah had questioned her faith and a god that would take her beloved daughter way too soon. Maybe it was time to forgive the Lord above and look at it as another step towards her healing.

❧

Scoffing the last of the sausage roll she'd bought at the servo instead of the bakery – a bad decision – it was just after lunchtime when she passed through the doorway of Saint Francis Xavier Church. Wiping the last of the tomato sauce on her jeans, she paused to dab holy water on her fingers while silently saying the Lord's Prayer and making the sign of the cross. Looking at the altar, memories of sitting in the church back in Malanda engulfed her. All she could picture was a tiny little coffin, and all the pain she'd felt that day thumped her hard in the chest. Slamming her eyes shut, she willed the image away. Her legs weak, she slunk into the empty pew at the back of the pin-drop quiet church. Emotions bubbling, she inhaled sharply, her stomach churning. She dropped her eyes to her folded hands and tried to shut out the horrible memories – they would do her no favours. A few slow, deep breaths later, and feeling ready, she stood on her shaky legs and walked up to the altar. Dropping to her knees, she joined her hands in prayer and stared up at the cross. And then she prayed like she'd never prayed before, begging God to take care of her daughter up in heaven, and for him to *please, please, please* do whatever he could to help Matt, and save their marriage.

Deep in prayer, at first she didn't hear the footsteps coming up behind her. She paused, turning to see a friendly familiar face. For a moment she was eight again, and preparing for her holy communion, and then she was fifteen, admitting to her sins in the confessional box. She offered a wobbly smile.

Heavy, white-as-snow brows scrunched together as the priest smiled, his blue-grey eyes gleaming and the crinkles at the corners ever so deep. 'Sarah Clarke, or should I say, Walsh, it's so lovely to see you.'

Sarah stood, the faint scent of camphor wafting from the priest. It reminded her of her dearly departed grandmother – mothballs had been in every cupboard. 'It's lovely to see you too, Father Donaldson.'

He reached out and touched her arm. His hand was cold and soft; so different from that of a man, like her father, who had spent his years working the land. 'How are you, my dear?' His eyes were full of compassion.

'Not the best, Father, but I'm slowly getting there.'

'Anything a keen ear would help ease?'

'Um.' Sarah paused, chewing her lip. 'Yes, maybe, but only if you have time … I don't want to bother you.'

'I have all the time in the world, my dear.' Father Donaldson motioned towards the front pew. 'Ladies first.'

Sarah took the invitation and the priest hobbled in beside her, groaning as he sat.

She helped steady him. 'You okay, Father?'

'Oh yes, the old knees don't work like they used to.' He chuckled. 'One could say they're in desperate need of re-greasing.'

Sarah's smile was easy and genuine now.

'So tell me, what's weighing on your mind?'

'My marriage is falling apart, Father, and I don't know what to do to save it.'

'I see.' He paused, looking down at his hands folded in his lap while nodding ever so slightly. He brought his gaze back to hers. 'And what's making you question your love for your husband?'

'You've heard about the accident?'

'I did, through your mother and father, and my condolences are with you and your family.'

'Thank you, Father.'

The wrinkles around his eyes deepened. 'The death of a child is never an easy thing to get through.' His voice was so calm, so steady, so comforting. 'But you will, Sarah, because as much as we may not like it, life does go on, and we have to go on with it.'

'It certainly does, Father, and it's brutal and heartbreaking and so hard to come to terms with.' Tears welling, she sniffled. Grabbing one of the tissues she'd shoved in her pocket, knowing full well she would most probably need them here, she wiped at the corners of her eyes.

'There there, love.' He tapped her arm, his gaze sympathetic. 'How is Matthew coping?'

'By drinking.' She didn't know why, but she half laughed when she said it.

'Oh, I see.' He paused once more, nodding slightly. 'Has he sought help for it?'

'Yes and no. He's out at his family's cattle station right now, trying to go cold turkey.'

'And how's that going for him?'

'Apparently so far so good.'

He smiled now, his entire face creasing with it. 'Good.'

'It is, but I can't help feeling like he's deserted me, and I feel angry and hurt because of it.'

'Yes, I can understand how you'd feel like that, but he's done what he needs to do to make himself whole again, just as you need to do what you have to do to make yourself whole again.'

At a loss for words, Sarah nodded as she tried to take in everything he was saying.

'Marriage is not always easy, Sarah, and sometimes, for one reason or another, it feels like it would be easier to give up on the other person. But let's strip all the hurt and troubles back, and simply focus on the vow you took the day you tied the knot. Through sickness and health, till death do us part. Remember that, Sarah, and stand strong in your vow, and you will make it through.' He sighed, shaking his head. 'Too many people throw the towel in the minute it gets too much, thinking it's easier to walk away, when in truth, they're just going to walk into another unsatisfying relationship until they learn what the true meaning of love is.'

Sarah found herself enthralled by his every word, everything making such perfect sense. 'And what is it, true love?'

He held his finger up, a knowing glint in his eyes. 'Ahhh, now isn't that the big question we all want the answer to?'

'Yes, it's what makes the world go round,' Sarah said with a gentle smile.

'It most certainly is.' Father Donaldson turned in his seat to face her, his expression now serious. 'True love is not a feeling, it's a choice … a choice to be in love every single day, no matter what. It goes beyond the pleasures of the flesh and what the other person can offer you. It's about loving each other without judgement and conditions, with trust and respect at all times. It's about letting go of expectations and any sense of possession. It's about stepping outside your ego, and seeing the value in someone else. True love stays with you, through all the good and bad times, and it knows no bounds.' He smiled now. 'You see, everyone is flawed, Sarah, and the secret of true love is seeing that, and accepting you're not perfect, and neither can your other half be. We all stumble and fall throughout life, and it's when we most need our loved ones there, to pick us up once we're ready to hold out our hands to stand back up again.'

Tears streamed down Sarah's face. She wiped them away with a fresh tissue she found in her pocket. 'Oh, Father, that's the most beautiful explanation I've ever heard.'

'Well, thank you, my dear, I hope that it's helped you somewhat, in your difficult time.'

'It sure has helped me to see things through different eyes.' She reached out and gently touched his hand. 'So thank you, from the bottom of my heart.'

'My pleasure, it's what I'm here for.' Holding the arm of the pew, he slowly eased to standing. 'I better get a move on. I've got a baptism in less than an hour and I need to get ready.'

Sarah stood. 'Okay, and thank you again.'

He pulled her into a hug. 'You take care of yourself now, and your husband,' Father Donaldson said. 'Because although it may feel one-sided at the moment, there will come a time in your life where he'll be there to carry you through, as you have for him.'

He was so right, and with that knowledge, Sarah allowed herself to see light at the end of the long and very dark tunnel she and Matt had been trapped in.

☙

Stacking the last of the bowls and utensils that had covered the kitchen bench from one end to the other into the dishwasher, and then popping the super-moist walnut and banana cake covered with cream-cheese passionfruit icing she'd made on a whim into the cake tin, Sarah felt a flood of satisfaction. Hands on hips, she surveyed the kitchen, making sure everything was back in its place and she hadn't missed anything – being super tidy was a trait she'd got from her mother, and one both women were proud of. Another quality she'd inherited from her mum was her love of cooking, a love that had vanished this past year. It felt good to be passionate about it again. The mouth-watering aroma of curried sausages filled the house and a pot of creamy garlic mash potato sat ready to go, but with no time to spare, Sarah decided it would be her midnight snack, or breakfast tomorrow morning. She hoped her dad left her some – he was a glutton when it came to good old-fashioned, homemade food.

Not that she minded, as an empty pot and a basically licked-clean plate were huge compliments in her eyes.

Her mobile phone buzzed from the pocket of her denim shorts. Plucking it out, she smiled at the good-humoured duck face Lily was deliberately pulling in the photo to make her smile – her mate knew how much she despised it.

See you soon, babe, and I hope you've got your dancing boots on. Yee-haa! Love ya! Lil Xo

Her stomach backflipped. She looked at the time. She knew it was getting on but not that quickly. *Shit!* Time had completely got away from her, so she raced up the stairs, clearing Harry and his step completely. She had a little over half an hour to shower, get dressed, and snazzy herself up a bit in the hair and make-up department. She really had to get her arse into gear. Skidding into the bathroom, she tore her clothes off while trying to turn the taps on. Diving beneath the steamy stream, she quickly washed her mop of hair, shaved her legs and armpits, deciding to leave her bikini line, brushed her teeth and then dried herself while running down the hallway and into her bedroom. Luckily, she'd already chosen what she was going to wear – her diamanté-encrusted jeans and ritzy belt to match, and a paisley patterned, button-up cowgirl shirt. It had been a lifetime since she'd dolled herself up for a night out, and now it was getting closer she felt a flutter of excited nerves in her belly. As long as she could make it to midnight, she'd prove to herself she wasn't such an old fart after all and still had it in her to go out and have fun sometimes.

At nearly five o'clock there was a *thump, thump* of music and the sound of tyres crunching on the gravel driveway, then Sarah heard the unmistakable country twang of 'Save a Horse Ride a Cowboy'. Lily honked short and sharp out the front of the house. Damn it, she still wasn't ready.

Hopping on one foot while trying to pull a sock on the other, she stuck her head out the window. Lily looked up at her bedroom from the driver's seat, her smile stretched from ear to ear. Her hair up and dangly western-style earrings on, she looked stunning, as always.

'I'll be two minutes, Lil.' Sarah had a feeling Lily wouldn't have heard a thing she'd just said.

The music fading away, Lily wound her window down. 'What'd you say, girlfriend?'

'I'm running a few minutes late, I'll be down in a sec.'

'Righto, babe, no rush ... but hurry the hell up, would ya! We got ourselves some bull-riding Wrangler butts to check out.' She grinned waywardly.

'I'll tell my brother on you.' Sarah returned the cheeky grin along with giving her the forks.

'You wouldn't dare.' Lily mocked shock horror, her mouth gaping open and her caramel-brown eyes wide.

Sarah laughed; she knew Lily would know she was joking. The love her best mate and Daniel had for one another had only grown deeper over the years, and although Lily might like to look at the goods, like any hot-blooded woman does at a rodeo, Sarah knew without a doubt she would never, ever, touch another man. She and Lily had strong morals and expected the same from their men. Matt had never failed her in that department, and she loved him for it.

'Good *married* cowgirls always keep their calves together,' Lily called out.

'Yes, you can look but you can't touch,' Sarah called back.

Lily gave her the thumbs up. 'Now, hurry up or we're going to miss the judging of the Beaut Ute Muster. One of my mates from work has his in for the Best Feral Ute.'

'Okay, okay, I'm a'comin.'

Tugging her other sock on, she rammed her feet into her favourite Dan Post boots. Tipping her head upside down, she scrunched some curl definer into her damp hair and flicked it back up, her head spinning a little from the motion. Chaotic long, blonde curly locks hung almost to her waist – a little unkempt and wild looking, but that's just how she liked it. Grabbing her make-up bag, she brushed on powder foundation, popped on some blusher, applied some mascara – cursing when she blinked too quickly and ended up with half of it on her eyelids, a quick lick of her fingertip and a wipe did wonders to remove it. And then a swipe of cherry-red lip gloss, and she was done. With a desperate deep breath she took one last look at her reflection, mostly satisfied with what she saw, and then picking up her wallet she dashed downstairs, leaping over Harry and almost ending up on her face, before tugging open the front door and stepping outside … right on five o'clock. Striding over to Duke, she gave him a quick goodbye pat, told him to stay put, and then made her way over to Lily's hot-rod.

'Hey there, cowgirl, going my way?' Her forearm resting on the windowsill of the black V8 commodore like she was a truck driver, Lily jokingly looked her up and down and then offered an over-exaggerated wink.

Hands on hips, Sarah flashed a toothy smile. 'If ya lucky.'

'I'm always lucky. And can I say, hot-damn woman, you've scrubbed up like a ridgy didge hottie patottie.'

'Why thank ya, cowgirl.' Sarah loved their banter. Slipping into the passenger seat, she watched Chilli make a mad dash across the driveway towards the chook pen, with eight chickens in tow. She was a born leader, that's for sure. Sarah's mum would lock them away for the night on her way home from feeding the horses.

'Oh shit,' Sarah said, tossing her tasselled western handbag onto the floor.

'What?'

'My mobile's back upstairs.'

'You wanna go get it?'

Ready to jump back out, she changed her mind. 'Nah, I don't really need it, less to carry anyway.'

'You can always use mine if you need to make a call, babe.'

'Thanks, so where's Danny boy?' She pulled on her seatbelt. 'He didn't cop out, did he?'

'He's already there, caught a lift with Brad.' Gravel flew from the tyres after Lily put pedal to the metal a little too quickly. 'Oops, shit, sorry.'

'Bradley Williams?' Sarah hadn't even stopped to think that her ex-boyfriend, the one she'd dated just before Matt, the same one who had let mutual friends know he'd do anything to rewind time so he could have her back – and Matt knew about this as she told him everything – would be there, and in close proximity. If Matt was a bit pissed about her going, he was going to be livid now.

Lily remained focused on the potholes in the drive, the dunnydoor (Commodore) not made for country driveways like this one. 'Uh-huh.'

'I thought he was working up in the Northern Territory?'

'Yeah, he still is. He's just come down for the rodeo.' Lily grimaced. 'I didn't think it would be a problem, seeing as you and him have kept in touch on and off over the years, and he and Daniel have always been mates.'

'Yeah, no, of course not … I'm just being stupid.'

Crossing the cattle grid at a crawling pace, Lily pulled to a stop. 'Sarah, spill now or forever hold your peace.' She folded her arms. 'Actually skip the last bit because I won't be able to hold my peace if you don't spill because I'm worried now.'

Sarah groaned. Why did there always have to be a drama in her life? She turned in her seat, looking Lily fair and square in the eyes. 'It's just that, well, you know how Brad has mentioned a couple of times how he'd give his right arm to have me back?'

'Yeah, and why wouldn't he? You're a bloody catch.'

'Thanks for that, but Matt knows too.'

Lily's eyes widened. 'Matt knows?'

'Of course he does, I tell him everything.'

'I think some things are best left unsaid, Sar, but knowing you like I do I should know you wouldn't be able to keep that from him.' She sighed. 'Matt must also know that you're a very trustworthy woman and he has nothing to worry about, especially when it comes to you and Brad. That was done and dusted almost ten years ago.'

'Yes and no … I *am* trustworthy, without a doubt, but Matt's not in a good headspace, Lily, and I'm afraid he might read way too much into it.'

'Well then, if that's the case, he doesn't need to know Brad will be there.'

'He doesn't?'

'No, not if it's going to cause a shit storm.'

'Oh, I don't know, Lil.' Sarah fumbled with her seatbelt; it suddenly felt tight and constricting.

'Sarah, you've had enough bloody drama in both your lives to last you a lifetime, so don't add to it with something that's not even really worth a mention, okay?'

Sarah nodded. 'Righto. Yup. Okay. You're right, I'm not going to gain anything by telling Matt.' She zipped her lips shut. 'They're sealed tight like a vault.'

'Good, because I don't want anything to ruin your night, Sar. You deserve to go out and have some drama-free fun.'

'I won't let it ruin our night, I promise.' Sarah forced a smile she was far from feeling. 'Now, come on, let's hurry up and get there. I'm dying for a dagwood dog smothered in tomato sauce followed by a cream-filled waffle cone.' She almost drooled with the thought.

'Good god, woman, what's happened to you? You used to say you're dying for a drink.'

'It's called growing up and getting older.'

'Oh you boring thirty-one-year-old fart, you.'

'I'm not officially thirty-one until midnight.' Sarah smirked. 'So get stuffed.'

'Ha-ha, I plan to … on dagwood dogs and waffle cones, and ribs, and maybe even a piece of deep-fried cheesecake if my stomach can handle it.'

'Oh, sweet baby Jesus, what's happened to the diet?'

'I've made this my cheat day.'

'Oh look out then, you rebel without a cause.'

Both women laughed as Lily turned onto the main highway into town. Music up, they sang out loud, Sarah feeling her mood lighten more and more the closer they got to the rodeo grounds. This would be a great night. She was going to make damn sure of it, if not for her sake then for Lily's.

CHAPTER
18

Mount Isa, Central Australia

The setting sun rippled on the surface of the dams and cast long shadows across the golden-hued landscape. His head throbbing like a jackhammer, Matt pushed his sunglasses on snugger and then turned the country music down a little so he could concentrate. If he were driving on his own he'd have turned it off, but he was thinking of Slim, who had his feet resting up on the dashboard while contentedly humming away to the catchy Hillbilly Goats' tune. If only he could be so relaxed, and in years gone by he would have been. But today he was wound up like a spring and was struggling to concentrate on the road. And it was imperative he did. It was the time of day to watch for the kangaroos that would appear out of nowhere, smack bang in the middle of the road, and although the station's beaten-up four-wheel drive had a bullbar, it wasn't uncommon for roos to be upended onto the bonnet and then ram straight through the windscreen if hit hard and fast enough – and that could end in tragedy. He couldn't bear to carry the responsibility of another lost life; the weight that was there already was too much for him to cope with. He'd offered to drive, but now he regretted it, still suffering from the effects of his binge drinking last night. He was tired and sore and grumpy, and possibly shouldn't be behind the wheel. But he was, and just had to suck it up. Thank god they were almost there. His plan was to have a counter meal and a couple of glasses of lemon, lime and bitters, staying just long enough to be social, and then sneak off to his hotel room. Ashamed he'd gone and ruined his cold turkey streak, all he wanted to do right now was have time to himself.

His knuckles were white as he wrestled the LandCruiser out of yet another patch of bull dust, and not only because he was holding the steering wheel tight. He was nervous about stepping foot into the pub, and wasn't as sure as Slim was about his ability to not have a drink. And on top of that, it was around about now Sarah would be arriving at the rodeo, without him, and no doubt looking hot as hell. He knew he should trust her, and deep down he did, but his own insecurities were making him conjure up images he really shouldn't. Damn his mind and all the torture it put him through – he was his own worst enemy. Without meaning to, he groaned as he stretched out his aching neck.

Clearly feeling the tension in the cab, Slim switched the stereo off. 'You all good, mate?'

'Yeah, just weary, that's all.' Matt glanced over at Slim and forced a smile. 'I'll pep up once I've had a chance to stretch my legs, don't you worry 'bout that.'

'Good, because I'm looking forward to kicking back with you, Walshee. It's been forever since we hung out, outside of work.'

'Yeah, true, huh.'

Slim rubbed his belly. 'I'm that bloody Hank Marvin I could eat the arse out of a low flying duck right about now.'

'Yeah, me too. I reckon I'm gonna have myself one of their famous T-bones with mushroom sauce, salad and beer-battered chips.' Matt's mouth watered with the thought of tucking into a juicy steak. 'And then if I have any room left, I'm going to grab a piece of warm apple pie with custard and cream.' His appetite was back and bigger than ever. That was something to be happy about.

Slim licked his lips. 'Oh stop, would ya, before I chew my own bloody arm off.'

Ten minutes later they stopped at a pedestrian crossing and the first set of lights for the entire trip. Leaning in and blasting the horn before Matt could stop him, Slim yahooed out the passenger window to the bloke crossing in front of them with his head buried in his mobile phone. Matt didn't know him from a bar of soap. The bloke's eyes suddenly focused on them, and fierce like a mickey bull, the short, stubby guy built like a brick shithouse went to give Slim the finger and a mouthful of what for, but then grinned from ear to ear.

He came up to the window and shook Slim's hand. 'Hey, bud, long time no see.'

'Shit yeah, Chook, it's been donkey's years. What ya doing round this part of the world?'

'I'm working at the mine, have been the past couple of months. You heading to the pub?'

Slim grinned like the joker from *Batman*. 'Is the Pope Catholic?'

'Last time I heard he was.' Chook laughed like a hyena, his beady little eyes almost closed as he did. He leant in further, hand outstretched to Matt. 'Hey, mate, Chook's the name and when I'm not working, partying's my game.'

Oh Jesus, so much for Slim having a bit of a quiet one with him. 'Matt Walsh, nice to meet you, Chook.'

Chook's brows shot up. 'Ah, you're Slim's boss.'

'Nah, not really, more like his partner in crime.'

Slim chuckled. 'Yeah, what happens in the Isa stays in the Isa, hey, Walshee?'

'Yeah, something like that.' Matt chuckled while trying to keep his gaze anywhere but the top of Chook's head. The brawny bloke had obviously achieved his nickname because of the crest of fiery red hair that perched on top of his head like a chicken's comb.

A honk sounded from behind them. Matt had all but forgotten they had stopped on the main thoroughfare in and out of Mount Isa. Cursing beneath his breath, he gave the driver a wave out the window to say sorry.

Chook turned his attention to the mud-splattered four-wheel drive behind them. 'Yeah, yeah, hold ya bloody horses, Gringo.'

'Hey, Chook, didn't see ya there, buddy,' the driver yelled back.

Chook looked back to Matt and Slim. 'Don't worry about him, he's just a bloody Mexican from down south that doesn't understand the road rules of a country town. Give way to whoever's in front or has the biggest bullbar, and you triumph with both rules, hey.' He slapped the windowsill and cracked up laughing again. 'Anyways, catch you both there. I'll whip your arse in a game of pool, and then you can buy me a round of drinks.'

Slim pulled a game face. 'Ha-ha, you're on.'

'You wanna lift there?' Even though there wasn't a lot of room between him and Slim, Matt thought he better ask.

'Nah, but thanks. I need to stop at the hole in the wall to get some dosh out.' He tapped the windowsill and stepped back. 'Catch yas in five.'

The sun all but gone and the stars hinting their arrival in the twilight sky, Matt pulled up in the parking area of the Mount Isa hotel. This had been like his second home when he'd lived at Rosalee Station. 'Oh shit, we forgot to get fuel. Remind me before we head out of town tomorrow, otherwise we'll be in trouble.'

'Yup, will do, buddy.' Slim slid out, groaning like an old man as he straightened. 'I'll get the bags, Walshee. You just drag yourself out.'

'Cheers, bud.' Reaching into the glove box, Matt pulled out his wallet and mobile phone – finally, they were somewhere with mobile coverage. He was a little sad to see there were no texts from Sarah. Without stopping to think about it, so he didn't talk himself out of it, he wrote her one instead. He couldn't say what he wanted to out loud to her – texting gave him the security of not having to hear the hesitation in her voice. His heart couldn't take it right now.

Hey Sarah, I've decided to come into Mount Isa with Slimbo for the night. I've got no intention of drinking so don't go worrying about me ... actually reckon I'll be in bed in the next couple of hours. Hope you're having a great time at the rodeo. Say hi to Lily and Dan for me. Missing you like crazy and loving you heaps. Hope you're missing me too, and still in love with me, even just a little bit. We'll get through this, baby, I promise.

I can't imagine my life without you. Love you, always and forever. Matt Xo

His finger hovered above the send button and before he could stop himself he pressed it. Now surely she wouldn't ignore a nice message like that? Sarah usually had her phone in her pocket or handbag at all times, so he held high hopes he'd hear back from her before his head hit the pillow.

Slim appeared at Matt's window and knocked on the glass. 'What the hell are you doing in there, Walshee? I'm starving to death out here.'

'Sorry, coming.' He leapt out, his butt numb from the drive, and taking his bag from Slim he followed his mate into the rowdy public bar. A band played up on stage, country rock blaring from the massive speakers on either side. Not used to any form of nightlife, the deafening noise of chatter and music hit him like a sharp slap in the face, and the stench of alcohol was both nauseating and enticing.

After checking in and then dumping their bags in their room with two single beds – they had to share as it was the last room left when they'd called to book this morning – Matt and Slim made their way into the dining room to order their meals. Then, with buzzer in hand, they both bought a glass of soft drink and pulled up chairs at one of the smaller tables. It was quieter in here, with more of a family feel – much more to Matt's liking.

A bit of a gambler, Slim swiped a keno slip from the middle of the table and crossed off some numbers. 'I'm gonna go put this in. You never know, we might not have to work a day in our lives again.' Standing, he sculled his Coke and then held up the empty glass. 'You want another?'

Matt looked to his almost full glass. 'Nah, but thanks, I'm good. You *can* order a proper drink, Slimbo.'

'Now that wouldn't be very supportive of me, would it?'

Matt could tell Slim was hankering for a rum and Coke, and after the backbreaking week they'd had in the saddle he deserved one, or several. 'Just because I'm having a hard time with it, doesn't mean you have to go without.'

Slim looked gravely concerned. 'Only if you're sure, mate?'

'Yup, a hundred and ten percent. I'm gonna feel guilty if you don't.'

'Righto, then, thanks, bud.'

While watching Slim make his way over to the betting counter, the buzzer chimed on the table. The service had always been top-notch here. Matt went off to collect their meals. They both arrived back at the table at the same time.

'Cheers, Walshee.' Slim took the full plate from Matt. 'Cor, this looks good. We got ourselves half a bloody cow each, by the looks of it.'

With the T-bone so big it hung over the edges of his plate, and half a garden of salad squashed in beside the tonne of crunchy looking chips, Matt had to agree. Eating in silence, the men devoured it all, both of them having to let their belts out a notch at the end of the feast.

'You still got room for that piece of pie, Walshee?'

Full as a bull in springtime, Matt groaned. 'Not a chance in hell.'

'You ready to head back into the public bar for a bit then?'

Feeling like a beached whale, Matt really just wanted to go to bed, but he couldn't pike out yet. 'Yup, let's head.'

Stepping into the public bar, the vibe went from wholesome to rowdy and drunken. Matt felt completely out of his depth, but did his best not to show it. Chook appeared out of nowhere, his face as red as his hair, and Slim yahooed the arrival of his mate – he and Slim could have passed for brothers, albeit for the massive difference in height. Then Showbags, Tumbles, Pothole, Hasselhoof and Whiskers emerged from the crowd, all of them clearly having enjoyed a few bevvies. After g'days all round, the group of blokes got chatting and thankful Slim had a drinking buddy for the night, so he could sneak off early, Matt looked for a place to rest his legs. Spotting an empty stool at the end of the bar, he walked over to it. That was going to be his perch for the next hour or so – if he lasted that long.

Settled on his bar stool, Matt ordered a ginger beer, actually enjoying being in a pub sober for once, so he could sit back and people watch. It was something he enjoyed doing at the healthy food cafes Sarah used to love dragging him to. Cafes he grew to enjoy too; the food was always weird, but wonderful. They never did that sort of thing anymore, and he made a mental note to take her out for a meal when he got home – that was, if she wanted him back there. With the thought of her, he pulled his mobile out and checked it. No messages. His heart squeezed. Maybe she just hadn't seen his yet with all the excitement of the rodeo going on around her.

Slim made his way over. 'You right, bud?'

'Yeah, just chillaxing.'

'Come over and join in, mate.'

'Nah, I'm happy sitting here, Slimbo.'

'Well, I'll sit here with you.'

'No, you won't. I don't need babysitting.' He gave his mate a gentle shove. 'Go and be merry.'

Slim hesitated, clearly torn between fun and obligation. Matt gave him another shove. 'Be gone with you.'

'Do I stink or something?'

'Yup, to high hell.'

'Ha-ha, good on ya, Walshee.'

A petite brunette woman came up beside them, her finger to her lips as if to tell Matt to not give her away. On her tippy toes, she leant into Slim. 'Hey, babe.'

Slim jumped so high he almost hit the ceiling. His face lit up like a Christmas tree when he spotted her. 'Sherrie, it's so good to see ya made it, babe.' Slim picked the woman up and spun her around.

Matt felt a rush of happiness. This must be the woman Slim had been going on and on about, the one he'd been a gentleman to when he was last here.

Sherrie kissed Slim smack on the lips, three times, and then once back on the ground she held her hand out. 'You must be Matt.'

'I sure am, nice to meet you, Sherrie.' He stood up and shook her hand, and gave Slim a subtle glance, as if to say how impressed he was. Slim grinned back at him like a lovesick teenager.

Oblivious to the men's silent conversation, Sherrie smiled wide, revealing a row of perfectly white teeth stark against her olive skin. 'It's really nice to finally meet you, Matt, I've heard lots about you.'

'All good, I hope.'

'Mostly.' She gave him a playful wink.

Matt liked her instantly. She gave off a warm, genuine vibe.

His arm wrapped around her shoulder, Slim stood beside her with not an inch between them, the look on his face letting everyone know he was proud as punch to have Sherrie by his side. The band began another song, an all-time favourite of the crowd, 'Country Boy' by John Denver. Grabbing Slim by the hand, Sherrie pleaded with him to come and dance. Quickly passing Matt his drink, he obliged while still trying to get out of it. Matt had to chuckle when he watched his friend's dance moves, Slim always having had two left feet. But he had to give him credit for effort, and Sherrie was having a ball.

The bar was a little less congested now, with most people having made it onto the dance floor, and Matt sat down again and enjoyed the space while he had it. A bikini-clad woman waltzed past him, the Akubra she'd just nicked off a bloke's head held high. Pushing through the crowd, she paused for blokes to deposit their hard-earned cash within it. Not wanting her to approach him, Matt tried to avoid her gaze, instead grabbing a glass and sculling it. He'd swallowed it before he realised it was Slim's rum and Coke. Damn it! He couldn't let Slim know, so he quickly ordered another, having to drink some of it because Slim had left a half-empty glass with him. Crisis avoided, and the delectable taste of rum in his mouth, he tried to go back to enjoying his ginger beer. A hard task – the rum and Coke sitting in front of him was like a carrot dangling in front of a horse. But he could damn well do it. Swivelling in his seat, he turned his back to it, doing anything he could to not pick the glass up again.

CHAPTER
19

The Mareeba Rodeo

The smells of horse, cattle, leather and show food wafted in the air. So far, with her brother and his mates watching the goings-on from the bar, Sarah had avoided running into Brad. Come the end of the bull riding, though, she'd have to pull her big girl boots on and deal with it. She wasn't doing anything wrong just by talking to him; she had to remind herself of that. It was Matt's insecurities, not hers, that made the situation uncomfortable. But on the other hand, she didn't want to do anything to upset him. It was a double-edged sword that she was honestly tired of trying to handle. As much as she would like to, she couldn't please everyone all the time. She'd have to go with the flow.

All around her, the grandstands were packed tight with people young and old; their eyes had all been glued to the action in the centre ring over the past couple of hours. Between the steer wrestling (Sarah liked to call it bull-dogging), barrel racing, buckjumping, a very flexible woman performing aerial acrobatics on a horse, and the clowns doing their usual side-splitting comedy routine with a three-wheeled motorbike, it had been an enjoyable show so far. Hoeing down on the last sticky sweet rib drenched in mouth-watering sauce, Sarah wiped her lips with a napkin. After devouring almost every rodeo treat on offer, she was so full she felt like she could burst. Lily sat beside her, a stick of pink fairy floss in hand. Her mate was going to be on a sugar high for sure.

Over at the chutes she could almost hear the spurs chink with each cowboy's defiant step, their chaps making even the scrawniest of them look sexy as hell to the young buckle bunnies screaming from the sidelines. The hard-core fans would be huddled at the back of the chutes in the hope of getting lucky with one of the riders. In between each bull ride, country music pumped out at ten thousand decibels, spurring the crowd on. Every now and then, a Mexican wave would ripple around the stands, and Sarah loved the sense of camaraderie and joined in the fun. With sideshow alley directly behind them, the screams of adrenaline junkies filled the air as they were thrown about in the air by huge mechanical arms. Sarah wouldn't be caught dead on one of the topsy-turvy rides, preferring to get on the back of a bull if she had to choose between the two.

The music stopped. With a slight crackle the announcer's twangy voice suddenly boomed over the speakers, letting everyone know it was coming up to the last ride of the night. Huddling closer to Lily for warmth, the temperature having dropped from thirty-three degrees to eighteen, Sarah felt a rush of both pride and excitement. Although she didn't know the rider, she still felt a flurry of butterflies in her stomach. All along the top railings of the chutes, testosterone-fuelled cowboys cheered their mate on. Inside the chute, the bull kicked and snorted as the brave cowboy slipped onto its back. Seconds later, he nodded, and the gate flew open. A Lee Kernaghan song blared over the speakers as the one-tonne brute exploded from the chute, at times with all four hoofs off the ground as it bucked and spun in mid-air. The protection athletes, who used to be called rodeo clowns back in the day, took positions front and centre in a bid to defend their bull-riding mate when he came off – putting their lives on the line was all part of the job. But with every buck the bull threw at the cowboy, the bloke hung on, his form perfect. The seconds ticked by like hours. The crowd stood, as did Sarah and Lily. The roar of the rodeo-lovers was electric. The eight-second horn blew, and lithe on his feet, the rider let go and landed upright, his smile dazzling as he tossed his hat in the air in triumph. But there was no time to stand around and bask in his winning glory as the bull charged and the man made a mad dash for the fence line, leaping up and over it just in time to avoid a horn to the rump.

Now close to ten o'clock and the show done and dusted, most people started to gather their things and make their way to the car park or the bar.

'You good to hit the dance floor?' Lily wriggled on the spot as if she had ants in her pants. Sarah smiled. Lily was most certainly on a sugar high. 'Let's do it.'

Carefully climbing down the massive grandstands, the two women made their way towards the bar area. A band was already playing, rocking out a Brad Paisley tune, 'Mister Policeman'. Following close behind Lily, Sarah made her way through the throng of partygoers, feeling a little like a fish out of water.

This used to be her stomping ground but, boy, oh boy, times had changed. Nearing the bar, the first person she ran into was Johnny Marsh, the farm manager. 'Hey, how's tricks, Johnny?'

'Sarah!' He grinned back at her, his face glowing a bright shade of red. 'I'm as crissed as a picket, but loving it.' He held his drink up, spilling half of it down his tomato-sauce splattered shirt – he'd clearly enjoyed a dagwood dog at some point. 'I wanna have a drink with you at midnight, to celebrate your birthday, so make sure you're still here.'

'Okely dokely, but pace yourself – otherwise you won't make it to midnight.'

'Don't you worry, I'll be here with bells on.' He turned unsteadily. 'Catch you laters, mate, the little boys' room is screaming for me,' he called over his shoulder, before disappearing in the sea of people.

Sarah was ninety-nine percent certain she wouldn't see him again tonight. He'd be passed out in his swag very soon by the looks of it.

Lily skidded in beside her, two shot glasses in hand. 'Here, drink this and be merry.'

Sarah had been hoping for a rum and Coke. 'What is it?'

'Sex on the beach, now drink.'

'Yes, ma'am.' Sarah chucked back the shot and squirmed. She tossed the plastic cup in the bin near her and then waggled a finger at Lily. 'No more of them, otherwise I'll be crawling out of here.'

'Spoil sport.' Lily grinned.

'Am not, I'm just being realistic.'

'True huh, we're such lightweights these days.'

'Hell yes we are.'

Daniel appeared beside his wife. 'Sis, 'bout bloody time you showed your face.' Reaching out, he tried to poke Sarah in the ribs but after years of playing this game Sarah avoided the prod with a stealthy backwards move.

Straightening, she folded her arms to avoid any more attempts to tickle her. 'How's your night going, bro?'

'Yeah, good, I'm pacing myself.' He leant on his crutches. 'I need to stay semi-sober to operate these bad boys, otherwise it could get really messy.'

'Good to hear, we don't want you breaking a leg.' She smiled. 'How's it feel, not being able to ride this year?'

'It sucks, but thems are the breaks.'

Sarah felt a tap on her shoulder and bracing herself for Brad's face, she was relieved when she spotted her old mate who owned the bucking bulls she'd just watched in the arena. He flashed her his customary Johnny Cash smile. He'd always reminded her of her country music god, the legendary Man in Black, same age, same looks. 'Greg!' She threw her arms out. 'It's been forever.'

After a tight hug she stepped back and he nodded sheepishly. 'Bloody oath it has been, Blondie.' His smile faded as he leant into her space. 'I'm so sorry I haven't been in touch much this past year, it's just, I don't know what to say about you know what.'

Sarah knew he was talking about Eve, and valued his honesty. Not many people knew what to say at such a traumatic time, so she understood where he was coming from. 'That's okay, mate. You rang and sent flowers to the funeral. What more could you do?'

'Yeah, I know, but it didn't feel like enough.'

She gave his arm a rub. 'It's all good.'

Greg put his arm around her shoulder. 'You're a beautiful soul, Blondie, you know that?'

'Why thankya … I do my best.'

'You most certainly do. I'll have to make a point of calling into Tranquil Valley next time I'm up this way. I could do with a couple more stud bulls and yours and Matt's are the best by far.'

'Do that, Greg, and plan to stay a few nights. We'd love the company. We'll have a BBQ and sit round the campfire.'

'Thanks, Blondie, will do.' He raised his beer. 'And happy birthday for tomorrow, sweetheart.'

'You remember?'

'Of course I bloody well do. I may be getting a bit long in the tooth these days, but how could I forget it's your special day.' He gave her a quick kiss on the cheek.

'Thanks, mate.' Sarah gave him another hug. A good man with a heart of gold, Greg was living proof to all the animal activists who believed rodeos were cruel that they were wrong in thinking this. He treated each and every one of his bulls like his children, putting food in their mouths before his. And when one passed away, he would shed a few tears – probably the only time he did.

'Anyway, I better get back to it. I left the boys loading up while I had a beer and caught up with a couple of mates. I've been gone almost half an hour so my dinner break is well and truly over.'

'Rightio, make sure you come and visit, Greg.'

'Promise I will.'

Greg said his goodbyes to Lily and Daniel as well, and then headed off. Sarah watched him go, noticing the limp he'd harboured for years after almost being crushed to death in the shutes by an irate bull. It had become more pronounced since the last time they'd caught up. But then again, he was nearing seventy, so what did she expect?

A woman brushed past her, knocking her a little, her heavily made-up face fleetingly visible before vanishing into the crowd. Her heart in her throat, Sarah swore it was Brooke, Matt's ex-girlfriend. But she couldn't be sure. She shook her head. Why would she be up this way when, last Sarah had heard, Brooke was living in New South Wales?

Before she could think about it anymore, Daniel came over and handed her a can of rum and Coke. Then another familiar face appeared, sending her heart rate skittering. The handsome, six-foot-tall man smiled at her. 'Hey there, stranger, how are you?' He leant in and brushed a kiss over her cheek.

Feeling like he was invading her space, Sarah took a step back. 'Bradley Williams, it feels like it's been years.' She had to silently admit he looked good, damn good, better than good. Age had done him a favour and turned him from a boyish looking guy into a very manly looking man.

'My bloody oath it has, Sarah.' Ignoring her bubble of space, he pulled her into a hug, spilling his beer down her back. 'It's so good to see you.'

Wriggling out of his arms as subtly as she could, she offered a smile. 'So how's life been treating you?'

'Not bad but not good. I had me a nice lady, but we broke up a few months back.' He shrugged. 'Just gotta roll with the punches.'

'That's it.' And didn't she know that all too well.

'So where's your other half?' He left the question hanging in the air.

Sarah thought Daniel would have already covered the subject of Matt's absence, but clearly not, or was Brad just fishing for information? 'Oh, he's out at Rosalee for the muster.' She took a glug from her drink.

'He is? Doesn't he have enough of a workload at home to keep him busy?' He tipped his head to the side as he waited for her response.

'We're in the quiet season now, so it gives him time to spend with the family on the station.'

'Ahh, I see.' He looked at her as if he knew much more than he was letting on.

She gave please-help-me eyes to Lily and her friend quickly came to her rescue. 'You wanna dance, girlfriend?'

'Yes, please.' Sarah had never wanted to dance so much in her life.

'Can I join?' Bradley boldly asked.

'Nope, this one's just for the sheilas.' Lily nodded towards Daniel. 'Stay and keep bugalugs company, seeing as he's an invalid and can't dance tonight.'

'Oi, fair go.' Daniel tried to playfully tap Lily with the end of one of his crutches but she skilfully sidestepped it before blowing him a kiss.

Talking on the dance floor was impossible, the music too loud to hear anything over it. Offering Sarah a smile, Lily gave way to the melody. Closing her eyes, Sarah moved in tune with it, the couple of drinks she'd enjoyed helping her to relax. Song after song, they danced to their heart's content. Every now and then she and Lily would spin each other around, their boot-scooting antics drawing cheers. When their drinks were finished, Lily dashed off and bought them another, so Sarah didn't find herself cornered by Brad again. Before she knew it, they'd been on the dance floor for over an hour and it was nearing midnight.

Covered in sweat, she said to Lily, 'I reckon I'm going to head off soon.'

'Wait until midnight, so we can sing you a happy birthday, and then I promise we'll call a cab and head off. Okay?'

Sarah looked at her watch. Only another fifteen minutes. 'Okay.'

'Good, now let's dance like there's no tomorrow,' Lily squealed.

Three songs later and they made their way over to Daniel. 'You look like you've just finished a session at the gym, sis.'

Sarah wiped the sweat from her brow. 'Tell me about it, I'm knackered.'

'It's midnight,' Lily shrieked as she pulled Sarah into a tight hug. 'Happy birthday, babe.' Before releasing her she kissed her on the cheek.

'Thanks, Lil.'

Daniel manoeuvred his way in beside her and wrapped his arm around her shoulder. 'Love ya, sis, happy birthday.'

Sarah smiled up at him. 'Thanks, bro, love you too.'

There was no sighting of Johnny Marsh, and hadn't been for a while. Her theory was right; he would have carked it in his swag hours ago. Brad appeared, a round of shots in his hands. 'Take one each, and let's raise a glass for Sarah's birthday.'

Not wanting to be rude, Sarah took hers, as did Lily and Daniel.

Brad raised his shot glass up in the air. 'To Sarah!'

'To Sarah!' they cheered, before throwing the shots back.

And then before Sarah could stop him, Brad wrapped his arms around her waist and bent her backwards, his lips landing fair and square on hers as he did.

Straightening, and then wrestling herself from his arms, she slapped him hard across the face, turned on her heel and stormed out of the bar with Lily racing after her.

⟡

Having left the blokes at the bar and now in the peace and quiet of the room, Matt checked his phone for the umpteenth time that night, his heart landing in his boots when there was still no reply from Sarah. What was she doing that was so important she couldn't text him? His mind began to play torturous tricks on him as he imagined her being wooed by all the eligible cowboys at the rodeo. He should be there with her, not here wallowing in self-pity. Fuck it. Fuck everything. Pacing the hotel bedroom, he looked to the darkness outside, at the stars that sparkled annoyingly.

'Please, Sarah, message me,' he whispered.

As if by a miracle his phone buzzed from the bedside table. He ran to it, and with shaking hands, looked at the glowing screen. His heart stalled. Stopped. What the? Brooke? What in the hell did his crazy ex want after all these years? He sat on the edge of the bed, readying himself for anything as he unlocked the screen. A picture message popped up, and it was like a sucker punch to the chest. Sarah was bent back in Bradley Williams' arms, his lips planted firmly on hers. They looked super cosy. The message beneath the photo read, *Thought you'd like to see what your cheating wife was up to ...*

What was left of his heart split in two. Wild rage filled him, anger so fierce and all consuming that for a moment the world seemed to distort and vanish. With adrenaline careening through him, a burning roar filled his ears. He fought to breathe as the room spun. He cried out, unsure of what he said. With a sudden start, he realised he'd punched the brick wall near his bed and blood now dripped from his knuckles. He needed to get out of here. Now. As if on auto-pilot, he picked up the LandCruiser's keys and stormed out the door, downstairs, outside, and to the drive-through bottle shop, hoping it was still open. The bloke was just closing up, but told him to quickly grab what he wanted. Scanning the shelves, he grabbed a bottle of scotch, stomped over to the counter to pay for it, and then made his way to the four-wheel drive. He wanted to be somewhere quiet and private, so he could drown his sorrows without getting the third degree. And why the bloody hell shouldn't he? There was nothing left for him to live for now that Sarah had clearly moved on. And all this time he'd thought they were going to be able to work things out, that he could trust her to never do anything like this to him. More fool him. He took big glugs while ignoring the little voice of reason trying to break through the fog in his mind. Sobs tried to escape him, but he fought them back. What good was crying going to do? He needed to tough this out and move on. Yeah right, it was going to damn near kill him to do that. Sarah was his wife, his life. Resting his head back, he squeezed his eyes shut, and stayed like that for a while, taking swigs from the bottle, and with each and every mouthful he cursed his pathetic life.

Suddenly he felt the desperate need to make a move. He knew it was stupid, reckless in fact, but at the moment he didn't give a stuff. Bottle in his left hand he turned the ignition, revving the old girl to life. He sat still for a few seconds, wondering what to do next. Where in the hell was he going to go at this time of the night, in the middle of the Australian outback? And what if he got caught drink driving? He couldn't afford to lose his licence. Just more fucking *what ifs* to add to his growing collection. He caught his reflection in the rear-view mirror. He looked like absolute shit. So much for getting himself back on the straight and narrow. Gripping the bottle between his thighs, he held his hands out. The tremor of an alcoholic was unmistakable. He sat back, staring through the bug and dirt-spattered windscreen. Is this what his life had come to?

With purpose, he slammed the accelerator to the floor, grinning like a madman as the tyres spun and then gripped the bitumen. He sat forwards and fought to keep the LandCruiser on the right side of the road as he headed out of the car park and onto the main thoroughfare. Reaching the outskirts of town, time seemed to stop, then rewind. Eve's face flashed before his eyes. He slowed and slammed them shut, squeezing the ridge of his nose. He was way too drunk to be driving, but the memories of her bloodied and broken body lying within his arms, of her chest falling and the final breath leaving her lips, tortured him, forcing him on. Eyes wide open, he switched on the stereo. Johnny Cash's version of 'Hurt' blared out, the lyrics fitting for a lonely, lost and desperate man. At the top of his lungs Matt sung the words about a transient life and graceless death, his hands clutching the steering wheel tighter and tighter as the road ahead got darker and darker. It was a song renowned for bringing people to tears, but not a drop would be shed from his eyes tonight. He glanced up. The rear-vision mirror showed nothing but deep, ceaseless black, as if mimicking the world he'd lived in since Eve's death, and was about to live in without Sarah by his side. He dared a glance at the butt of the shotgun resting beside his seat. He tried to remember Eve alive, as the happy, carefree little girl she'd been, but each time he tried to conjure up her pretty face, it would fade and bubble and blister, like a photograph left sitting in the baking Northern Territory sun.

As the miles and time passed, the landscape shifted to desert. Slowing and then taking a random turn, he headed off the beaten track. He had no idea where he was going, but he wanted to go somewhere he could yell out loud, to try to let all the pain he was holding inside free. He shook his head, trying to rid the blurry haze from his mind as the four-wheel drive rattled along the rutted dirt road, the headlights intermittently lighting up the track ahead. And then he spotted it – the glowing red fuel light letting him know he was almost empty. As if on cue the LandCruiser spluttered and eventually came to a full stop. He was out of fuel and in the middle of fucking nowhere.

'Fuck you!' he roared, his voice carrying. A deep, wrenching sigh escaped him, taking a part of his soul with it. Raging blood coursed through his aching heart. He plucked his phone from where he'd tossed it on the dash, and as expected, there was absolutely no service. He briefly considered calling 000, but then he didn't want the stigma attached to a bush rescue. He'd got himself into this mess; he needed to get himself out of it. Same as his damn shitty life.

Climbing out, he tossed the empty scotch bottle on the floor. Grabbing the gun and a couple of bullets, he slammed the door shut, shoved the bullets into his pocket and then kicked the tyre for good measure. A disconsolate walk back to Mount Isa seemed inevitable; the only problem was, he had no idea where he was. He looked to the sky, trying to work out his position from the constellations, but his drunken state of mind wouldn't allow it.

With one unsteady foot in front of the other, he took potluck and headed west, staggering left and right as he tried to walk forwards.

What felt like hours later, and with his mobile almost flat, he begrudgingly used the phone's torch to see what he'd bumped into. He glared at the *No Entry* sign as if it were a challenge. *Miller's Gold Mine, Private Property, DO NOT ENTER.* He'd heard of this place and from memory it was roughly the direction he wanted to be heading. It hadn't been used for twenty-odd years, and word was ghosts lurked around every corner of it – not that he believed in ghosts. The only life around was the thorny saltbush sprouting out of the red sand, catching the light of his torch. He recalled talking to an old bloke years ago, one who claimed to have mined here in his twenties, and Matt hazily remembered him saying the route back to Mount Isa from here was treacherously steep, rocky, and exposed to thunderous gusts of wind that seemed to come from nowhere. But there wasn't a hope in hell he'd make it the long way around, so this was his only choice and he wasn't about to buckle. Up shit creek without a damn paddle, and with no drinking water – a huge no-no in this type of country – he had to start walking. If he stayed put it could be days before someone found him here, if he was lucky.

Climbing the fence, he crossed a dry riverbed, the wattle trees that lined it stooped down as if waiting for a drop of water to appear. As the incline grew steeper, his breath sharpened. A broad vista opened up on the horizon, the weathered peaks reaching up to the heavens in sharp, rocky points. Beyond that, the lights of Mount Isa were faintly visible. It was a long way off but he couldn't focus on that, he had to keep moving while it was still night time and cool. Surely he'd come across a farm soon enough.

He ambled on, unsteady on his feet from the alcohol but the predicament he'd found himself in was somehow sobering. When needed, he used the shotgun for balance as he manoeuvred his way down the rocky slope. But with the incline growing even steeper, he slowed and tucked the gun under his armpit, deciding to go down on all fours, backwards, so he could gain some leverage by grasping the rocks embedded in the ground. But halfway down, he lost his grip and slipped. Desperately trying to stop his freefall, he reached out for anything, but only started to slide faster. His elbows hurting from the gravel, he braced himself for the thump he would undoubtedly feel as he hit the bottom of the ravine. And boy, oh boy, did he hit the ground hard.

Bent down on his knees, he sat on his heels and tried to catch his breath. Grabbing his mobile phone from his jeans pocket he tried to use the torch again but it was now dead as a doornail. Cursing, he stood up and dusted himself off, the shotgun in hand. Even with taking careful steps forwards, the ground suddenly gave way beneath his boots, and he was slipping, fast. Frantically grappling for leverage, he felt his fingernails lifting before clawing at empty air. Gravity heaved at his helpless body, pulling him deeper, faster, down the abandoned mine shaft. The ground was swirling up to meet him and he could do nothing to help himself. The starlit sky tilted as he tumbled. He was about to die.

Nauseating fear engulfed him. Hot currents tore through him. He slammed into a sidewall on the way down. The pain lanced his mind, sliced into his body. His muscles convulsed. It felt like an eternity, but seconds later he let out a strangled cry as he slammed into the earth below with bone-shattering intensity, the shotgun landing beside him. An excruciating pain coursed through him as something heavy landed on his leg. Unable to move, he cried out for help, knowing it was useless.

Wincing from the pain, he moved to sit up while trying to wriggle his leg free, but it wouldn't budge. Reaching out, he felt a timber plank across his leg, weighed down by a rock the size of a boulder. From the position he'd landed in, it would be impossible to move it. At the very least he had to sit up, no matter how much it hurt, but try as he might, he just couldn't. Like fire-hot razor blades, pain punctured him from head to toe. He'd undoubtedly broken bones, but how many he wasn't sure. Rocky shale dug into his back. He gritted his teeth, trying to come to grips with the agony and waiting for the world to stop spinning. He wasn't sure which part of his body hurt the most. Raising his hand, he touched the back of his head. It felt sticky with blood. Sarah and Eve's faces flashed through his mind's eye. His baby girl was gone forever, but now, because of his stupid recklessness, he might never lay his eyes on his beautiful wife again. No matter what she'd gone and done with Bradley Williams, he loved Sarah with all his heart and soul. After what he'd put her through, he had to forgive her for anything she might have done – honestly believing he'd driven her to it.

Drawing in slow, deep breaths, he tried to stop the spinning sensation, but it wouldn't ease. It was dark, so dark down here – he couldn't see an inch in front of him. He could hear small creatures scurrying around and half expected one to start gnawing on him. The thought chilled him to the very core. Clammy dampness closed in around him. He. Had. To. Sit. Up. Sheer strength of will got him to a sitting position, his cries of agony echoing around the enclosed space as he did. And then he heard Eve's voice, as clear as crystal, calling for him. Waves of dizziness claimed him as he slumped forwards, and then everything went black.

CHAPTER

20

Clarkes' Fruit Farm, Mareeba, Far North Queensland

Sarah sat up, her thin cotton singlet soaked through, the pillow damp, and her heart pounding – and it wasn't because of her slight hangover or what Brad had tried to do. Grabbing her mobile, she looked for a message from Matt, but there was nothing. Arriving home and seeing the beautiful message he'd sent her around seven o'clock, she'd tried to call him several times, but it had gone straight to message bank – very strange when he was in Mount Isa, which had full service. Maybe he'd fallen asleep and his phone had gone flat. It was a possibility, but her gut told her that wasn't the case. Something was wrong, she could feel it in her bones. Had he gone and drunk himself into a stupor, and was lying in a ditch somewhere, hurt, or worse? The thought pierced her heart. She looked at the digital clock glowing in the darkness of her bedroom, 3.46 am. Duke stirred on his rug in the corner, and she whispered to him that she was okay. But she wasn't. Fear had wedged itself in the pit of her stomach, and she couldn't quite put her finger on why. But it was real, and palpable, and frightening. Climbing from the tousled sheets she slipped out, using her mobile for light, and tiptoed down the hallway to get some water. The floorboards felt cold beneath her bare feet.

Reaching the kitchen she left the light off, the moonlight glowing through the window bathing the room in silvery light. Gripping the side of the sink she stared out into the darkness, her irrational state making her half expect to see a pair of menacing eyes peering back at her. Glancing upwards, a river of stars dotted the black sky. Why couldn't she shake this feeling of unease?

Shrill in the silence of the night, her phone rang. She quickly went to answer before it woke her parents upstairs. It was the homestead's number – maybe Matt had gone home. Her heart took off in a wild gallop regardless.

'Hello?' She was almost too afraid to hear the voice at the other end.

'Sarah, it's Judy.'

Her fear increased, tenfold. 'Hey, is everything okay?'

'No, I'm afraid it's not, love …' Judy's voice trembled. 'Matt's gone missing.'

The ground feeling as if it were giving way beneath her feet, Sarah held onto the bench for support. 'What do you mean, missing?'

'The boys all went to Mount Isa for the night, and Matt said he was heading off to bed around midnight. When Slim went to hit the sack at about three, he found the room empty and Matt and the LandCruiser gone.'

'But why would he drive off in the middle of the night?'

'We have no idea.'

'Was he drinking?'

'Slim swears black and blue he wasn't.'

'Is his stuff gone too?'

'No, apparently his bag is still there.' Judy finally broke down and sobbed. 'Sorry, love, I'm beside myself with worry. None of this makes any sense.'

The memory of Brad kissing her claimed her mind – but there was no way Matt could know what happened, could he? She would tell him, when the time was right. It wasn't something she'd want him to find out second-hand. Although she felt she was about to fall to the floor, Sarah stood strong and bit back tears. 'Okay, well, let's try and remain positive he's okay. I'm going to pack some things and catch the first flight out to Mount Isa in the morning. We can take it from there.'

'Yes, love, Steve and I are about to drive to Mount Isa ourselves. We'll make camp at my sister's place there for now. We'll pick you up from the airport as soon as you get in.' She sniffled and then blew her nose. 'Text me and let me know what time you're landing, and in the meantime I'll let you know as soon as we hear anything more, okay?'

'Okay, Judy.' Her heart in her throat, Sarah choked back sobs. 'We're going to find him safe and sound, you'll see.'

'I hope you're right, love. We've spoken to the police but we can't officially report him missing until he's been gone for twenty-four hours, so at the moment it's all on us to try and work things out.' There was a muffled voice in the background. 'Steve's ready to go, so I better run. Bye for now.'

'Yup, see you soon, Judy.'

The phone going dead, Sarah slid down to the floor and cradled her knees to her chest. Fear coiled around her heart and squeezed it so tight she could barely breathe. Tears rolled down her cheeks and she let them fall. She wanted to tell Matt how much she loved him, and how stupid they were being, and how she couldn't live without him by her side. She wanted to tell him he was her everything, and no matter what, she was going to stand strong beside him, and love him and help him through to the other side. She wanted to tell him how much she believed in him, and how much of a great father he'd been to Eve, and how much of a wonderful husband he'd been to her. She wanted to fall into his arms and never let him go. For within his embrace, she felt she was truly home. Was she going to get a chance to tell him all of this? Surely God couldn't be that cruel, first taking her daughter, and now her husband. Could he?

From where she sat, Sarah could see the tip of the big yellow M of the Macca's sign on the main street of Mount Isa.

'I'm so sorry I'm not there with you, Sarah. I feel so helpless here.' Maggie's voice was tired, strained.

A little hard to hear with the amount of comings and goings at the house, Sarah pushed her mobile in closer to her ear. 'It's not your fault that there was only one seat left on the plane yesterday, Mum, or the fact there's none until tomorrow night.'

'I've rung the airline to ask them to let me know if there are any cancellations, so I can get there sooner, and they've promised me I'll be the first one they call. Lily has also put in a request to be on the waiting list, after me, of course. We're all so worried and want to be there for you.'

'Hopefully it will all be sorted soon, Mum, and then there's no need for you to rush out here.'

'I hope so too, Sarah. Poor Georgia, going into labour as all this is unfolding.'

'Yeah, she's not coping very well, but Patrick is trying to keep her as calm as possible.'

'It's all so unfair.' Maggie cleared her throat, something she did when she was trying not to cry. 'I love you.'

'Love you too, Mum.'

'Please let me know as soon as you hear anything, okay?'

'I will.'

'Bye, love.'

'Bye, Mum.'

Ending the call to her mother, Sarah tried to draw strength from the earth beneath her feet. Her phone hadn't stopped ringing and text messages were coming in thick and fast from concerned friends and family. As much as she wanted to, she refused to break down, because if she did she'd be no use to anyone, especially Matt. Giving in to her fears and emotions would be like an admission to herself that there was something gravely wrong, and she wasn't going to acknowledge that. Matt would be okay, she had to find it within herself to believe that. But it was a struggle, especially when she saw the same fears she harboured reflected in the eyes of every single person she came in contact with.

It had been twenty-nine hours since Judy had called her, and there was still no sign of him, or the LandCruiser. It was as if he'd just dropped off the edge of the earth. Calls to his mobile went straight to message bank, so it was either flat, turned off, or he was out yonder where there was no service. Didn't he want anyone to find him? In his state of mind it was a possibility. Or had something untoward happened? Her gut wrenched with the thought. The outback was a colossal, mostly uninhabitable place, but surely someone would have to see something soon, wouldn't they? If and when they did, she prayed it wasn't going to be the news she was terrified of. Her heart couldn't take losing another loved one.

Squinting, she looked to the horizon. The sun had reddened the sky but the grass beneath her feet was still heavy with dew. Sighing, she rose from the rope swing that hung from the purple-bloomed jacaranda, tipped out what was left of her cold cup of tea, and then tiptoed across the back lawn of Matt's Auntie Mary's place, which was conveniently smack bang in the middle of town. With people everywhere, she'd needed to get out of the house for some fresh air and some quiet so she could think. But she hadn't come up with any reasonable answers to where Matt might have gone to in the middle of the night. She was bone-tired, but running on pure adrenaline, so she soldiered on. She'd become a master of doing so this past year. The hot shower she'd had at four this morning had been more of a necessity than a choice. No one in the house had slept at all during the night, and she'd needed something to wake her up – the countless cups of coffee weren't doing anything other than making her more jittery, so she was now drinking tea.

Walking back inside she found Slim, Whiskers, Showbags, Tumbles, Pothole and Hasselhoof sitting at the dining table with the two plain-clothed coppers she'd met yesterday, maps spread out in front of them. Bleary eyed, Judy and her sister stood behind them all, tissues in hand. No words were needed as Judy gave her a look that screamed hopelessness. Sarah felt exactly the same. Matt was now officially a missing person; his face was plastered all over the telly and his name was in every news report on the radio. Although surreal to see and hear, it was what they wanted, to get the word out there.

Even though she knew none of them had an appetite, Sarah busied herself making cuppas and sandwiches. They needed sustenance, and she needed to do something, anything, rather than just stay still. She spread out the entire loaf of bread and buttered each slice. Judy joined her and cut the cold roast beef in thin slices, to try to make it go round. Her sister, Mary, sliced some tomatoes. Then they placed it all on the buttered bread. It all felt so normal, too normal.

The crunch of tyres stopped in the driveway of the traditional Queenslander. Car doors slammed and Steve's voice could be heard over everyone's. He'd been out all night searching everywhere he could think of, with no success.

He stormed in, an air of urgency shadowing him. Sarah had never seen him look so pissed off and anxious. Three equally dishevelled, weary looking men followed him. They all huddled around the table, each of them pointing to areas on the map that they thought were worth a search. Steve focused on the fifty-something-year-old copper. 'So are you lot going to do something now that it's official?'

'Yes, Mister Walsh, we're doing everything we can to get the search underway.'

'Well, you need to hurry the hell up.' Steve glared at him. If looks could kill, the copper would have been dead.

The other police officer's phone rang, and everyone quietened, all eyes on her. Standing, she stepped away from the table with her back to them, her voice low. She nodded, hung up and then spun to face them. The room was so quiet Sarah would have heard a pin drop.

'A cattle farmer has rung in to report a sighting of the LandCruiser from the air, about five clicks outside of Miller's gold mine, but at the moment there's no sign of Matthew.'

Collective gasps were followed by what sounded like a million questions. Sarah stood back, her heart in her throat, not able to get a word in edgeways, even if she wanted to.

'Everyone quiet,' Steve roared, his voice so loud it almost echoed off the walls. Silence fell instantly. 'So what's the plan of attack?'

White as a ghost, Judy moved to his side.

Poker-faced, the copper joined her colleague back at the table. 'We're working on getting the search team out there.'

Leaning on the back of the chair Slim was sitting on, Steve blew a weary, angry breath. 'Working on it how?'

'We think he might have fallen down one of the abandoned mine shafts, and if he has, that's a very dangerous rescue to undertake. We've got a specialised search crew flying in from Cairns. They'll be here in less than three hours.'

'Three hours? Are you fucking kidding me? My son could die in that time, if he isn't dead already.'

Her entire body shaking, Sarah leant against the sink for support.

Judy placed her hand on Steve's back. 'Please take a breath, love, they're doing their best.'

'I know, Judy. I'm sorry. But I can't sit around twiddling my thumbs until the search team gets here.' Steve looked to all the grave faces in the room. 'Who's in?'

Every man voiced his agreement.

The older officer stood. 'Please, Mister Walsh, Miller's mine is well known for being a hazardous place. Please wait until the team gets here so we don't have more lives to save.'

Steve's gaze was challenging. 'Can you arrest me if I walk out of here?'

'No, sir.'

'Right then, let's head, you lot.'

Sarah finally found her voice. 'Can I come too, Steve?'

'Can you promise me you'll stand back and let us men do the dangerous stuff?'

'Yes, cross my heart.'

'Then of course you can, jump in with me.' He turned to a pale-faced Judy. 'I want you to stay here, love. It's no place for you, or your sister, out there.'

Judy went to argue but Steve shushed her. 'It's a treacherous spot and we don't need you hurting yourself. I'll let you know as soon as I know anything, okay?'

Nodding, Judy broke down. Mary ran to her side and wrapped her arms around her.

Steve was unnervingly silent the entire trip, as were Slim, Tumbles, Pothole and Whiskers, all four men crammed illegally in the back seat of the Toyota Sahara. Another carload of men followed in a beat-up, dusty old four-wheel-drive troop carrier. Breaking all speed limits, it was a little over an hour and a half to the deserted mine, Sarah had learnt that much. Every now and then Slim would give her shoulder a squeeze as if to say it was all going to be okay. No words could express how much it meant having him here – he was Matt's closest mate, and a very special one of her own too.

The mid-morning sun shone across the windscreen in a blinding yellow glare, making it nearly impossible to see the dirt track they'd turned onto almost thirty minutes ago. Why in the hell had Matt come out here? Pulling her sunnies from the top of her head, Sarah slipped them on. She stared out at the landscape, baked dry and heavy with heat. It appeared to stretch on into the never-never, shimmering in heatwaves. Even though the air-conditioner was pumping, sweat covered her and ran in rivulets down her back, and her legs stuck to the seat. Her gut wrenched and tied in knots. How could anyone survive if hurt and alone in this godforsaken country?

They spotted the tray-back four-wheel drive up ahead. Reaching it, Steve jolted to a stop and before he'd even cut the engine, he leapt out. Trying to open the driver's door of Matt's LandCruiser, which was obviously locked, Steve pressed his face up against the window and peered in. Sarah held her breath, hoping, praying, that if Matt was in there, he was okay. But then Steve stepped back and shook his head as though defeated. The blokes circled him and they started talking.

Stepping out the passenger side, she quickly made her way over. Coarse red dust rose with each step, and billowed around her legs. Standing deep in bull dust, she tugged her hat down to ward off both the sun and flies. Nearby, cattle stood in what little shade they could find. Their heads drooped, they chewed their cuds slowly; in this heat it seemed even eating was too much effort. Suddenly, the ground shook as if an earthquake had hit. All talk stopped. Eyes widened as they all looked this way and that. She grabbed Steve's arm and froze, holding her breath, as the source of the thudding emerged from a thicket of saltbush. A herd of emus, at least ten of them led by two huge old birds, sprinted past at a dizzying speed, their gawky eyes fixed straight ahead. Like pistons connecting to the ground, the power of their stick-thin legs was incredible. Sarah and the men all breathed a sigh of relief and got back to planning the next step when a four-wheel drive appeared up ahead, almost launching off the rise. With expert dexterity, the driver tore across the flat and came to a halt in a cloud of red dust. The white-haired driver, who Sarah guessed was in his seventies, leant on the window frame, his weathered face solemn. 'Name's Ron, Ron Donaldson. Which one of you is Steve Walsh?'

Steve stepped up to the driver's window. 'I am, why's that?'

'I think we may have found your son.'

'Alive?'

Terrified of the answer, Sarah almost pushed her hands over her ears.

Ron paused. 'We're not sure.' He thumbed to an Aboriginal man beside him, who looked like a beacon in his blue bushman's shirt and wide, old, curl-brimmed Akubra. 'After spotting the vehicle from the sky, I went and got Getty here and asked him to give us a hand. He followed the tracks and they disappear into one of the old mine shafts, but there's no response from the bottom when we call out.'

It was all Sarah could do to keep herself standing upright.

Steve's face now as pale as Judy's had been back at the house, he gripped the car door. 'Can you take me there?'

'Of course, all of you get up on the back.' He pointed to Sarah. 'Except you ... women ride in the front.'

All ten men aboard and Sarah squished in between Ron and Getty, Ron spun the four-wheel drive around and headed back from the direction he'd come. An assortment of rusty nails and screws rattled on the dust-covered dashboard. The ABC radio hummed in the background, the volume so low Sarah couldn't make out a word.

'How did you know where to look?' Sarah's voice was quiet, quivering.

'Getty knows every stone and tree in this land, because he belongs to it, is a part of it. He's well known for his tracking skills – it's in his bones.'

Getty offered her a gentle smile and she returned it.

They rattled over a cattle grid. 'And I mined the place in the seventies, so I kind of know my way around the shithole.'

Approaching a steep ravine that tapered down into a flat bit of land, Ron pulled to a stop and jumped out. 'We'll all have to walk from here. The ground's too unsteady to drive on it.' He waited for the men to pile out of the tray, and then hands on hips, he addressed them. 'And watch ya bloody step, you lot, there's shafts everywhere, even where you can't see them.'

Sarah followed Getty out the passenger door just as a gunshot fired.

Like a bull at a gate, Steve took off across the unstable ground. Calling out, Ron reminded him to be careful while the whole lot of them raced behind Steve, none of them really watching where they stepped other than sidewinding around massive, gaping abandoned shafts.

Another shot fired out, echoing around them, and they pulled up just shy of where the scent of gunpowder lingered, above a deep, dark hole.

'Don't shoot, we're up here.' On all fours, Steve lay on his stomach and warily stuck his face over the hole. The rest of the men stood back a little, watching, waiting. 'Matt, it's your dad. You okay, mate?'

They were met with an eerie silence. The thought that Matt might have just taken his own life horrified Sarah. Falling to her knees, she silently began to pray for a miracle. It was all she could do to stop from throwing herself into the cavernous hole to be with him. Slim came in beside her, and on his knees wrapped his arm around her shoulders. She collapsed into him, shaking as if she were freezing to death.

'If you can hear me, we're going to get you out, okay. Hang tight, Matt, we're coming.' Steve's voice was laced with fear and desperation.

Ron stepped up beside Sarah and Slim. 'We'll have to be careful, Steve, or we're going to knock the whole lot down on top of him.'

Steve looked frantic as he met Ron's eyes. 'How in the fuck are we going to do that without the rescue team here? And I need to get down there, to see if he's ...' Steve's fear-filled eyes met Sarah's. 'Hurt. To see if he's hurt.'

Getty finally spoke up, his voice quiet but at the same time commanding. 'We'll have to put a log across the middle, so we can lower someone down without disturbing the edges too much, hey. We got some rope in the ute we can use but we need the lightest bloke here to do the job.' He nodded. 'Which by the looks of things will be me.'

Steve slid carefully back and came to standing. 'I can't thank you enough, Getty.'

'If he's badly hurt I'm not sure I'll be able to get him back up without the help of the rescue team, but I can at least go down with the first-aid kit and a torch to see if I can help him in the meantime.' Getty pointed to a decaying lean-to, the corrugated-iron roof held up by three thick tree trunks. 'If we can pull one of them from the ground, it'll do the job, hey.'

Without giving it another thought, the men got to it, groaning and swearing and tugging until the log broke free and rolled to the ground. Sitting with her knees hugged to her chest, Sarah rocked back and forth, too scared to call out to Matt. She couldn't bear the silence in response. Haunting flashbacks of the day they'd lost their darling little Eve traumatised her even more. It all felt surreal and she was too numb to even cry.

Working quickly but carefully, they laid the trunk across the gaping hole. Returning from the ute with a huge roll of thick rope, a first-aid kit and a torch in hand, Ron knelt beside the hole and tied the rope firm and secure. Getty then looped it around his waist in a hangman-type knot. Sitting on the edge, he slowly eased his way across the trunk, the rest of the men hanging tight to the length of it, in readiness to lower him. Giving them a wave, Getty grabbed the rope above his head and then nodded to be let down. Sarah found herself holding her breath. The rope swayed and twisted as he slowly dropped from sight, the sound of his voice saying, 'Lower, lower,' slowly drifting away from them.

Voices once again stirred Matt from the dark place he was suspended in. Hovering between consciousness and oblivion he fought to blink open his lead-heavy eyes. He prayed the two shots he'd fired before losing consciousness again had caught the attention of whoever was above. His mouth drier than a desert, and the blackness suffocating, he tried to call out. But he couldn't. He was weak, so weak. Small stones tumbled and fell, and he covered his face to avoid being hit.

And then a torch shone out, almost blinding him. Blinking, he tried to focus. A man appeared. 'He's alive,' he bellowed upwards, before smiling a gentle smile, his teeth stark white against the dark colour of his skin. 'You hurt, pal?'

Matt nodded. 'Yeah, I think I've broken some bones.' His voice was faint, and husky with thirst, almost inaudible.

The man knelt down beside him. 'I'm Getty, nice to meet ya,' he said with a cheeky grin that made Matt smile.

'G'day, Getty,' was all he could muster.

'I'm going to get this boulder and timber off your leg, and then I'll check you out, okay? A rescue team is on the way, and I reckon we should wait for them to haul you outta here, in case you've hurt your back, hey. Sound good?'

'Anything's better than this,' Matt mumbled, trying his best to be light hearted. With the bottom of the mineshaft now lit up like daylight, he finally got to see what the tomb he'd been encased in looked like. Tiny to the point of being claustrophobic, and with decaying walls on either side of him, it was probably a good thing he'd lain in the dark. He could just make out joyous cheers above, and his father's booming voice, and then he heard Sarah's. She was calling his name, and telling him how much she loved him. Angelic and soothing, it brought him to tears.

With a groan, Getty moved the boulder, followed by the heavy plank, and grimaced. 'Lots of blood.' He leant in and looked closer. 'But your foot's still attached so that's a good thing, hey.' He grinned again and Matt was thankful for the humour. 'Can you move your toes?'

Matt tried, and although it was agony, he could.

Getty gave him the thumbs up. 'That's a good sign.'

With the *wop, wop* of chopper blades slicing through the air, Matt breathed another sigh of relief knowing he was going to get out of here real soon. He felt his heart reach up for Sarah's.

Getty sat down beside him. 'Not long now, brother.'

Feeling his eyelids drooping closed and fighting to keep them open, Matt tapped Getty's leg. 'Thank you, so much.'

Thirty minutes later and he was being lifted out of the ground. Moved from the rescue board and onto a stretcher, familiar faces surrounded him.

'It's good to see you, son.' His father had tears in his eyes.

'You too, Dad,' he murmured.

And then he saw Sarah, her face dirty and tearstained. He reached for her hand and she grasped his. Her fingers trembled against his own. All he wanted to do was pull her into his arms, and never, ever, let her go, but he didn't have the strength right now.

'I'm so relieved you're okay.' She rested her forehead against his, her tears falling and rolling down his cheeks. 'I love you so much, Matt.'

He choked back emotion as he pushed strands of hair from her face. 'I honestly believed I was going to die without being able to tell you how much I love you one more time.'

'Well, you can tell me over and over for the rest of our lives.' She kissed him gently on the lips.

'I love you, Sarah, so much. I'm so sorry I've …'

She placed a finger over his lips to shush him. 'No more sorrys, just please don't scare me like that ever again.'

'I won't, ever, I promise.'

'And no more drinking.'

'You have my absolute word.' He wanted to ask her about Brad, but not now. That time would surely come.

'Good, then you and I are going to be just fine.' She smiled, so lovingly, so tenderly, it reached in and caressed his aching heart. There was light at the end of the tunnel they'd been trapped in since Eve's death. Maybe just a single ray, but Matt truly believed they were on their way to coming out the other side of this more in love than ever.

EPILOGUE

Far North Queensland
Ten months later

There were no more sleeps until the most anticipated day of her life. Sarah took a few deep breaths. Excitement swirled in her belly. After eloping a few years back, this would be the wedding they never had. Glancing at her watch, she calculated it would be exactly one hour and fifteen minutes before her dad walked her down the aisle. She looked to where her wedding dress hung from the door – a satin gown with hints of lace throughout and tiny pearls stitched to the bodice. Lily and Georgia were busy getting their hair and make-up done, and her mum and Judy were running around like headless chooks, apparently making sure all the final details were covered. As much as it meant the world to her having all the special women in her life together, the hustle and bustle of the room began to unnerve her. Needing a few moments alone, she stepped out onto the balcony. She breathed in the salty air, the view from her beachside apartment breathtaking. Down on the private stretch of the beach, people were busy setting up the place where she and Matt would renew their vows. A path of red rose petals had been laid, and it looked striking against the golden sand. The bales of hay on either side set the scene perfectly.

'You ready, babe?' Lily's gentle voice caught her attention.

Turning, she smiled. 'I sure am.'

Her hair swept into cascading curls and her make-up done but not overstated, Sarah stood still as Lily and her mum helped her into her wedding dress. She slipped her arms through the spaghetti straps, loving the feel of the ivory satin as it slithered down her body.

'Let me get the zip, Sar,' Lily said.

Sarah held her breath as Lily pulled it up, hoping the tiny life forming inside of her wasn't visible just yet. Exactly twelve weeks to the day; she and Matt had decided to tell everyone at the reception that they were expecting – not even Lily or her mum knew their beautiful secret.

'Okay, you can take a look in the mirror now.' Lily sniffled and fanned her face, obviously worried about crying and ruining her make-up.

With her mother, Judy and Georgia also fighting back tears, Sarah found herself doing the same thing as Lily ... fanning her face. 'Stop it, you lot. We all promised we weren't going to cry today.'

'I know, I know. Sorry, love,' Maggie said with a tender smile.

Lily smiled. 'You look so beautiful, babe. I can only imagine how Matt is going to be when he lays eyes on you.'

Sarah stepped in front of the full-length mirror. For a moment, she was so taken aback she couldn't speak. With her hair done and the soft make-up she almost didn't recognise the woman staring back at her. The sweetheart neckline accentuated the cut of the ankle-length dress, and the split up the side, to just above her knee, added a hint of her cheekiness.

Maggie stepped in beside her daughter, her hand tenderly resting on her back. 'You happy, love?'

'I'm more than happy, Mum. I'm over the moon.'

Maggie cupped her cheeks. 'Good, because you and Matt deserve all the happiness in the world. I'm so proud of you both, getting through everything and coming out even stronger.'

Sarah sniffed back more tears. 'Thanks, Mum, for being there for us the entire way. I love you so much.'

'Of course, that's what mothers do.' Maggie pulled her into a hug. 'Love you, my sweet, beautiful daughter.'

Sarah took one last glance in the mirror while her mum bustled out to join the rest of the crew waiting in the lounge room. After double-checking she had everything and spraying on her delicate perfume, she joined them.

Daniel was sitting beside Lily on the couch, looking damn handsome in his tuxedo. 'Wow, sis, you've scrubbed up well.' He turned to Lily. 'And you, my sexy wife, look damn hot too.'

'Thanks, Dan, please tell me you've got the rings?'

'Yup, right here.' He patted his trouser pocket. 'How are you feeling, Sar?'

'Nervous as hell, but excited at the same time.'

'That's to be expected. I was shitting my daks on my wedding day.'

Lily threw him a sideways scowl.

Daniel grinned sheepishly. 'I was shitting my daks in a good way, Lil.' He jumped up and clapped his hands. 'Come on then, let's get this show on the road, ladies.'

After a perilous journey from the room to the beach, her dress having got caught in the lift door, Sarah stood next to her father. Waves curled and rushed to the shore. The music to cue her arrival started – 'Words Cannot Say' by Adam Brand. Butterflies filled her, and fluttered and swooped. Guests craned their necks to watch Lily and Georgia walk down the aisle. Then it was her turn. She took a deep breath as everyone stood to watch her head towards her destiny. She smiled as her father entwined her arm in his, the pride on his face immeasurable and the glassiness of his eyes almost bringing her to tears. Again. Ever so slowly, in time to the passionate country love song, he led her down the rose-scattered aisle. With every step there was a glimpse of her new boots, and her lace veil trailed along the sand.

Slim, Daniel, Liam and Patrick looked proud as punch to be standing by their mate, and Matt looked astonishingly handsome in his black suit and matching wide-brimmed hat. His smile was contagious – her prince charming, proof that fairy tales sometimes do come true. A radiant glow fanned throughout her, from her feet to her cheeks, and warmth spread through her chest. She was so proud of how far he'd come, not having touched a drop of alcohol for ten months now, and the love they shared was beyond anything she'd ever thought possible. She couldn't fathom how they'd come so close to walking away from each other.

Reaching Matt, her dad handed her over, and her heart skittered even more just by being near him. 'Howdy, cowboy,' she said with a wicked grin.

His smile from ear to ear, Matt gave her hands a squeeze. 'Hey, baby, you look amazing.'

'Thankya, and so do you.'

For the next ten minutes Sarah heard little of what was said, the pounding of her heart and the intense look of love in Matt's eyes drowning out the words of the celebrant. That was, until the celebrant announced it was Matt's time to speak his vows.

Clearing his throat, he held her gaze. 'My beautiful Sarah, you've been my best friend, my mentor, my playmate, my confidante, and were the most amazing mother to our darling Eve in her short time on this earth ...' He tripped over his words, tears filling his eyes. Sarah gave his hand a gentle squeeze, letting him know she was there for him as she blinked back tears. One slipped down his cheek and she reached out to wipe it away, the intense moment passing between them shared by all, many of the guests now wiping damp eyes too. He straightened and gripped her hands tighter. 'I have loved living and growing with you by my side. But most importantly, you're the love of my life and you make me happier than I could ever imagine. You love me in ways I never thought possible, and even when I deserve to be loved the least, you flip the tables and love me even more. And through it all you've made me a better man. I'm truly blessed to be a part of your life, and I look forward to all the happy memories we're going to make, together. I love you so much, baby.'

Sarah was struggling to keep it together, Matt's words touching her to the very core. And then it was her turn. Still holding his hands in hers, and looking into his eyes from beneath her veil, she offered up her vows.

'Matt, my love, we have already walked so many roads together, some so dark we couldn't see two feet in front of ourselves, but we made it through, and on this day, a new adventure begins. I want you to know how much of a wonderful father you were to Eve, and I also want you to know that I'll always stand by your side, no matter what life throws at us, as your partner in life and love. We'll laugh together and sometimes cry together. I'll inspire you and continue to be inspired by you.' Her voice trembling and tears filling her eyes, she took a brief moment to compose herself. 'I'll cheer you on as you follow your dreams, and I have no doubt that you'll always help me to achieve mine. I'll cherish you always and love you unconditionally. You are my one, my only, and the love of my life, now and forever.'

Matt's lips trembled as he smiled. And after a few more heartfelt words by the celebrant to round the ceremony off, she announced it was time to kiss the bride.

With a dazzling smile that made Sarah weak at the knees, Matt lifted her veil and pulled her into his arms. He placed a kiss on her lips and then spun her around in a dizzying circle. They were both laughing when he set her down on her feet, and Sarah had no doubt in her mind there would be many more years of love and laughter to be shared between them, because this man wasn't just her passionate loving partner, he was Eve's daddy, he was her rock, her best friend, her forever ... and once again was going to be the devoted father of their beloved child.

ACKNOWLEDGEMENTS

A standing ovation goes out to my remarkable cheer squad at Harlequin headquarters – my wonderful publisher Rachael Donovan, who makes me feel as though I can achieve my writer's dreams, no matter the barriers I need to jump or bowl over, my gifted editors ... Bernadette Foley, who totally gets me and my work, and Julia Knapman, a woman of many talents, the cover design wizards who've brought the outback to stunning life along with the inclusion of a very handsome bloke who looks oh-so-deliciously country front and centre, and the rest of the inspiring and supportive team who've helped make *Return to Rosalee Station* the very best it can be. I'm extremely blessed to be part of the Harlequin family and look forward to many more stories to come.

To my beautiful daughter, Chloe Rose. You're my everything, sweetheart. You brighten my every day, teach me so much with the way you view the world through such loving and innocent eyes, and inspire me to be the very best woman I can be in both my life and my career. It warms my heart to see you at your desk, writing your stories, so you can be like Mum – who knows, maybe you'll be a bestselling author one day too? Whatever path you walk in life, and whatever journey you choose, I will always be there, right beside you, loving you, cheering for you and supporting you through it all. Love you to the moon and back, darling, and then some. Xo

To my wonderful mum, Gaye, thank you for teaching me to always stand strong, and to fight for what I believe in. It's helped me to achieve every one of my dreams, and to also have belief in making future ones attainable. I love that we live so close now, and I enjoy every minute I get to spend with you. Here's to many more wonderful moments shared. Love you lots!

To my dad, John, your wise and gentle ways have guided me through so many journeys, both hard and happy. Thank you for always accepting me for who I am, and never judging me for the choices I make – both good and bad. Love you.

To my stepdad, Trevor – we may not see each other as often as we'd like, but our bond will always remain. You've been there for me since I was a little whippersnapper, and have instilled in me a belief that as long as I keep moving forwards, and smiling through it all, no matter how hard that might sometimes be, everything will work out just fine in the end. Love ya!

To my amazing sisters Mia, Rochelle, Karla, Talia and Hayley – thank you for being the wonderful, strong and inspirational women you are. I couldn't ask for better sisters, or more devoted aunties to Chloe – love you all heaps.

To Rachael Sharaz, what a beautiful shining soul you are! I'm so glad our mini-mes have introduced us to one another. I look forward to many more girls' nights shared over a bottle of wine and filled with enthralling conversations!

To my Soul Sister, Fiona Stanford, thanks for simply being you. I feel like I've known you for a lifetime and I couldn't imagine my writer's journey without you there, cheering me on along the way. Love and hugs xo.

To my German mate, Katharina (Katie), thank you for always being so excited to read my books – I'm sure they remind you of the all fun times we've shared in Aussieland over the years. Love ya, cowgirl! Xo

And lastly, but most importantly of all, a huge happy-dancing hurrah to YOU, the reader – a hug for each and every one of you! Thank you for plucking my book from the shelf, be it hardcopy or eBook, and diving into the pages – without you, I wouldn't be doing what I love day in day out. I hope Matt, Sarah and the rest of the motley crew have taken you on an unforgettable journey and that *Return to Rosalee Station* has taken you away from the pressures of everyday life, if only for a little while – to hell with the messy house, the unwashed dishes, the unkempt hair, and the pyjamas you might still be wearing well into the afternoon – we all deserve a little me time. ☺

Until my next book, keep smiling and dreaming … life is beautiful.

Mandy xoxo

Turn over for a sneak peek ...

Road to
Rosalee

by

MANDY
MAGRO

Available December 2021

mira

PROLOGUE

The fresh scent of the thousands of eucalypts the Blue Mountains were famous for lingered upon the air as dust-speckled dawn sunlight was snaking its way across the timeworn timber boards of the one-bedder farmhouse Lucy Harrison had called home for almost seven months. Her job as cook at the roadhouse out the front paid the rent.

She knew eighteen was too young to have a baby. She also knew she should have thought of that when she'd fallen into the charismatic stockman's swag at the B&S ball, a virgin and more drunk than she'd realised, but clued in enough to lie to him, both about her age and the fact she wasn't on the pill. It wasn't his fault she was in this predicament. She'd wanted him to want her, had spent half the night trying to woo him. If he didn't live thousands of miles away, she might have told him she was pregnant. In hindsight, she should have, but it was too late to harbour those kinds of regrets now. She'd made her decision and now she had to follow through with it. She just wished she had someone to hold her hand right now, to tell her everything was going to be okay. But she was very much alone, and terrified of what lay ahead.

Hopefully, the ambulance she'd called would be arriving soon because the contractions were coming faster, detonating inside her like fireworks. With each wave of primal pain, a deep intrinsic need to protect her baby grew, to the point that she knew now she couldn't put the child up for adoption. Her innate need to raise this child was almost overwhelming, ridding her of all her worries of not being able to handle motherhood.

Caressing the mound of her belly, she took in deep lungfuls of air, vowing to make her baby girl her life's purpose. Her girl would know nothing like the hellhole she'd grown up in, with a drunkard father and an absent mother. Her baby deserved the best life she could give.

With the next swelling contraction seizing her, she bent forward and gripped the verandah railings so she didn't buckle beneath the pain. After eight months of pretending, of covering it up with oversized clothes, it was really happening – she was going to be a mum. A single parent.

One day, she would move to the big smoke to be reunited with her best friend, Sally, and start a new life. But for now, this ramshackle house was her home, and would soon be her baby's home too.

One step at a time.

CHAPTER

1

Melody Harrison hated the fact today was her twenty-third birthday.

She didn't want anyone to say the word 'happy' to her. She wasn't happy, not in the slightest. Her mother was dying, her marriage was in ruins, she'd lost contact with her closest friends because of her insufferable husband and she was so bone-tired, she felt like curling into a ball and sleeping for a year. But she had to soldier on. One step at a time.

Finding a free seat amidst the chaos of commuters, she sank down and blinked back another onslaught of tears. Where had the strong, confident, happy young woman she'd been when she'd met Antonio four years ago gone? She'd give almost anything to find her again.

She was having a really hard time coming to terms with what the marriage counsellor had told her after their last session, on the quiet.

'Even though he's denying it, Antonio is a covert narcissist, Melody, and a very clever one. So don't blame yourself for not seeing it earlier, or for his cheating. I know you're hoping for a miracle, but he won't change. They never do. Even when they say they will. It's all a ploy to keep you tangled in their web. You can leave him, if that's what you feel you want to do. You're a strong woman. You can do this.'

Even though she'd lived through it, day in, day out, the words had been overwhelming in the moment. What was she meant to do with such information?

Once the fog has cleared, Melody had got to work. With a clinical diagnosis, she started researching on the web for countless hours. Now, she was starting to very clearly understand the demise of her marriage ... and of her self-worth. The intense love bombing, the devaluing, the breadcrumbs of false 'I'm sorry's and 'I promise to get help's, blow after blow to her trust, the crushing heartbreak, confusion, self-doubt. Then, when she was at her lowest point, manipulating her to believe in him again.

Even the fact he had declared his love so quickly, and they'd married within months, only for him to change tune the minute she moved in, going from 'I love you' to 'I choose to love you because you're hard to love.' Now she saw the pattern so very clearly.

Her heart had been crushed when she'd discovered that her husband wasn't the big romantic at heart he'd led her to believe he was. As a young married woman, she'd still held onto her high hopes for a happily-ever-after, even though a big part of her had screamed to run for the hills. So she'd stayed in the hope the romantic man she'd met would resurface. And here she was, years later, still waiting.

Golden sunlight and engulfing darkness mingled as the Sydney metro train sped through a maze of graffitied tunnels intermittently broken up by flashes of wintery fog, banked-up traffic and high-rises. Turning up the bluegrass melody playing from her AirPods, she sighed wearily. If only the view was instead of the endless countryside in which she'd spent her childhood in. Her days spent exploring the wilds of her backyard, the Blue Mountains, on foot or horseback had been filled with so much happiness. She and her mum had spoken about moving back there one day, if she ever unravelled herself from the clutches of Antonio and her beloved café, but then, in the blink of an eye, everything has changed. Her mum had been given the devastating diagnosis and everything in Melody's world had been tipped upside down and inside out. How was she meant to get through this? How could she come out the other side unbroken? The world was going to be a very lonely place without her mum to turn to.

She twisted her wedding band around her finger, and then, as she had many times the past couple of weeks, almost slipped it off. But as it wedged on her knuckle, she stopped herself. The thought of the mess that would follow if she asked for a divorce stopped her – she didn't have the strength for such turmoil right now, nor did she want the weight of it on her mother's already heavy heart. There were way bigger fish to fry in her turbulent life.

Melody was well aware that her focus needed to remain on her mum because as much as she didn't want to believe it, she knew they didn't have long left together. With that timely reminder, she found herself choking back sobs again. She'd made a promise to herself that she wasn't going to cry today, and a stickler for never breaking a promise to herself or anyone else, she had to try and hold it together. She owed herself that much.

Feeling as if the weight of the world was upon her small shoulders, she breathed in deeply then sighed it away. She'd never taken so many desperate deep breaths in all her life. Having sardined herself between an elderly lady with her nose buried in a book and a clean-shaven man in a suit whose attention was held fast by the glow of his laptop, she felt safe enough to allow her heavy eyelids to drop. She recalled Aunt Sally's advice and did her best to envision lying on a white sand beach, the rolling waves ebbing and flowing, seagulls floating on the gentle breeze above her. As nice as that fantasy was, it was tough to remain in such a beautiful place for long when her mother was living in daily hell of pills and chemo and the spectre of imminent death.

With her heart squeezing tighter, she tried to ignore the almost unbearable weight of fear and heartache. How she was going to handle the next chapter of her life was beyond her comprehension, but her mother had taught her from a very young age that it's one step at a time. That's all she could do.

Opening her eyes, she realised they were almost at her station. Standing, she tossed her handbag over her shoulder and, reaching up on her tippy toes, steadied herself with an overhead handhold as the train screeched to a halt. With the morning rush hour at its peak, as soon as the door slid open, she was propelled forwards. Elbows out to protect herself, she squished out among a sea of commuters. Then, one foot after the other, she turned left and strode towards the stairs that led up and onto the street. Racing up the stairwell and into the mayhem of Sydney's CBD, she glanced skywards as another crack of thunder reverberated off the skyscrapers engulfing her. After weeks of tempestuous weather, she yearned to feel the caress of sunlight against her skin. As if mimicking her tortured soul, the slate-grey sky was heaving with ominous black clouds aching to dump their heavy load. She sympathised with Mother Nature's need to unleash her vehemence, because she too felt like she was a pressure cooker about to explode. Or implode. She wasn't sure which would be worse.

The past three months had been her worst nightmare, and still, the worst was yet to come. She dared not to focus on it right now. That would come in the dead of night, when she lay awake, staring at the ceiling through teary eyes.

Frenzied people brushed past her, almost all of them walking blind with their gazes glued to their phones. If she had a choice, she'd toss her mobile in the bin – in her opinion, it had taken away people's need to really connect, eye to eye, heart to heart, soul to soul. The only reason she had the damn thing was for important calls, and to keep up with the social media avenues she used to promote her gastronomic masterpieces, or food porn, as Marianna, her business partner and mother-in-law, liked to call it. Posing and taking selfies for all the world to see to then tally up how many likes she got was worse to her than cutting off a finger. There was more to life than what other people thought of her. As long as they felt her emotion in the food, that was all that mattered. She'd made a name for herself in the foodie circles, and people came from far and wide to taste her culinary skills – ones she'd first learnt from her mum, then finessed in the years of her apprenticeship.

Antonio was well aware she was the reason their café was so successful – it was her only saving grace according to him. Whenever anyone asked what her secret was, she always said it was the love she poured into everything she cooked, and she firmly believed that, because in the grand scheme of things, love was what made the world go round.

As if on cue, her phone chimed her message tone – *The Dukes of Hazzard* horn. Had her mother taken a turn for the worse? Her heart leaping into her throat, she yanked it from the depths of her handbag, relieved to see it wasn't a message from Aunt Sally – not her real aunt but her mother's best friend – but from Antonio.

Hey, Lorenzo has called in sick and we're run off our feet. You were meant to be here already. Are you far away? See you soon?

Melody quickly checked the time. She was barely running five minutes late. *Far out.* She grit her teeth and groaned. No 'hope you're okay' or 'how is your mum?' No, even though she didn't really want to hear it but it was the principle that he'd clearly forgotten *again*, 'Happy Birthday'. Antonio Calabrese could be so damn selfish. The man she knew now was a far cry from the one she'd fallen for as an eighteen-year-old. Young love was so hopeful, so heedless. *So naïve.*

Strutting faster now, she shoved her mobile back into the seemingly endless pit of her handbag. Stuff him, she wasn't writing back. She was only minutes away and trying to walk and text would only slow her down anyway.

Her boots feeling as heavy as the eyelids she was fighting to keep open, she jiggled on the spot while waiting for a crossing to give the green go-ahead. After a sleepless night spent by her mother's bedside, she really didn't want to be doing this today, but she didn't have a choice. Her share in the café was the only thing keeping her sane, as if life could somehow continue on through the hardest of times. She needed the distraction of it to ground her. As her beautiful mother would say, you got this, my darling.

But did she?

Her hurried footsteps echoing off the sidewalk, she took the corner, barely avoiding a head-on with an equally frazzled-looking man. She was about to apologise when he glared at her. Argh! Stuff him too. His fault as much as hers. She resisted giving him a piece of her mind as she stormed away. Whatever happened to common decency, compassion, empathy? To make matters worse, half a block from her workplace, the heavens opened up like god was emptying his bathtub. The rain lashed down by the bucketful, instantly soaking the ill-prepared through to the skin. People ran this way and that, hands and newspapers overhead, as if the water would somehow make them shrink. Her umbrella swiftly overhead, and her somewhat rainproof jacket pulled in tighter, Melody had always been taught to be prepared for anything. But she sure as hell hadn't been prepared for the devastating news delivered by the family doctor, and definitely wasn't ready to say her final goodbyes. No twenty-three-year-old should be. *Cancer is an absolute bitch.*

Reaching her destination, she breathed a sigh of relief. She'd made it – one hurdle down – now she had to try to get through the day without crying or losing her already very thin patience with Antonio. Glancing to the stone plaque beautifully etched with *Café Amore*, she pulled her brolly down and shook the droplets of water off. With floor to ceiling glass walls and a deck that was used in the summer months, the eatery had stellar views of the Sydney Harbour and the iconic Opera House. Not that she got to enjoy the view much. Her place was at the back of house, pouring her passion into the dishes – cooking was her

way of escaping from everyday life, and boy oh boy, she needed
that right now.

She heaved the door open, the tinkle of the bell lost amidst
the chatter of the breakfast customers and the drone of traffic
behind her. The scent of strong Italian coffee lingered, and she
breathed it in – she couldn't wait to enjoy a double-shot latte.
Making a beeline for the back, she avoided Antonio, weaving
his way through the tables, collecting plates and schmoozing the
clientele – he was a master at winning people over, especially
women.

Tucking wisps of hair that had escaped her plait behind
her ears, Melody headed into the heart of the hip eatery – the
kitchen. A huge pot bubbled on the stove, the scent of her famous
oxtail and pork mince bolognaise sending her tastebuds dancing,
an impressive feat when she couldn't recall the last time she'd
had an appetite. She and Marianna had spent countless hours
perfecting the recipe and now, it was close to perfect. Grabbing
the wooden spoon, she gave it a stir, the bubbles of rich tomato
goodness still not dark enough in colour, nor thick enough – it
would be another hour before it was ready to be cooled, the oxtail
plucked from the bones, and then served over freshly made pasta
for the lunch rush. She was in the mood to make pappardelle
today. The thick egg pasta would be perfect slathered in the rich
sauce and topped off with some freshly grated pecorino, possibly
a little chilli oil, depending on the diner's palate.

'Thank god you're here, Melody.' Appearing out of nowhere,
Antonio dumped a tray of dirty plates and cups into the sink
then spun to face her – clearly they were extremely busy because
he rarely got his hands dirty. 'Oh, man, you look like death

warmed up.' He bustled over, leaning in to kiss her. 'Did you get any sleep at all last night?'

'Gee whizz, Antonio, don't go sugar coating anything, will you.' Rolling her eyes at his lack of tact, Melody turned her cheek to his inbound lips, deflecting his kiss to somewhere more platonic. 'Unless you count a couple of hours with your eyes closed as sleeping, no, I didn't.'

Sighing, he rested against the bench, his dark eyes on hers. 'So how is she?'

'Not good, but you know Mum. She refuses to have me sitting at her bedside all day long, waiting for her to die.' She half shrugged and smiled sadly. 'Her words, not mine.'

Antonio shook his head. 'I don't know how you do it, sitting with her most of the night then coming in here six days a week.'

'I do what I have to.' The shattering image of Antonio lip-to-lip with some girl from his gym flashed through her mind and she blinked back the threat of tears. She wasn't going to break down at work again. She'd done that too many times lately, and she'd made a promise to herself not to. Besides, he didn't deserve any more of her heartbreak. 'As you know.' She shot him a look.

'Come on, Melody. When are you going to stop being so pissed at me for my stuff-up?'

She and Antonio had been having this same conversation over and over since she'd caught him red-handed three weeks earlier, making out with some buxom blonde with lips bigger than hot air balloons and boobs to match. It made her wonder how many times he hadn't been caught. Melody was relieved of the need to reply as Marianna Calabrese bustled into the kitchen.

'Oh bella!' Marianna said in her sweet, singsong voice, thick with an Italian accent. 'You made it, my precious daughter-in-law.' Her long dark hair, threaded with streaks of grey and tied back into a tight ponytail, swung to land over her shoulder when she skidded to a stop. 'And the happiest of birthdays to you, sweetheart. Your present is still on the way. It got held up in the post, but it's coming.'

'Thank you, Marianna. Sorry I'm a little late.' Ignoring the panicked look on Antonio's face, Melody unwound her scarf and dumped it, her jacket and her handbag into her staff locker. 'I missed my first train by seconds and had to wait for the next one. Talk about frustrating.'

Wiping her hands on the red and white polka dot apron tied around her generous hips starched to a crisp, her megawatt smile radiating the genuine warmth she was renowned for, Marianna tutted as she closed the distance between them. 'Shush now, there's no apology needed.' She cupped Melody's cheeks, her big brown eyes filled with compassion. 'Because you, tesoro mio, are a blessing to me, to my son, and to this kitchen. I appreciate you being here with everything you're going through.'

Emotion lodged in Melody's throat making it impossible to reply. Instead, she smiled and nodded.

Marianna had always had Melody's back, and if she knew her son had been making out with another woman, just like Antonio's father had done so many year before, which had sent Marianna running all the way across the oceans to her family who had emigrated to Sydney, she'd lose it. That was why Melody had decided to keep her lips zipped. Marianna hated infidelity of any kind, and Melody didn't want a rift between mother and son on her conscience right now.

With his mother bustling back out of the kitchen, Antonio cocked his head as if pondering something. Melody could almost hear his brain ticking from where she was stood, putting her apron on. What the hell was he scheming now?

'What is it, Antonio?' She kicked off her boots and pulled on her chef's clogs.

'I know what you're thinking and no, I haven't forgotten your birthday. I actually planned to get your favourite from that little Lebanese place tonight, so would you mind if I called over to Sally's with it?' He took a tentative step forward. 'We can celebrate together with takeaway and a bottle of wine.'

'It's probably not the best idea.' She took her spot at the bench, eyeing the array of fresh ingredients she'd had delivered from the markets first thing this morning – a daily ritual.

'Please, Melody. It's been almost a month and I don't think I can say sorry any more than I already have.' He stopped on the opposite side of the bench, tipping his head to catch her eyes. 'Are you ever going to forgive me, pasticcino?'

'Please don't call me cupcake. You know I hate it.' Sighing, she brought her weary gaze to his. 'Honestly, Antonio, I don't know if I can ever fully forgive you, and if I do, I'm not sure I'll ever forget what you did.'

'But I've told you, it meant nothing and—'

She held her hand up to stop his excuses – she'd heard enough of them. 'I know, I know. It was just a stupid kiss, and she kissed you, not the other way around, yadda, yadda, yadda.' She met his gaze, hers fierce now. 'And like I've told you, it didn't look like that to me.'

'I know it didn't.' He regarded her like a wounded puppy. 'I've gone and stuffed everything up, haven't I?'

She offered a regretful smile. She almost wished that she could just magically forgive him. It would be simpler, easier. 'It's proving way tougher than I thought it would be, to forgive and forget, especially right now. All I want to do is focus on my mum.' Her hands went to her hips. 'You need to give me space, like I asked you to after our last marriage counselling session. You can't just push me to act like everything's going to be okay, because I honestly don't know if it will be.'

Antonio's mouth opened to say something, but then closed, as if he thought better of it. He regarded her for a few long moments, his gaze narrowing. 'I can't blame you, I suppose, but just know I'm here, waiting for you to love me again, like you should as my wife.'

'Mmhhmm,' was all she could muster for the raw anger rising in her throat.

Marianna's head popped through the doorway, a pen tucked above her ear. 'Antonio, we need you out here, pronto.'

'Coming.' Antonio turned and wandered back towards the hub of the café, his sway as cocky as ever.

His body language infuriated Melody, as did his expectation for her to believe his BS and simply get over it. Who did he think he was, making her feel bad for his selfishness? If she hadn't been his wife for four long years, she wondered if she'd have even tried to forgive him or would have run for the hills the second she'd caught him – like his mother had from his father. And through it all, she had to admit to herself that she felt cold, almost cut-off from feeling the emotion she usually would with such a betrayal, a by-product of what she was enduring with her mum. Numbness was way easier to handle than crying all the time.

Turning her attention to the vine-ripened tomatoes, purple garlic and bunches of basil, she decided to make some bruschetta topping, along with a Caprese salad. After that, the fresh pappardelle. The lunch rush would be upon her before she knew it, so she needed to get cracking.

Want to know how Matt and Sarah's story began?

Rosalee Station

by

MANDY
MAGRO

AVAILABLE NOW

talk about it

Let's talk about books.

Join the conversation:

 facebook.com/romanceanz

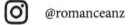 @romanceanz

romance.com.au

If you love reading and want to know about our
authors and titles, then let's talk about it.